"It was wrong of me to kiss you."

"I don't understand why you think it was wrong if I don't." Fortune said, perplexed. "I find I like kissing very much."

"You shouldn't say things like that," Kane answered hoarsely. Fortune's honesty made him uncomfortably aware of her innocence. She had no idea what rules society placed on a young woman.

"You've never been taught a proper young lady doesn't go around giving her kisses freely or expressing her feelings at the drop of a hat, especially to men. It's not respectable."

Fortune stiffened at his reprimand. A mutinous light glimmered in the depths of her eyes. "I'm not a proper young lady, as you've known from the first time we met."

# LADY FORTUNE

## Cordia Byers

FAWCETT GOLD MEDAL • NEW YORK

*To my wonderful readers with gratitude and love.*
*You have made the past ten years in publishing wonderful.*

# LADY
# FORTUNE

# Prologue

April 1777

*Tiny Bartholomew McQueen stilled when he caught the* scent of smoke upon the damp morning air. Every muscle in his large body tensed with warning as he peered cautiously through the greening forest and drew in another breath. He frowned when the pungent smell again filled his nostrils. Having lived in the wilderness of North Carolina since birth, his senses were attuned to the least aberration in his surroundings and he often depended upon his instincts to warn him of danger. It was no different now. Although he could see no threat to himself or his brothers, the hair rising at the nape of his neck warned him that it was nearby. He sniffed the air once more to determine the direction of the odor before he looked over his shoulder at his equally tense and silent brothers, Toft and Josh.

Without a word Josh raised a buckskin-fringed arm and pointed toward the east. Tiny agreed with a nod before he indicated toward the opposite direction. No verbal message passed between the three brothers but all were in silent agreement. In an area where white people had only just begun to settle, they knew from long experience that the smell of smoke could mean but one thing: Indians.

And they wisely chose not to confront the savages if they could avoid it.

The McQueen brothers were not cowards. No man could say that they were afraid of a good fight. Yet they were cautious men and used common sense in order to survive. To Tiny, Josh, and Toft, it wasn't smart to go looking for trouble when it was just as easy to evade it. In their opinion it was far better to detour around an Indian hunting party than to lose your skin by foolishly taking the shorter route.

As was the custom, Tiny led the way. He moved with the stealthful grace of a much smaller man, his agility belying his girth. His moccasin-clad feet made little noise upon the damp leaves as he made a path through the tangle of leafless muscadine vines that wound their way amid the underbrush and made an arbor of the tree limbs overhead.

Since the time when he was old enough to go trapping with his brothers, Tiny had been the leader. His keen senses gave him the ability to recognize danger before his brothers were even aware of it. Because of his sensitive nose and ears, he had saved their lives on many occasions in the past years.

No animosity existed between the brothers over Tiny's leadership. After realizing his ability, Josh and Toft put aside any sibling rivalry they felt toward their younger brother. They had come to rely on his judgment in such risky situations as the one in which they now found themselves.

The three mountain men moved like shadows through the woods blazoned with dogwoods in full bloom. The new leaves on the trees surrounding them emphasized the beauty of the white showy blooms while sweet shrub and honeysuckle filled the air with their heady fragrance. The trappers had just begun to breathe a sigh of relief when a shrill scream brought them to a halt.

"Tiny," Josh McQueen called. "That sounded like a woman."

Tiny's craggy features were set in a grim frown as he

turned and nodded at his brother. "It looks like we're going to have to meet up with them varmints after all, don't it?"

"Looks like it," Toft McQueen stated with a shrug. He had hoped that on this hunt he and his brothers could avoid any encounters leading to a fight. He wasn't getting any younger and he didn't enjoy brawling anymore. Toft eyed his two brothers with something akin to envy. It was different with them. Josh and Tiny were only a few years younger than himself but they seemed to relish the rough-and-tumble life they lived, especially Tiny, the largest of the McQueen brothers. Nothing pleased him more than a good fight. Toft shook his head. The very thought of a knockdown, drag out made all of his old battle scars throb.

Another scream pierced the still morning. Toft turned toward the sound but Tiny passed him on the run. With Josh, Toft followed quickly in his brother's wake. His bones already ached from the chill in the morning air but he put his own discomfort aside. No matter how he felt, he was a McQueen through and through. He could no more turn away from helping those in trouble than he could just lie down and die. Timidity wasn't in the McQueen blood.

A blanket of smoke hovered in the damp air, winding its way through the tree limbs and cloaking the bare branches in an eerie blue-gray mantle. The McQueen brothers crept forward, easing their way through the underbrush toward the new roadway that led across the mountains to the small settlement of Ashville. They could hear the low, guttural murmurings of the Indians when they approached the clearing and stealthily moved toward the sound. Their buckskin-clad figures blended with the winter-browned leaves scattered upon the ground as they crouched low amid the trees to survey the area.

Tiny, Josh, and Toft were fully aware of the danger that lay ahead, and they didn't want to alert the Indians of their presence. Noting only a small hunting party in the clearing beside the roadway where a coach lay overturned on its side, the brothers crawled the last few feet on their bellies.

From beneath thick clumps of mountain laurel they could see that they were already too late to help the people who had foolishly traveled through the mountains in the fancy vehicle with yellow wheels. They were already dead. The brothers knew there was nothing they could do now but watch the Indians rifle through the coach to steal what they thought valuable. After the Indians tired of their sport and departed, they would bury the savages' victims.

The Indians plundered the vehicle with wild abandon. They paid no heed to the two men and the woman who lay as they had fallen when the arrows pierced their flesh. One brave wore the coat and shirt of the man who was sprawled near the blazing campfire. Another body, dressed in fancy livery, lay near the tethered horses. With arms stretched over his head as if he had been reaching for the animals to escape, he lay facedown, an arrow protruding from the middle of his back. The third member of the party, a woman, looked as if she, too, had been trying to flee when she was struck down. She lay oddly doubled over with her arms folded beneath her and her face in the dust. Her sightless eyes stared at the nearby coach. Several arrows projected from her back.

Josh's face flushed a dull red with rage at the gruesome sight. Everything within him rebelled at the senseless slaughter. He raised his rifle and aimed it at the Indian brave sporting the dead man's coat.

"Don't," Toft ordered in a hoarse whisper. "It won't do them folks any good and could cost us our necks if there's a larger party nearby."

"Damn it, Toft," Josh grumbled. "They need killing for what they've done."

"I agree with you, little brother, but it won't do them people any good to get ourselves killed, too."

Josh looked to Tiny for support but saw him shake his head. "Then what are we supposed to do, run away and hide?" he whispered in disgust.

"Hell, Josh. A McQueen ain't never run and hid. But the reason we're all still alive is because we've used our heads. We'll stay here and when them Injun braves have what they want, we'll give them folks a decent burial."

Resenting the fact that he'd have to stand by and watch the savages enjoy their spoils, Josh cursed the Indians under his breath, lowered his rifle, and settled down to wait with his brothers. In less than a half hour the hunting party had draped themselves in their newfound finery taken from the victims' bodies and trunks. Then they left the campsite on the backs of the stolen horses, whooping their triumph over the booty and the destruction they had wrought upon the three whites who had trespassed into their territory.

The McQueen brothers waited in their hiding place until the sounds of the Indians died away and all was still. Once they were certain that the braves would not return, the brothers eased from beneath the mountain laurel and made their way to the clearing. Their craggy, weatherbeaten faces reflected their disgust at the senseless carnage but beyond that they displayed no emotion as they set about the task of tending the dead.

Death was not a stranger to them. In the wilderness the mountain men lived with it each day of their lives, and they accepted it as the natural order of things. It was something that finally caught up with a person no matter how hard he tried to outrun it.

Being the larger of the three, Tiny took on the burden of gathering up the dead for burial while Toft and Josh found a shovel amid the scattered camping equipment and began to dig the graves. After laying out the two men beside the hole his brothers worked to excavate, Tiny turned his attention to the woman whose body was slumped in the strange position near the coach. He snorted in disgust as he stood gazing down at what had been in life a beautiful woman. With raven hair and slender body, she would have turned heads in the fancy gowns that the Indians had stolen. He shook his head again and silently

damned the Indians' savagery once more. It was hard for
him to accept a woman's death.

There were only a few females in the mountain wilderness of the Carolinas, and most of those were already married or too young to have a man. Because of their rarity,
Tiny found himself in awe of the opposite sex. To him,
women were delicate creatures to be treasured by the men
who were fortunate enough to have one as their own. He
envied any man who had a wife and children. Tiny himself
wanted a family more than anything else in the world;
however, it was beginning to look as if he would never
have one.

Disgusted by the waste of such a precious life and the
prospect of never having a wife of his own, Tiny bent to
lift the woman into his arms. Rigor mortis had yet to set
in and the lifeless body moved easily as he turned her on
her side. His hazel-green eyes widened in shock at the
sight of the squirming bundle that had been hidden beneath the body.

"Well, I'll be damned!" Tiny exclaimed as he lay the
woman aside and drew back the material of the cloak that
she'd concealed with her body. He uncovered a red-faced
infant who let out a loud angry cry and began to flail the
air with its small balled fists.

"What in hell?" Toft cursed when he heard the cry. He
looked over his shoulder at his brother and his eyes widened as Tiny lifted the babe and cradled it in his brawny
arms.

Tiny gave him a lopsided grin. "It's a baby and it's
alive."

"I can see and hear that for myself," Toft said. He
dropped the shovel on the fresh mound of earth and
crossed to Tiny. He pushed his coonskin cap to the back
of his head and scratched his brow as he peered down at
the howling infant. "But what I'd like to know is how in
hell this little scamp survived? Injuns usually take white
young'uns with 'em."

"He was wrapped in a cloak under his mother's body.

I guess the Indians didn't know he was there or they would have stolen him, too,'' Tiny said, and glanced back toward the woman. His smile dimmed. She had tried to hide her child from the savages and had fallen over the infant to keep it quiet even as her own life was draining away. A small sigh of regret slipped past Tiny's lips as he drew his gaze away from the woman and looked down at the babe in his arms. The child's mother had been far more than a beautiful female, she had also possessed a valiant, unselfish spirit.

''Well, what are we agoin' to do with him?'' Toft asked, mystified.

''I guess we can take him down to the trading post but since we don't know who he belongs to or anything about his folks, I don't reckon that would do us any good,'' Josh said, bending to peer down at the infant in his brother's arms. He, too, was awed by the tiny being.

''I guess not,'' Tiny said absently, unable to take his eyes off the babe in his arms. He was fascinated by the squirming bundle. He'd seen children before but never one as small as the infant who thrust out its tiny hands and hit him on the chest.

''Then what do the two of you think we should do with him?'' Toft asked, edging closer to Tiny in order to see the babe better himself. The last time he'd seen a baby this size was when Tiny had been born.

''I don't rightly know what's best to do with him but I reckon we can take him home with us until we figure that out,'' Tiny said.

''Take him home with us?'' Toft gaped up at his younger brothers who towered over him by several inches. ''And what are we supposed to do with him once we do that? I fer one don't know nothing about babies and at my age, I shore don't intend to start learning.''

''Ah, Toft,'' Josh cajoled. ''You wouldn't turn this little 'un out, would you? He ain't got anybody exceptin' us to see that he makes it. His folks are dead.''

''His ma and pa may be dead but he might have other

relatives somewhere," Toft said. He had to bring a sane voice into this conversation since his brothers had both gone all sweet and syrupy over the young'un.

"Yeah, he might have some folks somewhere but they ain't here to take care of him now," Josh said, giving Toft a triumphant grin.

"We can't keep him, Josh. We need to take him down to the trading post and they'll see that he gets to a found-ling home," Toft countered.

"Foundling home?" Tiny's head snapped up and he quickly shook it. "No, he ain't going to no foundling home. We'll take him home with us and then I'll go alookin' for his relatives. Somebody ought to know who these people are. From the looks of that coach and the way they're dressed, they're somebody fancy."

"Well, I guess that's the end of it," Josh said. "Let's get them buried and get on home. The little tike probably needs food."

"Just you two keep in mind that I think you're making a mistake by not listening to my advice. You don't even know what a baby eats."

"It can't be much," Tiny said. "He's too little to have much of an appetite."

"I give up," Toft said, and threw his hands in the air to emphasize his exasperation with his brothers. A moment later he reached for the baby. "Give him to me while you help Josh finish up here." As Tiny turned away, Toft was unable to resist cooing and chucking the baby under the chin with his forefinger. The baby quieted and looked up at him through dark slate-blue eyes. A smile curled the cherubic pink lips as a tiny fist captured Toft's finger and drew it into the small toothless cavern.

"You're going to be trouble for us. I just know you will," Toft muttered under his breath as he smiled down at the babe. He wouldn't admit it but the infant had captured more than his finger, he had already captured his heart.

With their grim task complete, Tiny and Josh hunkered

down beside the log where their older brother sat holding the sleeping infant. With a gentleness that seemed foreign in one of his size, Tiny took the babe from Toft and cradled it in his arms.

"What you going to call him?" Josh asked, peering down at the cherubic little face exposed over the edge of the soft blanket.

"Hold on now," Toft interrupted before Tiny could answer. "It ain't our place to call him nothing."

"Well, we can't just call the babe, him or it. He deserves a name," Josh argued.

Toft came to his feet and hitched up his britches. "We ain't kin to the young'un and it ain't our right to name him. That's his folks' duty."

"Hell, Toft. He ain't got nobody but us. What if we don't never find any of his kin. You agoin' to let him go through life being called him or it?" Tiny teased.

"You know I don't intend no such thing. I just don't want the two of you to get attached to him. He has folks somewhere, and when we find 'em it won't be easy for you to let him go if you up and give him a name and start acting like he was your own kin." Toft tried to make his brothers see reason.

"Well, what do you suggest we do about it?" Josh asked.

"I don't rightly know." Toft scratched his head and scanned the surrounding woods before looking once more at his brothers. "I just know that we need to collect this little mite's belongings and get the hell out from here before we end up like his folks. Them Injun braves are still in the area."

"Well, I plan on naming him anyhow," Tiny said, ignoring his brother's warning.

Toft rolled his eyes heavenward. In all of his born days he'd never run into anyone as hardheaded as his baby brother. When Tiny got something in that mulish mind of his, nothing would detour him until he'd had his way. From long experience with Tiny, Toft knew it was far quicker to give in to him than argue the point.

"All right, damn it. Since you won't listen to reason, what do you plan to call him?"

"His name is going to be Fortune." Tiny smiled smugly at Toft and Josh.

"Now what kind of name is that for a young'un?" Josh asked.

"The kind I want to give him. Anyhow, he is fortunate to be alive so I figure that's a good name for him. Fortune McQueen. It has a good sound to it."

"Damn it, Tiny," Toft cursed. "That young'un ain't a McQueen."

"Toft—" Tiny began, and then paused abruptly. A stricken look crossed his face. His eyes widened and his mouth turned down at the corners in disgust as he slowly looked at the babe. Water dripped from between his fingers where he cupped the small bottom in his palm. It ran in rivulets down the front of his buckskins.

"I think the little 'un needs his nappies changed." Toft chuckled. The babe's heed to nature's call broke the tension between the brothers.

"Nappies?" Tiny asked, bewildered.

"Give him here and I'll do," Toft volunteered with a slow grin curling his lips. "Now that's what I've been talking about. Here you two are all up and ready to keep this young'un and you don't even know that a babe has to have his nappies changed ever so often or you'll end up like Tiny."

Tiny quickly handed the infant over to his older brother. "I thought you said you didn't know anything about babies."

"I don't" was Toft's short reply. "I just remember bits and pieces of what Ma done when you was born. And that ain't enough to take care of a babe properlike. Now go and see if you can find any of the babe's clothes. He's wet through to the skin."

"I am, too," Tiny grumbled, grimacing. He wiped at

his damp clothing as he turned away to do his brother's bidding.

Chuckling at the disgruntled look on Tiny's face, Toft squatted down and unwrapped the blanket from about the infant. He pulled up its soggy gown and untied the knots on the trifolded square of cloth. When it came free, he gaped at the tiny bottom. With eyes rounding from surprise, he muttered, "Well, I'll be damned."

"What is it?" Josh asked as he held out several tiny garments to his brother.

"It ain't a he we got here. It's a she."

Josh knelt on one knee and gently stroked the fine down upon the small head. His craggy features softened as he gazed down at the babe and smiled. "You're going to be a beauty when you grow up, Mistress Fortune McQueen. A real beauty."

"Damn it, Josh. You're beginning to sound like Tiny. We can't keep this babe."

Josh glanced over his shoulder at his younger brother before he looked back at Toft. "I don't know why not. We found her and now she's ours."

"You're out of your minds," Toft said as he dressed the baby in a dry gown.

"I don't think he is, Toft. If I can't find no trace of any of her kin, I plan to keep her," Tiny said. He paused and draped a companionable arm about Josh's shoulders. "As I see it, I ain't never going to have a family no other way."

"That's even more foolish since he has turned out to be a she. Girls ain't as easy to raise as boys. They need proper training and all sorts of things that we know nothing about," Toft argued.

"When the time comes we'll see that she gets what she needs," Tiny countered.

"I must be going crazy 'cause I'm beginning to believe what I'm ahearing." Toft shook his head. "But I ain't going to argue with you any more right now. We have to put some distance between them Injuns and us or we'll not be around to do anything for little Fortune in the future.''

''Fortune McQueen,'' Tiny murmured as he bent and took her from Toft. ''A right fine name if I do say so myself.''

# Chapter 1

April 1790, North Carolina

Tiny paused in the doorway of the curing shed and absently brushed away the flies that buzzed around him. The offending pests swarmed in a black wave over the furs he'd laid out to cure. By removing the hair and scudding it, he'd already prepared the deerhide to make into buckskin. Now all that was left was the tanning. Once that was done the hides would be ready for him to sell at the trading post down in the valley. Tiny glanced over his shoulder at the hides stretched out to air. His catch had been small this season without his brothers to help. In past years, the shed hadn't been large enough to hold all of their winter's work. Now, with Toft and Josh gone, it was only half full. The old grief rose up once more to gnaw at his heart. He gave a snort of disgust at his own sentimentality and turned his thoughts away from his brothers.

For a long reflective moment, he stood with one shoulder braced against the rough-hewn post of the shed and with his calloused hands pushed down into the pockets of his buckskin britches. His gaze fell upon the two-room log cabin that had been his home since birth. All was quiet. Tiny frowned. It was too quiet for his peace of mind when Fortune was in the vicinity. She was an active child who, if left too long on her own, could find more ways than one to get into trouble.

With the thought of the raven-haired, blue-eyed girl, Tiny couldn't stop the slow smile of affection that curved his lips up at the corners. Fortune was his life. Since that first day, thirteen years ago, she had been the focus of his and his brothers' lives and he couldn't love her more if she had come from his own loins.

Tiny scanned the area surrounding the cabin once more and stepped out into the midday sun. There was no sign of the young ragamuffin and he wondered where she had gotten herself off to since he'd left her that morning to fend for herself. Removing his coonskin cap, Tiny tucked it into the wide belt about his thick waist and wiped the sweat from his brow. It was too hot to wear the cap but, like his beard, it helped keep the bugs away from his skin. Tiny glanced up at the hazy blue sky and wondered when it was going to rain again to cool things off. It was only the first week in May yet an unseasonable hot spell had made it seem like late summer. The last time he could recall the weather getting so hot so early was the year he'd found Fortune.

"How times flies," he murmured to himself as he strode toward the cabin.

A high-pitched shriek sounded from above him at the same instant a small figure came sailing out of the large oak tree to land on his back. Long ebony braids swung like coiling black snakes as gangly arms and legs entwined about him and clung tightly.

"Dad blast it, Fortune McQueen! You'd scare the living daylights out of a man," Tiny grumbled as he pried the arms from about his neck and swung Fortune to her feet in front of him. With legs spread and hands braced on his hips, he looked down into the impish little face turned up to him and shook his head. "Girl, I'm getting too old for such horseplay."

"You're not ever going to get old, Tiny" was Fortune's jaunty answer. Like a mirror image of the man towering over her, she stood in her bare feet with legs spread and her small hands braced on her narrow hips. Her head cocked to one side, she regarded him through slate-blue eyes that sparkled with silver glints and held a mischievous twinkle.

"If that's true, I wish you'd tell my old bones about it," Tiny complained while rubbing his shoulder. He was nearing his fiftieth year and he felt every day of it. "They're getting crotchety of late and it makes it hard for a man just to get out of bed in the morning. Sometimes I wonder if I'll make it."

Tiny's apparent discomfort touched Fortune's soft heart and made her instantly contrite. She threw herself against Tiny, wrapped her arms tightly about his waist, and buried her face against his chest. "Don't you dare get old on me, Tiny Bartholomew McQueen. You're all I have since the fever took Josh and Toft."

"I'm not going to leave you, little one," Tiny murmured softly. He immediately regretted making her think of his brothers. After their deaths the previous winter, she had changed from the carefree little mite who had traipsed through the woods without a worry in the world. She had suddenly turned into a miniature adult who concerned herself with his welfare, as well as her own.

The thought perturbed Tiny. Fortune was growing up far faster than he had expected. She could still act the child, but he knew that deep down she was turning into a young woman. The changes in her life and those taking place within her body left her balanced between being a child and an adult. It was an unsettling time for anyone, much less a girl who had to worry about an uncertain future if something were to happen to him.

Tiny understood her feelings. He was all she had left. The secure little world in which she had lived with three doting uncles to protect her had suddenly vanished when Josh and Toft died. Though he'd allowed her to go with him to the trading post a few times in the past years, Fortune had never known any life beyond the tiny cabin in the mountains.

Tiny wrapped her in his arms and stared over her head at the verdant landscape beyond the cabin. Ever since the day when he'd found her under her mother's body, he had loved Fortune as the daughter he'd never had. Yet his brother's warning had come back to haunt him often in the last months. Toft had been wise enough to know that when Fortune began to grow into a woman she would need more guidance than they were able to give.

Tiny released a long, weary breath and felt a dull ache shoot across his chest. With his thoughts centered on Fortune, he ignored the light discomfort. For the first time, he was experiencing guilt over his actions. When he'd found Fortune, he had been near forty years of age and his hopes of ever having a wife and children of his own had been fading. Yet his need for a family had been so strong that he had not considered the consequences to the child. He had taken her as his own without thought of finding her relatives, though he had made the pretense of it for a time just to appease Toft.

Tiny tightened his arms about Fortune. He was beginning to fear that he had made an irreparable mistake. Nearly thirteen years had passed and it was far too late to begin searching for her relatives in order to ensure her a safe future. Even if he tried to find them at this late date, he didn't know where to begin. The Indians had stolen everything of value that might have led him to her kin. There had been only one trunk left untouched by the savages. It had contained a few articles of Fortune's mother's clothing and a few books. But since neither he nor his brothers could read, they'd had little use for them. So the trunk had been stored away for the child until she was old enough to understand what had happened to her parents.

Resigned to the fact that his selfishness could hurt the one person he loved more than anything else in the world, Tiny set Fortune away from him. It was far too late to worry over such things. Even if he managed to locate her relatives now, there was no guarantee they would believe him or want her. At least with him, she was loved.

"What have you been up to since this morning?" he asked, forcing a light note into his voice to quell any uneasiness he'd aroused in her. He captured one of her long, dark braids in his calloused hand and gave it a gentle, playful tug.

"Nothing much. I went down to the creek and tried to catch a mess of trout for supper but I didn't have any luck."

"Well, I guess we'll just have to have rabbit stew again, won't we?" Tiny said, and chuckled at the sound of disgust Fortune made. They'd had rabbit stew every other day for the past month and they were both getting tired of it. With his arm draped companionably about her narrow shoulders, they strolled side by side toward the cabin.

"I did spot some strawberries down near the creek when I was coming home. I thought I'd go back this afternoon and pick them. A pie would at least help improve our supper if it's to be stew again."

Tiny smacked his lips together and patted his bulging belly. "That sounds real fine. I can nearly taste it now."

"The real thing will be even better," Fortune said, grinning at Tiny's antics. With a burst of enthusiasm, she gave him a quick hug before running into the cabin to collect the small wooden pail that would hold the sweet, red berries. A moment later she came bounding out and set off in the direction of the small creek.

"You be careful, Fortune," Tiny warned as he did each time she left the vicinity of the cabin. The war between the colonies and Britain had been over for seven years but little had changed in the area. Indians still roamed freely through the wilderness, and he didn't want Fortune to end up like her parents or gracing some young buck's bark hut.

"I always am," Fortune said with all the confidence of youth. She waved as she took the narrow trail through the stand of maple and oak trees.

Tiny grinned and rubbed at his beard-stubbled chin. The

girl wasn't afraid of anything. He'd done his best to instill
some caution into that head of hers, and he was grateful
she had enough sense to listen to his warnings. However,
listening and heeding his advice did not mean she feared
man or beast. He had yet to see her intimidated by anything that breathed. She had enough courage in her gangly-
limbed body to face a wildcat on its own ground.

"You may need all of your courage, little one," Tiny
murmured then grimaced at the sharp pain that suddenly
shot across his chest as his heart began to flutter wildly
against his ribs. His breathing grew short and he sank
down on the rough-hewn bench beside the cabin door. He
laid his head against the logs and drew in several long
breaths. Nausea churned his stomach and beads of sweat
broke out across his upper lip and brow. He wiped it away
with a trembling hand.

Of late he'd been having chest pains and suspected that
his heart was acting up on him. He'd had several spells
like the one he'd just experienced. In the past he'd grown
so weak that he wondered if he'd be able to make it back
to the cabin before dying. The pains had only increased
his concern over Fortune's future. He knew his time was
growing short and that he'd be lucky to live another few
years.

Tiny squeezed his eyes closed and prayed, "Please,
God, let this tired old body live long enough to see her
safely settled."

Unaware of Tiny's tumultuous thoughts, Fortune
hummed a happy tune beneath her breath as she knelt in
the patch of strawberries. Clustered abundantly amid the
dark-green leaves of the plants, the berries were plump
and juicy. Unable to resist the temptation, Fortune popped
a berry into her mouth and sat back to savor the sweet,
tangy taste. It was delicious. Her mouth watered for another but she refrained from indulging herself further. If
she kept eating them she would not have enough to make
Tiny the pie she had promised.

With her pail only half full, Fortune lay back on the

mossy blanket that edged the strawberry patch and folded her hands beneath her head. She looked up at the cornflower-blue sky overhead as her musing turned to the large man who had raised her. Tiny had told her that he was her adopted uncle but she couldn't love him more if he was her own father. She had loved Josh and Toft but there was a special bond between Tiny and herself. She couldn't put it into words exactly but it ran nearly as deep as a bond of blood. Like a father, he had always been the one to comfort her whenever she was hurt and needed loving hands to mend her in body and soul.

With her thoughts on Tiny, Fortune's brows knit over her slender nose as she squinted up at the tall trees reaching toward the sky. She couldn't stop herself from reflecting upon the puzzling moods she'd experienced of late. Until recently she'd never considered anything beyond the moment. But after the fever took her uncles, everything seemed to change. She began to have strange feelings and her body had been changing in ways that surprised her and, at times, made her ashamed. Her breasts were beginning to fill out and were often tender and painful during that time of the month she feared. She loved Tiny but she couldn't tell him of the odd way her body reacted each month. The first time the bleeding came, she'd thought she was dying but when she didn't succumb to any illness, she had begun to believe that there was something terribly wrong with her insides. However, she was too embarrassed to let anyone know of her deformity.

Along with the changes in her body, she had also begun to think of things that would not have occurred to her several months ago. She'd had thoughts of her future and what the world was like beyond the Carolina hills. And oddly enough, she'd begun to have fantasies about having a husband and family someday. Because her own body was changing in so many ways, she'd also noticed the few men she'd seen when Tiny had taken her to the trading post last month. And she found she liked what she saw.

Fortune felt her cheeks grow warm and quickly sat up.

She had no business thinking such things. She had to stop daydreaming. She had to gather the strawberries for the pie and then get back to the cabin before Tiny began to worry about her.

The pail was brimming with luscious fruit when she first heard the man's cry. She froze and listened intently for a moment before she scrambled to her feet. Fearing that something had happened to Tiny, she dropped her pail in her haste to ascertain the direction from which the cry had come. She was already racing toward it when the second cry sounded. Fortune ignored the sharp sticks and thorns that pricked her bare feet as she ran up the steep hillside to the granite cliff. As a small girl she had named the jagged rocks Indian Head because they resembled a craggy face. Breathing heavily, she eased close to the precipice but could see nothing below. She then lay on her belly and peered over the rocky edge. There she saw a man hanging precariously, both hands grasping a small pine that had taken root amid the cracks in the granite surface of the cliff. For one fleeting moment a wave of relief washed over her as she realized it was not her beloved Tiny who was in trouble.

The man spotted Fortune at the same moment. Sweat beaded his brow and his face was pale with fear as he looked pleadingly up at her. His voice was strained as he begged, ''Help me.''

''Hold on, I'll go get help,'' Fortune said, beginning to scoot away from the cliff's edge.

''No! Don't leave. I can't hang on much longer,'' he cried in desperation.

''You'll fall if I don't go for help. I'm not strong enough to help you all by myself,'' Fortune called back to him. She was already running toward the cabin and Tiny.

Though it seemed an eternity to the man suspended on the scrawny pine, it was only a few minutes before Tiny stood above him. With one end of a rope tied about his stout middle, he lowered the other end down the face of the cliff to the distraught man.

"Grab hold and I'll pull you up," he ordered when the rope reached the pine and dangled in its short green needles.

The man's strained features grew several shades lighter at the order yet he obeyed. After a few fitful, nerve-wrenching tries, he finally managed to get hold of the rope and work his way up the cliff as Tiny pulled. He collapsed out of breath once he reached safety.

"Thank you," he panted, his voice faint from the exertion. "I'll always be in your debt. You saved my life."

"Now, I wouldn't go so far as to say that, Mister. I doubt if you would have died if you'd fallen into the creek. You might have been skint up and sore but that's about it."

"I would probably have died of fright if the fall didn't kill me," the man said, chuckling at his own fear. He pushed his way to his feet and dusted off his clothing before he extended his hand to Tiny. "I'm William Bartram, sir."

"And I'm Bartholomew McQueen but everyone just calls me Tiny." Tiny shook Bartram's hand vigorously.

"Well, who might this young lady be?" Bartram asked as he looked down at Fortune standing quietly at Tiny's side. "I seem to owe her my thanks, as well."

"This is Fortune," Tiny said proudly, draping an arm over her narrow shoulder.

"How do you do, Mistress Fortune," Mr. Bartram said, and extended his hand to Fortune.

She backed shyly away.

Noting the wary look she bestowed upon him, Mr. Bartram smiled to reassure her but made no other move. Like his father before him, he was a lover of all living things and had made his life's work studying them. The look he saw in her slate-blue eyes was the same as he'd seen in the eyes of other wild creatures of the forest. It was a silent message but plainly stated—keep your distance until you earn my trust—and he would abide by her unspoken rules.

"We don't see many people around these parts," Tiny

interjected into the strained silence that had developed between them. "And Fortune's a little shy around strangers."

"I completely understand, Mr. McQueen. I certainly don't want to frighten the young lady who helped save my life. I would much prefer to become her friend."

"Call me Tiny. It's hard to know who a body is talking to when I'm called Mr. McQueen."

"Then you must call me William, Tiny, since I'm going to be in the area for a while to collect specimens of plants." Bartram grinned. "That was why I ended up in such a predicament earlier."

Tiny frowned. What person in his right mind went around collecting plants? He could understand hunters and trappers and even the farmers who were beginning to come into the mountains, but a plant collector—that was foolish. "You were looking for plants on the side of the cliff?" he asked, bemused.

"Yes, I saw a lovely specimen of lady's slipper a few feet below on the small ledge. It was different from the others I've found and I fell when I tried to get a closer look at it."

At the ridiculous picture that rose in her mind, Fortune could not suppress the burst of girlish giggle that escaped her. A man picking flowers! She laughed again.

William smiled at the charming, childish sound. It was nice to hear a child's voice again after so many months in the wilderness. He loved his work but he sorely missed his family during the trips he took to record the plant and animal life in the Southeast.

Tiny could not suppress his own grin. He could nearly read Fortune's thoughts and knew exactly what had caused her sudden burst of merriment, but he would not offend Mr. Bartram by telling him that he was the reason behind her humor. Instead he took Fortune by the shoulders, turned her in the direction of the berry patch, and gave her a gentle shove. "Go get them berries for my pie, girl, and I'll invite Mr. Bartram to have supper with us."

Thrilled by the prospect of having Mr. Bartram stay

with them for even a few more hours, Fortune hurried back in the direction she had come earlier. She might find it hard to talk to him but she was bursting with curiosity.

"Perhaps they might even talk about the places that I've dreamed about," Fortune mused aloud as she gathered up the berries she'd spilled. Popping one of nature's sweet delicacies into her mouth, she smiled her pleasure at the taste, as well as the thought of Mr. Bartram's visit.

"Mr. Bartram might even know how to read and can tell me what is written in the books stored in the leather-bound trunk," Fortune said, slightly awed by the thought of finally having someone to read to her from her mother's books.

The leather-bound volumes were a mystery that she desperately wanted solved. Ever since Tiny had first shown her the treasures of the trunk, she had often sat by the fire in the evenings and thumbed through the books, marveling at the scribblings within them. Now if she was fortunate, she would finally know what the yellowed pages of her most prized possessions contained. She had never known her mother yet through touching the books, Fortune felt a closeness to the woman who had given her birth. With that thought in mind, Fortune hurried back to the cabin. She didn't want to miss a minute of Mr. Bartram's visit.

With a smile of satisfaction curling his lips, William leaned back in the straightback chair and patted his belly. "Fortune, I believe that was the best pie I've ever tasted."

Blushing at the compliment, Fortune cleared away the dishes. William Bartram had been at the cabin for several hours yet she still found it hard to speak with him. She wanted to ask him about her mother's books but each time she tried to bring up the subject she found her tongue had grown too thick to speak.

"Fortune does have a way with things," Tiny added proudly as he stood and took his clay pipe from the mantel. After filling the firebowl with tobacco, he lit it with a burning twig from the flames that popped and crackled in the fireplace. Drawing in several long puffs of the pungent smoke, he settled his large frame back in his chair and stretched his long legs out in front of him. As was his custom every night after supper, he relaxed to enjoy his pipe.

"You're a lucky man, Tiny. Few girls her age can cook that well."

"Fortune can do more than just cook. I've taught her to hunt and fish, as well as how to clean hides and cure them. She can shoot a rifle near as good as I can." Like a doting father, Tiny could not stop himself from bragging about Fortune's accomplishments.

"Well, it seems that you've done well by your daughter. I'm sure that her skills come in handy here in the wilderness," William said, smiling with pleasure at the glow of pride he saw on the mountain man's face.

"But I can't read," Fortune said, speaking directly to their visitor for the first time. When he glanced over his shoulder at her, she blushed with embarrassment and quickly busied herself washing the dishes. She used a rough cloth to wipe the excess moisture from the wooden plates that Tiny had made from a fallen poplar the previous winter. The white wood gleamed in the firelight when she stood it up on the shelf to finish drying.

"Then we need to correct that oversight. If Tiny has no objections, I'd like to repay your hospitality by teaching you how to read," William said, and glanced at Tiny who nodded his approval at the idea.

Wide-eyed with wonder, Fortune swung about. She glanced at Tiny and then at William Bartram. Her voice was little more than a breathless, wistful whisper as she asked, "Do you really mean it? Can you really teach me how to read?"

"I may not be able to teach you all you need to know while I'm here but I can give you a few rudimentary lessons." William glanced once more at Tiny. "If you will allow me to make camp here for a few weeks, I'll teach Fortune when I return each evening."

"I see no problem with that, William. And I'm grateful

for your offer. I ain't never learned to read or write and I don't want Fortune to be like me. I've done just fine without it, but she's growing up and will need to know more than I ever did.''

"Yes, that's how it is when raising children, Tiny. Each generation needs to know more than the last. And I doubt if it will ever change.''

"Can we begin now?'' Fortune was too excited to worry about the bad manners she was showing by interrupting the adults' conversation. Mr. Bartram was going to teach her to read her mother's books and she didn't want to waste a moment.

William chuckled at her eagerness. "Yes, we can begin now. Bring me the satchel lying by the door. Since I don't have any books or slate, I'll have to improvise with what I have with me.''

"I have books,'' Fortune said as she ran to retrieve the satchel and then hurried across the room. She knelt in front of the trunk and eased it open. With something akin to reverence, she lifted the books into her arms and carried them to William. "They belonged to my mother.''

William picked up the book on top of the small pile. It was a book of poetry. It would hardly do as a book of instruction yet he opened it out of curiosity. Tiny said he couldn't read and William couldn't stop himself from wondering why the man had books of such quality.

Perhaps his late wife could read, William mused to himself as he flipped open the cover and read the inscription on the first page.

*To my dear wife, Lorna Anne Northrop. The gift of our first child has made me the happiest man on earth. Like her mother, she is beautiful. From your loving husband, Sebastian Northrop, dated in the year of our Lord, 1777.*

William frowned down at the inscription. The name Northrop triggered a distant memory, but one that he couldn't quite grasp. He had heard that name before. Puzzling over the odd feeling, he looked up at Fortune. "You said these belonged to your mother?"

Fortune nodded. Her young face was lit with enthusiasm.

"That's odd," William said under his breath, and glanced toward the man who now sat with his bearded chin resting on his broad chest and snoring lightly. He looked once more at Fortune. "Then you and your father have lived here alone since her death."

"No," Fortune said, shaking her head. "My father died with my mother. Tiny and his brothers, Josh and Toft, found me after the Indians killed my parents."

"My word!" William breathed, recalling where he had heard the name Northrop before. It had been during the war with Britain. Lord Northrop had written his father at Kingsessing, requesting any information about what had happened to his son and daughter-in-law. Due to the uncertain times and John Bartram's age and health, William's father had been unable to give him any information. Unfortunately not long after the letter from Lord Northrop, William's father died.

"Mr. Bartram, are you all right?" Fortune asked. The look of shock that crossed the man's face made her uneasy.

"I'm quite all right, child. Now, where was I?" William asked in an effort to regain his composure. He could not reveal his suspicions until he was certain of the events that had transpired more than thirteen years ago. He would have to speak with Tiny and get all of the facts. It would not be right to disrupt the child's life and make her believe he knew of her relatives in England until he was sure of the truth himself.

William closed the book of poetry and set it aside. Slightly staggered by the realization that he may have found Lord Northrop's missing granddaughter quite by accident, William looked up at Fortune. If she was in fact a Northrop, she could be the next in line to inherit North Meadows.

"Now where shall we begin?" William asked, bracing his hands on his knees and cocking his head to one side. He smiled at Fortune. "I think the best way to go about this is to teach you the alphabet first. That will make it all much easier."

Eyes sparkling with anticipation, Fortune nodded and slid onto the small stool at William's feet. She waited with bated breath as he reached into his satchel and pulled out a piece of paper, a quill pen, and a bottle of ink. A thrill of excitement rippled along every nerve in her small body at the sight. She was going to learn to read and write!

Standing in the shade of the large maple, William braced himself for a good set-down from his host of two months. By the look on Tiny's face, he sensed that he had stuck his foot into his mouth by voicing the questions that had been preying on his mind since he'd read the inscription in the book of poetry.

During his stay with the McQueens, William had grown to like the large man and had begun to consider him his friend. Because of their new relationship, he had postponed asking Tiny any personal questions involving Fortune. He knew the man loved the girl, and it was hard to bring up a subject that might be painful to his friend. However, time had now run out for William. He had to know if what he suspected was true. He couldn't wait any longer for the answers. After today he would be on his way back to Pennsylvania with the new specimens he wanted to add to his collection.

"I'll answer you honestly, William. I don't rightly know who Fortune's parents were. She was just a wee mite when me and my brothers found her."

"Didn't you ever try to locate her relatives? Surely you knew that she had someone, somewhere?" William questioned, unable to comprehend the man's reasoning for keeping a child that belonged to someone else.

"You don't understand, William. Out here a man gets

lonesome for the same things you take for granted. On the frontier a man is lucky to see a woman once a year much less have one of his own. And to have a family, that's something different altogether. I know I was wrong in keeping Fortune, but she's the family I didn't have of my own.''

William placed a compassionate hand on Tiny's shoulder. ''I've traveled enough to know how lonely a man gets in the wilderness and I can understand your reasons, friend. But Fortune does have relatives in England. Do you realize that she is Lord Northrop's granddaughter and perhaps heir to North Meadows estate?''

''That don't mean much to me,'' Tiny admitted. ''I ain't never heard of no Lord Norththrop or North Meadows.''

''I'm sorry, Tiny. That was presumptuous of me even to think you had. I wouldn't know anything about it either if it weren't for friends of mine in England.''

''You've friends that know this Lord Northrop?'' Tiny questioned, suddenly realizing that the answer to his worries over Fortune's future might be solved.

''Yes, I do,'' William answered, wondering at Tiny's abrupt question.

''Then you'd be able to get in touch with this here lordship and tell him about Fortune?''

''I might, Tiny. Why are you asking?''

''I love Fortune, William, but she's come to an age when she needs more than I can give her here in the mountains. She needs learning like the kind you've given her,'' Tiny said.

''I can understand your reasoning, Tiny. I've never seen a mind as quick as Fortune's. In the last two months she's already learned more than most do after years in school. Her mind is like a desert waiting to absorb rain.''

''Then you'll write and tell this Lord Northrop about Fortune?''

''Are you sure you want me to do that? It could mean that he'd come after her and you'd never see her again.''

"I'll take that chance. I love her too much to let my own feelings stand in the way of her happiness," Tiny said. He did not add that if he thought he would live to a ripe old age no one on the face of this earth could make him let her go. However, he knew from the pains in his chest that he would not live much longer.

"Then I'll write to Lord Northrop when I arrive at Kingsessing," William said, somewhat surprised by the turn the conversation had taken. He had expected Tiny to be incensed by his questions instead of asking for his help in finding Fortune's relatives in England.

"Thank you, William. You're a good friend." Tiny extended his hand to William Bartram. He felt as if a heavy burden had been lifted from his shoulders. At least he now had hope that his beloved child would not be left alone to fend for herself once he was gone.

# Chapter 2

*The room was filled with greenery. From the tall exotic* palms in the corner to the tiny violets that sat on the shelves before the window, it reflected the dedication of William Bartram's life. His love for his work was apparent to any visitor to his home. Every vacant space was given to the plants that he'd spent so many years collecting and logging for posterity during his travels.

Kane Warrick relaxed back in the padded leather chair. He folded his long-fingered hands over his flat middle and stretched out his muscular legs, crossing them at the ankles. Thick black lashes shadowed his arresting silver eyes as he turned his regard to the verdant surroundings. He gave the room a critical inspection and then smiled his pleasure at finding that he was not disappointed by what he saw. Even after such a long journey, he did not regret his decision to come to America and visit the famed horticulturist. He had as yet to meet Bartram, but he already knew a great deal about the man from his peers in England. Kane was also acquainted with the book the horticulturist had written called *Travels*. And for that reason, he'd come to seek Bartram's advice about the best area in the colonies to grow cotton.

Kane's expression hardened at the thought of his venture, and he unconsciously clenched his fingers about the armrest of the chair. His enemy's name came in a low curse to his lips but he managed to suppress speaking it aloud. Nevin Manville and his partner, Orson Stoddard, were trying to force him and the other mill owners out of business by buying up all the cotton on the London market. Their plan was to deprive their competitors of the materials they needed to keep their mills open and their people working. Unfortunately, they had already succeeded in forcing several mills to close their doors.

"But I'm not going to be one of them," Kane muttered beneath his breath. He'd not allow Manville to force him to close the mills that his father had spent so many years of his life building. Before his death, Jason Warrick had tried to compete with Manville, and Kane believed that the strain had hastened his father's demise because Warrick mills had been nearly bankrupt when he took over. That fact made him determined to do everything in his power to see that his father's work remained in the family, no matter what Manville and his evil cohort did to try to shut him down.

The sound of the door opening drew Kane's thoughts away from Nevin Manville. He came to his feet and turned to see a thin middle-aged man who looked, from his rumpled appearance, as if he had dressed quickly and without concern over his attire. A smudge of dirt still darkened the skin beneath his ear as if he had pulled at the lobe while pondering some intricate question.

"Mr. Warrick, I'm sorry to have kept you waiting. I lose track of time when I'm in the conservatory with my plants. I do hope you will forgive the delay but I couldn't meet you covered in dirt and manure." William smiled and extended a hand with nails stained from years of working in soil.

"No need to apologize, sir. Your love and knowledge of plants are well known, and they are the reason I've come to see you," Kane said. He shook William's hand with genuine warmth.

"As I gathered from your letter. Shall we have a glass of wine and discuss what's brought you all the way from England for my help?" William crossed to the small inlaid table that held several plants, as well as a tray containing a crystal decanter of wine and several glasses. He poured the deep burgundy liquid into the tulip-stemmed wine-glasses and served Kane before settling himself in a large well-used chair opposite his guest.

"Now, what is it that I can do for you? I seem to recall something about cotton from your letter. Didn't you also mention a cotton mill?"

"Yes, I own a rather dilapidated mill near Bristol. Recently I've wanted to renovate it to steam but I'm afraid my neighbors at North Meadows won't sell me the land that I need for the project. But that's neither here nor there at the moment. My main interest is supplying my mills with the raw materials I need to stay in business."

"North Meadows?" William said, ignoring Kane's last remark. The name aroused memories that he treasured. He couldn't help but wonder how young Fortune was doing with her grandfather in England. "Isn't that Lord Northrop's estate? I've several friends in England who have written me about his interest in preserving the land. From what I've gathered he's well respected on his views."

"That might have been true a few years ago, but during the last years he's turned everything over to his nephew, Nevin Manville. And Manville cares little about the land. The only thing that he concerns himself with is his cotton mills." Kane's tone reflected all the contempt he felt toward the man.

William frowned at Kane. "You say that this Manville is in charge of the estate now?"

"Yes. Since he's Lord Northrop's heir, he's taken over management of North Meadows."

"Heir? But what about Fortune, his granddaughter?" William asked, surprised to learn that Lord Northrop had not made her his heir.

"Fortune?" Kane asked, wondering for the first time if

he had made the right decision about seeking out William Bartram after all. The man seemed to have little interest in his reason for coming to Kingsessing. "Lord Northrop doesn't have a granddaughter, as far as I know."

William set his glass aside. His brows lowered to shadow his eyes and he frowned. He gave a sad shake of his head. "I'm sorry to hear that's how things turned out. I had hoped that Lord Northrop would accept the girl. She is his granddaughter, no matter what he may believe."

"What do you mean?" Kane asked, his interest piqued.

"Perhaps I shouldn't discuss Lord Northrop's affairs but it does dishearten me to hear that such a lovely girl was not accepted by her own family. I wonder how the child is faring after being turned away by her only relatives."

"Sir, I'm afraid I don't understand a thing you're talking about. As far as I know, Lord Northrop has never seen or heard of the girl you speak of. Had he known, I'm sure he would have been more than happy to welcome her, having only Manville to inherit North Meadows at his death. Anyone would be preferable to that man." Kane refrained from adding several very descriptive words about what he considered Manville.

"I'm sure he's heard of her. I wrote him myself. I never received a reply but I assumed that Lord Northrop was too busy making plans to come after his granddaughter to answer my letter."

"How long ago has it been since you wrote him?" Kane asked.

"Let me see," William said, tapping thoughtfully at his chin with his fingers. "I believe it's been nearly four years. I was doing the last of my research for *Travels* and was on my way back to Pennsylvania from the Carolinas."

"The Carolinas?" Kane said, puzzled.

"Yes, that's where I came across the girl and her adopted uncle. They saved my life." William smiled at the memory and then told Kane of his adventure with the McQueens. When he finished with his story, he fell silent and waited for Kane to comment.

Kane shook his head, astounded by the what he had just learned. Lord Northrop had a granddaughter here in the colonies whom he did not know existed. Kane was sure he had never seen the letter William had written him. Knowing Nevin Manville as he did, he knew the greedy bastard wouldn't have shown the letter to his uncle. He would not chance losing everything if another heir to the Northrop estate were found.

After a long thoughtful moment, Kane smiled. A glimmer of an idea was beginning to form at the back of his mind. If things went as he hoped, he would gain far more from his trip to America than the knowledge of how and where to plant cotton. He would be able to renovate his mills to steam power and ruin Nevin Manville.

Peace reigned over the dark mountains. It was the hour of truce between night and day. The time before dawn lightened the eastern sky to awaken the daylight creatures of the forest; the time when the nocturnal animals crept back to their dens and, with bellies full from their night's hunt, snuggled down to sleep.

Nothing stirred when Fortune stepped from the warm cabin and closed the door behind her. She secured it with a strip of leather wound about the wooden peg that had been driven into the chinking between the logs and then glanced up at the indigo sky. This time of day was always the loneliest for her. It seemed as if no one else existed on the earth besides herself.

Fortune shivered from the thought, as well as the chill in the morning air, and quickly turned to the task at hand. There was no time to mull over the fact that she was now alone in the world. Tiny had often told her that there was little to be gained from self-pity. He had taught her how to survive without him and now she would put his lessons to good use. Today she'd take the furs that Tiny trapped last winter down to the trading post. The money from them would help see her through the coming months and by the time it was gone, hopefully she would have made some decision about her future.

Fortune hunkered down beside the bundle of raccoon, fox, and squirrel skins. She ran her hand over the silken furs and swallowed back the lump of emotion that rose in her throat. The furs were a sad reminder of all she had lost. It had been two months since Tiny collapsed and died in the curing shed, but time had not eased the heartache of his passing. There had not been an hour in the day that she did not think of him. Nor had a day passed when she didn't wonder what she would do with her own life now that he was gone.

Fortune was confident in her abilities to survive alone in the mountains. She had been taught from an early age how to live off the land, but she didn't think she could deal with the loneliness such a life presented. She was nearing her eighteenth birthday and her young heart ached to know again the feeling of being loved and cherished; the feeling of belonging to someone instead of just existing from day to day. Nor had she forgotten the dreams of having a husband and family of her own.

"But my dreams will never come true if I remain hidden away in the mountains," Fortune chided herself, fully aware of what had kept her from venturing far from the only security she had ever known. The uncertainties that arose within her each time she considered leaving the mountains had kept her a prisoner as surely as manacles about her ankles.

Fortune's slate-blue gaze swept over the shadowy landscape. The world beyond the mountain cabin was something that frightened her far more than anything she had ever encountered in the wilderness. She wasn't afraid of the wild animals or the Indians in the area. She knew what to expect from them and could handle any situation that presented itself. However, she wasn't sure that she could do the same in the civilized world. From what little she had read in her mother's books and heard from others who'd ventured into the towns and cities beyond the mountains, that world could be far more hostile than anything she would confront in the wilderness.

Seeing a less than encouraging future for herself, Fortune forced her thoughts back to her present situation. She would have time for decisions later, after she sold the furs.

Strengthened by this new determination, Fortune managed to heft the heavy bundle of furs onto her back. When she pushed herself erect, she staggered backward a few feet before regaining her balance. She shifted the weight around to adjust it to a more comfortable position before she gathered up Tiny's Brown Bess. She tucked the flint-lock musket firmly beneath her arm before resolutely setting off down the trail that would, by day's end, lead her to the trading post.

"I'll decide on the future when it gets here," she said, confident that she would make the right decision when the time came. Innocent of life beyond her mountain home, she was completely unaware that the world she would be entering was not one where women made choices. It was a world run by men, in which women were seen but not heard. And it was a world totally unprepared for a young woman who knew none of the rules she was expected to obey.

Weary of the two-day ride from the small settlement of Ashville, Kane dismounted and tied his horse to the hitching rail outside the trading post. His tired muscles screamed from the rigorous pace he'd set for himself. He'd had little rest since learning of Lord Northrop's granddaughter. If he was to succeed, he had no time to worry over a few minor discomforts. Each day that it took to find the girl was one more day that Manville had to further his stranglehold on the textile industry and push his competitors closer to ruin.

His mission was urgent and time was at an essence, yet at that moment he wanted nothing more than a cool drink to quench his thirst and a place to bathe away the layers of dust that coated him from head to toe. In the past two days he'd had his fill of dust. He had smelled dust, tasted dust, and felt dust beneath his shirt and around the edge of his collar for so long that he could think of little else except the annoyance of the dust.

His physical state made him less than congenial when he entered the trading post where he'd been told he'd get directions to the McQueen cabin. Kane paused upon the threshold to survey his surroundings. His gaze swept over the three burly trappers who sat at one of the two tables in front of the fireplace that dominated the left side of the room. Fortunately, the hearth was cool and a breeze seemed to be drawn through the room and up the stone chimney to help ease the heat. The rest of the interior of the trading post was reserved for trading. A youth dressed in buckskins added another bundle of furs to those already piled high in the corner. Barrels of flour, molasses, and salt were stacked against the walls that were not cluttered with every conceivable object, from beads to trade with the Indians to muskets, powder, and balls used to fight them. There was even a small space for cloth and kitchen utensils, though Kane wondered who would be in need of calico in the wilderness. He doubted if any of the trappers had a fondness for skirts without the female inside.

Kane smiled at the thought and crossed to the oak-planked bar where a large man with a beefy complexion stood polishing several pewter tankards.

"What can I do for you?" the man asked without slowing his polishing.

"Something to quench my thirst," Kane said, and slapped a coin down on the smooth surface of the bar. In his present mood he didn't care what he was served as long as it relieved him of the furry feeling in his mouth. The barkeep filled one of his newly polished tankards with ale and set it in front of Kane. However, before Kane could lift it to his lips, the buckskin-clad youth elbowed his way in front of him and threw several furs on the bar.

"If you think to cheat me, then you're mistaken, Harvey Mills," the youth began. He could not finish his statement because of the large hand that clamped down on the back of his collar and hauled him off his feet.

"It seems that you have need of a lesson in manners, you young ragamuffin," Kane growled, his temper snapping. Under normal circumstances the boy's actions would not have affected him in such a way, but in his present mood the youth wearing a mangy coonskin cap lit the fuse to make his temper explode.

"Gentlemen do not push in front of others, especially those who are their elders," he said with every intention of giving the boy a good shaking. However, a fraction of a moment later his intentions changed dramatically.

To Kane's dismay, the ragamuffin abruptly turned into a screeching wildcat intent upon doing as much damage to him as possible. He kicked and squealed at Kane until the large buckskin coat that Kane held firmly in his hand slipped upward to nearly bury the young boy. The action also served to dislodge the coonskin hat from his head and loosen two long ebony braids.

For one startled moment Kane gaped at the silken braids that fell down the youth's back before comprehension dawned on him. What he had thought to be a boy was in fact a girl. Years of inbred manners surfaced immediately and he set her away from him as gently as possible under the circumstances. However, she would have none of it. She came at him with fists and feet flying and when he grabbed her in an effort to protect himself, she left several deep marks in his arms with her teeth.

"Ouch!" Kane roared, to the amusement of the three trappers and barkeep. "You little hellion, stop it right now before I have to hurt you."

"You're the one who is going to get hurt," Fortune McQueen threatened even as he wrapped his arms firmly about her and forced her bodily toward the door.

"We'll just see about that," Kane said, pushing her outside with a less than gentle shove. Before she had time to regain her balance and turn on him again, he closed the door firmly behind him and strode back to the bar.

Fortune saw red. She felt her blood rush to her temples and thought her head would leave her shoulders from the burst of fury that shot through her. No one had ever laid a hand on her in her life. Tiny had always been there to assure her safety. Now that he was gone, she could depend upon no one to fight her battles except herself and she'd be damned before she backed down to the stranger dressed in the fancy clothes. She pushed the door open and, with fists balled at her side, she stamped back to the bar where he'd again tried to quench his thirst with the ale. Before he knew what she intended she lashed out at him again with a well-placed blow to his middle before adding a swift kick to his shins.

"You little fool"—Kane gasped—"I've had enough." He slammed the tankard down on the bar, splashing the ale across the smooth surface to puddle near the amused barkeep's elbow. Kane turned on Fortune, his face black with fury. With one arm he warded off her blows, with the other he imprisoned her against him until he could maneuver them both over to the straightback chairs the trappers had vacated to get a better view of the brawl. While his captive was still kicking and squirming and calling him every vile name under the sun, he managed to finally force her down into the seat and tie her hands behind the slatted back. He took his handkerchief from his pocket and stuffed it into her mouth to stop her screeching invectives at him.

Well satisfied that he had things under control, Kane wiped his sweat-beaded brow on the sleeve of his coat and turned back to the bar where the barkeep stood grinning. Smugly Kane dusted his hands together and flashed the men a triumphant, cocksure smile. With the vixen subdued perhaps he could now enjoy his ale.

"She's always been a little hellion," the barkeep volunteered while refilling Kane's tankard. He wiped up the excess froth with a rag and added as an afterthought, "Had her own way too long if you ask me."

Kane lifted the tankard to his lips and drank, ignoring the hellcat he'd tied up across the room. All he was interested in at the moment was quenching his thirst and then getting the information he needed to find Lord Northrop's granddaughter. From what Bartram had said, the McQueen cabin was nearby and if it were at all possible he wanted to reach it before night.

"I'd have to agree with your assessment. She *is* a hellion, but that's none of my concern once I leave here. As long as she stays tied up and out of the way until I find out what I need to know, she can remain a wildcat."

"What is it that you're looking for around these parts? From the way you're dressed and speak I doubt you're interested in trading with the Indians or buying furs from the trappers."

"An accurate assessment, Mr.—?"

"Harvey Mills. I own this establishment."

"Then, Mr. Mills, you may be able to tell me where the McQueen cabin is located. I have business with Mr. McQueen."

To Kane's bewilderment, the man threw back his head and laughed at his question. His large belly quivered like a pot of jelly from his mirth. Tears glistened in his eyes when he finally managed to control his amusement and look once more at Kane. He shook his head and wiped at his face with the back of a hairy hand.

"Mister, Tiny McQueen died about two months back. If you have business with him then you're going to have to deal with his niece." The man chuckled again. "And I'm afraid it's not going to go easy for you." He pointed toward the girl who sat in the chair, glaring her fury at Kane. "That's her."

For one fleeting moment, Kane felt a sinking sensation in the pit of his belly. The hellcat was Lord Northrop's granddaughter. That was all he needed to make his miserable day complete. After coming all this way, he had just manhandled the one person he needed to befriend him if he wanted to thwart Nevin Manville.

Suddenly Kane burst into laughter himself, seeing the humor of the situation. He'd really gotten off to a good start with Fortune McQueen, but at least he'd not have to deal with her for very long. Once he returned her to her family in England, she would be Lord Northrop's cross to bear and Manville's bane. Kane chuckled again at the thought of Nevin Manville being confronted by the wildcat sitting across the room. The man deserved everything he got.

Still chuckling, Kane crossed the few feet that separated him from the bound girl. His eyes glinted from the challenge before him. He had to make her understand that it was in her own best interest to return with him to her family in England. With his speculative gaze never leaving Fortune's furious face, he swung one of the vacant chairs about and straddled it. He draped his arm across the back and rested his chin on his sleeve. For several long, thoughtful moments he sat silently regarding Fortune.

His gaze moved over her from head to toe, assessing her strengths as well as her weaknesses. From what he had seen and heard since arriving at the trading post, he had his work cut out for him if he wanted to turn this mountain wildcat into a lady before they reached England. And that was a necessity. For Lord Northrop to accept her as his long-lost granddaughter, much would depend upon her behavior. She couldn't go to meet her grandfather for the first time acting like one of the American savages.

Kane frowned at the comparison. From what he'd already seen of Fortune McQueen, she had much of the savage in her. Dressed in buckskins and wearing her hair braided like a squaw's made it much harder to distinguish the difference between the two. However, it wasn't her clothing that concerned him. That could easily be remedied once they returned to New Bern where his ship awaited. Her manners were another matter completely. Kane released a long, resigned breath. The task he'd set for himself wasn't going to be an easy one, but he'd realized a long time ago that if you wanted something out of life, you had to work for it. His shipping business was a prime example. He'd had to work long and hard to make that venture succeed, and he was just as determined to do the same with his father's mills. No matter if he had to tame a thousand wild young girls to the leash.

"Mistress McQueen, it seems that you and I have gotten off to a poor start," Kane said, and bestowed one of his most winning smiles upon Fortune. As a man of experience, he was confident of his own good looks and the effect his charms had upon the fairer sex. "And if you promise to behave, I'll untie you. Perhaps then we can begin anew."

In no mood to be congenial to the stranger or give in to his request, Fortune moaned her protest through the handkerchief that gagged her and glared at Kane through narrowed eyes.

"Now, is that any way to treat someone who has come such a long distance to see you?" Kane smiled again at the spark of curiosity that he saw flare in her slate-blue eyes. "You heard me right. I've come all the way from William Bartram's home in Pennsylvania to see you."

Fortune tried to act nonchalant about his sudden announcement but found it impossible not to react to Mr. Bartram's name. Her curiosity overshadowed all else she felt toward the obnoxious man with eyes the color of polished pewter.

"Do you promise to behave?" Kane asked again, and waited for her to agree. When she finally gave him a reluctant nod, he untied her hands and took out the gag. For a long moment, neither spoke while Fortune sat rubbing her chafed wrists. A twinge of guilt stabbed at Kane when he saw the red line left from the piece of leather he'd used to bind her. He frowned at his own barbaric actions. She might be headstrong but that gave him no right to harm her.

"I didn't mean to hurt you," he said in an effort to apologize for his behavior. "I was only trying to protect myself from harm. Had you not attacked me, then none of this would have ever taken place."

"I don't know what people do where you come from

but around these parts when someone attacks you, then you fight back,'' Fortune said, her hostility still simmering just beneath the surface.

''Attack you? I beg to differ with you, young lady. You attacked me first. I was only trying to have a tankard of ale when you turned into a screeching madwoman.''

''After you hauled me off my feet and nearly strangled me,'' Fortune said, ready to defend herself again.

''This is getting us nowhere,'' Kane said, seeing the renewed light of battle in her eyes. ''Can't we just put the last few minutes aside and start over? I didn't come all this way to argue with a hot-tempered young girl.''

Seething with fury once more, Fortune came to her feet. She forgot her reason for agreeing to behave. All thoughts of her friend William slipped from her mind at Kane's remark. She glared down at him, her face set. ''For your information, I'm nearly eighteen years old and I don't think starting over will do us any good. Now, good day.''

Kane caught her buckskin-fringed sleeve. ''If you're Fortune McQueen, it might do you a great deal of good to listen to what I have to say. I know your grandfather in England.''

Fortune froze and looked sharply back at Kane. No one except Tiny and William Bartram knew of her relatives in England. She'd known of her parents from the inscription in her mother's books but had learned of her grandfather's existence just before Tiny's death. Concerned about her future without him to protect her, Tiny had finally told her of the letter he'd had William Bartram write several years earlier to Lord Northrop. Until his death, he'd not given up the hope that he'd receive a reply, acknowledging her existence.

However, Fortune had been more realistic. She didn't have any false hopes to that end. After she'd learned that it had been four years since William Bartram had written to her grandfather in England, she had reconciled herself to the fact that Tiny was the only family she'd ever have.

''I don't have a grandfather in England.''

"Oh, but you do, Mistress McQueen. Your grandfather is Lord Northrop of North Meadows Estate near Bristol and I've come as his emissary to bring you back to England."

"How do you know that he is my grandfather?" Fortune asked. Against her better judgment, her heart began to thump with the exciting prospect that Tiny's wish had finally come true.

"From your friend William Bartram. When I visited him, he told me of the meeting with you and your uncle that led up to him writing to your grandfather in England. He also confirmed you had several books that belonged to your mother to prove that you are in fact Lord Northrop's granddaughter."

"I don't believe you," Fortune said. She couldn't allow herself to hope what he said was true.

"It's true. I'm here at your grandfather's request."

Fortune shook her head. She desperately needed to belong to a family again yet she was afraid to even consider such a possibility. It would hurt too much to be left totally alone once more if the man was lying. With a sharp jerk, Fortune freed her sleeve from the stranger and turned her back on him. She'd listened to enough of his wild story. There were more important things for her to attend. She had to make Harvey Mills give her what she deserved for the skins she'd brought to the trading post to sell. He'd been trying to cheat her when the stranger arrived and all hell had broken loose between them.

"Fortune," Kane said, coming to his feet. "I'm telling you the truth. How can I convince you that Lord Northrop is your grandfather?"

Fortune glanced over her shoulder at Kane. "You can't." Putting the stranger with the silver eyes from her mind, she strode up to the bar and looked Harvey Mills square in the face. "Now, I want the same price for the skins that you gave Tiny last spring or I'll not sell them to you."

"Then you'll just have to lug them back home with you,

Fortune. The price of furs went down this season and I can't give you what you're asking. If you're smart you'll take what I offer. There ain't another market for your skins within a hundred miles of here," Mills said. He was well satisfied he had the girl at a disadvantage. She was not as astute as her uncle when it came to the selling of furs. She knew a good pelt when she saw it, but that was as far as her knowledge about the business went.

"You're a cheat, Harvey Mills, and you damned well know it. If Tiny was here you'd not offer me such a piddling amount. The pelts are all first quality."

"Keep talking like that, Fortune McQueen, and I'll take back the offer I've made you. Then we'll see how well you get by through the winter," Mills said, his beefy face flushing a deeper shade of red from his mounting annoyance. He might be lowering his offer a little to increase his profits but it didn't mean he liked to be told to his face that he was a cheat. He considered himself a smart businessman.

Fortune felt like screaming with vexation. She knew he was cheating her blind but there was no way for her to do anything about it. If she didn't agree to his offer, she'd end up without salt and flour during the coming months. When she finally spoke, her voice was filled with exasperation. "All right, damn you, you can have the pelts at the price you offered."

"I thought you'd see reason. You've been let run wild but there's one thing I have to say about the way ol' Tiny raised you. He taught you to use your head and be sensible."

"He also taught me to know when I'm being duped out of some of the best pelts we've trapped in years," Fortune muttered, and turned away from the bar. If she had to look at Mills's fat, gloating face much longer, she wouldn't be responsible for her own actions. She crossed to the vacant table and slumped down in a chair to wait while Mills counted the furs and dug into his precious coin box to pay her.

"I'll buy your pelts if you'll agree to come with me to England."

Startled, Fortune looked up at the tall man standing beside the table. Her business with Mills was still bearing upon her mind and it took her a moment to collect her thoughts. Already disgusted with how her dealings had turned out with the proprietor of the trading post, Fortune said, "Why don't you just leave me alone? I've enough trouble on my hands without you adding to it with all of your lies."

"I've not lied to you, Fortune. You have a family in England and if you'll let me, I'll take you to them. You'll never have to worry about selling furs and being cheated again. Your grandfather is a wealthy man."

Without being aware of it, Kane had struck Fortune's vulnerable spot. He had also caught her in a moment when she needed Tiny's help and knowledge in dealing with a man like Harvey Mills. It was for that reason that the word of family drew her like a magnet. She missed the closeness and security that her adoptive family had given her. She also yearned to experience again the love she had shared with Tiny and his brothers.

"How can I believe you when I don't even know your name?" Fortune asked cautiously. She might desperately need a family, but she had been taught to look before she leaped into any situation no matter how tempting it might be. In the wilderness her life could depend upon it.

"Kane Warrick at your service, Mistress McQueen, or should I now address you as Lady Northrop?" Kane bent at the waist, giving her a casual bow.

"I honestly don't know what you should call me," Fortune said.

"Does that mean you are considering my offer?"

Fortune looked up at Kane, unsure of what to say. Deep inside she wanted to believe that she had family in England. She was too young to be alone. And what he offered was enticing to the adventurer who had long dwelled within her youthful body. She felt the need to live life to its fullest and had no desire to bury herself away in the mountains with only the trees and animals to talk with. Nor had she forgotten her dream of having a husband and family. It lay just beneath the surface and rose with a pungent urgency, a gentle ache about her heart. But she still did not know how to answer the man who had just offered her everything she desired.

"I honestly don't know," Fortune said truthfully. She had been so sure that when the moment came she would make the right decision about her future. Now she was face to face with it and she couldn't decide what to do.

Strangely, Kane Warrick didn't help her feelings. No matter how tantalizing a picture he painted for her, there was something about the man that made her wary of him. He had an unsettling way of looking at her through those thick-fringed silver eyes. His glance made her heart do rapid little taps against her ribs, and her blood seemed to run much faster in her veins. She'd never reacted in such an odd way when talking to any of the other men she'd met in the past, and she didn't understand what it was about Warrick in particular that made her feel slightly giddy. Her instincts warned her that if she accepted his offer and let him take her back to England to meet the man he said was her grandfather, her life would never be the same again. And she didn't know if that was for better or for worse.

"You will be Lady Northrop if you come with me. It's as simple as that. Within a few weeks you'll be with your grandfather on his estate near Bristol," Kane urged her gently. He'd gained more ground with her than he'd expected after their first encounter, and he didn't want to push her too hard or he might frighten her away.

"It sounds very simple yet I know nothing about you or what you think to gain by taking me back to England," Fortune said cautiously.

"I assure you that I'll gain nothing more than Lord Northrop's thanks by returning his long-lost granddaughter to the bosom of her family," Kane said. In truth all he did expect was the man's gratitude for this gesture, and that was the way he wanted it at the present time. However, in the near future, he hoped Lord Northrop would feel indebted to him and be willing to sell him the strip of land that adjoined Warrick's property to the river.

"Here's yer money," Harvey Mills said, interrupting their conversation. He slapped the few coins down on the table in front of Fortune. "There's more there than they're worth," he added, insulting Fortune's ability to judge first-quality pelts.

Fortune looked at the coins and then back to Harvey Mills. Her temper flared white hot. The pittance he had given her would not last her through the winter. Face flushed and eyes sparkling with blue fire, she picked up the coins, pushed back her chair, and stood facing Mills. She threw the coins at him. "Keep your damned money. I'd rather see the pelts rot than let you make a profit from them."

"You little hellcat," Mills growled, and started to reach for Fortune when he caught sight of the pistol in the stranger's hand.

"I wouldn't do that if I were you, Mr. Mills. The lady has made her decision and I suggest you accept it. If you want the pelts then I would offer her double last year's price."

Mills backed away and shook his head. "Like hell I will. She can keep the damned pelts and go straight to blazes herself for all I care." He got down on his hands and knees to hunt for the precious coins that had rolled willy-nilly across the floor.

Fortune flashed Kane a grateful smile that lit up her whole face. Had he not intervened on her behalf, she had no doubt that Mills would have harmed her, if not killed her. Glancing back at the trading post proprietor crawling about the floor, she realized that the man's greed had finally made her decision for her. She had little choice left after her burst of temper. Without Mills's money, she'd go hungry in the coming winter months. She had no choice but to go with Kane Warrick to England. Fortune eyed Kane thoughtfully for a long moment and then said, "If you'll keep your word and buy my pelts, then I'll go with you."

"Agreed," Kane said, smiling. He'd managed to get her to go with him. Now the real work would begin. Once they were out of the mountains he'd tell her the entire story about her grandfather and convince her she'd have to change if she wanted to be accepted by him. However, for the time being, he'd leave things as they stood. She might change her mind if she thought that Lord Northrop didn't even know of her existence, and he couldn't chance that happening.

Fortune, too, was having her own thoughts about the coming journey. She'd made Kane buy the pelts for one reason alone: to give her a feeling of security in the event things did not work out in England. She had no idea what it would cost to get back home, but she'd at least have a little money to sustain her until she could find a way to return to the blue mountains of Carolina. "You always leave a way to escape when you confront a mountain lion in his own den" had been Tiny's sage advice, and she would heed it now when she entered the world where men like Kane Warrick lived.

# Chapter 3

*Steel-gray clouds obscured the vivid sunset. The gentle* breeze had freshened, changing the calm waves into roiling whitecaps that struck against the hull of the ship with enough force to make the vessel tremble from the impact. Caught up in her own reveries, Fortune stood by the rail completely unaware of the inclement weather approaching the ship called the *Mermaid*. As if to give her warning of what was to come, the wind whipped several raven curls loose from the ribbon that had secured them at the nape of her neck, and they momentarily webbed her profile before she absently brushed them away. Her thoughts were centered upon the dilemma she would face on her arrival in England. Her future now looked as bleak as it had before she left Carolina.

"After leaving everything I know, I may not even be welcomed by the man Kane said was my grandfather," Fortune said, voicing her worry aloud. Her tone reflected her mounting trepidation over the situation that had seemed the answer to her prayers when she'd first met Kane Warrick and believed he'd been sent by her grandfather.

Now, and quite by accident on Kane's part, she had learned that Lord Northrop knew nothing of her existence nor was Kane his emissary. When she reached England the man might disavow her claim to be his granddaughter. If that happened, she didn't know what she would do.

Her thoughts did little to build the confidence that had been slowly eroding under Kane Warrick's constant criticism. Since the day in New Bern when he'd purchased several gowns for her to wear on their journey, Kane had become her tormentor. Nothing she did pleased him. According to Kane, the list of her shortcomings was endless and there was no hope she'd ever correct them all.

Fortune had done everything she knew to please him in an effort to restore the amicable relationship they'd shared after their truce at the trading post. Until New Bern they had been like brother and sister, laughing and joking together as he accompanied her back to the cabin to collect her few belongings and her mother's books. However, once they left the mountains behind, something had changed the relaxed and easy rapport between them. And by the time she'd modeled the gowns, the tension was nearly tangible.

Now, on top of losing Kane's friendship, a friendship she'd come to enjoy during the past weeks on the trail, he'd accidentally let it slip that Lord Northrop knew nothing of her visit. Perhaps he would not want her even if he did know that she was in fact his granddaughter. This bit of information made her realize how foolish she'd been to trust a man she knew nothing about. Kane could have lied about everything he told her.

"But why would he come all the way into the mountains to find me if it was a lie?" she asked herself. "Even if it isn't a lie and I do have a grandfather in England, why would he go to such extremes to bring me and my grandfather together when Lord Northrop doesn't even know of my existence?" Fortune shook her head sadly. She could find no answers to her questions.

"I wish to God I'd never set out on this venture. I wish I was back in my tiny cabin at Indian Face Mountain. Then I'd not have to worry about Kane Warrick's reason for finding me or anything else," Fortune grumbled, turning away from the rail. In the same moment, she saw the man who was quickly becoming her nemesis striding across the deck toward her.

"Fortune, haven't you any sense in that head of yours? It's getting ready to storm and here I find you standing on deck. One wave could wash you overboard and no one would be the wiser," Kane scolded, even as he felt his heart give a sudden lurch at the thought of losing this wildcat he'd found in the Carolina mountains.

It was difficult for him to admit that in the last weeks the vixen had unexpectedly managed to insinuate herself into his life. He'd tried to ignore his own feelings and reaffirm his resolve never to become deeply involved with any woman again. The memories from his past were far too painful for him to allow any woman, young or old, to claim his heart. It had happened once, to his regret, and he didn't plan to indulge in that type of self-destructive behavior again.

Much to his chagrin and contrary to all of his resolutions, he found himself acting like an idiot concerning Fortune McQueen. Kane knew he had to put a stop to it. One way or the other he had to rid himself of the wild fantasies that had plagued his imagination since New Bern. After seeing Fortune gowned as a lady for the first time, his mind would give him no rest. Clothed in silks and lace and with her hair coiffed becomingly, she was no longer the backwoods girl he'd first met but a desirable woman who made his blood simmer in his veins.

Fortune held an attraction for him that was nearly too strong to resist, but he knew he couldn't give in to his desires. He reminded himself that she was nothing more to him than a business investment and he couldn't jeopardize his chances of gaining the land he needed by letting himself seduce Lord Northrop's granddaughter. It was far safer for all concerned if he kept his heated thoughts at bay.

"Leave me alone, Kane Warrick," Fortune said, breaking the train of unruly thoughts that had darkened Kane's swarthy complexion. "I've taken my last orders from you.

If I'd had any sense I'd never have let you talk me into coming along on this wild adventure in the first place.''

"You're still upset about what I told you about Lord Northrop, aren't you?''

Fortune nodded stiffly and looked away from him. Upset was too mild a word to describe how she felt at that moment. She was so angry with Kane that she couldn't carry on a polite conversation with him. If she opened her mouth at all, she feared she'd scorch his ears off with some of Tiny's choice invectives. He was the man at the root of all of her troubles. He'd given her a glimpse of what could be and now that it might not happen she was far more disappointed than she'd realized.

"There's no reason to worry about it. As his son's only child, I'm sure he'll welcome you with open arms,'' Kane said, hoping to lay her worries to rest. They would do neither of them any good. In the remaining days of their journey, she had to learn the finer points about being a lady if she was to be accepted in her grandfather's circles. They didn't have time to waste on problems that couldn't be solved until after they arrived in England and went to North Meadows. Kane placed a comforting hand on Fortune's shoulder and gave it a reassuring squeeze.

Startled by the touch, Fortune jerked away from him as if his hand had been fire. "Leave me alone, Kane. If you don't I won't be responsible for what happens. After all the lies you've told, I feel like skinning you like the polecat you are. Nothing you can say or do will ease my mind or make me forgive you for not telling me the truth from the beginning.''

"Cool your temper, Fortune. I did what I felt was right,'' Kane said as if reprimanding a recalcitrant child.

Fortune faced him with arms folded over her chest and her chin set at a pugnacious angle. "Right? How can you say such a thing? What excuse can you have for lying to me so that I would give up the only home I've ever known? If Lord Northrop decides I'm not his granddaughter then I'll be left with nothing. No home or family.''

"You had only a cabin in the woods and no family when we met, Fortune. You've risked little to gain much. I didn't tell you about your grandfather sooner because I knew you'd be upset and perhaps wouldn't come to England. You're too young and quick-tempered to realize the benefits of being Lord Northrop's granddaughter and the heir to his estate. Your grandfather may not welcome you, but as long as you can prove you are the rightful heir to North Meadows then you will inherit it. Someday you'll thank me for leaving out the few minor details that would have prevented you from going to England to meet your grandfather."

"I doubt that I'll ever feel that way," Fortune snapped, flashing him a contemptuous look. "I don't care about my grandfather's estate. All I want is to have a family. Can't you understand that money doesn't mean anything to me?"

"If you honestly believe that you're much younger than I thought. Anyone can have a family, but few can inherit an estate the size of North Meadows."

"What is it you hope to gain by taking me to my grandfather, Kane Warrick? Since you feel this way about family, I'm sure it isn't just to see us united after so many years."

"I've nothing against families. I have a son," Kane said, volunteering no further information behind his actions.

"Then I'm sure your wife and son mean more to you than a piece of property. No man could be so heartless." Fortune's heart had given an odd little twist within her breast when he mentioned having a son. Nor did she find it easy to speak of Kane's wife. Her own reaction puzzled her. Why she was behaving so oddly to such news, she couldn't fathom. She also didn't understand why his next statement filled her with such relief.

"My wife is dead. And if it is heartless to be more concerned about my estate than my son, then so be it. He has a nanny to see to his needs and I'm working to leave him an inheritance so he won't have to mortgage his soul to keep it," Kane said. He didn't add that this was far more than his own father had done for him.

"Then I feel sorry for you and your son. You don't know how fortunate you are to have a family of your own or you wouldn't put anything ahead of them. And I hope you never have to find out how lonely it feels to have no one."

"I don't need your sympathy nor do I want it," Kane said defensively. Fortune's statement made him uncomfortable but he shrugged it off. He knew exactly how it felt to be lonely, but because of Felicia it was by choice. His mistress, as well as a score of other women, would willingly end his lonely existence if he'd allow it. "I'm content with my life as it is and what I do with it is no concern of yours. But that's neither here nor there at the moment. However, the storm brewing on the horizon is of importance, so I suggest we go below. I'd hate to see you washed overboard before you could regain the family you want." Kane's sarcasm effectively ended their conversation before Fortune remembered he hadn't answered her question about what he thought to gain from her grandfather.

"You should worry more about yourself than me. With a heart of stone, you'd sink like a rock if you were washed overboard." With that parting barb, Fortune turned and stalked across the deck.

Kane chuckled at her show of spirit. His gaze never left her straight little back as he watched her walk away with her head held high. Right now he knew she was angry enough to skin him as she'd threatened, but in the last weeks he'd learned that her temper usually cooled quickly.

Kane shook his head, bemused. Fortune McQueen could be a true vixen at times. She spoke her mind and stood her ground without giving an inch yet he'd found another side to her nature, as well. She didn't hold onto her anger once she'd vented it. He had also been pleasantly surprised to learn that unlike most of the so-called ladies of his acquaintance in Bristol and London, she had a tender and caring heart.

He'd seen it at work the previous day when one of the seamen had cut his hand seriously while mending a sail. She'd been the only person among the passengers on the *Mermaid* to come to the man's aid. While the other so-called ladies gaped in horror and swooned at the sight of the scarlet blood covering the man's arm to his elbow, Fortune had taken charge of the situation. She'd thought nothing of raising the skirt of her new gown and ripping off a strip of her petticoat to use as a tourniquet to staunch the bleeding. The ship's surgeon had told Kane later that by her quick actions she'd probably saved the man's life. The seaman had severed a large vein and could have bled to death before the surgeon was summoned.

Tucking his hand into the pockets of his fawn-colored britches, Kane rolled back on his heels and watched her duck into the shadowy hatch that led down to the passenger cabins. He couldn't stop himself from admiring Fortune's courage. He'd begun to believe that she didn't possess fear. She had faced each obstacle placed in her path without blinking an eye, and he knew once they reached England she'd confront what awaited her there with the same dauntless and unflagging spirit. Kane smiled once more at the thought of Nevin Manville's reaction to his colonial cousin. The man was in for the surprise of his life when he tried to deal with Fortune on his own terms. From his own experience with her, Kane had learned that Fortune set her own terms and didn't back down.

The storm lashed the ship with high winds and needling rain. The vessel had no time to recover from one beating before the next ascended. The thick oak timbers creaked and groaned under the assault as the unmerciful waves pounded against the hull and washed over the deck. The furious wind rushed through the masts and tangled the rigging as if ridiculing the sailors who tried to battle the sea to keep their vessel afloat.

Unlike the brave souls on deck, Fortune sat curled on her bunk listening to the furor outside. With knees drawn up to her chest, she clutched one of her mother's books and Tiny's coonskin cap to her breast. White-lipped and wide-eyed, she held onto her treasures and waited for the end to come. The storm had been raging for more than an hour and each time the vessel dipped into a trough of waves and sea water dribbled down through the cracks in the ceiling to run across the floor in tiny streams, she thought the ship would never be able to right itself. Her heart felt as if it rested in her throat and her breathing had grown short and ragged. In all that had transpired since she'd met Kane Warrick, this was the most terrifying for Fortune. Squeezing her eyes tightly closed, she buried her face against her knees and sought desperately to think of anything but the storm beyond the cabin walls.

"Think of Kane," she muttered into the soft material that covered her legs. "He's the one responsible for all of my troubles since I left home."

At the thought of her home a sudden burst of homesickness swelled into an uncomfortable lump in her throat. No one knew how much she missed that tiny two-room cabin near Indian Face Mountain. In spite of the misery mounting in her heart with each passing day, she'd kept up a brave front. And until the storm struck and destroyed all of her defenses, she'd managed to keep all of her trepidation well hidden. Now with the storm raging outside and the new knowledge of what might await her in England, everything came crashing to the surface.

"Oh, God," she murmured, rolling her head from side to side against her knees. "Just let me live through this and I promise I'll never go off on another wild scheme, no matter how much I want something." Fortune jerked her head up when the ship shuddered and listed severely. She felt herself rolling toward the edge of the bunk but could not catch a handhold to save herself before she slid off her narrow bed and tumbled across the floor. She landed against the wall with a bang. At the impact of her hip against the planks, an involuntary cry of fear and pain escaped her white lips. When the ship righted itself once more she struggled to sit up but found her efforts impeded by the lawn of her night rail. Caught beneath her and wound tightly about her hips and legs, it bound her securely in place. She twisted to one side, jerked at the thin material, and heard it rip as it gave way. Paying no heed to the long expanse of leg exposed by the tear in her gown, she struggled to her knees and then pushed herself erect. She fought to remain upright but failed when the ship tilted sharply once more. With the deck roiling beneath her feet, she lost her footing again and slammed back against the wall. The collision knocked the breath from her and she sagged in a heap on the floor. Stunned and gasping for air, she was vaguely aware of the cabin door banging open to reveal a tall, tousle-haired man.

"Fortune," Kane said, his voice strained from the effort it took to keep himself upright. The floor swayed as if it had a life of its own. "Are you all right? I heard you cry out."

Fortune could not answer. At the moment she could find no breath or words to describe what she was feeling. Her back and hip ached from her fall but she thought little of her pain compared to the strange way her heart was behaving. It pounded erratically against her ribs as she looked up at Kane.

Bewildered, she found her thoughts abruptly centered upon the man instead of herself. Her gaze was drawn to the crisp mat of dark curls on the wide chest that was exposed by the deep V opening of his white lawn shirt. From there it moved downward to the fawn-colored britches hugging his lean hips and legs, and emphasizing the bulging muscles in his thighs as he tried to keep his balance. Her gaze traveled the length of him and then came back to rest on the shapely lips that were now firmed into a determined line as he braced himself in the doorway. The terror she'd felt at the storm mingled with other intense emotions that she could not identify and left her feeling hot and cold at the same time.

"Fortune, are you hurt?" Kane asked, beginning to move in a crooked path toward her. The ship shuddered and righted itself, making him stagger sideways a few feet before managing to regain his balance and move across to her.

"Are you hurt?" he asked again, kneeling at her side. When she remained silent, he grew worried. Concern etched a path across his smooth forehead as he cupped her chin and searched her ashen features for any sign of an injury. Seeing no visible evidence that she'd been hurt, he breathed a sigh of relief. His gaze traveled along the slender column of her neck to the pulsing hollow at the base of her throat and on down to the firm mounds exposed above the low neckline of the lawn night rail. For one uncontrollable moment, Kane found himself unable to take his eyes off the softness that peeked enticingly over the edge of the ribboned and laced edge. He felt his mouth go dry and swallowed hard before finally forcing himself to look once more into the slate-blue eyes of the girl-woman. Fortune McQueen was far too beautiful and innocent for her own good.

Despite his good intentions, Kane felt his blood heat up and he quickly let his hand drop away from her. He released a long breath, ran one hand through his tousled hair, and pushed himself to his feet. His gruff voice reflected his strain when he spoke. "Then if you're not hurt, I'll go back to my cabin."

"Please don't go," Fortune said, scrambling to her feet at his side. Without considering her own actions, she placed a restraining hand on his sleeve and stared up at him, her eyes pleading for his understanding. With the storm still raging beyond the cabin walls, she had no desire to be left alone again.

Kane drew in a sharp, agonized breath and silently prayed for the strength to keep himself from reaching out for her. She had no idea what a fetching picture she made with her raven hair hanging in a silken curtain about her shoulders and her bare feet peeking from beneath the thin lawn of her torn night rail. Nor was she aware of the self-control it took to restrain himself at such close proximity with her. He'd not bedded a woman since leaving his mistress in Bristol over three months ago, and Fortune McQueen's allure did little to ease the dilemma in which he was now finding himself. Kane disengaged Fortune's hand from his sleeve and shook his head.

"Go back to bed, Fortune. You've nothing to fear. The *Mermaid* is captained by a good man. He'll not let anything happen to the ship or its passengers."

"Please don't leave me here alone," Fortune said, and threw herself against Kane. She had not forgiven him for letting her believe her grandfather had sent him to find her, but she'd welcome the devil himself into her cabin to keep from being left alone in the hellish storm that raged beyond the room's walls.

Kane rolled his eyes heavenward, beseeching the Almighty to give him the strength to resist the warm young body pressed against his. Struggling to maintain his composure, he gently set Fortune away from him and peered down into her upturned face. At the unexpected look he saw in her eyes, he momentarily forgot his own resolve. The slate-blue depths revealed the emotion that he had believed Fortune McQueen did not possess. She'd never uttered one word to make him think she ever experienced the same kind of fear that other women so willingly displayed for the benefit of the opposite sex. With her chin up and shoulders squared, she'd faced each new situation without any sign of trepidation and now when she needed him, he couldn't turn her away. Even the strongest of souls needed support at times.

"I'll stay for only a short while. Now back to bed with you before you get a chill from this damp cabin." Kane spoke as if he were talking to his son, Price.

"Thank you, Kane." Fortune's relief was reflected in the smile she bestowed upon him. As she turned toward her bunk, intent upon following his orders, a huge wave hit the ship. The vessel listed severely and sent Kane crashing into her. His arms automatically came around her as they fell.

Sprawling together upon the bunk, Kane instinctively rolled his weight to one side to keep from crushing Fortune beneath him. Face to face and thigh to thigh, they lay with limbs entwined and breathing heavily. A moment later when the ship righted itself once more, they were too aware of each other physically to move.

Mesmerized, Fortune gazed up into Kane's silver eyes and felt her mouth go dry. Her heart began to race within her breast and all thoughts of the storm vanished under the current of heat sweeping over her from their intimate contact. Without realizing the invitation her action bestowed, she moistened her lips with the tip of her tongue.

Kane moaned inwardly at the simple gesture and accepted his defeat against himself. Resting on his elbows above her, he cupped Fortune's face in the palms of his hands and lowered his mouth to hers. Gently he tasted of her lips with his tongue, savoring the sweetness he had only imagined until that moment. His heart pounded against his ribs when he felt her first tentative response. She slid her arms up his chest and around his neck and opened her lips to his quest. He groaned his pleasure as he deepened the kiss and glided his hand down along the slender column of her throat to the beckoning mounds pressed against the thin material of her gown.

Fortune flinched at the first unexpected caress but soon found the warmth coming through the soft lawn too pleasurable to deny herself. She arched toward Kane, wanting, needing to feel the tingling heat that his touch kindled within her. The heady sensation traveled through her stomach to the pit of her belly and formed an ache that she did not completely understand but instinctively knew only Kane could appease.

"Oh, Kane," she breathed against his lips and tightened her arms about his neck to draw him closer. "I never knew I could feel this way."

Her innocent statement cooled Kane's ardor like a bucket of cold water poured onto a fire. It sizzled briefly and then died, leaving him tasting the ashes of his unquenched desire and calling himself every kind of a fool for allowing himself to succumb to his needs. A man of his experience had no excuse for losing control over a young innocent who knew nothing of the world. Disgusted with himself, Kane eased away from Fortune and sat up. He ran his fingers through his tousled hair and shook his head with regret.

"I'm sorry, Fortune. It never should have happened."

"Why?" Fortune asked, bewildered by his strange reaction to something that had felt so pleasant to her.

"It just shouldn't have. It was wrong."

"Why was it wrong? I liked it," Fortune said, coming to her knees at Kane's side. Her position emphasized the lush curves below the neckline of her gown.

Kane glanced at her and then quickly shifted his gaze to the wall in front of him. "Just take my word for it, Fortune. It was wrong of me to kiss you."

"I don't understand why you think it was wrong if I don't," Fortune said, perplexed. "I find I like kissing very much."

"You shouldn't say things like that," Kane answered hoarsely as he came to his feet. Fortune's honesty made him uncomfortably aware of her innocence. She had no idea about the rules that society placed on young women. She spoke her mind and voiced her feelings because she had lacked the influence of other females in her life. She possessed no guile, and it left him ill prepared to answer her questions, when in truth it took all he could do to control the urge to lay her back on the bunk and make love to her.

"Why shouldn't I tell you I liked your kisses? I'd be lying if I said otherwise."

"For God's sake, Fortune!" Kane exploded. "That's exactly why it's wrong of me to kiss you."

"I don't understand."

"You're too young to understand. You've never been taught a proper young lady doesn't go around giving her kisses freely or expressing her feelings at the drop of a hat, especially to men. It's not respectable."

Fortune stiffened her spine at his reprimand. A mutinous light glimmered in the depths of her eyes as she looked up at Kane. "I'm not the proper young lady, as you've known from the first time we met. And if I have to lie about how I feel to be one then I'm afraid I'm doomed to never achieve the high and mighty pinnacle you and your kind admire. I've tried to do everything you've told me since we left New Bern, yet no matter what I say or do I can't please you. Now even the truth makes you angry with me."

Kane drew in a long breath and turned toward the door. He had to get away from Fortune before he made an even greater mistake. Her honesty was making his will to resist her weaken by the moment.

"You said you wouldn't leave me," Fortune challenged when he reached for the latch.

"That was before our little encounter. Now if you know what's good for you, you'll go to sleep."

Kane's words brought home the fact that when he left, she'd have to face the storm alone. This thought effectively quelled her spirit for combat. Her tone reflected her feeling when she said quietly, "Kane, don't leave me. I promise to be good. I won't kiss you again."

"Damn it, Fortune. Go to sleep. The storm sounds as if it's letting up and I've no time to mollycoddle you. It's late and I want to get some sleep." Kane left the cabin without a backward glance at the white-faced girl on the bunk. He closed the door firmly behind him to put a physical barrier between himself and the young woman who made his blood run hot.

"Damn," he muttered beneath his breath, and turned

toward the steps that would take him up onto the drenched deck. Rain still pelted the ship but the fury of the storm had lessened. Kane welcomed the icy water that soaked him to the skin in less than a minute. He raised his face toward the dark sky, seeking the cooling effect of the downpour. He wanted to quell the fire Fortune had created in his blood and hoped the rain would wash the taste of her from his lips so that he could rid her from his mind as well. From the pressure in his loins and the way his heart hammered against his ribs, it wasn't going to be easy. He had no other choice or he'd never be able to stay away from her until they reached England.

God! How he envied the young swains who would seek her hand once her grandfather accepted her. Few would be able to resist her charms. Kane frowned at the thought of other men tasting the same sweetness he'd savored earlier. He felt something akin to jealousy rise up in his chest, but he quickly denied any such emotion existed within him. Jealousy was for men who cared about women beyond the bedroom. It wasn't for him.

He'd learned that lesson the hard way from his wife, Felicia. He'd cared for her in the beginning but after the vows were spoken, her coldness soon killed any love he'd felt for her. She had turned away from him, denying him his husbandly rights and antagonizing him when he insisted upon making love to her. But he hadn't let her coldness deter him from getting the heir he needed to carry on the family name. Now he had the son that he'd forced upon Felicia, as well as enough guilt from his wife's death in childbirth to last him through this lifetime. He didn't need any other complications now or in the future.

"I'm acting like a damned fool," Kane muttered into the wet, ebony night. His guilt rose up to block out all other feelings. "Fortune McQueen is nothing but a good business investment for me and that is all. When I deliver her to Lord Northrop and buy the land I need for the mills then she'll be out of my life for good."

Reassured that he had finally managed to get everything

well under control once more, Kane stepped back through the hatch and made his way to his cabin. He stripped off his soggy clothing and climbed into his bunk. Soon he slept, yet it wasn't a restful journey into land of Morpheus. His dreams were filled with images of the young woman with slate-blue eyes and raven tresses who lay alone in the cabin next door.

When the first rays of the sun peeped over the horizon it found Fortune lying wide awake, pondering the confusing turn of events from the previous night. After Kane left her cabin and the storm died away, she had been unable to sleep as he'd ordered. Kane's kiss had awakened her to a side of herself she didn't know existed until the hard pressure of his lips and tongue stirred it into life. Now she had to try to understand and deal with the strong emotions within her.

"Tiny, how I wish you were here to explain what I'm feeling," Fortune mused aloud. "Yesterday I thought I loathed Kane Warrick for not telling me the truth, but now his deception doesn't seem as bad as it did at first. What's wrong with me? Every time I think of Kane my stomach feels as if it has a swarm of butterflies in it. Oh, Tiny, I need you now more than I've ever needed you in my life."

Knowing that she alone had to work out the dilemma of her feelings toward Kane, Fortune restlessly turned from one side to the other seeking a comfortable sleeping position. She failed. Until she faced her tumultuous feelings, she knew she'd find no rest.

Never having learned to be coy, Fortune sat up and slid her bare feet to the floor. There was only one person on board the *Mermaid* who could help her with her confusion: Kane Warrick. She had nowhere else to turn. He had created the strange new feelings within her and now he'd have to explain what they meant.

Did the way she felt mean that she'd fallen in love with Kane? And as he had kissed her, did that mean he returned her feelings? Kane would have to answer those questions because, for the life of her, Fortune couldn't do it by herself.

Consumed by her dilemma, Fortune left her cabin and crossed the few feet to Kane's door. She spared no thought to her state of dress or to what anyone would think to see her going into a man's cabin wearing only her night rail. Before she lost her courage, she knocked and heard a muffled and less than welcoming "Come in and quit that banging."

Roused from the first sound sleep he'd had all night and thinking it was the cabin boy with his morning bath water, Kane bade him to enter. Disgruntled from the lack of restful sleep and without a glance toward the door, he threw back the covers. Naked, he sat up with elbows on knees and head bowed, rubbing the sleep from his eyes.

"What time is it?" he asked the silent figure who stood leaning against the door. "With no more sleep than I got last night, it seems my head just touched the pillow before you knocked."

"It's six o'clock," Fortune answered, her voice strained. Seeing Kane naked left her nearly speechless. The pure beauty of his masculine physique made her throat tight. Even from where she stood she could almost feel the strength he exuded. He was all sinewy muscle and ridges, and she had to control the urge to reach out and run her hand down his sleek body in appreciation.

Kane's head snapped up at the familiar yet unexpected voice. He gaped at her, momentarily shocked speechless by the sight of Fortune in his cabin. It took him a moment to collect his wits and remember his state of undress. He quickly covered himself.

"What in hell are you doing in here? Especially at this time of the morning," he growled, running a hand through his hair, his face flushing with annoyance. "Don't you have any sense of decency? Didn't McQueen teach you that a young girl doesn't enter a man's chamber uninvited?"

"You told me to come in," Fortune answered, nonplussed by his outburst. Tiny and his brothers had been like surly bears when they first awoke in the morning.

"That's not the point, damn it. I thought you were the cabin boy with the water for my bath. A lady would know that it is not proper to be alone with a gentleman in his bedchamber even if it is only a ship's cabin."

"I came here to talk with you," Fortune said, ignoring his criticism of her.

"Talk! At this time in the morning?" Kane exploded. "I'm in no mood to talk to you or anyone. Now go back to your cabin and stay there."

Undeterred, Fortune said, "I'm not leaving until I know exactly why you kissed me last night."

Kane rolled his eyes heavenward, once more beseeching the Almighty for help with this girl-woman who was driving him to the brink of madness. Here she was at an ungodly hour of the morning asking questions that he could not truthfully answer. "Fortune, this is no time to get into this. I apologized to you for my actions last night and I can promise it will never happen again. Isn't that enough?"

"No. It isn't enough, Kane. I want to understand what I'm feeling and you're the only person I have to ask. I know no one else." Fortune crossed to the side of his bunk and hunkered down in front of him. Her face was solemn as she looked up.

Unable to resist her expression, Kane reached out and cupped her face in his hands. His annoyance faded and his heart went out to her. She was on the brink of becoming a woman yet she was ignorant of her own sexuality.

"Fortune, this isn't something you should ask a man but since I'm the only person you have to ask, I'll try to explain things to you."

Feeling much like her father at that moment, Kane pulled Fortune up beside him and sat holding her hand. He absently massaged her palm with his thumb as he sought the right words. He wanted her to understand that her feelings were normal but she should wait until she found the man she wanted to marry before acting on them.

"What you're feeling is natural, Fortune," he began, then paused. He drew in a long breath to brace himself before venturing further into this unusual conversation. "Young girls are taught that they are not supposed to have sexual dreams—I mean—feelings toward the opposite sex until after they're married. But it wasn't the way nature made things." Kane paused again. Her expression and their conversation was having its own effect upon him. He felt his words of advice drying up along with his fatherly attitude.

Kane cleared his throat. "Does that explain things enough?" He prayed her answer would be yes. He didn't know how much more he could take.

"I understand what you're trying to tell me but it still doesn't explain what happened between us. Why did you kiss me, Kane?"

Holding the sheet about his hips, Kane awkwardly got to his feet and moved as far away from her as the cabin would allow. "What I did was a mistake, Fortune. I tried to explain that to you last night. Why are you still harping about it?"

"Because I want to know if you felt what I did."

Kane didn't look at her but stared at the spot above her head. "Fortune, you don't want to know what I felt. Now will you please go back to your cabin and get dressed. A lady doesn't run about in such *dishabille*."

Stubbornly Fortune shook her head. "Do you love me, Kane? Is that why you kissed me?"

"For the love of God! What on earth does one kiss have to do with love, Fortune? I just explained to you that women and men have sexual feelings toward each other but that doesn't have anything to do with love. It's the nature of things. Men and women both have needs. I can sleep with a dozen women and never love one of them. Now do you understand what I'm saying?"

Fortune blanched but her voice revealed none of her disappointment as she said, "Then you felt nothing for me except a momentary need?"

"That's right," Kane replied crisply. He wanted this conversation to come to an end as quickly as possible. "That's why I shouldn't have kissed you. You are innocent to the ways of men and I shouldn't have taken advantage of you in such a way. It was wrong of me."

Fortune stood and turned toward the door. "You've answered my question so I'll leave you to go back to sleep."

Unable to let her go with that heart-wrenching look on her face, Kane took her by the arm, halting her exit. "I'm sorry if I've hurt you."

Fortune looked down at the strong fingers on her arm and shrugged. "I've much to learn, Kane. And I would have expected no less from you after yesterday's awakening. You're the type of man who takes but never gives, and I'm grateful that you've taught me this valuable lesson before I meet other men."

Kane's grip tightened momentarily before he let his hand fall away from her. "Then at least something good has come out of this besides ill feelings. I would be your friend, Fortune. Should you ever be in need of one, then come to me."

The words were out of his mouth before he completely realized his own intentions. Never before in his life had he told a woman he would be her friend. Especially one he desired. But there was something different about Fortune that made him feel protective toward her. She was strong and capable in her own way, yet he had also just seen the vulnerable side of her she'd kept hidden until entering his cabin a few minutes ago.

"I prefer to have friends that I can trust, Kane. Not those who lie and use me for their own benefit." Without a backward glance at the man she left standing with a sheet draped about his lean hips and a bemused expression playing over his face, Fortune turned and walked out the door.

Fortune's brave front lasted until she closed the door of her cabin behind her. Then she let her tears fall. Anger and hurt mingled as she fell facedown on the bunk and pounded her pillow with both fists. When she'd gone to

Kane, she'd hoped, deep down, that he would return her feelings. Now she was left frustrated and feeling foolish. She didn't want to be affected by the man who had abused her trust in more ways than one, but she could not forget the way his kiss had aroused her. And to her shame, she was unable to stop herself from craving more of the same sweet torment.

"You're going to have to put yesterday out of your mind completely. Forget about Kane, as well as the fact that Lord Northrop may turn you away from his door. If you don't you'll drive yourself mad," Fortune muttered, slamming another fist into the already lumpy pillow. "Let the future take care of itself when it gets here."

Fortune spoke bravely but it would not be easy to wipe out the events of the previous day. She still felt giddy every time she thought of Kane no matter how hard she tried to deny it.

# Chapter 4

*Intimidated by the prospect of leaving the* Mermaid *and* entering the hive of activity on the docks, Fortune stood silent and tense at the ship's rail. From her vantage point, she had a clear view of the city that Kane had told her was the second largest in England. Though she didn't quite understand all he'd said, he explained that the triangular trade between England, Africa, and America and the West Indies for European goods, African slaves, and sugar, tobacco, and cotton had made the port the busiest in England. Although Bristol had a long history, it had come into prominence only during the past fifty years.

However, England's commerce meant little to Fortune at the moment. Paramount in her mind was the fact that she was only a short distance from North Meadows and her grandfather. Her concern over how she would be received had resurfaced to twist her insides into tight knots of worry. Her strained expression now reflected the turmoil she'd successfully kept at bay during the past weeks.

Ever since the humiliating morning in Kane's cabin she'd managed to avoid thinking of this moment by keeping her mind occupied with other things. She'd thrown herself into learning the intricacies of becoming a lady and in the time left on board the *Mermaid*, she'd spent every spare minute practicing Kane's instructions.

At the thought of her success, a tiny smile tugged up the corners of Fortune's lips. Though she considered many of the things she'd had to learn ridiculous, all of her hard work had paid off. She now knew the proper way to conduct herself in mixed company, how to eat, sit, walk, talk, and a dozen other silly little things that the English seemed to set such store in. She had been pleased with herself for managing to accomplish so much in such a short time, but her greatest joy had come when Kane praised her endeavors. At that moment she knew everything she'd endured to become like the ladies he admired had been worth the effort.

"Eager to get your feet back on dry land?" Kane asked, close at her side.

Startled, Fortune jumped and jerked about to face Kane. She'd been so preoccupied with her musings that she didn't hear his approach. "Yes. I was just thinking about going ashore."

Kane drew in a deep breath and turned his gaze to the city beyond the docks. Bristol's odor floated upon the wind and he took it in, welcoming each scent, assured that his journey had finally come to an end. He'd missed England far more than he'd realized, and it felt good to be home again. Once he had Fortune settled with Lord Northrop, then he could get back to business. Glancing once more at Fortune, he asked, "What do you think of Bristol?"

Fortune shrugged and, without realizing her gesture, grimaced.

"I know it's far different from the mountains of Carolina but I'm sure you'll like it once you get accustomed to it."

"But there are so many people," Fortune said, eyeing the throngs that worked on the docks loading and unloading ships.

Kane heard the apprehension in her voice and placed a comforting hand over hers on the rail. He squeezed it gently. He could understand her trepidation. Her life had been spent in the wilderness, coming in contact with only a few people in an entire year. Now faced with the crowded city, she found it frightening. "There's nothing to fear, Fortune."

"I'm not afraid," Fortune said, pulling her hand free from his and squaring her shoulders. "I'm just not accustomed to seeing so many people at once."

Kane smiled at her denial, admiring her mettle. It took courage to face one's fears. He proffered his arm to her. "Then if you're not afraid, shall we go ashore?"

Fortune swallowed back the lump of fear that had risen in her throat and placed her hand on Kane's arm. She walked down the gangplank to the docks with head held high. However, a few moments later, to her bewilderment and embarrassment, she found herself clinging to Kane's arm for support when they reached solid ground. Her head reeled and her knees turned to jelly beneath her. To her chagrin, she heard Kane chuckle at her predicament. She flashed him a look that seethed with her unspoken opinion of him and his ungentlemanly behavior.

"Forgive me for laughing at you but I couldn't help myself. You had the most amusing expression on your face as you tried to get your land legs back."

"Land legs?" Fortune asked, her vexation with Kane mounting.

"Yes. What you're feeling now often happens when you've been at sea for weeks. You'll be all right in a few minutes. Once you adjust to the lack of movement beneath your feet, your knees will quit knocking and your head will stop spinning."

Though Kane's explanation relieved her mind, Fortune was far too tense to find her situation humorous. Nor did it help her feelings to be the object of Kane's humor. Ever since the morning after the storm, she'd done her best to keep her mind away from what had transpired between them. Yet just beneath the surface of her thoughts, humiliation was fresh and waiting to taunt her for her foolishness where Kane Warrick was concerned.

Drawing in a deep breath and forcing her mind back to the reason she had ventured so many thousands of miles from the comfort and security of her home in the mountains, Fortune turned the conversation toward the man who had been in her thoughts since awakening that morning. "Are we going to North Meadows now? Will I meet my grandfather today?"

"Not today. We'll stay at the Red Rooster Inn tonight and then tomorrow, after we collect our luggage, we'll go to North Meadows."

"How far is the estate from Bristol?" Fortune asked as they traversed the maze of stevedores and cargo that filled the quay. The excess bales of cotton, barrels of molasses and rum, as well as a sundry of other crates, spilled over into the cobbled streets and made walking difficult.

"It's not far but I prefer that we wait until tomorrow."

"Wouldn't it be better if we didn't wait?"

Kane glanced down at Fortune and arched a brow inquisitively. "I didn't realize that you were so anxious to meet your grandfather. After learning that he isn't expecting you, I was sure you'd have second thoughts about meeting him."

"I was but I'm not anymore," Fortune lied, keeping her eyes straight ahead so Kane wouldn't guess the truth.

"What changed your mind?"

My need to get away from you, Fortune thought, but said aloud, "Since I've come this far, it would be foolish not to see Lord Northrop. He may or may not accept me, that's his choice. But as I see it, it's too late for me to have second thoughts about my decision to come here. I was taught that it's better to beard the lion in his den than to be afraid of what will happen when you confront him. The waiting and worrying is usually worse than what happens when you do. Wouldn't you agree?"

"You're right but I'm afraid it's too late in the day for you to beard your lion. Our luggage has as yet to be unloaded from the *Mermaid* so that makes it impossible for us to leave as soon as you want. However, when we reach

the inn, I'll send a message to North Meadows so that
Lord Northrop will be expecting our visit tomorrow.''

Tomorrow, Fortune mused as they entered the Red
Rooster Inn. One more day until I meet the man Kane
claims is my grandfather. One more day until I know if
he'll turn me away or accept me into his family. One more
day until I know exactly what lies ahead in my future.
And, she added, one more day until I'm free of Kane. The
thought did little to ease her anxiety. He might have turned
into her nemesis but he was the only person in England
that she knew.

The slice of lean roast beef lay untouched upon Fortune's plate. The afternoon she'd spent worrying over what
the following day would bring had successfully vanquished
her usually healthy appetite, and she could do little more
than force a few bites down her throat.

After Kane engaged their rooms for the night at the Red
Rooster, he'd left her to her own devices while he saw to
renting a carriage for the next day. She'd spent the entire
time thinking of her coming meeting with her grandfather.
Terrified by the prospect of facing a stranger and proclaim-
ing herself his granddaughter, she had sought to quell her
apprehensions by pacing her small chamber. However, her
efforts had been futile and as each hour passed, she had
grown more tense and uncertain.

Uneasily she glanced at the man sitting across from her.
Kane was enjoying his food with the enthusiasm of a man
long separated from the hearty English meals he loved,
and she was loath to disturb him even if she'd felt comfortable in seeking his advice. He had offered her friendship but after their encounter aboard the *Mermaid*, she
found that something within her refused to allow the sol-
ace of speaking to him about her worries.

Caught up in her own reveries, Fortune didn't note
Kane's close scrutiny as he finished his meal. Nor was she
aware when she set her chin at a pugnacious angle that her
tense expression and the ungiving line of her small jaw

told him far more of her thoughts than she realized. Her face was the window to her mind, and Kane had learned to use it during the past weeks to judge her moods. After finishing the last bite of the rare roast beef, Kane leaned back in his chair and took a deep sip of rich, red burgundy. "You should eat," he said, and watched Fortune gape at him for a moment.

"I beg your pardon. I didn't hear what you said," she said, using her new manners to perfection.

"I said, you should eat something. You've hardly touched your food."

Fortune glanced down at her plate and shook her head. "I'm not hungry tonight."

"Fortune," Kane said, leaning forward, his gaze searching her face, "I seem to recall you said this afternoon that worrying over something was usually worse than the fact. Am I correct?"

"I'm not worried," Fortune lied. Unable to look him in the eye and deny the truth, she turned her attention to redistributing her food about her plate. "I'm just tired."

Kane released a long breath and shook his head. "During the last weeks I had hoped we could become friends. Now I realize you still haven't forgiven me for not telling you sooner about your grandfather and, well, for other things."

Fortune's head snapped up and she blushed. "Friends? After all you've done?"

"Yes, friends. And as for what I've done to you I believe I apologized for my conduct and I won't do so again."

Fortune's cheeks burned from his reference to their single kiss. "I accepted your excuse for that but, because of your overbearing manner, I doubt we can ever be friends."

"My manner?" Kane asked. "You little idiot, I know you think I was rough on you because of some insidious plan that I'd devised just to make you miserable, but what I did was for your own good. I forced you to become a lady in a span of weeks when normally it takes years of education to achieve what you've accomplished. Had I left you in your buckskins and with the manners of a savage, then you'd have no chance of being accepted by your grandfather. I thought you understood that from the beginning.''

"I did," Fortune answered grudgingly. It was hard to admit that he spoke the truth. She'd realized it long ago but had been unable to accept it because of all the changes that had taken place in her life in such a short span of time. By fighting Kane, she'd been fighting to hold onto her identity. But she could no longer deny the fact that everything Kane had done had been for her own benefit.

"Then can we put the past behind us and begin again?" Kane asked. His heart seemed to still with anticipation while he awaited her answer.

"I—" Fortune began but before she could finish she was interrupted by a tall thin man dressed in black. He paused at their table to greet Kane.

"Warrick, old man. It's been awhile since I've seen you. Have you been out of the country or just hiding out at your mills?''

Kane's expression grew cold as he looked up at the intruder. "Manville, I don't see that my whereabouts or doings are any of your business. Now if you will excuse us." Kane turned his attention back to Fortune.

"Why so unpleasant?" Nevin Manville asked, his pale lips curling into a crooked smile. "Can't a man even speak to his neighbor without getting his head snapped off? Or is it that you're too concerned about the lack of work at your mills to be congenial?''

The taunt found its mark. Kane flushed with fury yet managed with great effort to restrain himself from throttling Manville and ending his troubles once and for all. "Now that I'm back, I will see that problem solved, be assured of that, Manville.''

"Glad to hear it," Manville said, his demeanor oozing false congeniality. Glancing at Fortune, he bestowed upon her what he considered his most charming smile before turning his attention back to his victim. "I just wanted you to know that Mr. Stoddard and I have just made several deals that will seal the final agreement for ninety percent of the raw cotton that comes into the country during the next month. I hope it doesn't hinder you in any way."

"I know you are aggrieved over my problems, Manville, but I can assure you that you've caused me no difficulty," Kane said, smiling for the first time. "And now I would like to return your congeniality by introducing you to Mistress Fortune McQueen." Kane paused for effect before adding sweetly, "Northrop, your cousin."

Recognizing the name immediately from the letter he'd destroyed years ago, Manville glanced sharply at Fortune and his already-pallid complexion turned a sickly white. He fidgeted with the black cape draped about his thin shoulders and turned his narrowed gaze back to Kane. "You may think you can get by with this hoax but you won't, Warrick. I'm the only living relative of Lord Northrop."

"I beg to differ with you, Manville." His enemy's name sounded like a curse upon Kane's lips. "Fortune is Lord Northrop's granddaughter, as you well know, or you wouldn't look so worried."

"I'm concerned for my uncle's health. He is not a well man, and it won't do him any good for you to try to pass this colonial off as his long-lost granddaughter."

"I don't have to 'pass her off.' She *is* Sebastian Northrop's child." Kane smiled his enjoyment at Manville's obvious discomfort.

Manville turned to Fortune. "If you know what's good for you, young lady, you won't go along with Warrick's little charade. I'm warning you now, if you continue, you'll find yourself locked in Newgate with the rest of your kind."

Fortune paled but showed no other sign that Manville's threats affected her. "I'm sorry that you feel that way, but I have proof that I'm Sebastian and Lorna Anne Northrop's daughter."

"Proof?" Manville exploded. "What kind of proof do you have? Warrick's say so?"

"No, Kane told me nothing," Fortune said, bristling in defense. "I have several books in my trunk that will prove who I am," she added triumphantly, disliking Nevin Manville more by the minute.

"Then let me see them," Manville challenged.

Fortune cast an uncertain glance at Kane before she said, "I—I don't have them with me now. They are still on board the *Mermaid*. When my luggage arrives tomorrow morning I'll be glad to show the books to you."

"Even if you do have the books that proves nothing. You could have stolen them. It will take more than that to convince me you are my cousin."

"She doesn't have to convince you, Manville," Kane interjected smoothly. "It's Lord Northrop who will decide the truth when we visit him tomorrow." At the expression that crossed Manville's rodentlike features, Kane felt like laughing aloud. Manville was already beginning to understand Kane's plan. He knew Kane had set out to ruin him, and he was desperately searching for a way to stop that from happening.

"Don't come to North Meadows, Warrick. You will not be received."

"I would think that is something else to be decided by Lord Northrop. Having you as his heir, I'm sure once he hears why we've come, he'll be more than glad to welcome us."

"We'll just have to wait and see, won't we?" Manville said, striving to retain his composure. He didn't want Kane Warrick to see how shaken he was over the girl's arrival. It would give the bastard too much pleasure. "And I promise you, Warrick, you will not succeed in breaking me, if that is your plan."

Kane smiled up at Manville, his expression triumphant. "Yes, we'll just have to see about a great many things in the next few days, won't we?"

Manville did not bid them good night but turned on his

heel and stalked away. The cape he wore fanned out about him like great wings and made his retreating figure resemble a giant black bird running around on stick-thin legs.

Fortune watched Manville's hasty exit before returning her attention to the man sitting across the table from her. From the crooked grin on his well-shaped lips to the victorious gleam in his silver eyes, she realized the answer to one of the questions that had been plaguing her during the past weeks. The hostility between the two men told her more than words. Now she knew Kane's reason for going to such trouble to unite her with her grandfather. His hatred of her cousin had driven him to seek her out.

"Is he the reason you've gone to all the trouble of bringing me to England?" she asked quietly. She needed to hear Kane admit that his actions hadn't stemmed just from his need to play the good Samaritan.

Kane took a deep sip of his wine before he nodded and answered without elaborating. "Yes."

Fortune released a long breath. Hearing the truth didn't help as much as she had thought it would. "I've suspected you had an ulterior motive from the beginning. And from past experience I'm not surprised to learn you've used me once more without considering how I would feel being thrown into the middle of your quarrel with my cousin. After your pretty speech about wanting to be my friend, I had begun to think there was an ounce of human kindness somewhere within you after all. It's sad to realize that I was wrong."

Fortune pushed back her chair and stood. "I won't be a part of your feud with Manville, Kane. I came here to meet my grandfather—not to foil my cousin's chances of inheriting North Meadows." Fortune turned to walk away but Kane captured her by the wrist, halting her.

"You're not a part of my quarrel with Manville, Fortune. You now have your own feud with him. He sees you as the enemy. You are the only person who can destroy his plans to own North Meadows, as well as all that goes with it."

"I didn't come here to battle with my cousin over Lord Northrop's estate. All I've wanted from the beginning was to find my family."

"But Manville doesn't realize that's all you want and he'll do everything within his power to make sure you're not accepted by Lord Northrop. You'll have to stand your ground and fight him if you ever hope to have a place in the Northrop family."

Fortune jerked her wrist free of his hold. "Once Manville learns that I have no intention of usurping him in my grandfather's eyes, he'll not feel threatened by me."

"Are you going to let Manville take what rightfully belongs to you? Had your father lived, he'd be next in line to inherit North Meadows; not that little weasel who just left us. I didn't think you were a coward, Fortune."

Fortune bristled. "I'm not a coward but I have no quarrel with Manville."

"Don't you understand I'm trying to warn you against Nevin Manville? He will stop at nothing in order to remain Lord Northrop's heir. He can't let you interfere in his plans. He has too much to lose."

"It's kind of you to warn me but it would have been kinder if you had told me the truth from the beginning. I don't like to be used, Kane, by you or anyone else." Fortune turned and walked away.

"Damn Manville to hell," Kane muttered, focusing his ire on his enemy instead of laying the blame where it belonged—in his own lap. His plan to ruin Nevin Manville had seemed perfect until he came to know Fortune McQueen. During the past weeks in her company something within him had changed. Her innocence compromised his ability to use her as he had hoped, and he now realized it would have been to his own benefit to have told her the truth from the beginning.

"What in the hell has gotten into me?" Kane muttered, disgusted with himself. He didn't know why he should care what happened to Fortune once she served his purpose. It was totally unlike him to react as he had with her.

He had always prided himself that he was a man of determination, one who would let nothing stand in his way. And, until recently, he had felt no qualms about how he gained his objectives.

Kane ran a hand through his hair in exasperation, pushed back his chair, and stood. It was all Fortune's fault. With only a few simple words she had a way of making him feel like a swine. There had been only one other woman who had caused him to feel guilty and that had been only after her death. Kane turned toward the stairs leading up to the rented rooms. For some strange reason he couldn't totally understand he needed to go to Fortune and be honest with her. As he ascended the stairs, he pushed the idea aside. He doubted if she would be in the right state of mind to accept anything from him, much less the news that he still intended to use her to gain the land he needed.

No matter how much he wanted to tell her the truth, he couldn't chance putting the fate of his mills into her hands. From the way she felt about him as she left the dining room, it was best to let things rest for a while. He would give her temper time to cool before he said or did anything that might jeopardize his chances to buy the land from Lord Northrop.

Through the door that joined their two rooms, Fortune heard Kane moving about, readying himself for bed. When Kane had rented the adjoining rooms that afternoon, she'd been relieved. It was reassuring in this strange, new environment to know he would be nearby should she need him. Yet after their argument in the inn's dining room, she felt he could not be farther away if he was on the other side of the earth.

Sitting alone in her room, staring at the cold fireplace, she felt abandoned and more uncertain than ever. The warm weather didn't require a fire and the ashes in the firepit were as gray as her hopes of finding a welcome at North Meadows tomorrow.

After her temper had cooled she rehashed the scene with

her cousin in the dining room. She couldn't find it within herself to blame Kane for his dislike of Nevin Manville. He was repulsive to her in appearance and manner. He reminded her of a rattler curled under a rock just waiting to strike at anyone, be it friend or foe, who attempted to trespass upon its territory.

She also knew that Kane's assessment about Manville's feelings toward her was right. During their short confrontation, she'd felt his hatred for her like a tangible force. Nevin Manville was Lord Northrop's heir and he considered her the interloper. She was a threat to his inheritance and he would do anything to keep her an outsider.

"An outsider who has traveled thousands of miles with the misguided hope she would be accepted into the Northrop family," Fortune murmured forlornly to the still room. Nevin Manville was a formidable enemy and she had no way to defend herself against him. Even with her mother's books as evidence, she feared he'd managed to convince Lord Northrop that she wasn't who she claimed.

Agitated by her thoughts, Fortune rose to her feet and began restlessly pacing her small chamber. A frown creased her brow and her worried teeth at her lower lip as she considered the future that awaited her after being turned away from North Meadows.

The thought made her shiver. She would have no place to go. She would be a stranger in a strange land with only the money Kane had paid her for the pelts. In the Carolina mountains, it was enough to last her an entire winter but from her observations that afternoon, she would find herself destitute in less than a week in Bristol. The amount Kane had paid for their rooms alone would have bought enough flour back home to last her two months.

"What am I going to do?" Fortune asked aloud. She knew so little of the world beyond the blue mountains surrounding her home in the Carolinas. After learning all Kane's lessons, she realized how little she knew of life. She felt ill prepared to face what would await her in a place like Bristol. And she suspected she would find herself at the mercy of those far more worldly. Her experience with Kane had proved that much to her already.

"I'll go home," Fortune whispered, suddenly deciding the course she would take if her meeting with Lord Northrop did not prove satisfactory. At least in her mountain home she didn't have to worry about being accepted or having enough money to live. She might have to do without some things but she could survive. She'd have a place to live and food to eat, and that was more than she could say she'd have if she remained in Bristol.

Her decision made, Fortune crawled into bed and snuggled down into the warmth of the woolen blankets. Her mind at rest, she soon slipped into a restful sleep.

"Damn you, Pitte. Hold that lantern up so that I can see, you fool," Manville growled, squinting down at the book in his hand.

"Is this good enough, Governor?" Pitte asked, raising the lantern shoulder high. The light spread in a circle about them and illuminated the yellowed inscription in the book.

Concentrating on the work in his hand, Manville didn't answer the ruffian he'd hired to do his dirty work. His heartbeat accelerated and a cold sweat broke out across his brow and upper lip at the sight of Sebastian Northrop's handwriting. The words scribbled upon the pages proved the girl's identity. Should Lord Northrop ever see it, Manville knew his chances of inheriting North Meadows would be ruined. A look of pure hatred pinched his thin face into an ugly mask as he slammed the book closed. His uncle would never see the pages nor the girl, if he had any say in the matter. Manville slipped the book into the pocket of his cape and turned to the villainous-looking pair who stood anxiously awaiting their pay.

"If that's all yer will be awanting of us tonight, Governor, we'd like our money so we can buy us a dram or two of rum," Pitte said, hunching his burly shoulders against the damp night air and burying his hands deep inside his tattered coat pockets.

"Not yet, my friends. I still have a small item that needs your attention. Once it is taken care of then I'll pay you double what I first offered."

Pitte's companion, a man called Bad Penny, spoke for the first time. "Wha' ye got in mind?"

Manville smiled at the eager expression on Bad Penny's face. He'd chosen these two well. They would do anything for a price, and once the job was done they'd vanish back into the shadowy underworld of the waterfront.

Roused from a sound sleep by a creaking floorboard, it took Fortune several moments to collect her thoughts enough to realize what had awakened her. Sensing a presence in her room, she strained to see through the darkness for any movement that might reveal the intruder's whereabouts. She could see nothing in the deepest shadows.

"Who's there?" she asked, her voice low and husky from the trepidation constricting her throat. After a few taut moments of silence, she began to relax. There was no one in her room. Her imagination was playing tricks upon her because of her strange surroundings. Releasing a relieved breath, she pulled the covers up and closed her eyes.

She had just begun to doze off when a floorboard creaked near the door that adjoined her room to Kane's. Fortune bolted upright, gripping the sheet to her breast.

"What kind of game are you playing now, Kane?" she challenged, instantly assuming the worst about the man in the next room. Prepared to give him a good set down for coming into her room while she slept and for frightening her nearly out of her wits, Fortune reached for the tender box to light the lamp.

Before she grasped the tin of flint and wadding, a large hand closed over her mouth. A strong, coarse-sleeved arm came about her waist at the same moment and she found herself jerked backward across the bed.

"Ain't nobody here by that name, little lady," whispered a man behind her.

Fortune tried to twist free of the suffocating hand by thrashing from side to side but the pain inflicted by the bruising fingers soon made her cease her efforts to escape. When she stilled, she heard him chuckle.

"Now are ye going to behave?" he asked.

Trapped and breathing heavily, Fortune nodded.

"Then ye are a smart wench who knows what's good fer 'er," he said close to her ear. "And if ye want to keep yerself all in one piece, I'd suggest ye keep behaving or ye won't like what me and me friend here will do to ye."

Fortune heard a low chuckle come from near the foot of the bed. She strained to see the second intruder but in the darkness could make out only his outline. She saw him move around the bed and a moment later felt his rough, calloused hands clamp down on her ankles.

Fortune recoiled at the touch but he kept a firm grip upon her, impeding all movement. Panic and fear of what the two men intended for her ate away at her courage. Her heart raced against her ribs, thumping hard with the realization that they had not come just to rob her. They intended to harm her and she was helpless to prevent it.

Fortune remembered Kane's reprimand when she'd tried to pack her musket in her trunk of new gowns before they sailed from New Bern. "Ladies do not carry weapons, Fortune. They have no need to defend themselves. They leave that to the gentlemen in their lives."

Foolishly, she had listened to him. She'd left all of her weapons back in the Carolinas. All, Fortune thought in disgust, except the small knife that lay beneath her pillow less than a foot away from her hand. Without Kane's knowledge she'd kept it secreted away, and each night she slept better for having it there.

Fortune's breath stilled in her throat. Now the small knife might be the only thing to stand between herself and death. If she could just free herself long enough to reach it, she would be able to keep them at bay until help could arrive.

Her decision made, Fortune breathed deeply, thrusting

her entire weight against her assailant's arm. The man, who was balanced awkwardly on the bed, fell sideways with her. Fortune used his moment of surprise to her own advantage and swiftly retrieved the narrow-bladed knife. She brought it around in one swift motion, stabbing her attacker in the leg.

"The bitch has cut me," he croaked, gasping from the pain. He released Fortune to grab his injured limb, clutching it tightly to staunch the flow of blood.

Fortune rolled to the edge of the bed and scrambled to her feet. She confronted the second man with knife held menacingly in front of her. Warding off his advance, she backed toward Kane's room. At the same moment, the door swung open and Kane stood upon the threshold with pistol in one hand and lamp in the other. The lamplight spilled into the room to reveal Fortune and her attackers.

"What the devil—" Kane began until his gaze came to rest on Pitte's scarred features. In a glance he took in Bad Penny sprawled on the bed. Before he could make a move to apprehend either, Pitte made a dash for the door, leaving his cohort to escape the best way he could. Kane had little time to take aim but raised his pistol and fired. The lead ball landed in the door frame, splintering the wood.

Bad Penny chose that moment to make good his own escape. He dove headfirst through the window, shattering wood and glass as he sailed out. His cry of fright and dismay briefly filled the night before a loud thud sounded and then dead silence. Bad Penny's neck had snapped when he landed on the cobbles.

Weak with relief, Fortune sank into the nearest chair and buried her face in her trembling hands. The knife fell unheeded to the floor at her feet. She was accustomed to living in the wilderness of the Carolina mountains and was prepared to face any danger that she encountered there. However, her assailants had caught her unawares. She'd not expected to be assaulted in her own bed.

"Did they hurt you?" Kane asked, kneeling at her side. His voice reflected his concern.

Fortune shook her head and then looked at Kane. "They planned to kill me."

"Damn it!" Kane exploded. "I knew Manville was a scoundrel but I didn't believe he'd stoop as low as to hire assassins."

"What do you mean?" Fortune began but before she could finish her question the innkeeper arrived with a crowd of men from the tavern.

"What's been going on up here?" the innkeeper inquired. His heavy-jowled face was flushed a deep crimson from his hurry to reach the top of the stairs and the room where the gunshot had sounded. "I run a decent establishment and I won't put up with murder or men fighting over their whores."

Kane bolted to his feet, incensed by the innkeeper's remark. His cold steel gaze made the man swallow nervously and try to back away. He could not move, however, because of the crush of men behind him.

"How dare you come up here and insult the lady and myself when it is your responsibility to see your customers are not murdered in their sleep." Kane strode forward and grabbed the innkeeper by the front of his shirt. He glared down at him and his voice was little more than a low growl as he continued, "Had I not been next door, the lady would have been killed by the thieves that you let roam freely through your establishment. And I hold you accountable."

"But, sir," the innkeeper pleaded, shaking his head from side to side and lifting his hands in a helpless gesture, "I can't be held responsible for what happened up here. I was busy downstairs at the bar." When Kane's angry expression did not change with his explanation, the man added rapidly, "But I'll be more than glad to do anything I can to make up for the inconvenience."

Kane shoved him away. "I've already taken care of things for myself but you can call the authorities and explain things to them. I think you'll find one of your thieves in the alley. Now good night.'' Kane closed the door in the man's face.

The innkeeper breathed a sigh of relief and swiped the sweat from his brow with his sleeve. He turned to the men gathered about him, his annoyance mounting as he noticed the smirking looks they gave him. Adjusting the soiled apron over his bulging waist, he growled, ''Didn't you hear what the gentleman said? One of you go get the constable while the rest go and check out the alley.''

As the group descended the stair, the innkeeper glanced back at Fortune's door. ''I wished they'd killed you for humiliating me in front of my friends, you high and mighty bastard,'' he muttered under his breath. He wasn't brave enough to say it to the dangerous-looking toff himself.

When Kane closed the door and turned back to Fortune, he found her sitting with head bowed and hands clasped tightly in her lap. Her young face held a strained expression. When he spoke her name and she looked up at him, her slate-blue eyes contrasted starkly with her pale skin.

''This is my fault,'' Kane said. Kneeling on one knee in front of her, he took her hands into his own. ''Had I kept your identity from Manville, you'd not have been placed in any danger tonight.''

''How can you be sure that it was my cousin who hired those two?''

''Who else could want you out of the way, Fortune? Tonight we frightened Manville, and he'll do anything to keep you from seeing Lord Northrop. He will lose too much to chance letting your grandfather know that Sebastian's child is alive.''

Fortune nodded her agreement. Although it was difficult to believe, she knew Kane was right. ''Tiny always told me it's better to know your enemies. Tonight has shown me mine. I'll be more aware in the future if he should try to rid himself of me. Manville will soon learn that I'm not that easy to kill.''

Kane brought her hand up to his lips and gently pressed

a kiss on it. His silver gaze held her immobile. "Then have you decided I'm not one of your enemies?"

"For now," Fortune said with a wobbly smile.

"Good," Kane said, and gave her hand a reassuring squeeze. "Now you need to get to sleep. You have a long day ahead of you tomorrow." He made to stand but Fortune wouldn't let go of his hand.

"Don't leave me alone tonight, Kane." Fortune's voice reflected her apprehension. Her encounter with the two ruffians had shaken her to the very depths of her courage and she couldn't bear the thought of being left alone again that night. She needed the reassurance of Kane's nearness to help her overcome her fright.

"Fortune, I can't," Kane said, his voice husky. Her request made him feel as if he'd been hit in the stomach by a solid fist. "It's not proper," he added. Pulling his hand free of hers, he stood. He didn't want to refuse her, far from it. All he wanted was to take her to bed and hold her so that nothing ever frightened her again. However, he knew he couldn't do that to Fortune. He'd brought her to England for one reason and he'd not use her further.

Cupping her chin in his hand, he bent and placed a fatherly kiss upon her forehead. His voice was strained with suppressed emotion when he said, "Go to bed, Fortune."

Determined to resist the temptation beckoning from her wide, brimming eyes, Kane turned to the door of his room. A moment later her soft, whispered plea "Kane, please don't leave me tonight" vanquished all his intentions to the contrary. He found himself crossing back to Fortune's side and taking her into his arms.

"Fortune, this isn't right," he murmured, still resisting the forces that had driven him back to her side. He had to stop before it was too late for them both.

"I don't care what's right or wrong. I don't want to be alone," she said, snuggling closer into his embrace.

A burst of desire shot through Kane at the feel of her young, thinly clad body nestled against his. His battered conscience retreated into the recesses of his mind before the onslaught of his passion. Surrendering to the strong forces that he could not deny a moment longer, he tightened his arms about Fortune and lowered his mouth to her trembling lips.

Fortune wound her arms about Kane's neck, entwining her fingers in his dark hair as she gave herself up to the kiss she'd been dreaming of since that fateful night on board the *Mermaid*. Although she'd tried not to believe Kane had any power over her, the mere touch of his lips upon hers now aroused the same intense feelings his first kiss had brought forth. All of her resolve to keep Kane at bay shattered and she soon forgot she meant nothing to him.

Molding her body to his lean frame, she opened her lips to his questing tongue and savored the wave of heat that washed over her as the kiss deepened. She felt as if she was drowning in the heady sensations. Her knees grew weak and she clung to Kane for support.

Lifting Fortune into his arms, Kane crossed to the bed and lay her down. For a long tense moment, he sat on the edge of the bed, poised above her. The expression in his pewter-colored eyes reflected the desire raging through him yet he made no move to take her. Gently he lifted a dark curl and wound it about his finger as he probed the slate-blue depths of her eyes with his silver gaze.

"Are you sure that you want me here, Fortune?" Kane asked, giving her one last chance to change her mind before he succumbed to heat in his loins. "Once I lie down, there will be no turning back for us."

"I know" was Fortune's soft reply as she raised her arms to him once more.

Unable to deny himself further, Kane shrugged out of his robe, stretching his lean body on the bed at Fortune's side. He raised himself on one elbow and gazed down at her, savoring the beauty he'd thought about since the night on board the *Mermaid*. His body throbbed with desire yet he made no move to fulfill his needs. He wouldn't rush.

He wanted to enjoy each moment of her—to know the exquisite fire that raged in his blood also raged in hers. He needed to carry her up with him to touch the stars of ecstasy and to share in that little piece of heaven all lovers are given at the end of their quest.

"My God, you're exquisite," he whispered in awe as he slowly slipped the night rail from Fortune until she lay naked beneath his burning gaze.

Kane lowered his mouth to hers, drinking in her sweetness. He glided his hand down the smooth line of her throat to the soft mounds of her breasts and fondled her, his thumb gently rousing the peak to a hardened bud. At her response to his caress, he moaned and tore his mouth free of hers to seek out the tantalizing orb beneath his hand. Capturing an aroused nipple in his mouth, he suckled greedily for several long, pleasurable moments before seeking its mate.

His lips and hand set Fortune aflame. The fire racing through her blood made it impossible to think coherently. She reacted on instinct alone. Arching her back to give him access to her burning flesh, she massaged his muscular shoulders and ran her hands through his silken hair, moving her hips against him in the ancient call of love. She now knew that only Kane could ease the strangely exciting ache deep within her. He alone could end the exquisite torment his touch had created.

Unable to continue the foreplay because of his own need, Kane answered her call. Recapturing her lips, his mouth absorbed her startled cry as he spread her thighs and gently slipped into her resilient warmth. He stilled, giving her time to accustom herself to him, and felt a thrill of renewed excitement when she began to move against him.

The moment of pain past, Fortune gloried in the heady sensations exploding through her. She moved her hips in rhythm with his and clung to Kane's perspiration-dewed shoulders as they soared toward the pinnacle of rapture. She gasped and arched toward him when she felt the trembling wave begin in the very depths of her being. It roiled over her in a swell of feeling so devastating that she was left panting for breath and trembling from head to toe. In the same moment she felt Kane's shuddering release and he collapsed over her, burying his face against her breast.

Tears of tenderness welled within Fortune's eyes as she lay cradling Kane's head to her. Gently she brushed the damp tendrils of hair away from his forehead and stared dreamily up at the ceiling. She'd dreamed about love but nothing had prepared her for the depth of emotion she was experiencing at that moment. She loved Kane with such an intensity it made her ache, and she wondered how it would feel to know he also loved her.

Fortune's happiness faded. She was too honest with herself not to admit she had leapt into bed with Kane fully aware that his feelings for her hadn't changed. She'd given herself completely to him without reservation and she didn't feel any guilt for loving Kane. It seemed too natural, as natural to her as breathing. During her lessons she'd learned that young ladies had to be virtuous, but she'd lived too long in total freedom to cage her feelings now. She loved Kane and the only regret she had was that he didn't love her in return.

Kane raised himself on his elbows above her and dropped a kiss on the tip of her nose before easing his weight from her.

"Fortune," he began, but she silenced his lips with the tip of her finger. Sensing his need to explain his feelings, she shook her head.

"You don't have to say anything now, Kane. I already know," Fortune murmured softly, unwilling to shatter the sweet glow left from their lovemaking. She wanted her time with him unspoiled by his apologies and regrets. The morning would be soon enough for that. "Just hold me," she whispered, snuggling closer to his side.

Fortune lay her head on his shoulder and closed her eyes. Tonight she'd savor her moments in Kane's arms because she knew they would be her last. Whether she was accepted by Lord Northrop or not, after tomorrow she would be out of Kane's life. She'd be left with only the memory of this night to treasure.

# Chapter 5

Sharp-fanged guilt gnawed away at Kane's insides as he eased from the bed where Fortune slept. He quietly made his way back to his room, crossed to the washstand, and gazed at his haggard reflection in the shaving mirror. What he'd allowed to happen was unforgivable. He was a grown man and he'd taken advantage of a girl who was little more than a child. This thought brought to mind the memory of a man he'd met in London who had enjoyed having sex with children. He didn't like the comparison.

"Damn it," he growled in defense of himself against the names that taunted him from his own imagination. "Fortune is a woman grown, not a child."

Yes, she has the body of a woman yet you were aware she knew nothing of the world beyond what you've taught her. You took advantage of her innocence to soothe your own desires, his conscience challenged him.

Running a hand through his hair in exasperation, Kane turned away from the image in the mirror and stalked to the window where the first rays of the sun were peeping through. Bracing his arm against the facing, he rested his brow against his sleeve and stared morosely out over Bristol's soot-blackened rooftops. He didn't feel good about what he'd allowed to happen between himself and Fortune, and he wondered how they'd managed to become involved when he'd not set out to seduce her.

"Damn it, I don't have any reason to feel guilty about what occurred," he defended aloud. "I gave her a chance to change her mind."

"You're right, Kane," Fortune answered softly from behind him. "You don't have to feel guilty about anything that's happened between us. I'd prefer it if you would forget about everything that transpired last night."

Kane spun around in time to see Fortune, with back stiff and head held high, walk through the doorway into her room. He caught up with her as she reached the bed. Taking her by the arm, he turned her to face him. "Fortune, let me explain."

"You don't have to explain anything to me, Kane. I'm young but I'm not stupid. I know that last night meant nothing to you beyond the moment so you needn't worry that I'll have a fit of vapors like one of your fine English ladies. I honestly doubt I'll ever manage to become that much of a lady."

A puzzled expression flickered over Kane's face before he flushed a dull, angry red. He felt as if Fortune had slapped him. He'd been ready to make excuses explaining his actions and also to ask her forgiveness. However, he wasn't prepared to have Fortune behave as if what had transpired between them meant nothing to her. It insulted him to the core of his masculinity.

"Damn it, Fortune," he began, but before he could finish, she interrupted him.

"Kane, there's nothing for us to discuss. I have no regrets about last night and neither should you. Now, if you'd allow me a little privacy, I'd like to dress," Fortune said, firmly ending their conversation before he could see through the brave front she constructed to protect her pride. She didn't want him to ever know that her insides were coiled into insidious knots and her heart ached to have him pull her into his arms and tell her he loved her.

But she knew better, and to save her own pride, she had to preserve his.

Baffled by his own conflicting emotions, Kane let his hands fall to his side. "Then I'll leave you to dress. After breakfast we'll collect our luggage and be on our way to North Meadows."

Fortune watched the door shut between their rooms and felt as if part of her own heart was also being closed off. Though the man she loved was only a few feet away from her, the distance between them had become so great in the last few minutes that she doubted it could ever be crossed again. She released a long breath and turned to the task of making herself look presentable to a grandfather who didn't know of her existence. She shook her head at the thought.

"He's not the only person who doesn't know I exist," she mused aloud to the reflection in the dressing-table mirror. Glumly she propped her elbow on the tabletop and rested her chin against her fist. After today she would have no reason to see Kane Warrick again. He would be out of her life for good. The thought did little to ease the ache in her heart.

Still vexed by Fortune's behavior earlier and in no mood to carry on a conversation, Kane ate his breakfast in silence. For the first time in his life he'd encountered a situation with a woman he couldn't control, and he didn't like the insecure feeling it left with him. He honestly didn't know what to think of Fortune McQueen. He'd known from their first meeting that she was unusual, but now he was beginning to believe she was unlike any young woman on earth. She hadn't ranted and raved about her lost virtue but accepted what had happened between them as if it were natural.

Natural, Kane mused, glancing at the young woman sitting across the table. Fortune McQueen was a creature of nature. From her beauty to her heart she didn't need to use the artifices that the ladies of his acquaintance so prided themselves upon. Her honesty had made their encounter as natural as breathing. She had given of herself and it had been beautiful, more beautiful than anything he'd ever experienced in the past.

Kane looked back down and shoved his plate away. He couldn't stop himself from wondering what his life would have been like if he'd been lucky enough to have a woman like Fortune as his wife. He envied the man who would woo and win her hand. He would have a prize indeed. Once she gave her heart, she'd never hold back anything from the man she loved.

Kane gave himself a sharp mental kick. Such musings were not for him. He'd set his course and he'd not change it because of one beautiful, strong-willed woman. Perhaps his life was less than perfect but he'd not chance another disastrous marriage. He had enough problems without adding one more with slate-blue eyes. He'd created one mistake by making love to her and knew he had to get Fortune to North Meadows before he ruined things further.

Kane pushed back his chair and stood. "While you continue your breakfast, I'll go see if our luggage has arrived from the docks."

"I'm finished," Fortune said and pushed back her plate. The food hadn't been touched.

"You've eaten very little," Kane remarked as he reached to retrieve her cape from a peg on the wall beside their table.

"I'm too excited about meeting Lord Northrop to eat," Fortune lied. She couldn't tell him the real reason behind her lack of appetite was the thought of not seeing him again after he left her at North Meadows.

"Then we should be on our way." Kane draped the cape about Fortune's shoulders and proffered his arm to her. "We should be at North Meadows within the next couple of hours."

Fortune forced a smile to her lips and accepted his arm. Two hours was all she had left to her. Two hours to brand

Kane's image upon her brain. Two hours that had to last her a lifetime.

"Mr. Warrick, sir," the coachman said, interrupting Fortune's musings. Standing with hat in hand he gave her a courteous bob of his head then turned his attention back to Kane. "There's been a problem with your luggage down a' the ship."

"What kind of problem, Flemming?" Kane asked, setting his wide-brimmed hat rakishly on his head.

"It ain't there. Neither yours nor the lady's."

Kane stilled, his expression hardening. "What do you mean?"

"The captain says to tell you that it's been stolen by some of the stevedores. Yours and several other passengers' trunks were taken."

"Damn!" Kane swore and slammed his fist down on the table, upsetting the mugs of coffee. The dark-brown liquid spread unheeded across the marred surface and then dripped into a puddle on the floor at his feet. "I should have known Manville would try something like this when he learned that the evidence to prove your identity was still on board the *Mermaid*."

Fortune sank back into the chair she'd vacated a few moments earlier. The import of her loss made her pale. Her chances of being accepted as Lord Northrop's granddaughter had vanished.

Seeing her stricken expression, Kane knelt in front of her and took her hand. He gave it a comforting, reassuring squeeze. "This changes nothing, Fortune. We're still going to North Meadows."

"But," Fortune began before Kane silenced her with a tip of one long, elegantly shaped finger to her lips.

"Shhh. Now is not the time for doubts. We're not going to let Manville win. He may think he can stop us by stealing your mother's books but he's mistaken. His hired assassins didn't succeed and neither will he."

"But how can we prove that I'm Lord Northrop's granddaughter without my mother's books?'' Fortune asked, still unreconciled.

Kane stood and drew her to her feet. ''I honestly don't know at the moment but hopefully by the time we reach North Meadows I'll have thought of something. If I haven't, then all we can do is tell Lord Northrop the truth and hope that he believes us.''

As Kane helped her into the coach, Fortune feared her stay in England would be far shorter than she'd first imagined. Without any proof of her identity, Manville could make Lord Northrop believe that everything she said was a lie.

As the coach traveled past the fountains and rolled up the graveled drive to the three-story mansion known as North Meadows, Fortune sat with mouth agape and eyes wide with wonder at the sight before her. Her insecurities were momentarily forgotten as she viewed Lord Northrop's home. Nothing had prepared her for such grandeur. The house, built of handmade brick, their color muted by time and the elements, was an imposing structure with beveled glass windows trimmed in white Italian marble. It sat amid manicured lawns and gardens like an aged ruby broach upon green velvet. Marble steps fanned down to the cobbled courtyard from the recessed doorway where more intricately carved marble emphasized the two heavy oak doors with gleaming brass lion's-head knockers.

''This is where my grandfather lives?'' she asked, unable to believe that a normal man could reside in such impressive surroundings. In her opinion North Meadows was an appropriate setting for England's king.

Kane read disbelief on her young face and grinned. ''Yes, this is Lord Northrop's home and will also be yours once he accepts you as his granddaughter.''

Fortune slowly shook her head as she looked back to the man sitting across from her. ''I'm afraid that will never happen, Kane. Lord Northrop will never take our word over Manville's.''

Before Kane could say anything more to reassure her, the coach rumbled to a halt in front of the wide double doors. The coachman leapt down from the driver's seat and opened the door to allow Kane to step down. He turned and extended his hand to Fortune but before their fingers touched an angry voice came from the entrance way behind them.

"Warrick, get off of my land. I've already told you that you'd not be welcome at North Meadows," Manville ordered.

Kane ignored the thin little man who stood puffing and fuming on the steps above him. He helped Fortune safely down from the coach before he turned the full power of his steely gaze upon his adversary. "As you already know, we haven't come to see you, Manville. Fortune has come to meet her grandfather."

A look of shock momentarily flickered over Manville's thin features when he saw Fortune but he quickly regained his composure and turned his attention back to Kane. "Damn you, Warrick. Have you no conscience? My uncle is unwell and your lies could very well kill him."

"Then it is even more imperative that Fortune see Lord Northrop. It isn't right to keep him from his only grandchild and heir when he has so little time to live." Kane smiled at the look of pure venom Manville shot at him.

Manville glanced at the liveried servant guarding the doorway behind him. "Get the grooms, Balfor, and have them escort these two from North Meadows. If Warrick gives you any trouble, you have my permission to horsewhip him." Manville flashed Kane a triumphant smile.

"If you think your threats will stop us any more than your hired assassins then you're mistaken, Manville. We're not leaving North Meadows until we've seen Lord Northrop."

"Do as I say, Balfor," Manville ground out between clenched teeth. Casting Manville an uncertain look, Balfor turned to comply with his orders at the same moment an aged, belabored voice came from the doorway behind them.

"What's the meaning of this, Nevin?"

Manville spun about, his already-sallow skin turning ashen at the sight of Lord Northrop relying heavily upon his valet's assistance to stand upright. "Uncle, you shouldn't be down here. I've taken care of the problem with these two and you mustn't worry yourself about it."

Lord Northrop turned his faded slate-blue eyes upon the couple at the foot of the steps. He spared Kane only a brief glance before his gaze came to rest upon Fortune. The wrinkles in his aged brow deepened as he studied her features with eyes that saw the past in her lovely face.

"Lorna Anne." He gasped as if he'd been struck. He took an unsteady step forward before he managed to collect his shaken wits and realize that he wasn't looking at Sebastian's wife. The girl resembled his daughter-in-law but she was far more beautiful. Although she possessed the sweet curve of Lorna Anne's mouth, she had eyes that had come directly from his own bloodline through his son Sebastian.

"My God," he breathed, grabbing his valet's arms for support. "After all these years of praying, God has finally seen fit to forgive me and answer my prayers. It's Sebastian's child."

"No, Uncle," Manville said, hurrying up the steps to Lord Northrop's side. "She's only someone Warrick brought here to upset you. You know that Sebastian's child disappeared with him."

"Out of my way, Nevin," Lord Northrop growled, his voice stronger than it had been in years. "That is my granddaughter you're trying to keep away from me."

"Uncle, I'm only trying to spare you more pain. In your condition, I can't allow you to upset yourself over someone who means nothing to you."

"Damn it, if you don't get out of my way, I'll summon the grooms myself and have you whipped, you young pup.

Now move, Nevin.'' Lord Northrop raised a blue-veined hand and brushed Manville out of his path.

"Come here, child," he urged, extending his hand palm up toward Fortune.

Manville flashed Fortune a hate-filled look and tried again. "Uncle, you can't mean to accept this—this girl without any proof of her identity. She could be anyone that Warrick found in Bristol's gutters."

"Don't be a fool, you ninny. All you have to do is look at her and you'd know that she is Sebastian's child. She has his eyes and her mother's mouth but she also has my chin and hair. The girl is a Northrop, through and through."

"V-very well, Uncle," Manville stuttered into silence. His thin features set in a bitter mask as he stepped back to allow Fortune to approach Lord Northrop. Now was not the time to press the old man. His uncle was known for his stubborn disposition, and if he tried to force the issue of the girl's identity with him at this moment, it could push him in the opposite direction. He'd let the first thrill of excitement wear off before he pursued it further.

Fortune glanced briefly at Kane before she slowly ascended the marble steps. She dropped into a graceful curtsey in front of Lord Northrop.

"Rise, child. I'm only a lord of the realm and your grandfather, not the prince regent," the old man said, and chuckled with pleasure at the girl's grace and manners. "But I daresay you do that nicely enough to be introduced to the prince on his next visit."

Uncertain of what to say or do, Fortune cast a pleading look to her mentor. Everything that Kane had taught her during the past weeks vanished completely from her mind. She found herself left speechless and bewildered by the swift turn of events.

"Speak up, girl, and tell me your name," Lord Northrop said, his voice growing weaker by the moment. The excitement over finding Sebastian's child was leaving him and the exertion it took to remain standing, even with the support of his valet, was now draining away the stamina that had taken him days to build.

"This is Mistress Fortune McQueen, Lord Northrop," Kane said as he strode up the steps to her side. He gave Fortune a reassuring smile.

"McQueen?" the old lord asked, puzzled. "Why is she called that? The girl is a Northrop."

"Yes, she's a Northrop but I'm afraid until recently she didn't know it."

"Take us inside, Vincent," the old lord said to his valet. "I suspect there is much that I have to learn about my granddaughter." He glanced at Fortune once more and raised a gnarled hand to cup her chin. He smiled down at her. "There is much I need to know and explain now that God has granted me a second chance."

"Yes, Grandfather. There is much we both need to know," Fortune said, smiling up at him for the first time. Gazing up into blue eyes so much like her own, it felt right calling Lord Northrop grandfather. Everything seemed so natural. She sensed an instant rapport with the man who claimed her as his kin and knew in that moment that all her worries had been over nothing. She'd made the right decision to travel to England with Kane Warrick. She had come home.

"You need some time alone," Kane said. "Manville and I will join you shortly." He pinned Lord Northrop's nephew with a look that spoke volumes.

"We have nothing to discuss, Warrick," Manville said, shifting uncomfortably from one foot to the other like a small boy who's been caught with his finger in the pie.

"I feel certain that we do. While Lord Northrop and Fortune use this time to get better acquainted, I think we should discuss business."

Manville cast a nervous glance at his uncle and then nodded. "Yes, I agree. Shall we go into my study?"

Kane winked at Fortune and followed Manville into the house.

Wheezing from the exertion of the short walk into the

drawing room, Lord Northrop drew an unsteady hand across his brow and smiled weakly at his newfound grand-daughter. "Now, young lady, it's time to tell me how you have come here and what happened to my son and your lovely mother."

"I know only what I've been told, Grandfather. When my adoptive uncles found me hidden in a cloak beneath my mother's body, I was only a few months old."

Lord Northrop nodded sadly. "I can understand that, child. But I would appreciate your telling me what you do know of your parents. It would finally ease my old mind after all these years of worrying."

Fortune understood her grandfather's request. From experience she knew how hard it was to lose someone to death, but it would be harder to live with the uncertainty that Lord Northrop had for nearly eighteen years. The knowledge that somewhere in the world a loved one might be alive and suffering was too horrible to contemplate.

"My parents died in the spring of seventy-seven." Fortune began the story of her life and left out nothing of her years with the McQueen brothers in the Carolina mountains except for Tiny's letter four years earlier. In her grandfather's fragile state of health, she wanted nothing to shadow their reunion. It was in the past. They were now together and this was all that mattered.

Lord Northrop's eyes glistened with tears when Fortune concluded her story. He now knew the fate of his son, but there was one question that prayed upon his mind and had to be answered before he could find any peace. "Fortune, do you know if a letter from me was found in my son's possession?"

"I'm sorry, Grandfather. Tiny never mentioned any letter but that doesn't mean there wasn't one. My uncle said the Indians burned or stole everything except for the trunk holding my mother's books."

Lord Northrop nodded, releasing a long breath. Fortune had brought him so close, but now he'd never know if Sebastian went to his death despising him for being a foolish old man. Lord Northrop drew in a shuddering breath, resolutely closed away his grief, and turned his attention back to the present. He couldn't dwell on the past when he had been blessed with his granddaughter.

"I have much to thank young Warrick for," he murmured softly. "He's given me back the granddaughter that I thought lost for nearly eighteen years."

Fortune shared her grandfather's sentiments.

"Close the door behind you, Warrick. My uncle has already experienced enough excitement for one day," Manville said as he crossed the study and put the large mahogany desk between himself and his steely-eyed visitor. Like a hare ready to spring out of harm's way, he didn't sit down. Nor did he offer Kane a seat. "Now, what is so important we need to discuss? I know we don't have any business dealings that need our combined attention."

Kane closed the door and leaned back against it, blocking Manville's only exit. "I think you know exactly what kind of business we have to discuss."

"Must you talk in riddles, Warrick? I for one don't think we have anything to say to each other." Feigning indifference, Manville turned his attention to the stack of papers on the desk. He perused the top page, then scribbled his name at the bottom.

"We have much to say about your hired assassins."

Manville's head snapped up and he shifted uncomfortably. "Again, Warrick, you're talking in riddles. I don't know anything about hired assassins."

"I think you do, Manville."

"You're mad," Manville accused, adopting an injured air.

"Perhaps I am but that will only make it easier to wring that weasely little neck of yours if you attempt to harm Fortune again."

"Get out of my house, Warrick. How dare you stand there and accuse me of such horrendous things when you're the one who is trying to ruin me out of spite? Your mills are nearly bankrupt and since you're not as good a businessman as I am, you want to blame me for your problems.''

"It's true that I have my reasons for wanting to see you ruined. My father's death is one of them, yet that has nothing to do with what happened last night. I'm warning you only once, Manville. Your life now rests with Fortune's safety. Should anything happen to her then you will forfeit more than your wealth. It will mean your death."

"Then I have nothing to worry about," Manville said, and smiled cynically. "As you had planned all along, the girl has been taken under my uncle's wing. Out of his misconception that she is in fact his granddaughter and not some tramp you picked up in Bristol to play the part, poor fool that he is, he'll see nothing happens to her."

"How like you to play the offended party when in truth you know she is Lord Northrop's granddaughter and heir."

"I know no such thing."

"You found the proof of her identity when you had our trunks stolen from the *Mermaid*."

"Warrick, I've had just about enough of your wild accusations. First you accuse me of attempted murder and now of robbery. Can you think of nothing more you want to lay at my door? Perhaps stealing babies or raping young innocents? But that's more in your line, isn't it?"

Manville's taunt hit too close to home for Kane. After his bout of guilt that morning, he was in no mood to overlook the man's insulting remarks. With face flushing a dull red and fists balled at his side, he took several steps across the study before he managed to regain control over himself. His full attention centered on Manville, he didn't hear the study door open behind him.

Manville's eyes widened in surprise at Kane's reaction. Without even realizing it, he'd hit upon something that could render Warrick vulnerable: his relationship with Fortune. He smiled triumphantly at Kane and could have laughed aloud a moment later when he saw his other adversary standing quietly in the doorway. Never a man to surrender easily, Nevin's brain instantly began to formulate a plan to save himself and North Meadows. He would divide and conquer. If he could get Warrick to admit he'd used the girl for his own purposes, he might drive a wedge between them before it was too late.

"So that's how the land lies between the two of you," Manville said, eyeing Fortune over Kane's shoulder. "I should have known that there was more in your relationship with my dear cousin than your need to play the good Samaritan. You want more than just to ruin me, you want all of North Meadows for yourself, don't you?"

"Damn you, Manville. You know I have no designs on North Meadows. All I want in return for bringing Fortune to her grandfather is that strip of land I need to build my canal from the river. If her presence also ruins your chances of inheriting North Meadows, so much the better."

Manville felt like shouting with joy at the stricken look that crossed Fortune's pale features. His assumption had been right. There had been much more to their relationship than Kane wanted to admit. The girl's face told the story of what had transpired between them, and he was going to use it to his own advantage. "I now understand how your mind works, Warrick. You didn't want to leave anything to chance, did you? If you couldn't get the land one way, you'd seduce Fortune to get it another. I admire your ingenuity."

"If that was your intention, then your plan has failed, Kane," Fortune said quietly.

Unable to control his glee any longer, Manville threw back his head and let loose his mirth. His laughter seemed to echo like a death knell through the halls of North Meadows as Kane turned to face Fortune.

"Warrick, it seems my cousin has put an end to your machinations."

"Fortune, it's not as you think," Kane said, ignoring Manville.

"You mean you don't want the land for your canal?"

she asked calmly. She showed no outward sign of the pain tearing at her heart.

"No, I—mean, damn it. Yes, I do want the land for the canal," Kane answered truthfully.

"That's all I wanted to know," Fortune said without emotion. She glanced toward Manville and then back to Kane. "Grandfather wants to thank you for bringing me to North Meadows."

"Fortune, there is more here than what you overheard," Kane said, attempting to explain his motives before it was too late.

"Perhaps there is, Kane, but it's none of my business. I came here for one reason alone and that was to find my family. I'll have nothing to do with trying to ruin Manville for you nor will I help you gain the land that you prize."

"Damn it, Fortune," Kane said, growing defensive. "That land I prize could well mean the life and death of my mills. If wanting to keep my people working so they can put food on their tables makes me guilty of some horrendous crime, then so be it. I'll not apologize for it." Kane glanced back at Manville.

"You think you've won but you haven't. I won't allow you and Stoddard to drive me out of business." With that he turned and stormed out of the study.

Baffled by Kane's explosion, Fortune looked at Manville who sat on the edge of his desk, smiling smugly. "What did he mean about his mills?"

"Nothing of importance, cousin," Manville said. "Warrick has a tendency to overlook his own faults as a businessman and lay the blame for his troubles on others." Manville dusted his long-fingered hands together and stood. "Now that you've come to North Meadows to live, let me be the first to welcome you."

"You're welcoming me to North Meadows?" Fortune said, puzzled by the sudden change in his behavior toward her.

"Of course," Manville said, smiling. "I beg your pardon for my actions last night at the inn but I was only trying to protect my uncle. He's been ill for some time now and I am the only person to see to his affairs."

"You don't really expect me to believe that you want me here, do you?" Fortune said, eyeing her cousin dubiously. "Especially after you tried to have me killed."

Manville feigned ignorance. "My dear cousin, you and Warrick both have vivid imaginations. He told me of what transpired at the inn last night but I assure you I had nothing to do with it. I was horrified that something like that could happen."

"I don't believe you. You're the only person who has anything to gain from my death."

"Poor, misguided child," Manville said, shaking his head. "Warrick has as much to gain as anyone from what happened."

"Kane couldn't gain anything from my death," Fortune said in Kane's defense.

"True, but you. didn't die did you?" was all Manville said.

"What do you mean?"

"He wanted to make sure you were in his debt in order to get the land he needs."

"But he shot at the men."

"If they were dead there would be no one left to identify him as the man who hired them."

Fortune shook her head in denial. "Kane might not have told me the reason he brought me to England, but I won't believe he is that devious."

"It's up to you, cousin, but give me the same courtesy. Don't accuse me of crimes until you have proof of my guilt."

"I'm sorry," Fortune said, flushing with embarrassment.

Manville came around the desk and crossed to Fortune. "I'm the one who should be apologizing. I've said several harsh things since we met and I want you to know I didn't mean them. If you can forgive me, cousin, I'd like for us

to be friends. We are family now.'' He held out his hand
to her.

''It's been a trying time for all of us,'' Fortune said,
and took his hand. ''I think we all say things we don't
mean in the heat of anger.''

Manville placed her hand on his arm and smiled down
at her. ''Shall we go and have tea with Uncle? I know it
will please him to see we are getting along after our encounter upon your arrival at North Meadows.''

''Yes, I would like that,'' Fortune said. For now she'd
accept Manville's offer of friendship, but she'd never be
able to trust him. There was something about the man that
repelled her, and she couldn't rid herself of the sensation
that her hand lay on a snake. Instinct told her to draw away
from him but she forced herself to calmly walk at his side
to the drawing room. An unspoken truce had been nego-
tiated a moment earlier and she'd not be the first to break
it. She was home and she wanted to live in peace.

''Then I'll bid you good day, Lord Northrop,'' Kane
said as they entered the drawing room. ''If I can be of
further service to you, please don't hesitate to call upon
me.'' He bowed and turned toward the door. He paused
only briefly to incline his head to Fortune and flash Manville a look of loathing before he strode from North Meadows.

''A good man,'' Lord Northrop said, smiling up at
Fortune and patting the seat beside his chair.

Lord Northrop glanced out the window to see Kane
climbing into the coach. He rambled on as if he'd not
changed the subject. ''But it's odd that he wouldn't accept
anything for all his trouble. I wanted to compensate him
for the expense of his journey but he refused to take a
penny. He said his reward was knowing that he'd brought
our family back together.''

Fortune's gaze followed her grandfather's and she watched
the coach drive away down the winding drive. She felt her
throat constrict with grief—a grief for something that had
not truly been born, only dreamed. And she wondered

what had made Kane refuse her grandfather's offer of re-payment. Had he accepted, it would have been a simple matter to gain the land he needed for his canal.

Bewildered by the strange turn of events, she frowned. She'd never understand Kane Warrick. With his mercurial moods, he changed from moment to moment and she never knew what to expect. He could be her gentle friend as well as her enemy, her lover, and her nemesis. Her heart ached to learn all of his sides, to understand him as only a woman understands the man she loves.

"Nevin," Lord Northrop said. "I'm proud to see that you've decided to accept your new cousin. It does my heart good to know that the two people who mean the most to me can live amicably together. I'd hate to know you disliked each other because then one of you would have to leave."

The unspoken threat well taken, Manville swallowed back his ire and seated himself across from his uncle. He smiled pleasantly at Fortune. "Fortune and I have come to an understanding, Uncle. She now understands I had only your best interest in mind when I reacted so strongly to her arrival. I think since that's all settled we can live here without any problem."

"Good to hear it," Lord Northrop said, and reached out to pat Fortune's hand. "You'll never know how much your arrival has helped me, child. After nearly eighteen years of not knowing what happened to Sebastian and Lorna Anne, it is a blessed relief to be able to put it out of my mind. I still grieve for them but time heals all wounds to some degree. I'll not forget my son or his wife but you will give me peace in my old age. For that I'll be eternally grateful."

Fortune squeezed her grandfather's blue-veined hand. "I'm grateful you've accepted me, Grandfather."

"How could I not, child? I made too many mistakes with your parents and I don't intend to do the same with you." Lord Northrop pulled the servants' cord and a moment later Vincent came hurrying into the drawing room.

"Have a maid to show my granddaughter to her rooms and then take me to my bed, Vincent. I need to rest."

Lord Northrop patted Fortune on the cheek and brushed his bluish lips against her brow before hobbling from the drawing room with the aid of his valet. By the time they reached the master bedchamber and he was safely tucked back beneath the silken sheets, he was breathing heavily from the exertion. He was tired but he couldn't sleep. Fortune's arrival had brought back memories that he'd long tried to forget. It was his fault that Sebastian and Lorna Anne were dead. Had he not taken it into his mind to have Lorna Anne for himself, he'd not have lost the past eighteen years with the girl downstairs.

"Oh, God," he muttered. His thin yellow-nailed fingers fidgeted with the covers. The child downstairs was the image of her mother, the woman he'd loved, the woman he'd lost his son over. For Sebastian had never forgiven him for loving Lorna Anne. He'd taken her and their child to the colonies, determined to build a new life without his father or his wealth. He'd written Sebastian, begging his forgiveness, but he now knew his letters had never reached his son. Sebastian had died with the hatred for his father still burning in his heart. Lord Northrop knew he'd go to his own grave guilty that his lust for his son's wife had driven Sebastian to his death.

"Sebastian," Lord Northrop whispered, his aged face damp from his tears. "I pray that I can make it up to your daughter for all she missed because of me. She didn't know you or Lorna Anne but she will know her roots, her place in society, that I promise. When I die, she will have North Meadows in your stead."

# Chapter 6

*From Fortune's vantage point on the hilltop overlooking* North Meadows, she could see the dark haze of smoke that rose from the distant chimneys of the cotton mills at Northington. Her grandfather had told her that the village had been named after his family in the fifteenth century and had once been called Northropington but with the passing of time changed to its present name. She couldn't remember which ancestor had founded the village. There had been so many to learn about since her arrival at North Meadows a month ago that she couldn't keep them separated. Her grandfather had used the time they'd spent together to impart all of their family history to her. He seemed determined to make her familiar with every Northrop who had ever lived.

Fortune smiled. She understood what her grandfather was trying to do and she loved him for it. He wanted her to feel at home at North Meadows, to be proud of her family's heritage. He had succeeded. During her short stay, she had grown to love Lord Northrop and the land her family had claimed for generations.

Only one thing had shadowed her happiness during the past weeks at North Meadows: her feelings for Kane Warrick. They had not lessened, and she was even more confused about his hasty exit from North Meadows without asking her grandfather for the land he needed for his canal. Before that had happened she'd thought she could finally kill any feeling she had for him; however, his unselfish act served only to fuel her turmoil.

She couldn't find any answers to solve her dilemma, so Fortune turned her thoughts from Kane and glanced at the land to the west of her. It was Warrick land. After learning from her grandfather that the boundaries of his land bordered Warhill, the Warrick estate, she'd first come to the hilltop to feel closer to Kane. But now it served a different purpose. In the past weeks she'd come here often to escape the restrictions placed on her by English society. The hilltop with the tall oaks and thick grass afforded her a haven where she could enjoy her privacy, as well as a feeling of freedom that she had missed since coming to England. The hill was a place in which she could be herself without worry that someone would see through her guise of a well-mannered lady.

Fortune frowned and glanced down at her lovely sprigged muslin gown. The girl from the Carolina mountains may have been hidden beneath the layers of silks and satins of her fancy gowns but she hadn't disappeared. She still existed, as did her yearning for the independence she'd known with her uncles in the tiny mountain cabin.

Fortune's expression grew thoughtful as she looked in the direction of her new home. Although she had to admit it was wonderful to live at North Meadows and have her every need attended to, she had found that there were also some disadvantages to such an existence. Her indolent lifestyle left her feeling restless.

"I need something to occupy my time besides deciding what gown to wear and watching the flowers grow," Fortune mused aloud to the soft breeze that molded her muslin gown to her lithe body. Her tone reflected her mounting irritability.

Fortune stilled as a new thought occurred to her. She was sure her grandfather would know how to help her find something useful to do with her time. Excited at the prospect, she decided to see Lord Northrop immediately. Lifting her skirts in one hand, she hurried back down the trail to where she'd tethered her pony cart to the limb of a small oak. Humming a happy tune, she gave the furry little beast a pat on the neck as she passed by him to untie the reins. However, the sound of soft crying in the nearby bushes stilled her fingers before she could undo the knot.

Forgetting her mission to see her grandfather, Fortune automatically turned in the direction of the heart-wrenching sounds. She paid no heed to the limbs and briars that snagged her gown and hair as she pushed her way through the thick underbrush to the source of the weeping. She found a small boy hunkered forlornly with his face buried in his hands, sobbing brokenly at the base of a tall oak. His entire body shook from the force of his anguish. Fortune needed no further encouragement to give comfort to the small unhappy child. She knelt at his side and gently brushed back the dark hair that lay in ringlets about his head.

"Are you hurt?" she asked softly. "Can you tell me what's wrong?" Fear of frightening the child into running away suppressed Fortune's urge to pick him up and cradle him to her breast as instinct bade her to do.

Sniffling loudly and shuddering from his sobs, the child raised his head and looked at her through misty silver eyes fringed in thick dark lashes. Fortune's breath stilled in her throat. When their eyes met, she had no need for anyone to tell her the child's identity. He was the image of his father, Kane Warrick.

"Can I help you?" she asked, tenderly brushing a tear from his damp, chubby cheek.

"I-I'm lost," he stuttered as new tears brimmed in his eyes.

"That's no problem. I'll help you get back home," she said.

"I don't want to go home," the little boy said, pressing

his lips into a tight moue even as more tears cascaded down his cheeks.

Fortune's lifestyle in the Carolina mountains had left her better prepared to fight Indians and kill bears than to deal with small children, yet her instincts told her that only gentle persuasion would get Kane's son to tell her why he didn't want to return home. His weeping revealed his fear of being lost but he seemed determined not to go back to Warhill.

"Do you mind if I stay here with you for a while?" Fortune asked, settling herself on the ground at his side and leaning back against the rough barked oak.

He shook his head.

"Good," Fortune said. She lay her head back against the bole of the tree and gazed up at the patches of blue that could be seen through the leaves. "It's such a nice day. I love to come here where it's quiet and peaceful."

Imitating Fortune, Kane's son settled his small body against the tree and turned his smudged face toward the sky. "I love it here, too," he said, liking the strange lady of the wood. She was much nicer than Nanna.

Fortune glanced down at her small companion. "It seems we haven't been properly introduced. My name is Fortune. What is yours?"

"Price," he answered quietly, all his bluster disappearing as he told her his name.

"Price," Fortune repeated and nodded. "That's a nice name for a young gentleman." She smiled as her words brought life back into his face. His chubby cheeks deepened in hue and he squirmed with delight at her compliment.

"Fortune. That's a beau-ti-ful name," he said with all the dignity that lay in his four-year-old heart. He'd stretched the word beautiful out to make his new friend as happy as she'd made him.

"Now that we've become friends, can you tell me about yourself? I've never known any other small boys before."

"Really?" Price said, looking up at her in wonder.

"Most certainly. Where I come from, there are few grown-ups and even fewer children. Until today I've never been fortunate enough to have a friend your age."

Price seemed to swell with pride. This beautiful, gentle lady considered him her friend. "I've never had a friend your age before either. All I have is Nanna and she's not my friend." The happy expression faded from Price's cherubic face when he mentioned his nanny.

"Why isn't she? I would think she would be honored to have such a fine young man as her friend," Fortune said. The look on Price's face tore at her heart.

Price lowered his head and began to draw in the dust with his finger. "Nanna doesn't like me. She gets angry with everything I do."

Unable to stop herself, Fortune placed her arm about his small shoulders and drew him against her. "Perhaps you've misunderstood. I'm sure your nanny likes you. I don't see how she could do otherwise."

"Nanna's not nice like you. She hits me with the birch rod when I do something that she doesn't like."

Laying her head against his dark ringlets, Fortune felt tears of sympathy well in her own eyes at the thought of anyone touching Kane's son in anger. She'd known him only a few minutes but in that time his sweet nature had stolen her heart completely.

"Is that why you ran away from home and became lost?" she asked softly.

Price nodded. Feeling secure in her arms, he snuggled closer. "Nanna was going to beat me for getting dirty," he said, his voice catching in his throat.

"Does your father know how your nanna treats you?" Fortune asked, unable to believe that Kane could knowingly allow his child to be abused.

"Papa's too busy to have time for me," Price said, his little voice tinged with adult cynicism. "He leaves me in Nanna's care because he doesn't want me . . . or love me."

"I'm sure that's not true. Sometimes we grown-ups do

get so busy we forget to do certain things but that doesn't mean we don't love our children or want them."

"Really?" Price asked, turning to look up at Fortune, his young face alight with hope.

"Yes, really." Fortune laughed and ruffled Price's hair. "Now will you let me take you back to Warhill? It's nearly time for tea and I'm sure a growing boy like you is hungry."

Price shook his head. "No. Nanna will beat me for running away."

"Price, I promise that won't happen. I'll speak with your father about how your nanna's been treating you and I'm sure he'll have a talk with her."

"All right," Price agreed reluctantly. He pushed himself to his feet and swiped at his runny nose with the back of his hand. He stood trustingly before her, tear-reddened silver eyes reflecting the innocent faith he placed in his new friend's ability to protect him.

Fortune felt honored to be looked upon by this small boy in such a manner and she determined at that moment to fight for him. After her last encounter with his father, the odds were not in her favor, but she wouldn't let that stop her. This child needed someone to care for him. Getting to her feet, she held out her hand to Price Warrick. He took it eagerly, giving her a wide happy smile.

Using the pony cart to return Kane's son back to Warhill, Fortune had to take the road that led through Northington. What she saw appalled her. From the distance the little hamlet looked enchanted resting on the banks of the glistening river; however, upon closer inspection it was little more than a maze of dismal little houses crowded about the large Northrop mills.

After weeks of living in the luxury of her grandfather's home, she was stunned by the poverty she saw. The soot-blackened cottages reflected the grim lives of those who lived within the meager shelters. Bleak and tired faces peered from the grimy windows and sagging doorways as she passed. Raw sewage ran in the open drainage ditches to the river that the villagers used for drinking water. Its stench was nearly unbearable, and it took all of Fortune's willpower to keep from disgracing herself by losing her luncheon.

Unlike his silent companion Price, with the honesty of a child, made a face of disgust and pinched his nose together with two fingers. "It smells bad here," he added to ensure that Fortune was aware of the tainted air.

"I know, Price," Fortune said, choking back the bile that rose in her throat. "We'll soon be at Warhill and you won't have to smell it any more." Fortune cast one last puzzled glance at the village before snapping the pony's reins and sending him trotting across the bridge along the road to Warhill. Price chattered constantly and she nodded her head in agreement or said, "Oh really," to keep him satisfied that he had her full attention. However, her thoughts were not upon the child at her side but the miserable little village named after her family.

It was a disgrace for people to live in such squalor. Her little cabin in the Carolina mountains had been a mansion compared to what she'd just seen in Northington. She didn't understand how her grandfather, who had been so kind and generous to her and had more wealth than he'd ever need, could allow his mill workers to live in such pitiable conditions. But she was determined to find out. As soon as she returned to North Meadows she would confront him with what she'd seen today.

"That's where I live," Price pointed out to Fortune, jerking her thoughts back to the present.

She turned the pony cart onto the graveled drive that snaked its way through a tunnel of gnarled oaks. Exiting the cool shade provided by the trees, the drive abruptly veered to the right around a sprawling lawn and small fish pond. Winding past manicured gardens with white graveled paths gleaming in the afternoon sun, the drive ended in a cobbled courtyard in front of a beautiful two-story mansion. Like North Meadows it, too, had been built of handmade bricks, and its color was a soft muted rose that blended well with the dark crimson blooms from the gardens on each side of the portico.

Fortune drew the pony to a halt and sat gazing up at Kane Warrick's home. Its clean Georgian lines reminded her of its owner. He endured no excess in his architecture or his life if what she'd learned of him in the past months was true. She glanced down at the small boy at her side. From what Price had said, that included his son.

"Where have you been, young man?" a shrill-voiced woman said as she came running down the front steps and jerked Price from the pony cart and shook him. "How dare you worry me like this."

"Nanna." Price gulped, his throat clogging with fear.

"Mistress," Fortune said, her tone reflecting the anger that ran in a white-hot current through her. "Put Price down."

Harriet Ward glanced up at the young woman climbing resolutely down from the pony cart. "I don't know who you are, but Price is my concern, not yours."

"I am a friend and I've come to see his father about the treatment he has been receiving at your hand," Fortune said. "Is Mr. Warrick home?"

The nanny set Price on his feet. "Mr. Warrick has gone to London and isn't expected back for several days. I'm in charge of Price and his house in his absence."

"Does that mean that you have his permission to beat his son until he flees from his home?" Fortune questioned. She restrained the urge to deal with the shrew-faced woman as the nanny had dealt with Price.

"As I've said, Mr. Warrick leaves Price's welfare in my hands, and you have no right to come here and interfere." Harriet Ward drew herself up and folded her arms over her flat chest. Raising her pointed chin in the air, she stared down her thin hooked nose at Fortune.

"I know Mr. Warrick and I seriously doubt he is aware of your treatment of his son, but I intend to remedy that as soon as he returns from London." Fortune turned her attention to Price who had eased his way back to her side and stood huddled against her skirt, eyeing his nanny with fear. "Price, run along to your nursery. You will not be punished for today."

Price glanced uncertainly up at Fortune and then at Harriet Ward. With lips pinched tightly into a narrow line, she nodded. He looked back to Fortune. "Will you come to see me again?"

Fortune ruffled his dark curls and bent to give him a kiss on the brow. His small arms came about her neck and he hugged her tightly. "I most certainly will come to see you again," she said, returning his hug. "We are friends, and friends visit each other. Now run along and have your tea while I speak with your nanny. Everything is going to be fine."

"Bye, Fortune," he whispered into her ear. "Hurry back to see me." Price turned and went into the house.

"Now, Mistress," Fortune said, turning her full attention back to the nanny who stood stiff with anger. "I gave Price my word he would not be punished, and I intend to see that my promise is kept. I will return tomorrow and if you have touched one hair on that child's head, then you will answer to me personally. If you know what is in your own best interest, you'll heed my advice. Do you understand?"

All the resentment that Harriet Ward felt toward Fortune was reflected in her narrowed gaze yet she reluctantly nodded her head. Something about the younger woman intimidated the nanny. Until she was certain of Mr. Warrick's reaction to this little twit's accusations, she'd make no move to punish the boy. If he told her to mind her own business, then the little brat would be the one to pay for the girl's interference.

"Good, I'm glad that we understand each other. Now I'll bid you good day." Fortune climbed back into the pony cart and clicked the reins.

However, before the pony could move, Harriet Ward said, "Mistress, you failed to tell me your name."

"Fortune Northrop. I'm Lord Northrop's granddaughter."

Harriet Ward nodded briskly and turned away. She swallowed back the uneasy lump that had formed in her throat upon hearing that Price's new friend was a member of the powerful Northrop family. This changed things dramatically in Harriet's view. Even if Mr. Warrick told the girl his son was none of her concern, Harriet wasn't stupid enough to go up against a Northrop. Harriet knew her place in society. It would be wise to do as the girl bid if she ever wanted to find another position after Warhill.

From the look on the hateful woman's face, Fortune felt sure her threats had saved Price a beating. She drove happily back down the road to Northington. After weeks of inactivity it felt good to be doing something useful again.

Until Kane returned from London, she could do no more for the child, but she could begin the tremendous job of trying to correct the deplorable conditions that existed in the village. Turning her thoughts to the improvements needed to be made at Northington, Fortune glanced toward the blackened streambed that ran alongside the road. This was the first thing she would have her grandfather rectify. No one should live near such stench and contamination.

Engrossed with her plans, she failed to see what caused her pony to jerk to a halt. The sudden stop nearly sent Fortune tumbling headfirst to the ground. Startled and seeking to retain her seat in the cart, Fortune finally caught a glimpse of the obstacle. Her eyes widened in shock at the sight of a pregnant woman stumbling blindly past her, clutching her distended belly. She didn't glance up at Fortune but kept her lint-covered head bowed and her eyes on the ground as if she had to force her feet to move. Her gray face was already contorted into a grimace of pain as she turned her ankle on the loose pebbles at the edge of the road. She fell headfirst down the embankment. Her cry of agony echoed eerily through the still afternoon air as she rolled like a warped ball toward the fetid drainage ditch. The oozy slime splashed up and over her on impact before she lay still.

Everything had happened so swiftly that Fortune had not been able to react in time to save the woman from her fall. Her shock, however, was only a fleeting thing. She jumped to the ground and made her way, slipping and sliding in the muck, into the drainage ditch where the pregnant woman lay. Heedless of the sewage blackening the slimy water, she strained to pull the woman from the vile mud. The woman moaned once and then was quiet.

"I didn't mean to hurt you," Fortune apologized. "But we have to get you out of this filth. Are you able to get up?"

Oblivious to everything except her own agony, the woman paid no heed to Fortune's question but grabbed her bulging stomach and drew up her legs. "My baby." She groaned helplessly.

Fortune's eyes widened in horror. The woman was in labor. Frantic to get help before the babe could be born in the sewage, she scrambled back up the bank and ran toward the thatched-roof cottage she'd passed only a few minutes earlier. She banged on the leather-hinged door with both fists. "Someone, help me, please," she cried.

A stooped old woman, followed by a gray-haired man, came to the door. At a glance both looked to be in their nineties but Fortune took no time to consider their great age. Her only thoughts were of helping the pitiful creature in the drainage ditch.

"You have to come with me. A woman has fallen into the ditch; she's in labor." Fortune panted, out of breath from her run. She pointed in the direction she'd just come.

The old woman turned to the shadows behind her. "Henry, there's a girl here that needs your help."

A red-haired man who looked to be in his mid-thirties appeared behind the stooped old woman. He took a clay pipe from between his tobacco-yellowed teeth and cocked a red brow at her. "What's yer trouble, Missy?"

Fortune repeated what she'd just told the two older people.

Henry Reed paled. "My God, that sounds like little Mary Beth. Her firstborn is due next month." Before the words were completely out of his mouth, he was already on his way toward the ditch. Wide of shoulder and powerfully built, he loped easily down the embankment and lifted the girl he'd called Mary Beth from the mire. Tears glistened in his hazel eyes as he turned back to Fortune with his dripping, smelly burden. "She's dead and so is her babe. That bastard killed her."

Henry Reed's ruddy complexion deepened to a beet red as he strode up to the roadway where Fortune waited. He stood shaking his head, gazing down into the girl's still features, absorbed in his grief and fury. "I've known this child since the day she was born and no sweeter girl has there ever been." He looked at Fortune. "How am I to tell her man his wife and child are gone because of that black-hearted bastard who runs that sweat pit of a mill?"

"Put her in my cart and we'll take her home," Fortune said, touched by the man's emotional display.

Henry Reed glanced toward the cart before focusing his narrowed, tear-reddened eyes once more upon Fortune. "That cart came from North Meadows?"

"Yes, my grandfather gave it to me."

"Yer Lord Northrop's kin?"

Fortune nodded, immediately sensing the change in the giant's manner toward her.

Henry Reed drew himself up and eyed Fortune hostilely. "Mary Beth won't be riding in yer fancy trappings. It's yer fault that she's dead and I won't insult her nor her family by bringing her home in something a Northrop owns. I'll carry her meself." He spat at her feet and turned away.

"I don't understand," Fortune said, stunned by the man's reaction upon learning that she was a Northrop.

Reed stopped and looked back over his shoulder at Fortune. "Ye and yer kind never do. That's why this child in my arms is dead. All yer kind wants is the money to be made off of our sweat. Ye don't give a damn about the conditions we have to work in nor the hours girls like little Mary Beth have to put in to have a few bites of food on their tables for their families. Mary Beth asked for an easier job but even in her condition that bastard kin of yours wouldn't let her have one. He kept her on her feet and lifting the heavy bins of thread until it cost her life.''

Contempt for Fortune and her family was written on Henry Reed's flushed features as he continued his tirade. ''Ye high and mighty nobs would work us all to death if we'd let you. And when somebody like me speaks up against the way ye treat us, then it's no more work and out the door to starve.''

Henry Reed turned away again. He carried the dead girl toward the dismal little cottage where he'd lived with his parents for the past thirty years.

Fortune watched Reed walk away. With a sinking heart she knew that his accusations were true. The lifeless burden in his arms was evidence of his claims, as was the smelly dilapidated village that housed the people who worked for her grandfather.

Fortune pensively bit down on her lower lip. Although she'd witnessed the girl's death and saw the condition of the village, she couldn't believe that her grandfather would allow these things to happen. Such actions were contrary to everything she'd learned about the man who had welcomed her into his home and life.

Bewildered by the contradictions that were suddenly shadowing her new life, Fortune climbed back into the cart and snapped the reins against the pony's back. She turned the animal in the direction of the Northrop mills. Before she condemned her grandfather, she had to see the conditions of the mills for herself.

Smelling of sewage and giving no thought to her own appearance, Fortune drew the cart to a halt in front of the three-story building with the Northrop name painted boldly in red letters on a sign that spanned the entire second floor. As she climbed down from the cart, she cast only a cursory glance up at the sign and walked purposely into the dimly lit, humid interior of the cotton mill. The spinning and weaving machines hummed from within the cavernous structure.

"May I help you, Mistress?" a large man asked, stepping from the shadows to block her path.

"I've come to see my cousin," Fortune said, and attempted to pass by the man.

"Mr. Manville has already returned to North Meadows for the day, my lady." The man made no move to let her inside.

"Then you may show me about the mills," Fortune said, unintimidated by the man's size or the large stick he tapped against the leg of his britches.

"I'm sorry, my Lady. I'd have to have Mr. Manville's permission to do that. Mr. Stoddard and Mr. Manville don't allow no one to go in the mill without their say-so."

"Then I'll go in without their permission. My grandfather owns this mill and I'm sure he would not object. Now step out of my way." Fortune made to pass the man again. He did not budge.

"I can't allow that, my lady. No matter what your grandfather would say. I have me orders and must follow them."

"Then be prepared to answer to my grandfather when you throw me bodily off the property. I intend to see what goes on inside this mill with or without your approval."

"My lady, please. It will cost me my job and I have six little ones to feed. If you go in there without Mr. Manville's permission, he'll see that I don't work another day."

"My foreman is right, Fortune," Manville said from the doorway behind her. "I have given Wilson strict orders to allow no one, and that includes you, in the mill."

Fortune turned to her cousin. "Then I'm glad you've returned to show me about so I won't have to make Mr. Wilson lose his wages."

"Now why would I want to do that?" Manville wrinkled his nose in distaste at the odor emanating from Fortune's soiled gown. "I suggest you forget about this foolish whim of wanting to tour my mill. You need to go back to North Meadows and have a bath. You stink to high heaven, Fortune."

"I stink because I was in the drainage ditch with one of your workers. She died there less than an hour ago and you have been accused of working her to death."

"I'm sorry to hear that," Manville said, unconcerned. He pressed his handkerchief to his nose to ward off the offensive smell. "Now will you please go and get yourself cleaned up. It's not proper for you to be seen in public in such a state."

"Nevin, I don't give a damn about how I look or smell. I came here to see the mill and I'm not leaving until I do." Fortune braced her hands on her hips and squared her shoulders.

Manville glanced at Wilson and waved him away with the flick of his handkerchief and a curt "That will be all for now." When he looked back at Fortune, his face was set with anger.

"My dear cousin, you seem to forget that you are a stranger here and know nothing about how we do things in England. And if you are smart you will mind your own business and keep out of my affairs. I run this mill the way I see fit, and it is none of your concern."

"Does Grandfather know that you are working his people to death or that they live in squalor?"

"He leaves it to me to do as I please with the business," Manville said with a smirk of confidence. He lied as easily to Fortune about his uncle's involvement with the mill as he had to the bankers when he'd first used Lord Northrop's money to invest in the cotton venture with Orson Stoddard. It was much easier to raise capital from investors by using his uncle's name and influence. Legally the mill was his uncle's until his death but that didn't concern Nevin. To him the mill was already his, and he would not let this little chit's interference cause him problems.

Manville's answer reaffirmed Fortune's determination. Undeterred, she turned back to the door leading into the large spinning room.

"Where do you think you're going? I've already told you that I don't allow anyone inside the mill except my workers."

"I'm going to see if the accusations leveled against you and my family are true."

Manville grabbed Fortune's arm and jerked her about to face him. "Don't be a little fool. If you have any sense in that beautiful head of yours, you'll mind your own business and keep your nose out of mine."

"I'm going to see the mill now, Nevin, or later after I've spoken with Grandfather."

Seeing her determination, Manville realized it was in his own best interest to change his strategy. He was a firm believer in the old adage that you catch more flies with honey than vinegar. He'd give her the tour and then send her on her way. From her own lack of knowledge about the cotton industry, she'd find no fault with what she saw. She would return to North Meadows assured that everything was normal and it was only disgruntled workers who accused him of mistreatment. Manville forced a smile to his lips and made to drape his arm companionably about her shoulders. However, he had second thoughts as the smell reach his nostrils once more. He stepped back and nodded. "I'll give you a tour of the mill today but from now on, I want you to mind your own business. A cotton mill is no place for a lady.

"You have women who work here," Fortune said.

"Yes, but they are not Lord Northrop's granddaughter. Your place is at North Meadows, not in the mill or"—he paused and glanced down at the soiled bottom of her skirt—"in drainage ditches. Now let's get this over with so you can rid yourself of that stench." Taking her by the arm, he escorted her through the door that led to the next room.

"This, my dear, is the spinning room," Manville said

with a sweep of his hand. "As you can see, it's here the cotton is made into thread. Upstairs in the weave room is where the looms make the thread into fabric."

Fortune swiped a damp curl from her brow as she looked down the rows of spinning machines. In the short time she'd been inside the stifling atmosphere, she felt perspiration bead and roll down the curve of her back. She found it hard to catch her breath and wondered how the women and children lived in such an environment.

The air was humid and thick with the lint that covered everything. Like furry legless animals, layers of lint roiled about the feet of the workers whose jobs were to keep the raw cotton wound through the spinning machine and onto the bobbins. The employees themselves were also covered in lint from head to toe. It stuck to their hair, lashes, and clothes, making them look like large gray fuzzy beasts instead of human beings.

After seeing the spinning room, Fortune didn't believe conditions could get any worse as they ventured further into the mill. She was appalled to find the large storage room that held tons of baled cotton also served as the sleeping quarters for several children whom Manville had purchased from their parents. He boasted that for a mere fifteen shillings he owned them for six years of their life. They worked for him from six A.M till eight at night unless business was brisk. Then they worked sixteen hours a day. After putting in their long day's work, they were given meat and potatoes or porridge and locked up in the storage room until the next morning.

Sickened by what she had seen and heard, Fortune was ashen-faced and silent when they stepped out into the fresh afternoon air. Before she could speak she had to draw in several deep breaths to rid her nostrils of the lint and dust. The very thought that her family's name was associated with something so vile made her want the mills burned to the ground.

Satisfied with the way things had gone, Manville smiled down at Fortune. "Now that you've inspected the mills, I hope you realize what you've been told is completely unjust. You shouldn't concern yourself with the mills again, Fortune. You can't listen to a few disgruntled workers or they would have you believe we treat them no better than animals. But as you've seen, the Northrop mills are just like any other mill in the area. As a matter of fact, I'm better to my people than most employers. I take the orphans from Bristol and give them food and a place to sleep in return for their services, and I also give my indentured people a wage. That's far more than other mill owners can say they do.''

Fortune swallowed back a few of Tiny's choice invectives. "What I've seen today is a disgrace, Nevin. How can you sleep at night knowing that you're using children as slaves?''

The congenial expression left Manville's face. "Go back to North Meadows, cousin. You're still upset about what you saw earlier in the afternoon and it's affected your judgment. Once you're cleaned up and have rested, things will look better to you.''

"I'm going back to North Meadows and I'm going to speak with Grandfather. I can't believe he approves of what I've seen here today.

"I forbid you to say anything to Uncle that might upset him,'' Manville said. His thin face grew pale at the thought of his empire collapsing because of this hussy's interference.

"Forbid me, Nevin? You are my cousin, not my guardian. I can speak with Grandfather if I please.''

"Then do as you like, cousin,'' Manville snapped. "His death will be upon your conscience.'' Manville smiled to himself at the confused expression that flickered across Fortune's face. That would give her pause. She'd not risk her grandfather's life to improve a few workers' lives.

"Now, if you'll excuse me, cousin,'' Manville said, taking her by the arm and escorting her toward the pony cart. "I have work to do.''

He helped her up to the padded seat and handed her the

reins before pausing to look up at her. "As I've said before, I'm not an ogre, Fortune. I know you don't believe it but I do deal with my people fairly. Instead of criticizing me, they should be grateful I keep them working so they can put food in their bellies."

"Go home and rest, Fortune," he said. He gave her hand a pat and then walked back into the mill. He chuckled to himself as he entered his office and closed the door behind him. He was well satisfied his dear, stupid cousin wouldn't rush back to North Meadows to speak with her grandfather. The threat of Lord Northrop's death would give her something to consider. In the meantime he'd see no one was able to interfere in his business again.

Settling his thin frame behind his huge mahogany desk, Manville opened the top desk drawer and withdrew a folded document from its hiding place. He smiled as he opened it and read the name on the deed. Soon the name on the heading would read Nevin Manville instead of Lord Northrop.

Manville's smile deepened. Perhaps he should have allowed Fortune to run to his uncle about the conditions in the mills. The old man would have died of shock upon learning his money had built the cheap-labor cotton mills he detested.

Manville chuckled aloud. It would serve the old devil right after taking in that little hussy on her say-so alone. He'd weep no tears if the old bastard had an attack and died.

"Perhaps I should help matters along before the old bastard also ends up changing his will in favor of the little chit," Manville mused aloud. He stilled, his expression growing thoughtful. He couldn't allow that to happen. He had worked too long and hard for the Northrop estate to let it slip through his fingers because of his uncle's misguided need to have his granddaughter with him. A speculative light entered his dark eyes and he smiled. His uncle's death wouldn't be a difficult matter to arrange and once the old man was out of the way, he could rid himself of the girl.

Tapping his thin, long fingers against the smooth polished surface of the desk, Manville considered his options. He'd already learned that it wouldn't be easy to kill Fortune, but there were other ways of dealing with her. Ways that wouldn't draw suspicion to him if she suddenly disappeared or had an accident. His smile deepened. Without Kane Warrick as her champion and with no way to prove her identity, it would be a simple matter to have the courts rule against her. Once that was done and he was in complete charge of North Meadows, Fortune McQueen would be at his mercy. He licked his lips at the thought. She'd have no place to go and he'd be very magnanimous after his triumph. He'd generously offer her a place to live in exchange for her services in his bed. Feeling himself swell at the thought, Manville shifted in the chair and reached for the decanter of brandy sitting to his right. He poured himself a drink, downing it quickly. After wiping his mouth free of the excess liquid, he replaced the deeds in the drawer. He locked it and dropped the key in his waistcoat pocket.

Patting the embroidered material confidently, he pushed back his chair and stood. He needed to see Stoddard. He'd heard Warrick had gone to London with the hope of purchasing the cotton he needed to put his mills back into operation. Stoddard had just returned from the same destination, and he hoped that the man had been successful in buying up the raw material before Warrick had a chance to get his hands on it. As long as Warrick had his mills to worry about, he'd keep his nose out of Manville's affairs. He'd be too busy to worry about Lord Northrop's sudden demise or how the old lord's granddaughter was faring under Manville's protection.

# Chapter 7

$A$ *steady drizzle fell from the leaden sky to drench the* mourners who attended Lord Northrop's funeral. Beneath her black bombazine cloak, Fortune's shoulders shook from her silent sobs and her face was wet with tears behind her black veil. No one offered any comfort to the grief-stricken girl.

Standing stiff and silent at her side, Manville watched as the gravedigger shoveled the first spade of wet earth onto his uncle's shiny black coffin. He felt no grief for his uncle or pity for his cousin—only relief that it was finally over and he could get on with his life now that North Meadows was to be his.

Through narrowed eyes he cast a surreptitious look at Fortune and fought to suppress the urge to laugh at how well things had worked out. His beautiful, impetuous cousin blamed herself for her grandfather's death.

Manville mentally rubbed his hands together with glee. Fortune's guilt would only advance his own plans where she was concerned. Without Lord Northrop's protection she was now vulnerable to his manipulations, and when the will was read she would learn she was at his mercy. She would be destitute and without friends to give her aid.

Engrossed with his evil musings, Manville wasn't aware

of the tall figure who had arrived late to the cemetery. He stood to the rear of the crowd of mourners with his hat pulled low over his brow to protect him against the elements while watching his enemy intently with his penetrating silver eyes. Nor was Manville aware that the expression in his own beady little eyes revealed the direction of his thoughts to Kane Warrick.

Clenching his fists at his sides, Kane fought the urge to push his way through the crowd and throttle Manville before he could carry out his evil scheme. Without being told, Kane knew that the little weasel had some evil plan concocted for Fortune before Lord Northrop was completely cold in his grave.

A muscle in Kane's square jaw twitched from vexation. The thought of Fortune being used by someone like Nevin Manville sickened him to the very core of his being. She was too innocent and too beautiful. And she was—Kane stopped himself before he could finish the thought. He wouldn't say or even think that she was his. He had no claim on Fortune, nor did he want one. He only wanted to see her protected from vermin like Nevin Manville.

Kane's gaze came to rest upon the black-gowned figure at Manville's side and he searched the tearstained face behind the sheer lace veil. His heart went out to Fortune as she stood immersed in her grief over her grandfather. From the silent shudders that shook her slender frame he could feel the depth of her loss and knew the pain she suffered. In the elaborate coffin decorated with shining brass handles lay her grandfather, a grandfather for whom she had left everything to travel so far to find, a grandfather she'd had so little time to come to know and love before he was taken away from her. Now she was again left alone to fend for herself.

Unable to keep his distance as he had planned, Kane remained at the grave site after the mourners began to disperse. Something deep within him urged him forward to give comfort to the grieving girl. He judged his own feelings as sympathy, yet while he looked down at Fortune's bowed head he found that there were other confusing emotions mingling within him.

"Fortune, I'm sorry about your grandfather. Is there anything I can do?" he asked softly.

Slowly Fortune raised her head and looked up at him, her eyes glistening with her tears. "No, Kane. There's nothing anyone can do now. I—" Her words trailed off and she turned away. She couldn't tell Kane how she'd ignored Manville's warning about her grandfather's health, and because of her he now lay in his coffin. It was her fault and no one else's. After her visit to the Northrop mills three days ago, she'd returned to North Meadows and had gone directly to her grandfather with the tales of the horrors she'd witnessed. He'd seemed in better health than usual and he'd asked her to send Nevin in to see him as soon as he returned from the mills. And until the next morning when her grandfather was found dead by his valet, Vincent, she'd mistakenly believed her cousin's warnings had been used as a guise to keep her quiet about the deplorable conditions in which the villagers worked.

The doctor had said her grandfather's death had stemmed from a seizure. Something had overtaxed his already weakened heart and it hadn't been strong enough to handle the strain.

Kane raised a hand to draw her back to him but a skinny little man wearing a tall beaver hat and rain-fogged spectacles on the end of his hooked nose stepped between them. He took her by the arm and, without a glance at Kane or an apology for his rudeness, led her toward the closed carriage. Fortune did not look back at Kane.

Wanting to ease the agony he'd seen in her brimming eyes, Kane turned to follow her but found his path blocked by Nevin Manville.

"What are you doing here, Warrick? Can't you leave my family in peace even in their time of grief?"

"I came to pay my respects, Manville, and to give Fortune my condolences for her loss," Kane said, stepping around Manville. Again his enemy stepped in front of him.

Kane drew in a deep, steadying breath and sought to keep a tight rein on his temper. Lord Northrop's funeral was no place to fight with Manville. No matter how he felt about the bastard, he wouldn't allow the little weasel to badger him into an argument here. Fortune already had enough to contend with without adding their quarrel to her grief.

"Stay away from my cousin, Warrick. She's my responsibility now that my uncle is dead and I don't want you anywhere near her or North Meadows."

"Manville, I frankly don't give a bloody damn what you want. You forget that I know what a scoundrel you are, and if you think I'll stand by and let you use Fortune then you're mistaken. I didn't bring her here to be your pawn."

"Jealous, Warrick?" Manville questioned snidely as the carriage pulled away. "Are you afraid I'll get to taste that luscious body? Or are you just afraid that she might find out what a real man is like in bed?"

"You bastard," Kane growled, and took a step forward before he managed to regain control of himself. His face set and eyes flashing with ire, he regarded Manville contemptuously. "You'll answer to me if you ever touch her."

Shaken by the look of pure hatred he saw in Kane's eyes, Manville nervously readjusted his cape about his thin shoulders and cleared his throat before gaining enough courage to say "Whatever happens between Fortune and myself is none of your affair. But I suggest that you heed my warning, Warrick. North Meadows now belongs to me, and I'll have you horsewhipped if you set one foot upon my land again. Is that understood?"

"I wouldn't be so certain that you will inherit North Meadows, Manville. Fortune is the true heir to Lord Northrop's estate."

Manville shrugged and gave Kane a superior smile. "No court in the land would go against my claim. Without her mother's books, the girl has no proof of her identity."

"Perhaps that's so but I wouldn't be so smug if I were you. Lord Northrop might have changed his will in favor of his granddaughter." Kane grinned at Manville's reac-

tion to his taunt. The little man paled as he pursed his thin
lips and glanced uneasily away from Kane's mocking silver eyes.

"He didn't," was Manville's flustered reply before he
turned and strode toward his horse. He could still hear
Kane's mocking laughter as he mounted and rode away.

Manville kicked his horse in the side, urging him to a
faster pace down the muddy road. He knew how his uncle's will had been made but he wanted to get back to
North Meadows before Rutherford read it. As he rode
through the rain-drenched afternoon he told himself there
was no need for haste, but he didn't want to miss the look
on Fortune's face when she learned her grandfather had
bequeathed everything he owned to his nephew.

Lord Northrop's solicitor withdrew several papers from
his black bag and shuffled them together before seating
himself behind the large mahogany desk. "I'm afraid I
can't wait any longer on Nevin. I've urgent business in
London in two days and I'll be pressed to make my ap-
pointment as it is. I hope you understand, Lady Northrop?"

Fortune nodded, too miserable to care if Nevin missed
the reading of her grandfather's will. A few moments later,
however, she sat staring dumbfounded at Harry Rutherford, unable to believe what he had just read.

"Do you understand what I've said, Lady Fortune?"
the solicitor asked uneasily as he looked at the young
woman before him.

Mouth agape, Fortune just looked at him, unable to answer even his simple question.

"Lady Fortune, are you all right?"

Finally Fortune managed a nod.

"Then you do understand what I've just read to you?"
Rutherford asked again.

"I can't believe it," Fortune finally managed to croak
over the lump in her throat.

"Well, it's true. The will is exactly as your grandfather stipulated. Nothing has been changed."

"What can't you believe?" Manville asked as he strode into the room still wearing his rain-soaked cape.

"Grandfather's will," Fortune said, her voice still faint with disbelief.

Smiling at her shocked expression, Manville tossed his wet cape across the back of a leather wing-backed chair and nonchalantly straightened his cuffs. "What's to believe? I'm sure my uncle knew exactly what he was doing when he had Mr. Rutherford make out his last will and testament."

"I'm not sure, Nevin. It has to be a mistake."

"I doubt it," Manville said confidently. He settled his thin frame into the chair opposite Fortune's and relaxed back into the soft padded leather as he looked to the solicitor. "Is there any mistake, Mr. Rutherford?"

"I'm afraid there isn't. Lord Northrop made out this will the day before his death."

"What?" Manville exclaimed with a start and abruptly sat upright. His face paled and his eyes grew round with astonishment. "That's impossible," he gulped out. "My uncle made his will out years ago, as you well know."

"That's true, my boy, but that was his first will. This one was finalized three days ago."

Manville's face flushed a beet red as he swung about to glare at Fortune. "What did you have to do with this?"

"Nothing, Nevin. This is the first I've heard of it. I swear this comes as much of a surprise to me as it does to you," Fortune said, bewildered.

"What does my uncle's will state, Mr. Rutherford?" Manville said, striving to compose himself even as a ripple of dread crept chillingly up his spine.

"Everything Lord Northrop owns goes to Lady Fortune with the codicil stipulation that she marry within six months of the day of his death. If that doesn't take place or should she return to America instead of remaining in England, then it reverts back to you as it was in the first document he made out. And should she die without issue, then the same holds true. The estate and all that comes with it will be yours, Nevin.''

"The old bastard," Manville swore, coming to his feet. "After all the years I spent caring for the old fool, I'll not allow him to cheat me out of everything that is rightfully mine." He turned and pointed at Fortune. "You'll not get North Meadows away from me. You have no proof you are my uncle's granddaughter and I intend to see the will broken in court."

"My boy, calm yourself," Rutherford said. "Lord Northrop left you a healthy stipend of your own. You'll have five hundred pounds a year to do with as you please."

"Five hundred pounds!" Manville exploded. "That is nothing compared to what I will have once I prove her a fraud."

White-faced from Manville's sudden attack, it took several minutes for Fortune to comprehend everything the solicitor had told her. "Nevin, I know it is unfair but you still have the mills."

"No, I'm afraid he doesn't. In the last day I've gone over all of Lord Northrop's papers. Quite by accident I found that the Northrop mills go with North Meadows since Lord Northrop's money was invested in them. When I checked with the registrar's office, I also discovered that the deeds had been registered under his name completely without my knowledge. The mills are now yours as well, Lady Fortune."

Face flushed with fury and balled fist braced against the top of the desk, Manville leaned forward and glared at the solicitor. "Damn you, Rutherford! Those mills belong to me."

"I'm afraid that's not correct. As long as Lord Northrop's name is on the deed books, the mills go with the estate to Lady Fortune."

Manville turned on Fortune, his eyes wild. "I'll see you dead and in hell before you keep my mills. I may have used the old man's money to invest in them but they are mine, do you hear, mine! I'll not rest until I get them back. The courts will see I get what I deserve.''

"I'm afraid you're wrong, Nevin," Rutherford said, interrupting his tirade. "The will is legal and binding and no court in the land will break it, no matter what you claim. It was Lord Northrop's right to bequeath his holdings to anyone he chose. Nothing he possessed was tied up by primogeniture."

"We'll just see about that. I won't stand by and do nothing when everything I own is at stake." Manville turned and stalked from the room, slamming the study door behind him. The sound echoed eerily through the still room as Fortune and Mr. Rutherford sat stunned and silent.

"Well now, Lady Fortune," Rutherford said, clearing his throat. "It seems Mr. Manville abused your grandfather's trust and is now having to pay for his duplicity." Shuffling the papers before him, he looked up at Fortune. "But I can assure you that you have nothing to worry about. Now shall we get down to the business at hand? Do you have any suggestions about what you want done with your property or whom you want to act as your solicitor during this affair?"

"Mr. Rutherford, I'm afraid this has come as a complete shock to me and I don't have the faintest idea of what I want done with anything. But if you wouldn't mind, I would like for you to remain as my solicitor. I feel I can trust you since you've been loyal to my grandfather."

Rutherford's thin lips spread into a warm, cordial smile and he nodded. "Then that much is settled. Now let's turn to the will's codicil. Do you have anyone in mind for your husband?"

"My husband?" Fortune said, baffled. During Manville's outburst she'd forgotten all about the codicil Mr. Rutherford had mentioned. "I don't wish to marry anyone at the moment."

"Then I suggest you begin looking, young lady. It's imperative if you want to keep North Meadows and the Northrop mills. Your grandfather's will must be fulfilled six months to the day of his death or you'll lose everything.''

''But I don't even know any men, much less one that would be willing to marry me.''

Rutherford gave Fortune a reassuring smile. ''Lady Fortune, I don't mean to be bold, but with your looks and wealth I doubt you'll have any problem in finding a husband. Now, if you'll excuse me, I need to get back to Bristol before the weather gets any worse.'' He stood and shuffled the papers once more before returning them to his leather bag. ''I'm not getting any younger and this type of weather makes my old bones ache.''

Tucking his satchel beneath his arm and settling his beaver hat on his head, he looked once more at the young woman. ''If you should need me, please fell free to send word.''

''Thank you, Mr. Rutherford, for all that you've done,'' Fortune said, coming to her feet and extending her hand to him. He took it within his own gnarled fingers and gave it a reassuring squeeze. ''Don't worry, Lady Fortune. Nevin has always had a temper but I'm sure he'll come round once he has time to think things over.''

''I hope you're right,'' Fortune said, sensing that the solicitor knew Manville wouldn't change his mind in this matter. He would fight her for North Meadows and the Northrop mills.

Settling herself beneath a tall, gnarled oak, Fortune lay her head back against its rough-barked bole and closed her eyes against the sunlight spilling through the thick green leaves overhead. She'd retreated to her haven on the hilltop hoping to clear her mind of her troubled thoughts long enough to get a few minutes' rest. The shadows beneath her eyes reflected her lack of sleep since her grandfather's death. Each night she'd tossed and turned in her large feather-ticked bed until she thought she would wear holes in the sheets.

Guilt had kept her awake. It gnawed at her insides and

taunted her with the knowledge her stubbornness had been the cause of her grandfather's demise. Had she only listened to her cousin's warning, he would still be alive. Yet that wasn't the only thing which made her nights miserable. Since the will had been read, she had been torn with indecision about the new responsibility placed on her shoulders: the Northrop mills.

Fortune drew in a ragged breath and sought once more to rid herself of thoughts regarding the horrid mills. At the moment she had enough problems without complicating her life further by involving herself in something she knew nothing about. Although she wanted to forget what she had seen and what her stubbornness had caused, she failed to do so.

Even the fresh, clean air seemed to taunt her. It reminded her of the dusty, lint-filled chambers where she'd watched the small children struggling to keep up with the work demanded of them. An involuntary shudder shook Fortune as the images again rose in her mind.

Each time she closed her eyes she saw the small haggard faces—faces that were a mixture of youth and age. Their features were those of children yet from their lack of food and ill treatment their expressions were as tired and old as time itself. There had been no happiness in the large eyes that had turned upon her when she passed them, only a world-weary look whose memory made her heart ache.

"Grandfather, I'll try to be strong enough to bear the responsibility you've left upon me," Fortune murmured softly. But even as the words left her mouth she feared she'd be unable to fulfill the commitment her heart urged her to make. She knew nothing about business or managing cotton mills. No matter how much she wanted to help the poor wretches who slaved twelve to fourteen hours a day, she didn't know how to go about doing so. And there was the other problem she had to deal with before the end of six months. She had to find a husband. Fortune frowned. When she married she wanted it to be for love and not money, yet her grandfather hadn't given her a choice.

"There has to be a way that I can change things without losing everything to Nevin," she said aloud. During the past week she had become determined to keep her inheritance. Upon first learning of the change in her grandfather's will, she'd felt sorry for her cousin. However, those feelings had changed after learning of the way he'd misappropriated the funds to finance the mills. Her pity had quickly turned into anger. The man was little more than a common thief. He'd taken advantage of her grandfather's illness and trust to enrich himself. And she'd not allow him to take North Meadows or the mills he claimed from her. They were now hers, and he'd never get another chance to make her people suffer because of his greed. She would improve the bad working conditions that Manville had perpetrated and see the children smile once more.

Her frown deepened, her brows knitting over her nose as she sought a solution to the dilemma in which she now found herself. She didn't want to marry but she had to stop Manville. The main problem was to find a man who would want to marry her and champion her cause against her cousin.

Uninvited, Kane's name rose in her mind. He was the one man who would know how to deal with Nevin, but she feared he would not be willing to help her now. She had rejected his offer of friendship the day he'd brought her to North Meadows and he'd made no effort to mend the rift between them. He'd been kind to her at her grandfather's funeral yet she'd turned away from him again because of her own guilt.

"Why am I thinking of such a thing in the first place?" she muttered and pursed her lips, disgusted with herself for allowing such farfetched thoughts to even enter her mind at a time when she needed reality, and not girlish dreams.

She had already accepted the fact that she meant nothing to Kane Warrick, and she couldn't dwell on things that would never be. She had been only a means to an end, and he was probably glad to see the last of her since he'd not gained the strip of land he needed for his canal.

Fortune's flagging spirits sank even lower. She tried to put Kane out of her thoughts and concentrate on the problems at hand yet at that moment she longed to see him more than anything else on earth. She needed his strength and support as she prepared to do battle with Nevin Manville.

"What shouldn't you be thinking?" was Kane's soft question as he hunkered down at her side and picked a blade of the sun-dappled grass.

Shocked to hear Kane's voice, Fortune snapped her eyes open and found herself peering up into his entrancing silver gaze. His expression made her mouth suddenly go dry, and she had to swallow several times before she could speak. To her chagrin only a throaty whispered "Oh" emerged as she watched his lips curl up into a provocative grin.

Drawing her thoughts away from the lips that had given her so much pleasure, she gave herself a sharp mental kick. She couldn't let Kane have this effect upon her. She had to keep her wits or she'd end up making a fool of herself again. Forcing calm into her voice, she rearranged the skirt of her gown and lowered her eyes as she asked, "What are you doing here?"

"Before I answer your question, will you answer mine?"

"It's nothing that would concern you," Fortune said, praying her voice didn't reveal the turmoil his nearness created.

"I'm absolutely sure that you're telling me the truth because of that woebegone expression you're wearing. Now why don't you tell me what's troubling you?"

Fortune picked a blade of grass and twisted it between her fingers. She looked up at Kane. "I inherited North Meadows and the Northrop mills."

A perplexed frown creased Kane's brow as he looked down at Fortune. "And that's a problem?"

"Yes, it is when Nevin is determined to take me to court to prove I'm not my grandfather's legal heir."

Kane nodded in understanding. "I would expect as much from Manville."

"I'm going to fight him, Kane," Fortune said, a spark of her spirit returning. "I intend to see he never steps foot in the mills again."

Kane relaxed back against the tree trunk. One corner of his sensuous mouth curved upward as he gave her a crooked grin and cocked his head to the side. "I see that living at North Meadows hasn't changed the stubborn little wildcat I first met. She's still alive and well beneath all the trappings of society."

"I'm afraid she's here to stay, Kane. For a while I thought she was gone, but now I know a part of her will always be with me and she'll never completely fit into polite English society."

"I'm glad to hear it," Kane said, and tweaked her playfully on the chin. "You'll need all that indomitable spirit if you intend to do battle with Manville. A faint-hearted miss would never succeed against him. He's more savage than any Indian you ever encountered in the colonies."

"I already know exactly what Nevin is without having to be told. The account books prove he is a thief and much worse—he has been monstrous in his treatment of the mill workers yet there is nothing I can do about it now that grandfather is gone. If I bring him up on charges, he'll only say he was doing Grandfather's bidding."

Kane looked at Fortune with new respect. "Then what do you propose to do?"

Fortune shrugged. "Mr. Rutherford advises me not to worry. He says the courts won't go against my claim to North Meadows even if I'm not who I say I am. Once everything is settled I'll decide about what I will do in the future about Nevin."

Kane arched a curious brow at her. "Do you intend to keep the mills?"

"That's my intention," Fortune said, turning to gaze in the direction of Northington.

"Do you think it's wise?"

She looked back at Kane. "It may not be wise but I have no other choice. The people of Northington depend upon the mills to live. They have little enough as it is without me taking more away from them."

"You've already thought this out, haven't you?"

Fortune nodded.

"I admire your courage but I'm afraid you've made the wrong decision, Fortune. You don't know the first thing about how a cotton mill works. You'll be bankrupt within three months."

Fortune stiffened and raised her chin to a haughty angle. "If I can learn to be a lady, I can learn anything."

Kane chuckled. "Managing a cotton mill is a far cry from learning proper manners. Furthermore, business is no place for a woman. Women don't have the acumen for it. They should be at home having babies and tending to their household duties."

Incensed by his condescending attitude, Fortune came to her feet. She stood with hands braced on her hips, glaring down at him. "For your information, ladies aren't supposed to know a great many of things that I know, Kane Warrick. And whoever said I was a lady? I told you only a short while ago I'm still the girl you met in the mountains of Carolina."

Kane came to his feet in one graceful movement. "Don't get angry at me because I'm just trying to save you the heartache of failure."

"Don't do me any favors, Kane Warrick. I can stand on my own two feet, just as I've always done. Tiny didn't raise me to be a coward nor did he teach me how to be a weakling. If I were you I'd look to my own affairs before trying to run other peoples'."

"Now what is that supposed to mean?"

"Exactly what I said."

Kane's face hardened with irritation. "What are you talking about?"

Fortune's blue eyes flashed with vexation. "Your son, you fool. Price ran away from home last week because he was afraid Mrs. Ward was going to beat him for getting dirty."

"I wasn't told anything about any beating. Mrs. Ward only told me that Price ran away and you were responsible for his safe return to Warhill. That's the reason I stopped by North Meadows this afternoon. I wanted to thank you."

"There's no need to thank me. Price is a wonderful little boy, but that woman is another matter. It doesn't surprise me she didn't tell you the reason Price ran away from her," Fortune said, shifting slightly away from Kane. He was far too close for her to relax. Even after all these weeks of trying to get him out of her thoughts and heart, the very smell of him made her heart race like a hunter within her breast.

"Price is a handful for anyone. He keeps poor Mrs. Ward on the verge of pulling out her hair."

"And his," Fortune added, unable to stop herself when she heard Price blamed for all the trouble.

Kane cocked his head to one side and raised one dark brow. "Is that comment supposed to mean something, Fortune? I can tell by the look on your face something is on your mind."

Fortune looked up at Kane. He was so handsome it made her ache, but his blindness about his son infuriated her nearly as much as did his condescending attitude. He had no right to side with that mean old witch against Price. "You don't have to believe what I've said but you could at least listen to Price's side of the story before you make your judgments."

Kane shook his head. He didn't look at Fortune as he dusted the grass from his fawn-colored britches. "I don't have time to listen to his tales. He's Mrs. Ward's responsibility."

"How can you stand there and say something like that,

Kane Warrick? The child is your son and he needs your love and understanding.''

"O sage, should I take your venerable advice on how I should treat my own son? Since you know so much about children and are so old I'm sure it would be wise of me to heed your words," Kane said, mocking her.

"Damn you, I don't have to be old to recognize an unhappy little boy when I see him. All you have to do is notice his tears."

"Price is merely spoiled. He's had his way for so long he expects everyone to jump to his tune."

"Then he takes after his father, doesn't he?"

"Fortune, I didn't come here to argue with you about my son. I came to thank you for returning him into the care of his nanny. And now that I have, I'll bid you good day." Kane turned to leave but before he could take a step, Fortune took a firm hold on his arm, her temper unappeased.

"You can't leave things as they are at Warhill, Kane. Your son is miserable."

"Fortune, you're interfering in places you're not wanted. Price is my concern, not yours."

"He is your son but I'm the one who held him while he cried his heart out. He was afraid of being lost yet he was even more afraid to go home. He doesn't think you even love him."

"My, you certainly got to know my son in a short time. Is there anything else you want to tell me about him? Perhaps his favorite food or toy?"

"Don't mock me, Kane. I know your son is none of my concern, but he's a wonderful little boy. Since he doesn't have a mother, you're all he has and he needs you. I may not know much about children but I do understand that need. I was raised by three loving uncles but I still missed not having a mother's and father's love."

The tension and anger left Kane as abruptly as it had come. Fortune's defense of his son touched a cord within his own heart, vanquishing any hostility he felt at her interference in his life. Her actions brought back the memory of her bent over the deckhand on board the *Mermaid*. He'd seen her compassionate nature and had admired her for it, but during the last weeks he'd done his best to put everything about Fortune McQueen Northrop from his mind. He didn't want to remember her generosity, her warmth, her caring, or her passion.

One corner of his sensuous mouth curved upward as Kane gave her a crooked grin, raising his hands palm upward. "Truce, Fortune."

Fortune shook her head and folded her arms stubbornly across her chest. "No. There'll be no truce between us until you do something about that woman."

"God! How stubborn can one woman be?" he asked no one in particular. "Don't you understand I'm doing my best for my son? I don't want to see him unhappy."

"Then get rid of Mrs. Ward before she manages to break his spirit."

"Fortune, you're being unreasonable. What am I supposed to do with Price if I fire Mrs. Ward? He needs a woman in his life to give him a sense of stability."

"He doesn't need her, Kane. He needs love and understanding from his father more than anything else. Children can endure nearly anything except the lack of love. Love to a child is like rain to the rose; without it they wither and die."

"Now you're being melodramatic. Price won't die."

"Perhaps not physically but emotionally he will. He's already hiding all of his pain inside himself or you would have seen it."

"This conversation is getting us nowhere. In the future I'll attend to my son and you see to your own affairs."

"If the past is any example, my heart goes out to your son." Fortune turned away. She had tried to help Price but his father was too blindly stubborn to listen to her advice.

It was Kane's turn to stop her. He took her by the arm and turned her to face him. He opened his mouth to tell her he didn't want to argue with her about his son. Gazing down into her lovely face, no words could pass his lips. He swallowed hard and felt himself drowning in the slate-blue depths of her eyes.

Against all of his resolves to the contrary, he found himself drawn to her like a magnet to a lodestone. He brought his hand up and cupped the smooth curve of her cheek in his palm and gently brushed it with the pad of his thumb. His gaze came to rest on her soft lips and he felt a burning need to taste their sweetness once more. Over and over he'd told himself he could stay away from Fortune without any trouble, but now with her so tantalizingly close he was finding it difficult to keep himself from pulling her into his arms and taking what he craved.

Fortune stood mesmerized by the expression she saw in his molten eyes. Something deep inside of her quickened in response to the look. Her problems with her cousin and the Northrop mills seemed to melt away as her own blood caught fire and began to sizzle through her veins. She drew in a ragged breath and tore her eyes from his as she stepped away from him. She couldn't give in to her wayward heart again. She had managed to salvage her pride once, but if she surrendered to her feelings for Kane once more, she feared she would never recover.

"Fortune, I've missed you," Kane said. All thoughts of Price vanished from his mind as he closed the space between them.

"I don't see why you would miss me," Fortune answered sarcastically, trying to break the tension between them. "I would think you were glad to see the last of me, especially since you didn't get the land you needed for your canal."

"I should have been," Kane said, imprisoning her with a hand on each shoulder. "I went to a great deal of trouble to bring you to your grandfather."

"I know you did and I can't understand why you didn't ask for the land you needed when my grandfather offered to reimburse you for your expenses."

Kane glanced toward the river winding its way through the Northrop land. How could he tell her he didn't request the land in return for his services because he didn't want her to believe Manville's accusations? For some strange reason he couldn't soil the memory of the time they'd shared together. It had been too beautiful an experience. "I'd prefer not to go into my reasons, Fortune."

"But you admitted you needed the land for your canal," Fortune said, unwilling to accept his answer.

Kane let his hands fall to his side. "I need the damned land if I'm to improve my mills and keep my people working. Does that satisfy your curiosity?"

"No, Kane. It doesn't. I want to know why you denied yourself the very thing you wanted most in the world," Fortune said intently.

"Damn it, Fortune. You won't let it go, will you?" Kane said, running a hand through his hair in exasperation.

Fortune shook her head. "It's because of what happened between us, isn't it?"

"This conversation is getting us nowhere," Kane said, turning away before he admitted things that he didn't even want to face himself.

Fortune circled in front of him, blocking his path. "Didn't it mean anything at all to you, Kane?"

"My God, woman! I came here to thank you for helping my son, not for the third degree on something that should never have happened in the first place."

"Why shouldn't it have happened, Kane? I needed you that night and I think you needed me, as well."

Kane let out a long breath and rolled his eyes heavenward. This conversation was bringing back too many memories. He could nearly feel her silken flesh beneath his hands. His palms seemed to itch with the need to cup her firm round breasts, and he could feel the heat of desire stirring in his loins.

"Damn it, Fortune. Don't you realize I didn't have any intention of seducing you when we left the Carolinas? But damn you," he said in a hoarse groan of defeat as he reached out and drew her against him. "You turned into a desirable woman along the way and you wouldn't let me keep my distance."

"Then you don't find me repulsive?" Fortune asked, suddenly realizing the solution to her problems and Price's was holding her within his arms. Kane also would gain from their union.

"I find you far from repulsive," Kane said, tipping up her chin with the thumb and forefinger of his right hand while he kept her imprisoned against his throbbing body with his left.

"Then will you marry me?" Fortune asked simply.

Taken completely by surprise, Kane stared down at Fortune as if he'd never seen her before that moment. Her question successfully quelled any desire he felt, and he let his arms fall away from her so suddenly she staggered backward. He shook his head and turned away from her. His gruff answer reflected the painful memories her question had brought to the surface. "No. I won't marry you or any woman."

"I'm not asking you to love me, Kane, just to marry me. It will be a business deal that will help both of us," Fortune argued, unwilling to accept his rejection. It hurt but she wouldn't let herself lose everything to her cousin because of her feeble emotions. She and Kane needed one another.

Puzzled and oddly incensed by her suggestion, Kane glanced over his shoulder at Fortune, arching one dark brow. "A business deal?"

"Yes. Even if the courts uphold my claim of ownership to North Meadows and the mills, I could still lose them because of the stipulation in my grandfather's will that says I have to marry within six months of his death."

"I'm sure within that time you'll be able to find some young man who will be more than eager to marry an heiress with your wealth."

Fortune felt her bristles rise at the mockery she heard

in his voice, yet she forced herself to remain calm. She'd never gain Kane's help if she lost her temper. "I don't want some young fop who will pretend to love me just to get his hands on my grandfather's wealth. I know where I stand with you and there will be no surprises."

Kane shook his head. "It's still out of the question, Fortune. I don't ever intend to marry again. I've been through it once, and once is enough."

"I'm willing to give you the land you need for your canal in exchange for your help," Fortune said, holding her breath as she awaited Kane's answer.

"Is that the business deal you were talking about?"

Fortune nodded.

"If I marry you, you'll deed over the land I need?"

Again Fortune nodded. "And I'll try to be a good mother to Price."

Kane's expression grew thoughtful as he looked back toward the river glistening in the distance. In his imagination he envisioned the steam that would come from the chimneys of the Warrick mills once the canal was built. He also could see a prosperous future for himself and the people he employed. With the mills renovated, there would be no lack of work.

I can make a few sacrifices for the canal, he rationalized. At least Fortune would go into their marriage with her eyes open and without expecting his undying love. He would make sure of that before any vows were spoken between them. She had to understand he would not change his lifestyle for her; their marriage would be exactly as she had proposed: a business deal.

Turning back to Fortune, he smiled and gave her a sweeping bow. "Lady Northrop, I accept your proposal of marriage. When shall we set the date for our nuptials?"

Fortune breathed a sigh of relief. "If it is all right with you, I'd like it to be as soon as the banns can be read."

"I see no problem with that since this is a business deal. We'll send word to your solicitor today so he can draw up the papers for the land. I want to get started on the canal as soon as this affair is settled.''

''As you wish,'' Fortune said, inwardly wincing at his cold attitude. She knew Kane didn't love her and their marriage would be nothing more than what she had stated, a business deal, yet it still hurt to hear him speak so unfeelingly about their union. However, she didn't reveal any of her emotions to Kane. She was determined never to let him know her true feelings. They would live together under the same roof and share his son, yet there would be no involvement between them. Perhaps in time they could become good friends, but they would never be lovers again. The one night she'd spent in his arms in Bristol would have to last her a lifetime.

# Chapter 8

$A$ *dark curl fell over Kane's brow as he slammed his fist* down on the top of the desk. The forceful current of air swept the papers off the polished surface, scattering them across the floor at Fortune's feet. "I won't hear of it and that's the end of the matter."

"I'm afraid it's not the end of it, Kane," Fortune said, not giving an inch of ground to her future husband. Word had come earlier that Manville's attempt to break the will had failed in the London court, and now she was trying to make Kane understand her feelings about her responsibilities before they were wed. "I fully intend to manage my own mills after we're married."

"Then there will be no marriage," Kane threatened in an attempt to make Fortune see reason.

"That decision is yours to make, Kane, but before I send the minister away be sure your mills can survive without the canal."

"You'll also lose North Meadows if you don't marry," Kane replied acridly.

"You were the one who said I would be able to find a husband before my six months were up. Surely in that time I'll find someone who'll be willing to overlook the fact I intend to handle my own affairs after we're married."

"Damn it, Fortune. Ladies do not meddle in business. They concern themselves with their homes and families."

"Ladies who marry for love concern themselves with those things, but as your written agreement has made very clear to me, our marriage is a business deal and nothing more," Fortune shot back, too angry to note the pained expression that flickered across Kane's face.

At that moment she didn't care what she said to him, her own hurt was too new. He'd had Mr. Rutherford make out the papers for her to sign, stating that she understood he was marrying her in exchange for the land but he would not change his lifestyle in any manner. That meant he'd keep his mistress in Bristol, as well as his home at Warhill.

Fortune felt as if she were going to explode from the unbridled emotions his audacious request aroused. Jealousy and hurt mingled as one to trample the practical side of her nature and she let her anger take reign.

"How dare you expect me to sign an agreement like that when you are demanding I live my life to please you," she spat, her blue eyes blazing with ire. Unless Kane agreed to her terms, as well, she would never sign such a humiliating document.

"You will be my wife, Fortune, and I can't allow you to work like one of the village women."

"As these papers confirm," Fortune said through clenched teeth as she bent and picked up the papers scattered at her feet. "I'll be your wife in name only, and you have no say in what I do with my own affairs. Under English law when we marry everything I own will become yours, but since this is a marriage of convenience for both parties involved, I want to ensure my property remains in my control at all times and I will be free to do with it as I see fit in the future."

"Blast it, woman! This entire conversation is ridiculous."

"You're right, Kane. It is ridiculous to argue about something you can't change. Shall I send the minister away or do you agree to my terms?"

Kane ran a hand through his hair in exasperation. He opened his mouth to tell her she and the minister could go jump in the river but his son's sudden entry stayed his words. Price burst into the room and grabbed Fortune about the skirt. He stood glaring up at his father, his small mouth set in a mutinous line.

"You don't talk to Fortune like that. She's my friend," Price said, pressing protectively back against her legs.

Kane pressed his lips into a thin line of annoyance as he saw Fortune's expression change from one of anger to tenderness. The look tugged at his heart when she laid a gentle hand on his son's curly head and caressed him. To his vexation he couldn't stop himself from wondering how it would feel to see that look bestowed upon himself. Nor could he stop himself from feeling a twinge of envy for his son. He had gained Fortune's love without even trying. Disgusted with his train of thought, he snapped, "Price, return to Mrs. Ward this minute."

Price shook his head. "No, Papa. I want Fortune to be my new momma."

"Son, this is between Lady Northrop and myself."

Again Price adamantly shook his head. "No, she's to be my new momma and I won't let you make her go away."

"For Christ's sake," Kane swore beneath his breath, wondering how he should handle the situation in which he now suddenly found himself the villain. Again he ran a hand through his already-tousled hair. Looking from one young face to the other, he knew he couldn't deny the bond that had already been forged between his son and Fortune. She was young and exasperating to the very limit of his patience, yet she did make Price happy. Even as determined as she was to manage the Northrop mills, he knew she would make his son a good mother. Her gentle-hearted nature would assure that Price would have her love even if their marriage was a sham.

Convincing himself his son's happiness was the motive behind his decision, Kane released a resigned breath and told himself he would go through with the wedding because Price needed a mother.

"All right, Price. I won't make Fortune go away." Kane shifted his gaze away from his son and back to Fortune. For one, long intense moment their gazes locked and clashed in battle before he surrendered. "If you will agree to my terms then I will also agree to yours."

"Agreed," Fortune said, and flashed him a triumphant smile as she stepped around Price and placed the papers on the desk in front of Kane.

Kane bent and scribbled Fortune's requirements at the bottom of the page before he signed his name and pushed the paper across the desk for her signature. His expression was grim as he looked back at Fortune, his silver eyes momentarily revealing the emotions he refused to recognize himself.

Fortune reached for the paper but before her hand touched it, the look she saw in Kane's eyes made her pause. Her heart quickened within her breast at the feelings mirrored in the silver depths. For one fleeting moment she thought she saw love reflected in his thick-fringed eyes. She knew, though, that it was only an illusion, something she had imagined because she wanted so desperately to see it.

A look of sad futility entered Fortune's eyes as she looked down at the paper and read what Kane had written. In the few brief lines she had gained her independence yet she hadn't obtained what her heart truly desired: Kane Warrick's love. When she signed her name, they would go into the drawing room where the minister waited to marry them. In a matter of minutes Kane would be her husband, but they would be no closer now than they had been the morning after he'd made love to her at the Red Rooster Inn.

Suddenly flustered by the memory of the night she'd spent in Kane's arms, Fortune felt the heat rise in her cheeks. She nervously cast a surreptitious glance at Kane to see if he had noted the chaos that only the memory of his touch created within her. She was relieved to see he hadn't.

For a long moment, she studied his handsome features, absorbing their beauty and searching behind them for the man she had grown to love. She couldn't find him in the stiff, forbidding person standing before her. The Kane Warrick who stood with arms folded over his chest, an implacable expression on his face, wasn't the gentle lover she had known or the man who had befriended the lonely mountain girl. He was a stranger, willing to saddle himself with a woman he didn't love to gain a strip of land.

What am I doing? was her silent question as a wave of confusion swept over her. Why am I forcing Kane to marry me? And what's more important, why am I willing to marry him without his love? Fortune quickly lowered her gaze back to the agreement. I'm doing what I have to do to keep North Meadows, she told herself and scribbled her name below Kane's.

"Now that that's settled, shall we join the minister and Mr. Rutherford in the drawing room?" Kane asked. Like a cool, distant stranger, he courteously proffered his arm to Fortune.

Fortune nodded and blinked rapidly to stay the tears that sprang into her eyes. She couldn't speak. The lump of misery in her throat made it impossible.

Price grinned up at Fortune as he eagerly took her other hand, his young face alight with excitement. "Can I call you momma now?"

"I think you should at least wait until after the ceremony, Price," was Kane's gruff answer as he escorted his bride out of the study and down the hall to the drawing room.

The marriage ceremony was a blur in Fortune's mind while she sat before the dressing table, staring at the reflection of the pale-faced girl in the mirror. How ironic life is, she mused silently. She was now a married woman, yet her husband had deliberately made her aware that they would each have the freedom to live their lives as they pleased.

Tears brimmed in Fortune's eyes and spilled over her lashes making a crystal path down her cheeks. They splashed unnoticed onto the lace table covering. Heedless to the fact it was their wedding day and that she'd had the cook prepare a delicious meal to celebrate the event, Kane had asserted his rights as soon as the last vows were spoken. He'd dropped a perfunctory kiss on her brow, then said a gracious good-bye to the minister and his wife before ushering Mr. Rutherford into the study to collect the deed to the land he'd given his name to gain. Afterward he'd made no apologies to her when he'd mounted his horse and rode in the direction of Warhill.

Fortune swiped at her eyes with the back of her hand and sniffed loudly. Her lower lip quivered as she drew in a ragged breath. It was her wedding night but as the agreement had stated, she would be a wife to Kane in name only.

After pushing herself to her feet, she crossed to the window and pulled back the sheer lace curtain to view the moon-drenched grounds that spread out before her like a dark velvet mantle. North Meadows was now hers. Mr. Rutherford had explained to her that by English law any money she possessed or gained would be her husband's, but the land would always be hers and her children's.

"What children?" Fortune muttered. "If it's left to my husband, I'll never have children of my own." Dejected, Fortune let the curtain fall back into place and turned to the elegant room that was only one out of dozens she now owned. Thick carpets covered the parqueted floors, silk wallpaper decorated the walls and was enhanced by gold-leafed wainscotting. As she had learned from a book in her grandfather's study, the furniture was of the English Rococo design and had been made by Chippendale. The high tester bed, dressing table with its oval bevelled glass mirror, and the ribbon-backed chairs upholstered in blue and white striped satin were crafted of rich, gleaming mahogany. The room exemplified the meaning of wealth and the prestige of the Northrop family, yet without future generations to call it home, it meant nothing to Fortune.

Fortune released a long breath and sank down on the bed. Her thin silk night rail spread about her as she absently brushed her hand across the velvet counterpane and her thoughts turned once more to the man she had married. At least she was grateful to Kane for one thing. He'd seen fit to leave his son with her at North Meadows instead of returning him into the custody of that hateful woman, Mrs. Ward. Price now slept down the hall in the room her father had used as a boy.

"He's rid of both of us now," Fortune mused aloud. Flopping down on the bed, she buried her face in the depths of her folded arms and wept openly for the first time in months. She'd managed to keep up a brave front outside of the privacy of her room but now alone, where no one could see, she allowed herself to become the eighteen-year-old girl with a broken heart.


By the firelight Kane's shadow stretched across the drawingroom floor as he braced his hands against the mantel and hung his head. He closed his eyes against the light. Shutting out the sight of the jumping flames was much simpler than shutting out the thoughts of the woman he'd left at North Meadows.

Kane bit down on his lower lip and his brow wrinkled with consternation. For the life of him, he didn't know what had gotten into him of late. Today he'd married a beautiful, desirable woman and he'd run away from her like a pubescent schoolboy who had never known a woman.

"I know exactly why I ran," he ground out before arching his head back and drawing in a deep breath of air. "I ran because I was afraid that if I stayed, I couldn't keep my part of our agreement."

Rubbing a hand across the back of his neck to ease the tension that had his muscles tied in knots, he crossed to the decanter of brandy sitting on the side table. He poured himself a dram, then tossed it down his throat and for a moment savored the burning sensation as it slid smoothly to his stomach. He needed to relax. The day's events had his insides wound as tight as a coiled spring.

Kane refilled his glass and, with drink in hand, crossed to the window, thoughtfully peering out into the moon-silvered night. He automatically looked in the direction of North Meadows, his thoughts centering once more upon his bride. The moonlit night was one of enchantment. It made his imagination torment him with tantalizing images of Fortune nude upon the dew-moistened grass, beckoning him to her. Kane snapped his eyes closed and pressed his fingers against his lids as he shook his head.

"Damn, I have to quit this or I'll never make it through the night, much less be able to continue with this sham of a marriage," he mumbled, even as he felt his body responding to the imagery his mind had concocted to torture him. "She's made it clear she wants nothing to do with me. I'm only her means to keep Manville from inheriting her mills."

Kane looked once more out into the night and smiled cynically. "I may suffer but at least I know that bastard has lost everything."

Kane gave a sarcastic chuckle. He'd wanted to ruin Nevin Manville and gain the land he needed for the canal, yet marriage had never been in his plans. But the irony in the situation was that he found himself liking the thought far more than he would have ever imagined when he'd accepted Fortune's proposal less than a month ago.

Kane chuckled again and rubbed his hand across the back of his neck once more. Ever since he first met Fortune, his own wants had seemed to change. She had a way about her that crumbled all of his resolutions.

Felicia's image rose in his mind and he shifted uncomfortably from one foot to the other. His life would have been so simple had he first married a woman like Fortune. Where Felicia had been cold, Fortune was full of warm passions. They seethed within her in everything she did, from her determination to manage the mills herself to her sexuality. She was of the earth, a child of nature, and the kind of woman any man would be proud to claim as his wife.

"And I'm a fool for not going to her and claiming my rights as her husband," Kane muttered into the night but made no move to fulfill his desires.

Absently Kane swirled the amber liquid about the round bowl of the brandy snifter and looked once more toward North Meadows. He knew he'd acted like a scoundrel after the wedding ceremony that afternoon. But his anger and fear of his own weaknesses had made him leave Fortune as soon as the vows were spoken.

"It's better this way," Kane said aloud, but the words sounded hollow even to his ears. Annoyed with himself, he tossed the brandy down his throat before he turned away from the window and crossed back to to fireplace. He tried to convince himself it was best if Fortune never learned the true reason he'd returned to Warhill. Yet as he slumped down in a chair and buried his head in his hands, he knew at that moment he'd do nearly anything to make amends for the humiliation he'd caused her earlier.

"God, how I want her," he muttered beneath his breath and splayed his fingers through his thick dark hair. His entire body ached to feel her lithe form pressed against his hard, throbbing flesh.

Kane drew in a shuddering breath and raised his head. His eyes were haunted as he stared into the leaping flames and recognized the truth of his own feelings. He recoiled as his heart told him that he had fallen in love with his Carolina wildcat. He shook his head in denial.

He'd made the mistake of loving Felicia, and he wouldn't allow himself to make the same mistake with Fortune. She was his wife but he couldn't give in to his emotions. The pain after the dreams fell apart was too great and he knew he'd not survive such heartbreak again.

"I feel nothing for her," Kane said aloud with the hope

that if he heard the words, he'd believe them. It didn't work. He knew the truth deep down in his soul and his fear rose again within him in a blinding wave.

"It's not true," he said, coming to his feet like a frightened rabbit ready to flee the fox. "I desire her but I don't love her." And he would prove it to himself that night.

Denying he was using any excuse to go to Fortune, he strode from the drawing room and ordered a servant to have his mount saddled.

Fortune stirred at the light touch of Kane's lips. She didn't open her eyes but rolled away from the annoyance and curled into a ball on her side with her back to him. Her movement made her silk night rail slip up to the swell of her hips giving Kane a tantalizing peek of her soft round bottom. He smiled his pleasure at the sight.

"My beautiful Fortune," he murmured softly. He quickly shed his clothing and slipped into bed beside his wife. She did not stir as he eased her night rail from her and then cupped her naked body with his. He relaxed with one arm draped possessively over her. Feeling more content than he had since the night in the Red Rooster Inn, he closed his eyes.

When he'd left Warhill he'd been determined to make love to Fortune to prove he hadn't fallen in love with her, yet at that moment, with the feel of her warmth snuggled against him, he knew he had lied to himself. He was in love with his wife but until he knew she returned his feelings, he would keep the secret to himself. He'd not make a fool of himself with her as he'd done with Felicia. She had known of his feelings and had used them to hurt him. He'd not give Fortune that same kind of power over him.

The sun was streaming through the east window when Fortune stirred. The morning chill made her instinctively snuggle closer to the warmth at her side. She yawned drowsily and arched in a sensuous stretch against Kane. Her sleepy expression vanished in an instant and her slate-blue eyes opened wide with surprise as she stared up into

Kane's smiling countenance. Dumbfounded to find her heart's desire lying next to her and unable to believe her wishes had come true, she gazed up at him with mouth slightly agape. Her throat worked but no sound emerged.

"Good morning, wife," Kane said before he dropped a light kiss upon the tip of her nose and used his finger to tip up her chin to close her mouth. "You can catch flies like that if you're not careful." He chuckled at his own jest.

"What are you doing here?" Fortune finally managed to blurt out.

"You should already know the answer to that question," Kane said, and bestowed upon Fortune one of his most charming smiles.

She shook her head. "But I don't know why you're here. This is my bedchamber."

Kane briefly scanned the room before he rested his gaze back upon Fortune's face. "True, it's your bedchamber but since I don't have one at North Meadows at the moment, I didn't know where else to sleep when I returned last night."

"You've been here all night?" Fortune asked, feeling her cheeks burn with embarrassment. She'd slept with Kane and hadn't even known it.

Kane nodded, a wicked light entering his silver eyes.

Kane's expression suddenly made Fortune aware of her state of undress and she eased away from him. "You still haven't answered my question, Kane. What are you doing here?"

Kane lay back, folding his arms behind his head as he watched his wife. He cocked one dark brow at her and gave her a roguish smile. "Where else should a newly wedded man be but in his bride's bed?"

"You know you don't have any right to be here." To defend herself against Kane as well as the emotions warring within her own body, Fortune drew the sheet up to her chin. She could feel her heart pounding against her ribs and prayed Kane could not see the effect he was having upon her.

Kane rolled onto his side and propped on his elbow. He cocked his head to one side and his lips curled up at the corners in a provocative smile as he gazed at Fortune through half-closed lids. "I am your husband" was his simple answer.

"In name only, Kane."

Before she could thwart him, Kane reached out and captured Fortune at the nape of the neck with one long-fingered hand. His smile never wavered as he drew her purposely toward him. "That can easily be remedied."

Fortune shook her head to deny him even as her own heart leapt from the thrilling prospect of Kane's lovemaking. "We can't do this, Kane. We signed the agreement."

"The agreement cannot stop us from making love, Fortune," Kane said softly, his gaze resting on her parted lips. "I want you." His voice was husky with emotion as he drew her down to taste the sweetness of her mouth.

Wanting nothing more in life than his kiss yet knowing she shouldn't surrender to his allure, Fortune made one last, halfhearted attempt to free herself from him. She didn't succeed. His mouth claimed hers in a fiery kiss that made her toes curl up and her blood sing through her veins like a siren's song, drawing her instinctively toward the source of pleasure. A brief defiant shudder rippled through her before she molded her body against the lean muscular frame stretched out at her side and she wrapped her arms about his corded neck. She entwined her fingers in the dark curls at the nape of his neck and pressed her breasts against his furry chest. She gasped from the shock of electricity that shot through her from the contact.

"My God, how I've missed you," Kane whispered as he buried his face in the curve of her neck and inhaled the sweet scent of her. His body felt on fire and he drew in several deep cooling breaths to keep a rein on his passion. When he made love to Fortune, he didn't want to rush. He wanted to rouse her to the peaks of ecstasy so that she, too, could share in the glory he would experience once he was deep inside her velvet softness.

"Love me, Kane," Fortune breathed, surrendering to her needs. She could lie to herself or him no longer. She craved Kane's touch with every sinew of her body and she couldn't deny herself the pleasure he offered, no matter what happened between them in the future. She was his wife and for the moment—if only fleetingly—she would savor their union to the fullest.

At her throaty plea a thrill of excitement shot through Kane. It tingled its way down the length of his lean body and made his heart pound against his ribs like a caged beast. He felt himself swell achingly against her soft thigh yet he held himself back. He wanted to savor their union for as long as possible.

Gliding his hand down along the swell of her hips to the silken apex of her thighs, he gently caressed her until she voluntarily opened to him, her hips arching up to meet his hand.

"My beautiful Fortune," Kane murmured, leaning back to devour her beauty with his eyes as he continued to tantalize her with his fingers. To him she was perfection, her slender body flawless. Her breasts were proportioned just to fit his hand, and her softly curving hips were ideally suited to mold against his when she wrapped her legs about his waist to draw him deeper inside the sweet passage hidden beneath the curls of silk.

Fortune gave a moan of protest when he took his hand away and slowly moved it up over her belly to her breast. She gasped with pleasure when he captured one entrancing globe within his palm and lowered his head to taste the sweetness of the dark-pink bud. She trembled as his mouth closed over the nipple and he began to tease her flesh with his tongue and lips. He gave its mate equal attention before he slid between her thighs. The dark hair on his chest and legs rasped against her midriff and belly as he inched his way down, teasing each inch of her with the tip of his moist tongue as he made his way to her womanhood.

The morning sun streamed in across the bed to bathe the lovers in gold as Kane raised her hips to his questing lips. He moaned softly against her as he tasted her essence and knew in that moment that no other woman but his Lady Fortune could ever satisfy him again. He savored the smell of her, the feel of her, and the taste of her and wanted to possess every inch of her until she belonged to no one but himself.

"You're mine," he breathed, covering her with his hard body. His mouth once more claimed hers as he slid into the welcoming warmth of her resilient flesh.

Fortune reveled in the words she'd longed to hear. The knowledge that he claimed her as his own served to heighten her passion. She gave herself up to the glory of his lovemaking, soaring with Kane on the torrid winds of their quest for fulfillment. And when their bodies exploded with the pleasure of their release, the sun seemed to become only a dim shadow in contrast to the golden rapture they shared. She was his wife and his lover and her dreams had finally come true.

Kane's body glistened with perspiration as he rolled to one side and drew Fortune into his arms. He was content for the first time in years. He'd made love to other women since Felicia's death yet he'd failed to find true gratification with any of them. They had appeased his sexual needs but it had gone no further than that.

Kane tightened his arms possessively about Fortune and laid his head against her dark hair. He couldn't honestly say he'd ever found true contentment with any woman before Fortune. He'd loved Felicia but her frigidity had kept him from finding any satisfaction with her. Nor had anything changed after her death. He'd been too afraid of being hurt again to allow himself to become too deeply involved with a another woman.

A smile tugged up the corners of Kane's sensuous mouth. That had all changed. He had a passionate, loving wife and he'd never let her go. She belonged to him and no one else.

"It would seem, my Lady Fortune, that we suit well in bed," Kane said, lifting a dark curl and twirling the silken skein about one long finger.

Feeling much like a well-fed kitten, Fortune turned to look at Kane. A smile of contentment curled her passion-bruised lips as she playfully ran the tip of her finger through the mat of dark hair on his chest. "I would say, sir, that is a severe understatement."

Kane caught her hand and brought it to his lips. He pressed a teasing kiss to her palm before rolling away from her and sitting up. He smiled when he looked back at Fortune and saw her petulant pout. Giving her nose a playful tweak, he shook his head. "I would love to stay in bed with you all day, wife, but I'll never get any work done that way."

"Work!" Fortune grumbled as she, too, sat up and slid her feet to the floor. Showing no embarrassment at her state of undress, she stood and crossed the room to retrieve her dressing gown. The sun's golden light outlined her lithe body and emphasized her firm breasts as she raised her arms to slip on the silken garment.

Kane groaned inwardly at the sight of her naked, long-legged beauty. He could feel his desire rekindle and knew if he didn't get away from her immediately, he'd not be able to leave her at all. Fortune's uninhibited passion was like an addictive opiate. The more he had of her, the more he wanted.

Kane cleared his throat and forced his gaze away from Fortune. "Yes, work. I have to go into Bristol to see the engineer about the time it's taking on the canal. I want it finished as soon as possible because I've already ordered the steam engines for the mill."

"Then I guess that means I'll just have to go to work, also," Fortune said, hiding her disappointment about Kane's decision to work on his canal instead of spending time with her. She'd already received more from him than she'd ever expected and she'd not drive him away now by acting the shrewish wife. Settling herself at the dressing table, she picked up the brush and began to untangle her long hair.

A muscle twitched in Kane's cheek as he stood and pulled on his shirt. Her nonchalant attitude piqued him. He had work to do but he wanted her to at least act as if she wanted him to stay with her.

"Damn," he said, muttering his vexation beneath his breath.

"What did you say?" Fortune asked, looking at Kane's reflection in the mirror.

"I said I thought you might have changed your mind about the mills."

Unaware of Kane's darkening mood, Fortune turned her attention back to unsnarling her hair. "No, I haven't changed my mind. There are several things I intend to right immediately."

"Pray tell, madame, what might they be?" Kane questioned sarcastically as he jerked on his boots.

Fortune was too content to recognize the storm clouds gathering and blithely answered, "The first thing I want to see changed in the mill is the use of child labor."

Kane exploded. "For God sake, madame. Don't you realize what you're really suggesting? The children are often the only thing to keep some families from starving."

Fortune placed the brush on the dressing table and slowly turned to look at her husband. Her expression reflected the surprise she felt to find that he condoned such an abhorrent practice. In all the time she'd known Kane, she'd thought many things about him, but she would never have believed he would use children for his own greed.

"You can't honestly approve of such things, can you, Kane?" she asked, unable to reconcile herself to the fact that her own husband could be as brutal as Nevin Manville.

"No, damn it. I don't approve of it, but it is the way things are done. You can't expect to change everything because you object to it."

"I most certainly can. I could never forgive myself if I

let matters go on as they have without at least trying to do something to improve the things I find abhorrent," Fortune said. Her face reflected her sentiments about Kane's acceptance of practices he didn't approve.

"Don't look at me like that, damn it," Kane swore. "I'm not the villain here. I'm not doing anything all the rest of the mills owners don't do."

"Maybe you're not but I don't have to be like you or the others because I won't sanction such cruelty to line my pockets with gold."

"You may try to change things but you won't succeed. Even the mill workers won't go along with you on this. Those children you're so set to protect will go hungry without their jobs at the mills."

"No, Kane. They won't go hungry as long as I have any say in the matter."

"I suppose you're going to turn North Meadows into a poorhouse and give out alms," Kane replied sarcastically.

"If I have to, I will," Fortune said, and turned her back on him.

Suddenly feeling like a brute for haranguing Fortune because of her gentle heart, Kane crossed the few feet that separated them. He lay his hands on her shoulders and pulled her back against him as peered at her reflection in the mirror. "I understand what you're trying to do, but it won't work. You're only going to bring trouble upon yourself if you go against the way things have been done since the beginning."

"I don't know how things have been done from the beginning, Kane. All I know is what I plan to do in the future."

"Don't say I didn't warn you when your mill is shut down from lack of labor," Kane said. He gave her shoulder a light, harmless shake to vent his exasperation at her continued stubbornness.

"I'll have to take that chance," Fortune said. "I don't believe Grandfather would rest if I let things remain as Nevin left them." She didn't add that by helping the mill workers she would in some small way be absolving herself of the guilt she still felt over her grandfather's death. He had been a good man and she knew he would approve of her plans for the workers.

"Since you won't listen to me, then you'll have to learn it the hard way, madame," Kane said, his tone sharp with criticism. He'd not argue with her further about the matter. She was determined to do as she wished, and he'd let her see it wasn't going to be as easy as she thought.

"You let my momma go!" Price shouted as he ran into the room. His fists were balled and ready for battle as he attacked Kane about the legs. "You won't hurt my momma," he screamed, flailing at his father.

Unaware their raised voices had been overheard by Price who had misconstrued the scene, the two adults were taken by surprise at the child's abrupt entry. They had no time to do anything but react on instinct. Kane grabbed his young son by the nape of his collar and shook him. "How dare you burst into our bedchamber like some young jackanapes who has no manners. It seems I've neglected to teach you how to behave, but I can remedy that immediately."

Without considering Fortune's feelings, Kane dragged Price across the room and sat down on the bed. He pulled his son across his lap and raised his hand to give him the first spanking he'd had from his father.

"Don't, Kane," Fortune cried, coming to her feet in defense of the child who kicked and thrashed about beneath his father's heavy, imprisoning arm.

"Price is my son, Fortune, and he will learn how to behave," Kane said, his hand stayed in midair.

"Not this way, please," she pleaded, unable to stand the thought of Price being hit again, especially by the man he already believed didn't love him. Kane's actions would only serve to prove to Price that he was right about his father's feelings toward him.

Kane let his hand fall to his side and then released his son. No matter how much his son needed to be disciplined, he couldn't punish him in front of Fortune. "Price, go to the stable. I'll attend you there."

Instead of obeying his father, Price scrambled to his feet and ran to Fortune. He buried his face in her dressing gown and wrapped his arms in a death grip about her legs. His silent sobs shook his small shoulders.

Gently Fortune pried away his clinging arms and sank to her knees at his side. She brushed back his unruly curls and wiped the tears from his damp cheeks. "Now you run along and have Vincent show you the kennels. Grandfather's spaniels have had a new litter of puppies and I know they want a young boy to play with," she said comfortingly.

Price cast an anxious glance in his father's direction before he turned pleading, tear-reddened eyes back to Fortune.

"There's no need to worry. I'll talk to your father, and I'm sure the two of you can come to an understanding without you having to be spanked."

"He won't hurt you, will he?" Price asked, concerned more for Fortune's welfare than his own.

"No, Price," Fortune said, lowering her voice to keep Kane from overhearing her words. "Your father is a good man and he'll not hurt either of us."

"Are you sure?" Price asked dubiously.

"Yes, now you go and play with the puppies and I'll talk with your father."

After another glance in Kane's direction, Price ran from the room.

Kane came to his feet and stood with hands braced on his hips and face dark with anger. "What was that all about?"

"I merely told Price he should have Vincent show him the new spaniel puppies."

"You had no right to usurp my authority, madame!"

"Your authority? You mean I had no right to stop a grown man from beating a small child? I beg to differ with you, sir."

"Fortune, you're now my wife, but Price is my son and I will handle him as I see fit," Kane said, his temper inching a degree higher.

"Handle him, Kane?" Fortune exploded. "Like one of your horses? From what I've seen, you treat your animals with more love than you do your own son."

"Woman, you are pushing me too far. That child needs to be disciplined and he will be."

"Over my dead body! I'll not stand by and let you vent your ire with me upon Price's head. He needs love instead of your so-called discipline. The child has done nothing wrong. He was only trying to protect me from his brutish father, and I'll be damned if you will harm a hair on his head because of it," Fortune spat, ready to defend Price physically if necessary, and unwittingly erecting battle lines between herself and her husband.

Kane momentarily saw red before it was shadowed in a deep virulent green. Like a disease, his jealousy had begun as a tiny germ the first time he'd seen his son with Fortune. It had laid dormant, waiting for the right environment to make it grow into this thing that now consumed him. It ate away at his reasoning with jagged fangs and made him feel slightly feverish from the power it had over him.

Without asking, Price had succeeded in capturing Fortune's love when his father could have only her passion. The thought made Kane clench his fists at his sides. He wanted all of her, not just a few moments in her bed.

They were bound legally by their marriage but, to Kane's regret, not emotionally. The only thing they shared was their lovemaking. He couldn't deny it was wonderful, yet when it was over, Fortune reverted to being his business partner. She was more concerned with her mills and his son than with her husband's feelings. The thought hurt more than Kane liked to admit.

Unable to endure his feelings any longer, Kane turned to follow his son.

"Kane, don't do this," Fortune said, blocking his exit.

"Take out your anger on me. I'm capable of handling it but your child isn't. He needs love, not anger."

"Move out of my way, Fortune," Kane answered gruffly as he eyed his wife. She came only to his chin in height yet she faced him with all the courage of a man twice his size.

Fortune shook her head. "Not until you promise me you won't punish Price."

"Woman, you would try the patience of a saint," Kane growled.

"Then you're safe," Fortune shot back, making no move to step out of his path.

To Kane's vexation he found himself smiling down at his stubborn little wife. She had the uncanny ability to alter his moods with only a few words or a glance. One moment he would be angry enough to throttle her and in the next all he wanted was to make love to her for the rest of his life. It was unnerving to realize the power one small woman could have over him.

"All right, damn it. This time I won't give him the spanking he deserves for his insolence, but I won't be as lenient in the future. Price has to learn that he can't get away with murder by hiding behind your skirts. I am his father and I will have respect from my son if nothing else." Kane didn't add he intended to make sure his son didn't ever come between him and Fortune again.

"Thank you, Kane," Fortune answered simply as she stepped out of his path and let him pass. She had no other words to say at that moment. Something in his tone and the look she saw in his eyes made further conversation impossible.

Puzzled, Fortune watched Kane descend the stairs. She'd seen the same look in his eyes the previous day, and it had confused her as much then as it did now. There had been a haunted expression in the silver depths of her husband's eyes, and she wondered what ghosts from the past had been roused by their confrontation.

Fortune bit down on her lower lip, and her brows knit

into a thoughtful frown as she pondered the strange relationship between herself and her husband. Everything had been wonderful between them that morning. Even when they'd talked about the mills they had disagreed but there had been no strain between them. It wasn't until Price burst into the room that the change had come over Kane. She suspected his anger with his son stemmed from more than Price's actions. There was something that kept Kane away from his son, and she was determined to find the answer to solve their problems or they'd never become the family she wanted.

# Chapter 9

*Still consumed with the problems between her husband* and his son, Fortune failed to notice the strange silence that greeted her when she reined the pony cart to a halt in front of the Northrop mill. She wasn't aware of anything amiss until she entered the weave room and found the machines still and the workers missing.

"What in the devil is going on here?" she mused aloud, her brow furrowing into a perplexed frown. The mystery deepened as she went through the entire building and found not a soul on the premises.

Suspecting her cousin was somehow responsible for her workers' absence since he'd lost his battle to regain the mills in court, Fortune climbed back into the pony cart and turned it in the direction of the village. She didn't know where any of her workers lived but if it took her all day, searching from house to house, she was resolved to find out why none of them had reported to work.

By the end of the day Fortune was beginning to believe determination alone would not solve the riddle of her missing workers. She'd stopped at nearly every cottage and asked if anyone who lived there worked at her mill. She'd had no problem in locating her employees, but she'd not learned any satisfactory reasons why none were working.

Each had used illness as an excuse. Their lies had not been convincing enough to make Fortune believe a strange malady had descended overnight on the village of Northington. By the time she stopped at the cottage where the old man and woman lived with their giant red-haired son, she was tired and had nearly reached her limit of patience.

She knocked on the cottage door and a moment later the old woman opened it only a crack and peered out at her.

"Go 'way," she muttered through toothless gums.

"Madame, I would like to speak with your son if he's at home," Fortune said, her voice tinged with the exasperation she felt over her fruitless day.

"He ain't got nothing to say to likes of you. Now, go 'way and stop causing us trouble."

"I don't want to cause you any trouble, madame. I only want to speak with your son."

"All your kind is trouble fer the likes of us. Me boy is a fine man but because of ye and yer kind, he's not able to get enough work to put food on our table."

"I want to see your son, madame," Fortune said, not giving an inch of ground under the woman's condemnation and putting her foot in the door to keep the old woman from closing it in her face.

"Then I guess you'll see him," Henry Reed said as he opened the door and draped a comforting arm about the old woman's stooped shoulders. "Rest, Ma. There's nothing for you and Da to worry about here." He gave her a reassuring hug, then stepped out of the cottage and closed the door behind him. With arms folded over his barrellike chest, he stood regarding Fortune through speculative hazel eyes.

"What business do ye have with me and mine?" he asked after a long moment.

"I've come to ask you if you know anything about the closing of the Northrop mill. I've visited nearly every cottage in the village today but I can't get any answers from anyone."

"Why did ye think I'd be willing to tell ye anything when yer own workers won't?"

Fortune looked Reed directly in the eyes. "From what you said the day of Mary Beth's death, I suspected you might know why my workers have left their jobs at the mill."

Henry Reed grinned down at Fortune, unable to stop himself from admiring her spirit. Few of her kind would care enough to try to find out anything about the people they employed. If they didn't show up for work they'd hire an entire new crew to replace them without a second thought. "Then ye suspected right. I do know why yer mills have been closed down."

At the man's ambiguous answer Fortune tapped her foot rapidly against the hard-packed earth with mounting exasperation. She regarded him thoughtfully through narrowed lids before she said, "I had suspected my cousin of being at the root of my problems but I now think I might have been wrong. Mr. Reed, did you have anything to do with the mill closing?"

Henry Reed chuckled. "Ye give me far too much credit, Lady Northrop. I only wish I could have shut ye down a long time ago; it would have saved a lot of grief if I had. But unfortunately, I'm not responsible for yer troubles now."

"Then who is responsible for keeping my workers away from their jobs?"

"Yer first suspicions were right. Manville's hired ruffians have made sure the people wouldn't go to work."

"Damn," Fortune muttered beneath her breath. Manville was determined to regain the mills at any price. If he couldn't get them legally through the courts, then he hoped to get his hands on them after he ruined her financially with his sly methods.

"I won't let that happen," she muttered to herself and turned away, too consumed with this new problem to note the look of interest that crossed Reed's face.

"Lady Northrop," he said, limping along in her wake.

His old injury didn't bother him except when he needed to walk faster. Then the limp became pronounced enough to be noted. "It would seem you have a problem on yer hands."

Fortune glanced up at the tall man who was now walking at her side down the dusty two-wheeled track that led back to the village. She noticed his awkward movements but was too worried about her own affairs to wonder why she'd not noticed his limp the first day she met him. She spoke before she realized she was voicing her feelings to a man who hated her family. "If you mean that I have a problem because my cousin has set out to ruin the Northrop mills, then you're right."

"Why would he want to ruin his own mills, my lady?"

"The mills now belong to me, Mr. Reed. When my grandfather died, I inherited North Meadows, as well as the cotton mills."

Henry Reed came to an abrupt halt. "Ye now own the mills?"

Fortune nodded. "Now if you'll excuse me, I don't have time to explain my family's affairs. I have to find a way to get my people to come back to work."

"They won't come back as long as they're afraid of what will happen to them from Manville's men," Reed said.

"Then what do you propose I do? I can't just leave things as they are. My people will starve without work, and I can't give them work without reopening the mills."

Henry Reed frowned down at Fortune. She was a strange one, all right. She seemed to care about the people who worked for her. He scratched his bushy red head in wonder at this new specimen of mill owner he'd discovered in one young woman.

"Lady Northrop, your people want to work but until they know they won't suffer retribution from Manville, they won't come back. It's better to starve than to be beaten to death."

At her wits' end and determined not to ask for Kane's help, Fortune looked up at the giant man at her side and asked, "Do you know what I can do to persuade them that nothing will happen if they come back to work?"

"I'm not sure, my lady. I'll go into the village and try to convince them they've nothing to fear. But I'm not saying they'll agree to come back to work. Few make enough money to take the risk of crossing Manville and his hirelings."

"Mr. Reed, will they come back if I raise their wages?"

Henry Reed gaped down at the young woman before him and shook his head as if to clear it. He knew he hadn't heard her right. No mill owner raised employees' wages. Employers argued that wages had to be kept low to keep the people coming back to work. They also believed more money in the workers' pockets would only increase the size of families, as well as the drunkenness that seemed prevalent in mill towns. They felt confident their decision to give their workers only enough money on which to subsist without increasing their species was the right one for all concerned.

Henry knew the mill owners' beliefs well. He had lost his job trying to bring about changes. He'd been the first to ask for an increase in wages and when he didn't succeed, he'd then tried to improve the conditions in which he worked. That had ended his days at the Northrop mill. Manville had had him thrown bodily from the premises after a severe beating, which had broken his leg and left arm. Fortunately, his mother had been able to set the arm so he'd suffered no aftereffects, but the leg was different. Every day his limp served as a reminder of how much he hated Manville and the rest of his kind.

Disturbed by the odd look Reed was giving her, Fortune shifted uncomfortably from one foot to the other. "Mr. Reed, I asked you a question and would appreciate an answer."

"I'm sorry, Lady Northrop," Henry said. "But I don't believe I heard ye right. Did ye say ye'd raise yer workers' wages if they come back to the mill?"

"Yes, I did. Is there something wrong in that?" Fortune asked, unable to understand the man's strange reaction.

"Well, I'll be damned," Henry said, and burst out laughing.

"I beg your pardon," Fortune said, further confused by his laughter.

Henry's face turned as red as his hair when he flushed with embarrassment. "Forgive me, my lady. I didn't mean to use such language in front of ye."

Raised by three men far rougher than any she'd found in England, Reed's curse hadn't been what affected Fortune. It was his laughter she didn't understand, and she said as much to him.

"My lady, I don't mean to laugh but it's a joy to my ears to hear that someone is willing to raise the wages of mill workers. I had begun to believe I wouldn't live long enough to see that happen."

"There are a great many things that I intend to change about the Northrop mill, Mr. Reed, and the daily wage is only one of them."

Henry chuckled again.

"But I can't do anything if the mills are shut down," Fortune added.

"I'll see that yer workers get the word, Lady Northrop. I've a feeling even Nevin Manville's threats won't keep them away when they know you now own the mill."

"Thank you for your help, Mr. Reed," Fortune said, and turned away. She had taken only a few steps before she paused and looked back at the tall red-haired man. From what she'd seen of his home, Henry Reed and his parents lived in poverty, yet he'd asked nothing for himself. He had only been concerned with the people who worked in her mills. The thought made her smile. Henry Reed would be an asset to the Northrop mills and to her when she started to change things.

"Mr. Reed, would you come to work for me? As Seth Wilson is my cousin's hireling I can no longer allow him to work for me, and I'm going to need a new foreman,"

Fortune said. She watched as he frowned thoughtfully for a long moment before his face lightened and he smiled at her.

"I could use the work, my lady."

"Then you'll start tomorrow," Fortune said, and happily made her way back to the pony cart. The day had turned out much better than she would have believed. And she suspected she'd not have to face another silent morning at the mill with Henry Reed working for her. Snapping the reins on the pony's back, she urged it back in the direction of North Meadows.

Fortune was proud of herself. She'd managed to deal with the situation without having to turn to Kane for help. Now if she could also deal with what awaited her back at North Meadows, she would feel her life had finally begun to settle down. However, she wasn't sure she could handle the problem between her husband and his son as easily as she had the problem with her workers. There would be no Henry Reed to take charge and intercede on her behalf. She would be left to bring them together, and for the life of her she didn't know how to go about it.

"How did she take it?" Manville asked, cocking a curious brow at his hireling.

"She didn't take it too well," Seth Wilson said with hat in hand. He glanced nervously away from his employer's scrutiny.

Manville chuckled. "That's exactly as I intended when I shut the mill down. Now I hope she realizes the futility of owning a mill that she can't keep running." He chuckled again. "I'll give it a few days before I go to North Meadows and offer to buy her out."

"The m-mill, uh," Wilson stuttered, dreading to divulge the information he'd gleaned from one of the Northrop spinners. "It'll be open tomorrow morning."

"What did you say?" Manville asked, sitting abruptly upright. He frowned and eyed Wilson through narrowed lids.

''Uh, Mr. Manville, I said the mill will open tomorrow morning.''

''Like hell it will. If the bastards know what's good for them they'd better stay at home. I won't hire a damned one of them back if they go against me.''

''They already have, sir,'' Wilson said, shifting uncomfortably under Manville's blazing stare.

''The workers know you don't own the mill any more and Lady Northrop has told them she'll give them an increase in wages if they'll come back to work.''

Manville stared at Wilson for a long moment before he threw back his head and burst out laughing. His shoulders shook from his glee as he leaned back in his chair and savored his triumph. When his mirth subsided, he wiped at his damp eyes and looked once more at the confused Wilson.

''That bitch has fallen right into my hands.''

Wilson frowned, unable to understand his employers mercurial moods.

Seeing his hireling didn't comprehend the magnitude of Fortune's folly, Manville chuckled again and then said, ''Don't you see, Wilson? All I have to do is to stand back and let the other mill owners shut her down. By increasing the workers' wages, she'll have every owner in the area up in arms against her. They'll fight her tooth and nail before they agree to coddling their workers like my dear cousin seems intent to do.''

Wilson's face seemed to lighten as he began to understand Manville's elation, but instead of joining in with his employer's enthusiasm he voiced his reservations. ''Sir,'' he said, then hesitated. ''What if the others decide not to do anything about her?''

''You don't have to worry about that. They'll consider her a troublemaker and they'll do their best to stop her. However, I've ways of dealing with her if they don't succeed.''

Seeing the curious light in Wilson's eyes, Manville shook

his head. "It's none of your concern at the moment. When the time comes I'll tell you what you need to know."

"Now, let's see," Manville continued as he drew several blank pieces of paper from the desk drawer. He picked up the quill pen and dipped it into the inkwell. "I think I'll do my friends a favor and warn them of the dissension my dear cousin's actions are going to create among their workers if they let her succeed with this foolish endeavor." He glanced up at Wilson and smiled smugly. "I seriously doubt if any of them will approve of her plans once they read my letter and see the trouble it could cause every manufacturer in England."

When Manville finished writing, he sealed the letters and handed them to Wilson. "Deliver these to every mill owner in the area with the exception of Mr. Kane Warrick and make sure they're read before you leave. And no matter how late it is, I want a full report when you return. Is that understood?"

"Aye, sir," Wilson said, bobbing his head rapidly up and down. "I'll see that it's done."

Exhausted, Fortune sank into the hot tub of water and lay back to relax her tired body. She was satisfied with her day's accomplishments yet she felt as if she'd tangled with a wildcat and had come out the worst for wear. Every muscle in her body ached from weariness.

"I've grown soft," she mused aloud as she envisioned what Tiny's reaction would have been if he could have seen her since she'd come to England. She doubted if he'd even know her after all the changes that had been made in her appearance, as well as her actions. Fortune gave a mental shrug and stopped herself from thinking of Tiny. She had to put that part of her life behind her and look into the future her grandfather had left to her. She'd always love Tiny and she still grew homesick when she thought of the Carolina mountains, but her life was no longer there. She had inherited responsibilities from Lord Northrop that she could not turn away from. They were her life now. Lifting the large sponge, Fortune squeezed it and dribbled soapy water down one outstretched arm.

"And I for one am glad," Kane said as he bent and nuzzled the side of her neck. He'd come to speak with her about the decision he'd made that morning about his son but once he'd seen her in the tub, all thoughts of Price fled as a wave of desire washed over him.

Fortune jumped. Her action sent water splashing over the rim of the tub and onto the floor. She squealed in dismay as she peered at the soapy water that puddled on the shining parquet wood.

"Kane! Look what you've made me do."

"I've far more pleasant things to look upon than bath water," Kane murmured, his gaze moving down the smooth line of her bare back before venturing to the firm mounds exposed to his view as she raised her arms to clasp the sides of the tub. Her breasts peaked enticingly through the soap bubbles that obscured the bounties he knew to lay hidden beneath the water.

Unashamed of her nakedness in front of her husband yet flushing from the hot light she saw in his eyes, Fortune reached for the large towel laying on the chair beside the tub. However, she wasn't swift enough to retrieve it before Kane saw her intentions. He grabbed the towel and draped it about his neck before he picked up the sponge and cocked a jaunty brow at her. "Surely you aren't through with your bath so soon, my lady?"

"I'll finish it later," Fortune said, making to retrieve the towel again. The action served to bring her breasts into full view.

"Madame, I think you should finish it now," Kane said, leaning out of Fortune's reach. "And if it will please you, I'll act as your maid tonight." Kane didn't wait for her response to his proposal. He dipped the sponge into the warm water and, with a wicked grin curving his lips up at the corners, began to bathe her.

"Do I have a choice, sir?" Fortune asked shamelessly as she relaxed and let Kane's soothing ministrations ease the tiredness from her limbs. He plied the sponge along her aching shoulders and down her back before venturing to the entrancing globes of her breasts. Gently he caressed them, rotating the softness around each firm mound before gliding it down to her flat belly. Unable to deny himself the pleasure of touching her with his hand, the sponge popped to the surface unheeded when he released it to knead her belly with his strong fingers.

Their gazes locked—slate blue and silver—as Kane's hands glided over her flesh and sent all thoughts but pleasure from their minds. Fortune gasped audibly when his fingers brushed against her womanhood and then felt deprived when they ventured past to stroke her thigh.

Kane ran his hand down her slender leg and lifted it out of the water. He massaged her wet flesh with experienced fingers and smiled when he felt the tension ease from her muscles. His eyes never left her face as he bent to give the bottom of her foot an erotic kiss before beginning a slow and mesmerizing journey along her silky wet skin. When he could go no higher because of the water, he stopped and turned his attention to its mate. And by the time he made the same journey upward and raised his mouth from her flesh, Fortune was quivering with anticipation.

Seeing the fire glowing in her blue eyes, he rapidly discarded his own clothing and lifted her from the water. He carried her, wet and dripping, across the room to the bed. Fortune lay naked and glorying in the hot light of desire that burned in his eyes as he stood over her, feasting upon her beauty until he could no longer deny himself the pleasure of touching her. He came to her on the bed.

Taking her mouth for the first time, he delved into the sweet cavern, exploring it fully with his tongue and savoring the taste of her as she satisfied her own craving of him. She wound her arms about his corded neck and arched her back to press her breasts against the crisp curls that furred his chest. Her nipples hardened with the contact and her nostrils flared as she drew in a sharp breath of air, his scent igniting the tinder already smoldering from his touch.

Her blood seemed to explode into rivers of fiery sensation and she moaned and brought her hips up against his, silently beseeching him to give all of himself to her.

The muscles in Kane's back rippled beneath his tanned flesh as he raised himself above her and plunged into the welcoming warmth of her body. She brought her legs up and wrapped them about his waist, holding him deep inside her, enraptured by the exquisite feel of him touching the very depths of her being. She moved with him as he slowly stroked her resilient flesh, tantalizing her and making her want the heady torment to last forever. A cry of dismay escaped her lips as he slowly withdrew from her and lowered his head to her breasts.

Tormented and aching with need, she thought she'd reached the peak of desire. His mouth proved her wrong. His tongue played its erotic game with her nipples until she arched against him, her hips rubbing against his. Still he did not take her fully but instead lowered his mouth to the valley between her breasts and traced a fiery path down to her navel. He circled it with his tongue before he moved slowly downward.

An elated moan escaped him as he wrapped his arms about her hips and buried his face against her, savoring her woman's smell and feeling himself burn to know all of her. He sated himself on the sweet musky taste of her and felt her flesh ripple with ecstasy before he once more covered her with his hard body and sought his own paradise.

They moved as one, hip to hip, mouth to mouth—souls united. They were mythical creatures—lovers blessed by Venus, love's enchantress. She bound their souls and sent them on the fiery quest through the splendors of the heavens. They traveled higher and higher until nothing existed in their universe beyond the velvet sweetness of the flesh and the gilded rapture that dewed their bodies with jeweled droplets when they reached the pinnacle where only lovers are allowed to dwell.

A deep sated moan escaped Fortune as she whirled amid

the myriad sensations that filled her before gently floating back into mortal man's world. Her smile reflected her satisfaction as she wrapped her arms about Kane's neck and hugged him close. She felt as if her heart would burst from the love that welled within it.

Kane raised himself on his elbows above her and dropped a light kiss on the tip of her nose. He smiled, replete, and wondered how he had ever imagined he was satisfied with the life he'd led before he'd met Fortune. The years he'd spent with Felicia and the years since her death had been emotionally barren for him. His love had been like the rain and Felicia had been like the desert sands. She had absorbed all he had to give yet had given nothing in return.

He'd made the mistake of not realizing from the beginning of their marriage that nothing would help solve the deep-seated problems. Yet he had not been willing to give up his dreams of a family. Kane frowned and shifted to Fortune's side as his guilt rose up to shadow the glow left by their lovemaking. He'd forced Felicia to have his child and it had cost her life.

A shudder passed through Kane and he quickly drew Fortune into his protective embrace. Until that moment his desire for his young wife had not let him consider the consequences of their lovemaking. His child had killed Felicia, and his seed might already be growing within Fortune. Kane felt gooseflesh form on his arms with the terrifying thought, and he tightened his embrace about the young woman who lay content and sated at her husband's side.

Sensing the sudden tension in Kane, Fortune turned to look up at her husband. In the silver eyes looking down at her, she saw an anguish that made her heart stop. Instinctively she reached out to him. "What is it, Kane?"

"What is what?" Kane said, forcing a lightness into his voice.

"There's something troubling you," Fortune said, her eyes imploring him to share his problems with her.

"There's nothing troubling me," Kane said, and sat up. "As a matter of fact, I couldn't ask for things to have gone better today."

"Don't draw away from me," Fortune pleaded, sensing the distance her husband was putting between them.

Kane turned and lay a caressing hand against her cheek. She pressed a kiss into his palm as she looked up at him, silently begging his confidence so that she could help him over the pain she saw reflected in his eyes.

Kane shook his head and smiled. "I'm here, Fortune. I'm not drawing away from you. You're my wife."

Fortune released a resigned breath. She would have to accept his answer and be grateful for what he did want to share with her. It was far more than she expected after the agreement she'd signed on their wedding day. All she could do was hope that in time, he would come to care enough about her to feel free to share all of his life with her and not just his passion.

"I want to be your wife in every way, Kane. I—" Fortune's words dried up on the tip of her tongue. No matter what they had shared during the last twenty-four hours, she couldn't tell him she loved him. Their newfound relationship was too tenuous to risk expressing her feelings. He'd told her a man didn't have to love a woman to make love to her, and until she knew that he felt more for her than just a moment of passion, then she'd keep her secret.

Kane arched a brow at her curiously. "What were you going to say?"

Fortune shifted uneasily. "I was going to say I also want to be a good mother to your son because I love that little boy with all of my heart."

Kane let his hand fall to the bed and stood. The jealousy he'd felt that morning now rose again to tear at him. He retrieved his britches from where they lay in a crumpled heap by the tub and slipped them on. His expression was grim as he buttoned them and then shrugged into the white silk shirt. The dark hair on his chest peeped over the edge of the V neck opening when he turned to look at his wife.

''I had come to speak with you about Price before other things claimed my attention.''

The serious expression on Kane's face made Fortune uneasy, and she pulled the counterpane up to shield her nakedness as if it would protect her in some way from the bad news she sensed was coming. ''What did you want to discuss about Price?''

''I didn't come here to discuss anything. I came to tell you that I'm sending him back to Warhill tomorrow,'' Kane answered bluntly. There was no easy way to tell his wife he was sending his son away to keep him from coming between them again.

''You're going to do what?'' Fortune asked incredulously, coming to her feet.

''Exactly what I said. Price is my son and I feel it's best that he be under Mrs. Ward's supervision.''

Fortune thought she would explode. She trembled visibly from the rush of anger that shot through her. ''How dare you even consider doing such a thing to the child? Don't you have a heart? My God, Price is but a baby and you want to turn him out of his home.''

''I'm not turning him out of his home but sending him back to it. Warhill is my son's home as it is mine; not North Meadows. And as for your objections against Mrs. Ward, she has the firm hand he needs. He needs discipline instead of mollycoddling. His actions this morning proved that. What he did was unconscionable.''

''Get out of my sight, Kane Warrick. You disgust me,'' Fortune spat. She turned and, dragging the counterpane with her, strode across the room in an effort to put as much distance between herself and her coldhearted husband as possible. If she didn't she wouldn't be responsible for what she said or did.

Kane's temper snapped under her condemnation. He closed the space between them in three strides and took Fortune firmly by the shoulders. He turned her to face him. ''Damn it, Fortune. I'm doing what I think is best for all concerned. We have enough dissension between us without my son's interference.''

''You are the one who is creating the dissension and not Price. You're the one who can't love your son.''

''Damn it, Fortune. I do love my son,'' Kane ground out.

Fortune jerked away from Kane's imprisoning hands and regarded him skeptically. ''If what I've seen is what you call love, then you really don't know what love is, Kane. And I'm grateful our marriage was made on a business arrangement instead of your type of love. No one could live with that.''

''No one is asking you to,'' Kane spat, then stalked from the room furious with his wife to the point of madness. Hurt and anger mingled as one as he descended the stairs and stormed into the study, determined to make use of Lord Northrop's stock of fine brandy. He needed something to wash away the pain Fortune's words aroused. They cut into his soul and made him realize that no matter how much he loved his wife and no matter what he did to try to stop anything from coming between them, she didn't return his love.

Kane's hand shook so badly from the emotions tearing away at his insides that the rim of the crystal decanter rattled against the brandy snifter as he poured himself a drink. Drawing in a steadying breath, he downed the fiery liquid in one gulp. He poured himself another drink before the first reached his stomach. At the moment, he didn't appreciate the flavor of the cognac or the soothing warmth it created in his stomach. All he wanted was to drink enough to forget he'd allowed himself once more to fall in love with a woman who didn't return his feelings.

At the thought, Kane downed the second drink and refilled his glass. His shoulders sagged under the weight of his misery as he crossed the study and slumped into the leather chair behind the desk. Fleetingly he recalled that his enemy had probably concocted many of his schemes to ruin his competition exactly where Kane now sat. How-

ever, Manville's days at North Meadows were over. After
Mr. Rutherford read the will, he'd removed himself to the
small house outside of Northington that his uncle had bequeathed to him along with his five hundred pounds a
year. As Kane had once planned, Manville had lost everything, yet in his present state of mind, he couldn't find
any satisfaction in his enemy's misfortunes.

"Manville was the lucky one. He has only lost his inheritance to Fortune, but I lost my heart," Kane mused
sadly, laying his head back against the soft worn leather.
He knew if he had any sense he'd take his son and go back
to Warhill and never look back. He had the land he needed
for the canal and there was nothing to hold him at North
Meadows.

"Nothing but my heart," Kane mused aloud, and
squeezed his eyes closed. The stem of the crystal glass he
held snapped under the pressure of his hand as he reflected
on Fortune's accusations. She'd accused him of having no
heart, yet the very thing he wasn't supposed to possess
now felt as if it were being torn asunder. She'd also accused him of not loving his son, yet he did love Price. He
loved both his son and Fortune with equal intensity, but
each love was different. And it wasn't the child's fault he
felt such guilt about Felicia.

Kane's eyes snapped open and a look of astonishment
crossed his face as he realized Fortune's accusations did
have some merit after all. In truth he'd never been able to
conquer his own guilt enough to show his love to his son.
Because of the way his child had been conceived, he'd
treated Price as if he was to blame for all that had transpired.

"My God, what have I done?" he asked the empty study
as he fully comprehended the magnitude of his actions.
He'd irrationally allowed his past to cast a shadow over his
relationship with the most precious thing in his life, the
son he had wanted more than anything else on earth.

"I've been a damned fool," Kane muttered, gingerly
setting the broken glass on the desk. Price was innocent

of any crime and he didn't deserve the treatment he'd received. Kane pushed the chair back and stood. Perhaps his life with Fortune was doomed to another loveless relationship, but it didn't have to be that way with his son. He intended to begin to correct the mistakes he'd made with his son, and he'd not wait until the morning to begin. He would speak to Price tonight if he was still awake.

His resolutions made, Kane ascended the stairs and made his way along the carpeted hallway to the room where his son slept. He glanced at Fortune's door as he passed but didn't succumb to the urge to enter. At that moment he had to begin setting to right his life with his son. Once that was done, hopefully he'd be able to turn his attention to the other important person in his life: his wife.

In the soft glow of the lone bedside candle, Kane stood silent and still beside the bed that had once belonged to Sebastian Northrop. His silver gaze rested gently upon the child who lay curled on his side with his small hands folded beneath his chin, sleeping peacefully and completely unaware of his father's presence. Price's thick lashes cast spiked shadows upon his pudgy baby cheeks and his cherubic lips were slightly parted as he breathed.

Looking down at his son, Kane felt himself swell with pride and love for this child of his blood. From the top of his curly dark head to the bottom of his small feet, Kane could never deny that he was his son, the resemblance was too strong. He was the image of his father when Kane was of the same age.

"My son," Kane breathed quietly, easing himself down on the bed at his son's side. Tenderly he brushed a wayward curl back from his son's brow. A rueful smile touched his lips as it sprang back into place. How many times had he wanted to touch his child in that manner but had turned away, unable to look at him because of his own guilt.

"I wonder if you'll ever be able to forgive me my mistakes?" he asked quietly. "Had not Fortune made me realize what I was doing to you, I would have continued to treat you as if you were the one responsible for Felicia's death.''

Fortune eased back into the hallway and quickly made her way back to her room. She quietly closed the door behind her and leaned back against it for support. Tears welled in her eyes and she blinked rapidly to stay them but she failed. They slipped over her dark lashes and ran unheeded down her cheeks.

She'd heard her husband's soft tread in the hallway and had quietly followed him to his son's room, afraid that he intended to take Price back to Warhill without waiting till morning. However, when Kane had stood watching his son with an expression that reflected all of his heartache, she had been unable to leave. Now she wished she'd left before she'd learned the answers to the questions that had puzzled her about her husband's relationship with his son. Kane had blamed his son for his wife's death. It was Felicia's ghost who still haunted him. It was his love of his first wife that kept him from loving her.

Fortune drew in a ragged breath and wiped at her damp cheeks. A feeling of futility filled her as she crossed to the bed and fell facedown upon it. She buried her head in her arms but couldn't vent the misery that now consumed her. She had hoped Kane would come to love her as much as she loved him, yet now she feared it would never happen. She couldn't fight a ghost for his affections. Flesh and blood could never rival a memory. They were always perfect while their human counterparts had visible faults.

Fortune rolled onto her back and stared numbly up at the ceiling, unable to focus on the elaborate scrollwork that fanned out from the base of the chandelier like waves upon a blue sea. Many a night she'd lain there visualizing the ships that sailed upon the imaginary ocean. But not tonight. Her thoughts would not leave the man who sat quietly talking to the sleeping child.

A rueful smile touched Fortune's lips. At least some good had come out of her relationship with Kane. He had finally realized the way he had been treating his son and hopefully in the future they would be happy. The thought eased her mind for Price's future but not her own. She still had a ghost to defeat before she could win the battle for Kane's heart.

# Chapter 10

*The gloomy overcast sky matched Fortune's mood as she* descended the stairs and crossed to the dining room where Kane sat at the head of the table enjoying his hearty breakfast of kidneys and eggs. Feeling as if Felicia's ghost sat on his right, where his living wife should sit, Fortune filled her plate from the buffet and seated herself at the opposite end of the long table. After the restless night she'd spent, she had little appetite.

Kane frowned at his wife's choice of seating but didn't voice his need to have her near him. He knew the reason she'd put so much distance between them and hoped that the decision he'd made in his son's room the previous night would rectify her low opinion of him. Clearing his throat, he said, "I thought you would like to know that I've reconsidered my decision to send Price back to Warhill."

Fortune lifted her eyes from her plate and looked at her husband. A semblance of a smile touched her lips and she nodded. "I'm glad to hear it."

Kane's frown deepened. He'd expected more of a reaction from her. He'd hoped his decision would at least make her realize he wasn't the ogre she thought him to be. Annoyed by her lack of response, he pushed back his chair and stood. His voice was gruff as he said, "I'll be at the construction site if you should need me."

Fortune nodded and turned her attention back to her plate. She didn't look up as Kane paused at her side but continued to redistribute her food about her plate. This morning she didn't feel up to battling with her husband. She'd slept little and when she did manage to doze off, her dreams had been filled with images of Kane and his first wife. She'd awoken that morning feeling tired and depressed.

"Good day, madame," Kane said shortly when his wife refused to look at him. He turned and strode briskly from the dining room.

Fortune's hand clenched about her fork and she squeezed her eyes closed as she listened to Kane leave the house and summon a servant to bring his horse. From the sound of his voice she knew he was annoyed with her but in her present state of mind, she really didn't have anything to say to him. After what she'd learned last night, the futility about her marriage to Kane weighed her down. They had been wed less than a week yet it already seemed as if she'd spent a lifetime unsuccessfully battling Felicia's ghost.

"I can't keep doing this to myself," Fortune said, exasperated. She'd gone into this marriage with her eyes open, fully knowing that Kane didn't love her and the only reason he'd agreed to their match was to gain the land for his canal. Now she sat hunched up like a beaten animal, cowering in her own despair.

The thought made Fortune straighten in her chair. Her slate blue eyes snapped with indignation as she tilted her chin in the air. She'd not allow a ghost to defeat her. She was alive and could fight for Kane's affection. And, if need be, she'd battle Felicia's memory for the rest of her life to gain her husband's love.

Feeling more like herself, Fortune shrugged off the last of her maudlin mood. She slammed her fork down on the table and pushed back her chair, then stood and squared her shoulders. This morning she would concentrate on reopening the Northrop mills, but tonight she'd put all of her energy into seducing the man she loved.

Fortune smiled. "I might not be able to fight a memory but I'm going to try my damnest." With that encouraging thought, she ordered her pony cart readied to take her to the mills.

Already mentally primed for battle, Fortune reined the pony to a halt in front of the mill and climbed down. In a glance she took in the group of well-dressed men who stood blocking the entrance while her workers wandered around, too frightened to go to their jobs.

"What's the meaning of this?" she asked, her temper already beginning to simmer just below the surface.

A heavyset man stepped forward. He raked Fortune with a contemptuous glance before he said, "We're not going to allow you to reopen your mill, Lady Northrop."

"And who are you, sir, to tell me that I can't open my mill?"

"I'm Trevor Waring, the owner of the spinning mills south of Northington. These other owners and I have come as a delegation to stop you from reopening the Northrop mills."

His manner and tone set Fortune's teeth on edge and she bristled even more. She glanced past Waring to the group who murmured their agreement to his statement. "What do you mean that you're not going to allow me to reopen my mill, sir? As I see it, you have no authority here. This is my land and my mill and I'll do as I damned well please."

"I beg to differ with you, my lady," Waring said, flushing at her unladylike manner. "We can't allow that to happen."

"Out of my way, sir," Fortune ordered, but the large man made no move to obey.

"Lady Northrop, I'm sorry but you have to understand that if we allow you to continue with this folly, then we will all have to follow suit to keep our own mills in operation."

A perplexed frown knit Fortune's brows as she stared up at Waring, wondering what the man was rambling about. "Folly, sir? I see no folly in wanting to put my people back to work."

"Lady Northrop," Waring said as if she were slow-witted. "You must understand that putting your people back to work under the circumstances is impossible."

"I certainly do not," Fortune snapped. "Now, if you will be so kind as to take yourself and your friends off my property, I have work to do."

Trevor shook his head. "Madame, unless you agree to rescind your decision about raising your workers' wages, you'll not open this mill today or any other time."

"So that's what this is all about," Fortune snapped as she finally comprehended the situation. "You fear if I raise the wages of my workers then you'll have to do the same. Well, sir, you and your friends can go take a leap into the river. I won't change my mind about my decision now or in the future."

A rumble of approval came from the workers who stood listening and waiting for their futures to be decided. "That a' way, me lady. Tell 'm like it is," one worker called from the rear of the crowd. "It won't hurt the nobs to give us a little extra fer our work."

Trevor Waring's beefy features hardened. "Then, Lady Northrop, you will not reopen your mill."

"I am now Lady Warrick, sir. And I will reopen my mill."

Shocked, Trevor Waring blinked down at her, completely baffled by the news that she was married to Kane Warrick. "Surely your husband can't agree to this outrageous scheme of yours. It will also hurt him."

"My husband doesn't handle my affairs, sir. I inherited the mills from my grandfather and they are my concern."

"I can't believe it, my lady."

"Believe what you will, but I am in charge of the Northrop mills now and I intend to make several changes you're not going to approve of."

"I'm going to speak to your husband about this. He will be able to take you in hand and keep you from making this horrendous mistake. And if he doesn't control you, then we will make sure that you do not continue."

"There's no need to trouble yourself, Waring," Kane said, stepping through the crowd of workers. He'd stopped by his mill before going to the canal construction site and had heard that the mill owners were organizing to keep the Northrop mills shut until Fortune decided against raising her workers' wages. Kane's first reaction to the news of his wife's decision had been pure, undiluted rage. She'd told him nothing of her resolution, which would ultimately be detrimental to his finances, as well as those of the other mill owners. But no matter how hardheaded she was, Fortune was his wife, and she needed his support even if he didn't approve of the changes she'd already set into motion. He'd be damned before he let anyone try to run roughshod over her.

"Warrick, from that I assume you approve of your wife's shenanigans. Don't you realize what this will mean to all of us? If this takes root here and spreads, it could cause a depression in the textile industry all over England."

"I think you're exaggerating, Waring," Kane said, draping a protective arm about Fortune's shoulders. "You do not have to follow my wife's lead if you don't want to. That is your choice. But I for one don't see how it will make a great deal of difference in my profits to give my workers a raise in wages."

"Then you're as much a fool as your wife. The two of you deserve each other."

"Thank you, Trevor, for the compliment," Kane said and smiled, his cool gaze raking over the heavyset Waring. "From that I assume you and your friends won't give my wife any more trouble."

"I haven't said any such thing," Waring blurted out.

"This isn't over. If you and your wife know what is good for you, you'll stop this ridiculous plan right now."

Kane looked down at Fortune. "Do you want to change your mind, madame?"

Fortune shook her head.

"I didn't think you would," Kane murmured for her ears only then turned his attention back to Waring. "I suggest you rethink any decisions you have made concerning the Northrop mills. I will hold you personally responsible if something untoward should happen here or at North Meadows. Is that understood?"

Feeling slightly intimidated by the younger man, Waring glanced over his shoulder at his silent companions for courage. He saw them nod reassuringly before he looked back at Kane. "Warrick, your threats don't frighten me. Nor will we stand by and let one woman ruin everything we've built over the years. You need to take her home and put a babe in her belly so she'll have something to occupy her time instead of sticking her nose into men's business."

"The mills belong to my wife, not me," Kane said. "And she'll run them as she sees fit."

Waring smirked at Kane. "I thought you were a better man, but I should have known from your last marriage that you don't know how to handle women."

"Damn you, Waring," Kane growled. It took every ounce of willpower he possessed to keep from throttling the man, then and there. "Get the hell off Northrop property before I throw you off."

"We'll go this time, but as I've said, we won't let you ruin us." Waring turned away and mounted his horse. The group of mill owners followed suit. They wheeled their mounts around and rode back toward the village.

The roar of approval rending the air a moment later was staggering. The mill workers crowded around Fortune and Kane, deferentially showing their gratitude to the couple before turning toward the mill, laughing and clapping each other on the back in celebration of their triumph. In only a short while the steady hum of the spinning and weave machines could be heard from where Kane and Fortune still stood.

With Kane's arm about her shoulders, Fortune looked up at her husband, her eyes alight with wonder at the strange turn of events. She still couldn't believe that her husband had come to her defense when she knew he objected to the changes she planned to make at the mills.

"Thank you for your help, Kane," she said in an effort to voice a small measure of her gratitude.

"I should wring your neck," Kane exploded. "You should have had the courtesy to tell me what you intended to do. But no! I had to hear a rumor from my own workers that my wife was raising the employees' wages."

Startled by his outburst, Fortune stiffened and moved away from her husband. "If you feel this way, why did you come here?"

"Damn it, you're my wife. I couldn't let Waring and his group threaten you and get away with it."

"Then you should have stayed away. I could have handled the situation myself."

"I assume by that remark you considered that scene the best way of handling the situation?"

"No," Fortune admitted grudgingly. "But—"

"There are no buts to it, Fortune," Kane interrupted. "Had I not arrived when I did, your mill would not be operating now. Men like Waring think women can't run their affairs, and he wouldn't have backed down."

"It's not only men like Waring," Fortune snapped. "As I recall you also feel a woman's place is having babies and wiping snotty noses."

"Your language, madame, ill befits a lady."

"Damn it, Kane," Fortune swore, and turned on him with fists braced on her hips. "I've told you before I'm not one of your fancy English ladies. Nor will I ever be one."

"I'm becoming more convinced of that each day," Kane snapped.

"Oh, you—you—" Fortune stuttered. Unable to express

her fury in words, she drew back her fist and hit K.
the belly. "No one is asking you to put up with som....
like me. Go back to your fancy English ladies and leave
me alone." Without waiting, she turned and stormed into
the mill.

"Blast it!" Kane swore as he stood rubbing his aching
midriff and watching his wife stalk away. "I come to her
rescue and what thanks do I get? A punch in the stomach.
From this moment she's on her own. She has her inheritance and I have the land for my canal."

Kane's face clouded as he turned and strode back to the
horse he'd tethered to the limb of a small tree. Fortune
had told him to go back to his fine English ladies and he'd
do exactly that. He'd allowed himself to become so involved with her he'd not considered going to visit his mistress, Madelene Deveau. But Fortune's attitude had
changed all that today. He had been pushed too far. He
was tired of fighting; tired of needing a woman who cared
not a whit what happened to him.

Kane smiled cynically, turning his mount in the direction of the construction site. Perhaps there was no love
between himself and Madelene, but at least she'd be glad
to see him and would appreciate his company for an evening. That was far more than he could say about his wife.


Kane stretched his long legs out to the warmth of the
fire. It might be summer but the rain that had begun earlier
in the day had left the evening chilly. Sipping the deep-
red burgundy Madelene's maid had served him upon his
arrival, he glanced toward the darkened window. The rain
had begun soon after he'd left Fortune and had continued
throughout the afternoon, making it impossible to work on
the canal. However, he'd not returned to North Meadows
but had gone to Warhill, changed into his evening clothes,
and rode directly to Bristol. Now he awaited the appearance of his lovely mistress. He didn't have long to wait.
Even as his thoughts turned to the lady, the double doors
that led into her boudoir opened to reveal the woman.

Fully aware of her beauty and the power she possessed over most men, Madelene poised with the candlelight behind her to display her many charms. Gowned in translucent silk, the curves of her beautiful, voluptuous body were visible through the sheer material. She stood unashamed of her seductive display, and, with chin proudly raised in the air, she drew in a deep breath to emphasize her bountiful breasts.

Kane smiled with pleasure. Madelene never changed. She didn't pretend he had come to court her like a lady but acted the seductress she was. Slowly she crossed to him, her hips swaying sensuously as she moved. She gazed at him through half-closed lids and moistened her red lips with the tip of her tongue in a silent invitation.

Kane set the glass of wine aside and lifted his arms to her. She came into them, wrapping herself about him, pressing her breasts to his chest and capturing his mouth in a hungry kiss. The aggressor, she ran her fingers through his ebony curls and wriggled her bottom against his corded thighs in mute appeal.

The scene varied little from time to time. Madelene was always ready for him any time of the day that he chose to visit her. She never seemed to tire of their lovemaking, and he wondered again tonight, as he had in the past, what she did to appease her sexual appetite when he was unable to pay her regular visits.

Feeling the desire that viewing her unclothed body had created dissipate, Kane withdrew her arms from about his neck and set her away. She groaned in protest and tried to reinstate herself against him.

"Madelene, give me a little time. I've had a hard day."

Her red lips in a sullen pout, his mistress scooted off his lap and settled herself at his side on the lounge.

"I've never seen you too tired to make love, Kane," she grumbled petulantly.

"I've never built a canal before," Kane replied.

"So you finally managed to get the land you needed?"

Madelene asked. Her voice revealed none of the annoyance she felt at being denied Kane's lovemaking.

Kane shifted uneasily and nodded. "That's what I've come to talk to you about."

"I don't know anything about canals. My forte lies in other directions, as you well know," Madelene replied huskily, running her hand down his stomach to the apex of his thighs. She cocked a curious brow at Kane when he didn't respond immediately to her touch.

Kane captured her hand and brought it to his lips for a brief kiss. "As I well know," he murmured but didn't release her hand to return to its play.

"Then why are we discussing canals? There are far more pleasant things for us to do with our time."

"Madelene, I'm married," Kane finally blurted out, unable to find an easy way to tell his mistress.

"You're what?" Madelene asked, incredulous. Her passion was momentarily cooled by his sudden announcement.

"I'm married."

Madelene gaped up at Kane. In all the years they had been lovers, she had been sure he would never marry and she'd not have to worry that he'd toss her out of the secure little world she'd built for herself in Bristol. She enjoyed the benefits of being a rich man's mistress. He paid her expenses and when he didn't visit her she was free to have as many lovers as she wanted as long as she was discreet. And discreet she'd been, so discreet, in fact, that Kane hadn't discovered her liaison with Nevin Manville.

Madelene knew her relationship with Kane would come to an abrupt end if he should ever learn that she'd shared his enemy's bed. But she couldn't stop herself from seeking out other men and the excitement in the risk involved should she be caught. One man could never keep her needs satisfied. Which was why she'd never married. Her body craved sexual variety as much as it needed air to live.

Madelene drew in an unsteady breath. She had to tread carefully. Her present life was too perfect to chance finding herself without a sponsor. It was difficult for a woman to find a man like Kane Warrick. He was one of those rare men who had looks, money, and also could please a woman in bed until she cried out with pleasure.

Although Madelene was distressed with the thought of losing her security, she wasn't emotionally involved with Kane or any other man. However, when she looked up at him with brimming cornflower-blue eyes, she achieved the desired effect.

"Madelene, you've no reason to be upset. Nothing will change between us. My marriage was a business agreement and that is all." Kane felt his heart flutter at the lie but he couldn't tell his mistress or anyone his true feelings. He'd be the biggest fool who had ever been born if he revealed he'd let himself fall in love with his own wife. Especially when she felt nothing for him but contempt.

Feigning heartbreak, Madelene threw herself dramatically against Kane. "Oh, I couldn't stand it if someone kept you from me. I believe I would die if your wife came between us."

A little shocked and oddly touched by her display, Kane wrapped his arms around his mistress and held her close. As long as he'd known Madelene, he'd never suspected she was so attached to him. They had always enjoyed each other but he'd always made sure she understood that he didn't love her. And she had never uttered one word of love for him.

"I'm afraid you don't have to worry about that ever happening," Kane said with a sinking heart. Hadn't his argument with Fortune earlier proved it?

Desperately needing to get away from his thoughts, Kane buried his face in the hollow of Madelene's perfumed neck and sought to rid himself of his torment in his mistress's arms.

"Love me, Madelene," he pleaded huskily.

A deep satisfied laugh rumbled from Madelene as she pressed Kane back against the satin lounge. Her experienced fingers made swift work of the fastenings of his shirt and britches and soon his magnificent body lay naked to her heated gaze.

Madelene felt her insides quiver in response to the beauty of him. She never ceased to be amazed at the reaction the mere sight of Kane roused within her. Each ridged, sinewy muscle in his whipcord lean body excited her until she ached with such intensity that it was physically painful. She could feel her heart beat in the very depths of her being. She throbbed there, hot and moist, needing no further stimulation to bring her near the peak of ecstacy.

She didn't straddle those lean hips as her body urged her to do. Instead she enjoyed her torment, lavishing caresses upon his hard body in an effort to rouse him to meet her demands. She stroked and fondled until Kane captured her hand within his own and sadly shook his head.

"It's no use," he said, and drew her back onto the lounge at his side.

Madelene felt like screaming in frustration. Her body cried out to be fulfilled, and she squirmed unconsciously against the smooth satin of the seat.

"I'll make you want me," she whispered hoarsely, and began an erotic trail of kisses down his furred chest to his firm belly. Kane stopped her before she could reach her destination.

"I'm sorry, Madelene," he said, reaching for his britches. His face was grim as he stood and slipped them on. At that moment he felt as if his world had suddenly gone out of kilter. He was humiliated in the deepest sense. In a world that often judged a man on his prowess in bed, he had always stood tall and proud of his accomplishments. He had always been able to respond to a beautiful woman's caresses.

Until now, Kane mused silently and jerked on his shirt. It was his misfortune to want no other woman but his wife.

A streak of lighting lit the black sky and a rumble of thunder made the house tremble. Madelene watched from the window as Kane rode away into the darkness beyond

the street lamps. Her red lips were pursed where she stood
with brow pressed to the cool glass, her body still burning
with need.

"Damn you, Kane Warrick." She groaned and moved
her hand to the ache he had created. Her breathing became
rapid and her eyes grew glazed with the fire in her blood.
She felt the swell of her release building at the same instant a knock sounded on her door.

"Kane, you've come back," she said, her voice thick.
She quickly drew her silk robe together and hurried to the
door. When she swung it open, her smile wavered for only
a fraction of a second before she threw her arms about the
bony shoulders of the man dressed in black.

Without preamble, he thrust his foot against the door
and slammed it closed. By the time the sound died away
in the room he'd already shed his coat and unbuttoned his
britches to expose himself to Madelene's hungry gaze. She
took him in her hand and wrapped her voluptuous body
about him. They sank to the floor, arms and legs entwined
and no word passing between them as they sought to
quench their desire.

"Damn, if Warrick didn't get you all fired up." Manville chuckled as he pulled away from Madelene and readjusted his clothing. "I'll have to make sure that I visit
more often after he's been here."

Madelene brushed a lock of blond hair back from her
brow as she sat up. She drew her robe over her sated body
and pushed herself to her feet. After crossing to the table
where a decanter of brandy sat with several crystal glasses,
she poured two drinks and then turned back to Manville.
"I can't afford for you to do that, Nevin. You took too
much of a chance coming here tonight. What if Kane had
still been here when you knocked? How could I have explained your sudden appearance on my doorstep this late
at night or, for that matter, any other time?"

"Don't worry, I saw the bastard ride away, but I still
waited to make certain that he wasn't coming back. I don't

want to mess up your little game any more than you do, my dear Madelene.''

"But what if you hadn't seen him? How would you have known he was here?''

"My dear, I keep a close eye on my enemies. Much more so than Warrick does, or he would know that I've been sharing your bed for the last six months.'' Manville's thin shoulders shook with mirth as he savored the thought of taking Warrick's mistress right beneath the man's nose. It didn't matter to him that Kane was unaware of the fact. What counted was that he had taken something Kane owned.

And soon I'll take everything the man possesses, including his bitch of a wife, Manville thought as he downed the brandy and reached to pull Madelene upon his lap. He slid his hand into her robe and fondled her large breasts. His thoughts, however, were not with the mistress whose passion had already begun to mount once more. They lay with the young woman who now resided on the estate she'd taken away from him.

Manville tightened his fingers about Madelene's breast and felt her wince from the pain. He paid no heed to her discomfort. His mind was centered on one person, Fortune Warrick. She would pay for all the trouble she'd caused him. If she thought her problems were over since Warrick had backed the other mill owners down that morning, then she was sadly mistaken. She had managed to reopen the Northrop mills but there was no guarantee they would remain open.

An ominous gleam entered Manville's dark eyes. Fortune thought she had won, but this morning had only been the first skirmish in the battle for control of the mills. It didn't mean she'd triumph over him in the long run. He had too many ways to make her suffer. Manville mentally rubbed his hands together with glee. When Wilson carried out his orders tonight, his dear cousin would see that she'd taken on more than she could handle.

Manville smiled up into the glazed, pale-blue eyes of

Warrick's mistress. Even this hot-blooded bitch could be used as a weapon against his cousin, he mused. Dear Fortune wouldn't be too happy to learn that her husband still visited his whore while she slept alone at North Meadows. That knowledge would severely strain, if not end, their marriage.

Manville chuckled. He wrapped his long, skinny fingers in Madelene's tousled curls and drew her head down to capture her red lips in a savage kiss. Yes, Madelene could be of service to him out of bed as well as in it.

The porcelain clock on the intricately carved mantle chimed off the hour as a streak of lightning lit up the countryside with its ghostly shimmer. Thunder cracked overhead, shattering the stillness of the night and bringing Fortune out of her chair in alarm. The thunder had jerked her abruptly awake after she'd dozed off while awaiting Kane's return to North Meadows.

"It was only thunder," she reassured herself as she rubbed the sleep from her eyes and concentrated on getting her heart to stop hammering against her ribs. She'd crossed to the window and peered out into the darkness, her thoughts turning once more to her husband. A frown of worry creased her brow while she stood listening to the downpour beyond the leaded glass. She knew she shouldn't be concerned about Kane, yet she couldn't stop herself from worrying. The weather was foul and any number of things could happen to a person out on a night like this.

Her mind on her husband, Fortune found her gaze drawn to the glow appearing above the trees in the distance. For a brief, unthinking moment she breathed a sigh of relief. At least Kane could see his way in the moonlight.

"There can be no moon on a night like this," she said as a streak of lightning abruptly brought her back to reality. Straining to see what caused the light in the distance, Fortune realized with a sinking heart that it was in the direction of Northington.

"My God, the mills!" she breathed. Even as the words

left her lips, she was throwing off her night rail and hurrying across the room to the armoire. With no thought to her appearance, she dragged out the buckskins she'd been unable to throw away when she left Carolina. She didn't have time for all the fripperies required of a lady to wear. She quickly slipped into the smooth worn leather britches and shirt and then dug out her sturdy boots and tugged them on. Without a glance in the mirror, she pulled on her rain cloak and raced out into the foul night.

After calling for the grooms to notify the servants that there was a fire in the village and every able body would be required to help, she slipped the reins over her grandfather's bay mare and, mounted bareback. A swift kick to its sides sent her and the spirited animal down the drive at full speed.

Fortune's heart was in her throat as she reined the mare to a skidding halt and slid to the ground in front of the mill, fears realized. The warehouse was ablaze. Horrified, she watched as flames shot through the windows and sizzled as they licked toward the wet, black sky. Smoke, made worse by the dampness, billowed in huge plumes through the cracks in the walls and roof. A bucket brigade had been formed by the villagers, but their efforts had little effect upon the fire. The bales of cotton stored within were tinder that fed the flames and made it impossible to save the building.

Tears of futility brimmed and mingled with the raindrops on her cheeks as Fortune realized the structure was lost. There was nothing more they could do but let it burn. Resigning herself to the loss, she glanced in the direction of the building that housed the spinning and weave machines and sent a silent prayer heavenward to spare the mill. Then she turned and began giving orders.

"We have to keep the flames from spreading to the other buildings," Fortune shouted, taking her position alongside the villagers in the bucket line. "If the mill goes up, we're all in trouble."

"We won't let that happen," Henry Reed said at her

side and handed her a bucket filled with water. "The fates won't do that to us, not after we're finally getting a few of the things we deserve."

Fortune attempted to give him a smile of assurance but failed. She clamped her jaw tightly together and clenched her teeth to keep her tears at bay. She was afraid to depend upon the fates to show her any kindness at this late date. Ever since her grandfather's death and even before that, when Tiny had died, the fates seemed determined to make her suffer. What she'd done to earn their animosity she didn't know, but she prayed they wouldn't take their hostility out on the poor souls who depended upon her for their livelihoods.

Mud oozed into their shoes and boots as the workers sloshed back and forth through the ankle-deep mire that sucked at their feet and hindered their steps. They passed the buckets of water along to the man or woman at their sides and ignored any discomfort they felt from the rain or mud. The plight that awaited them should they fail to save the mill gave them impetus, and their haggard faces reflected determination as they continued battling the flames.

Each man, woman, and child along the line knew if the fire destroyed the mill, they would starve. There would be no work for them in the area if the Northrop mill crumbled into ashes. The mill owners wouldn't hire Northrop workers out of fear they'd expect the same treatment as they'd been given by Lady Warrick. They would be considered troublemakers and ostracized.

Although the future was at stake, there was much more involved than just their own welfare. Lady Warrick had defied her own kind for them and they owed her their loyalty in return. Each man, woman, and child would stand on the bucket line until the fire was out or they dropped with exhaustion.

Fortune ached from head to toe. The muscles in her arms, legs, and back screamed from the torture of lifting the heavy buckets yet she didn't leave the line. She felt proud to stand with her people and battle a force that could tear all of their lives apart. She sensed their feelings and couldn't let them down by retreating behind the mantle society expected her to wear because of the blood in her veins. Her people depended upon her, and she'd stay and fight at their sides for as long as it took.

"Fortune, you're going to drop if you don't rest," Kane said, taking the bucket and passing it to the man beyond her before she could touch the handle.

"I can't stop," Fortune murmured, absently rubbing her aching arm as she looked up at her husband. "If the mill goes up everything will be lost."

"You can rest. My people are here to help. I saw the fire on my way back from Bristol and rode to Warhill for help."

"Thank you, Kane, but I'm afraid I still can't rest. It will take all of us to save the mill," Fortune said, swaying with fatigue. Until that moment she hadn't realized the extent of her exhaustion. Now with Kane there to shoulder some of the burden it came rushing over her in a trembling wave. Her knees seemed to turn to liquid and she reached out to her husband for support.

"Take over here," Kane called to Henry Reed as he lifted his wife into his arms and carried her a short distance away.

"Put me down, Kane. They need me," Fortune ordered weakly.

"I'll put you down but you're not going back to that line. We have enough men to finish putting out the fire without you falling over from exhaustion," Kane said, setting her on her feet. "Now, you stay here and that's an order." Without waiting for her answer, he turned and strode back to the line of volunteers.

Fortune sank down on the wet ground and watched helplessly as the fire continued to consume the warehouse. The roof caved in a short time later and a momentary shower of fiery cinders rose in a cloud above the hulled-out structure before the rain turned them into ash. Floating over the workers, the ashes coated them in black, streaking their rain-drenched faces into grotesque looking masks.

It took several more hours before the last flame died and the mill was safe. The workers' drooping shoulders and flagging steps mirrored their exhaustion as they turned weary faces back toward home. They didn't speak when they passed Fortune yet she sensed their satisfaction for a job well done. They had worked together, hand to hand, to fight one common enemy, and they had prevailed.

She, too, felt the same sense of unity with her workers as they felt among themselves but something more grand had happened during the waning hours of the night. She had, for the first time, felt a oneness with her husband. He had labored through the long rainy night to save the very thing he objected to, her mill. And she watched with love and pride as he came toward her, his face and clothes soot-blackened and his body drenched to the skin.

Wiping a weary hand across his face, smearing it further with ash, Kane gave Fortune a wobbly smile and extended a hand to her. She took it, grateful that this strong man was her husband. She walked at his side to where the bay mare and his horse were tethered.

"It's been a long night," he said, hoisting himself into the saddle. Again he extended a hand to her and she let him help her up in front of him. At that moment she had no desire to ride the mare back to North Meadows.

"Too long," Fortune replied. Content, she leaned comfortably back against her husband's wide chest. It had indeed been a long and terrible night, but something good had come out of it.

# Chapter 11

*The new day was already shedding its dark mantle when* Kane reined his mount to a halt in front of North Meadows. He raised a grimy finger to his lips to silence the groom who ran forward to assist him and then eased himself and the burden in his arms from the saddle.

The movement didn't fully rouse Fortune. She shifted, murmured something inaudible, and snuggled closer to her husband's hard chest without awakening. The steady gait of his horse had lulled her to sleep as soon as they'd started back to North Meadows, and Kane didn't have it in his heart to wake her after all she'd been through that night.

Carrying his sleeping wife up the winding stairs to her chamber, he couldn't take his eyes off her soot-blackened and rain-drenched features. In the eyes of those who set such store in a lady's manner and appearance, Fortune would be considered totally unfit, yet Kane didn't believe he'd ever seen anything as beautiful as his wife at that moment. His heart swelled with pride and love while he recalled how he'd found her working side by side with the villagers. Even through the grime that had covered her lovely features, her undaunted spirit had glowed brightly.

Kane's soft expression reflected his feelings as he lay

Fortune upon the bed and tenderly brushed his lips against her brow. He eased her soggy buckskins from her and then tucked her beneath the soft down comforter before he shed his own filthy clothing and quickly slid beneath the covers at her side. The rainy night had left a damp chill in the room but he was too exhausted to rekindle the fire in the grate. He cuddled his wife, cupping her body with his to share her heat, and closed his eyes. He slept immediately.

Fortune snuggled close to the warmth at her side, instinctively trying to escape the damp chill that had invaded the room during the night. When she felt a hand steal along her side to cup her breast, her eyes snapped open and she found herself looking into molten silver.

"Good morning, wife," Kane murmured softly as he lowered his head and took her lips in a gentle, caressing kiss.

Fortune moaned her pleasure and molded herself against the hard length of him. She wound her arms about his neck and entwined her fingers in his dark curls, imprisoning him within her embrace. Well rested and instantly aroused by the mere touch of Kane's lips, she became the aggressor.

Delightfully surprised, Kane brought her on top of him, then lay back to enjoy his wife's attentions. Her dark hair spilled about them, curtaining off the world beyond, as she hungrily recaptured his mouth and sucked greedily at his full bottom lip. She teased him with her kisses and moved her hips provocatively against his, tempting him until his blood felt like liquid fire.

Unable to stand the sweet torment a moment longer, Kane, with a deep throaty laugh rumbling from his wide, furred chest, flipped her onto her back and slid into the welcoming warmth of her resilient body. Her long legs wrapped about his hips and drew him inside her velvety softness. His lean muscles rippled beneath his tanned skin as he matched her rhythm and they soared upward, joined body and soul. They gloried in the exquisite sensations that held them spellbound in a world where nothing existed beyond the pleasure they were giving each other. Together they reached the ultimate plateau and frolicked there amid the stardust, savoring the wonderful thing known as love.

Kane's heart still pounded against his ribs when he raised himself above Fortune and gave her a sated smile. To his chagrin the gesture made her burst into laughter. Puzzled, he eased to her side and cocked a curious brow. Propped casually on one elbow and resting his chin in the palm of his hand, Kane gazed down at his wife and asked, "Pray tell, what's so funny, madame."

"You—" Fortune managed to say before another bout of laughter exploded from her. She clutched her stomach and her eyes misted with tears of mirth as she stared up at her husband. Giggle upon giggle erupted until she was weak from laughter and her husband lay frowning down at her.

"I've made love to many women but you're the first to laugh at me," Kane said, forcing a lightness into his voice. For in truth, his wife's gaiety had slightly insulted him.

"Oh, you," Fortune said, her spirits high as she tapped him playfully on the nose with the tip of one finger. "If those women could see you now, I doubt they would admit to sharing your bed. I doubt they'd even recognize you."

Kane's brows lowered over his silver eyes. "What are you talking about?"

"Look in the mirror and you'll know exactly what I'm talking about."

Kane's expression lightened and he arched a brow at his wife. "I'm not the only one who wouldn't be recognizable, madame. Have you taken your own appearance into consideration?"

Fortune raised a hand to her cheek and stared at her husband. "You don't mean—"

Kane nodded smugly.

Fortune scrambled from the bed and crossed to the mirror. The image that greeted her made her eyes widen. She looked as if someone had used her head to sweep out the fireplace. Her face was sooty and her hair was matted with ash and standing on end.

When Kane's deep, resonant laughter filled the room, Fortune spun about to face him, hands braced on her hips. "How could you have put me to bed in such a state?"

"Easy. After I took off your clothes, I just pulled back the covers and tucked you in," Kane answered simply.

"Kane Warrick," she said and stamped her bare foot against the polished flooring in exasperation. A moment later the impish look on his face caused a reluctant smile to tremble at the corners of her lips. "We ruined the bedding."

Kane glanced down at the gray sheet and nodded solemnly. "I think we have."

Fortune's laughter once more pealed through the room as she bounded back to the bed and made a dive for her husband. She landed on top of him and, with a mischievous grin curling her lips, began to wriggle her fingers into his ribs. Laughing, he pleaded for mercy but Fortune was relentless.

"Woman, you're going to regret it if you don't stop," Kane panted, unable to catch his breath before another bout of laughter seized him.

"How am I going to regret it?" Fortune asked, digging her fingers into his armpits.

"Like this," Kane said at last, grabbing her wrists and tossing her facedown on the bed. It was his turn to enjoy himself at her expense. Straddling her legs to keep them still, he held her foot and began to tickle her. Fortune squealed and tried to wiggle from beneath him. Her actions served to rouse other interesting means of making her pay for tormenting him. A cunning smile tugged at the corners of Kane's sensuous mouth as he bent and placed a kiss on the sole of her small foot.

Fortune stilled instantly, the kiss a subtle reminder of the night that Kane had found her in the tub. She felt his weight ease from her and she gasped with anticipation when his breath stirred the silken hair at the nape of her neck. A moment later his lips lightly brushed against the sensitive skin at the hollow of her shoulder. His hand glided down the curve of her spine and cupped her round bottom, caressing it with his long, tanned fingers.

"My Lady Fortune," he murmured as he began to trace the path his hands had made with his lips.

Fortune's skin seemed to burn where his mouth touched her. The sensations radiated out from the point of contact and settled achingly in the core of her being. She panted for breath and tried to turn on her back but Kane wouldn't let her. He gave her no reprieve from the heady torment of his lips. He moved down to her round bottom and then on to the downy thighs beneath. His lips traveled the length of one long, slender leg before moving up its mate. He nuzzled her soft flesh and she thought she would die from the rush of excitement that filled her.

"Love me, Kane," she murmured against the pillow and felt him lift her hips to join with his. She arched to him and he wrapped her in his arms, capturing her sensitive breasts in the palms of his hands and teasing the hardened peaks with his fingers.

Fortune threw back her head and savored the sweetness of his lips upon the side of her neck as they moved together. She reveled in the feel of him deep inside her.

Together they soared into paradise.

Lying cuddled together while their breathing and heartbeats returned to normal, Fortune smiled up at her husband. "You're a randy goat this morning, Kane Warrick."

"Where did you ever hear such language?" Kane asked, arching a curious brow at his wife.

Fortune turned on her back and gazed up at the ceiling as if seeing into her past. "From Tiny. Every few months he'd make an excuse to go down from the mountains to the settlement. He said he had a lot of randy business to take care of and for me not to worry."

Flabbergasted that a man would tell a young girl he was

going looking for sex, Kane said, "I can't believe your uncle would tell you any such thing."

Fortune chuckled and turned her head to look at her husband. "I didn't know what Tiny meant until you explained things to me on board the *Mermaid*. Then I began to put two and two together and realized Tiny had been a man and needed the comfort a woman could give him."

Fortune giggled again. "I thought Tiny was doing business with a man called Randy."

Kane laughed and shook his head in amazement at how innocent his wife had been before he'd taken her out of her blue mountains. She'd known nothing of the world yet she'd had the strength of character not to let that stand in her way. She'd bravely confronted all obstacles by sticking out her small chin and diving headfirst into the fray whether it dealt with her mills or with his own son.

"There's no reason to laugh at me. There was a man named Randy who came to the trading post once a year so I just took it for granted Tiny was seeing him when he left me," Fortune said defensively. She didn't like Kane making fun of her ignorance.

"I'm not laughing at what you believed. I think it's charming that you were so innocent."

"You do?"

Kane reached out and drew Fortune into his arms. "I wouldn't have it any other way."

"I'm glad," Fortune whispered, her throat constricting with joy. At that moment she didn't believe she could be happier. She had dreamed that someday Kane might begin to care for her, and now his words made her believe her dreams would soon become a reality. She snuggled close and pressed her cheek against his furred chest, content to remain in his arms forever.

Kane dropped a kiss on her smudged brow and chucked. "Madame, I think we had best order our baths unless you prefer looking like one of London's street urchins."

Reminded of her disarray, Fortune clambered up and out of the bed. She rang for her maid and, without allowing her into the chamber, ordered two baths prepared, one for herself and one in the adjoining room for Kane. Her husband gave her an offended look when the maid left to do her bidding.

"Modesty, madame? I would think we might share a bath together since we are husband and wife."

"We could if I didn't think it will probably take more than one bath apiece for us to get rid of our soot." Fortune made a moue of disgust as she held out her hands and looked at the dirty nails.

Kane laughed at her expression and then let his gaze slowly assess her ivory body. There were only a few smudges to mar her perfection. Their clothing had protected all but their faces and hands from the soot. He chuckled again at his wife's reaction to a little dirt. For a person who kept reminding him that she was far from an English lady, she was terribly upset about a little soot. "I'm sure one bath would have sufficed but as you insist, it's probably best I have mine in the adjoining room. If I bathed with you, we'd never get to the mill today."

Slipping on her silk robe, Fortune arched a brow at her husband. "Why do you want to go to the mill with me?"

Kane pulled on his grimy britches and buttoned them. Bare-chested, he shrugged. "I just thought we should see if we can find any clue to why the warehouse went up in flames last night."

"Someone said it was probably struck by lightning." Fortune turned back to the dressing table and lifted a matted strand of her hair. She wrinkled her nose in distaste.

"Perhaps it was but I'd like to make certain it wasn't intentionally set."

"Do you think the other mill owners would try to burn me out of business?" Fortune asked, looking at her husband's image in the mirror.

"After the little scene we had with them yesterday morning, I can't be certain they're *not* responsible. You've stirred things up with your decision to raise the workers' wages, and from this point you can expect anything to happen.''

''Surely my decision wouldn't push them to do something that terrible,'' Fortune said, unable to believe that something so minor would cause such bad feelings.

''Fortune, I tried to warn you. What you're determined to do is going against everything that has made them wealthy. They won't stand meekly by while you tear down everything they've built. They're going to try to stop you.''

''Do you still feel the same about my decisions?'' Fortune asked softly. After the previous night, she had to know where she stood with her husband.

Kane ran his hand through his tangled hair and shook his head. ''I don't disagree with your ideas, it's the way you've set about putting them to work that I object to, Fortune. It takes time to bring about change without upsetting the balance of things. You can't rush in headfirst and expect not to get a few bruises along the way.''

''But I didn't have time on my side. My mill was closed and wouldn't have been reopened if I hadn't taken the bull by the horns and raised the workers' wages.''

''You may have taken the bull by the horns and led him to slaughter. Men like Waring won't rest until they shut you down.''

''Then they'll get no rest,'' Fortune said with a new show of determination. She rose to her feet and faced her husband. ''That's exactly what Nevin hopes. He wants to put me in financial difficulties with the mills, so I'll fight Waring and the rest of them. And that includes my dear cousin who's sitting back and waiting until the other mill owners do his dirty work.''

A speculative light entered Kane's pewter-colored eyes as he rubbed a hand thoughtfully over his beard-stubbled chin. ''You could be right about Manville. After we visit the mill, I think I will pay a visit to Waring and see if I can find out who told him about your decision to pay your workers more.''

"You'd do that for me?" Fortune asked, feeling her heart swell with a new burst of love for Kane.

"I'm doing it for all of us, Fortune. If Manville succeeds in regaining the Northrop mills, then every mill owner in the area will suffer. Waring and the rest of them seem to have forgotten what the man has done in the past, but I haven't. Your plans are nothing compared to that little weasel's schemes. He'll have free rein since he doesn't have to work behind the scenes as he did when Lord Northrop was alive."

Kane's answer didn't fully satisfy Fortune. Her heart had wanted to hear a different reason, but she wouldn't complain. Her relationship with Kane had already come much farther than she would have imagined less than twenty-four hours ago. He'd been furious with her when he'd ridden away from the mill. But something had changed while they battled the fire. The rain had washed away their animosity and they had become allies and hopefully friends. And she prayed that the rest would come in time.

The servants bringing their bath water stopped further conversation between Kane and Fortune. He bid her adieu and brushed his lips against her brow before he followed the servants into the adjoining room.

When Kane came downstairs he found his wife sitting on the drawing-room floor, playing toy soldiers with his son. For a long moment he stood watching them. He listened with interest to their chatter and his heart ached at the years he'd lost enjoying the boy. He hadn't fully reconciled himself to everything that had happened in the past but he would no longer punish himself by staying away. Thanks to Fortune, he had seen his mistake.

"Now what do we have here?" Kane asked, strolling into the drawing room.

Price immediately came to his feet and moved closer to Fortune. He regarded his father through large, wary silver eyes.

Kane noted his son's reaction and drew in a deep, steadying breath to brace himself for Price's rebuff. After the years of neglect, he couldn't overcome his son's feelings toward him instantly. It would take time. He accepted that fact though it tore his insides apart to see the look on his son's face.

"Price and I have been playing soldier. Would you like to join us?" Fortune asked, smiling up at her husband.

"I would love to but we must ride to Northington if we intend to inspect the warehouse."

Fortune frowned. "You don't have time for just a short game?"

"I'm sorry, but I don't. However, I thought Price might like to go with us if you think the weather isn't too bad for a young man's outing."

Price stared up at his father, bewildered.

"Would you like to ride into Northington on your pony, son?" Kane asked, reaching out to ruffle Price's dark curls. The boy recoiled instantly, closing the space separating him from Fortune.

"Can I really go with you?" he asked, looking to her for affirmation.

"Of course you can. Your father just asked you, didn't he? And shouldn't you give him an answer?"

Price nodded and glanced once more at his father. His eyes glowed with excitement and a wobbly little smile trembled on his cherubic mouth. "I'd like that, Papa."

"Good. I'll have your mount saddled and I'll meet the two of you out front as soon as you have on your rain cloaks. From the look of the clouds, it could become a downpour anytime and I don't want either of you getting sick on me," Kane said, raising his hand to ruffle his son's hair again. He reconsidered the gesture in midair and let his hand fall back to his side. For now he wouldn't push. He turned and strode out of the house.

"Papa's really going to let me go with you," Price squealed. He grabbed Fortune's hand and danced a jubilant little jig on the carpet before her.

"Didn't I tell you your papa was a nice man?" Fortune said, unable to hide her pleasure with her husband.

Price nodded as he began to pull Fortune across the drawing room. "Oh, do let's hurry before he changes his mind."

"I don't think you have anything to worry about, Price. From what I know of your father, once he decides something his mind is not easily changed." Fortune silently reaffirmed her words with the thought of her own attempts to gain Kane's love.

A short time later the three rode side by side down the muddy road to Northington. Fortune glanced over Price's head at Kane riding silently beside his son's short-legged pony and for the first time she felt a sense of belonging. She was Kane's wife and Price's mother and the three of them had finally become a family.

Tearing her eyes away from the man who held her heart, she looked down at the small boy at her side. It hadn't been a simple thing to achieve. Kane's reluctance to admit his son was not to blame for his first wife's death had been nearly too great a barrier to overcome. However, he had finally managed to put the past behind him and was willing to be a father to Price.

Although Fortune hadn't gained her husband's love, Price had. She'd seen his feelings in the silver depths of Kane's eyes when he'd asked Price to join them. It was Kane's first tentative step to bridge the chasm the years of neglect had created. He loved his son and wanted his son to love him in return.

Fortune felt her throat constrict with happiness. Together they would be the family she'd always wanted and, hopefully, in the future she would be able to give Kane more children to share their life.

At the thought of having Kane's child, Fortune found herself yearning to feel his babe within her, to know that her love for Kane had created a new life. Unconsciously, she rested her hand on her abdomen and wondered if her wish hadn't already been conceived.

Kane noticed her gesture and the faraway look that had entered her slate-blue eyes. His breath stilled in his throat and his heart seemed to stop, as his fears once more rose from the depths of his subconscious. He yearned to have a child with Fortune but he wouldn't take the chance of losing her.

Fool, Kane silently berated himself. You've taken that risk since the first time you made love to her and each time thereafter. You sated yourself on her passion without a thought to the consequences.

Kane broke out in a cold sweat and he raised an unsteady hand to wipe his brow, glancing once more at his wife. He couldn't relax until he knew if she carried his child. Swallowing hard, his heart pounding uncomfortably against his ribs, Kane maneuvered his mount alongside his wife's. Leaning across the space that separated them, he took her hand. He gazed down into her beautiful face, his eyes searching for an answer to his unspoken question. Unable to find it, he swallowed again and cleared his throat before he managed to ask, "Fortune, are you pregnant?"

The shocked expression that flickered across Fortune's face gave Kane a sinking sensation in the pit of his belly.

"I'm afraid it's far too early to know that, Kane, but I don't think I am," Fortune finally answered. It had taken her a few moments to recover from the unexpected question. It was uncanny how both their thoughts had centered upon the same thing.

The relieved expression on Kane's face at her answer made Fortune's heart give a sudden lurch, and she quickly looked away to keep him from seeing the hurt he'd unwittingly caused her. She focused her attention straight ahead and fought to contain the tears that burned the backs of her lids. Without a word, she knew that Kane didn't want a child with her. He already had a child by the woman he loved, and he was satisfied.

Unaware of his wife's thoughts, Kane gave her hand an affectionate squeeze and maneuvered his mount back alongside his son's. Her answer had not eased his mind completely. If she hadn't become pregnant in the last few days then he had to make certain she would never conceive.

Kane frowned, wondering how he could accomplish that feat if he remained at North Meadows and continued to share his wife's bed. There was only one way he knew to assure she didn't conceive his child: abstinence. It was a staggering thought. How could he be close to Fortune and not make love to her? He knew it was an impossibility—he didn't have that much fortitude.

Glancing once more at the young woman who had suddenly become so important in his life, Kane came to a decision that tore at his heart. He would have to find an excuse to move back to Warhill. Hopefully the distance would ease the aching loneliness he'd already begun to feel. Kane's eyes rested briefly upon his wife's delicate features before he looked down at his son.

He'd only just started to mend the rift between Price and himself, but he knew he couldn't take his son back to Warhill. It was best for Price to remain with Fortune at North Meadows. Her love gave him a sense of security that he'd never known before in his life, and Kane couldn't take it away from his son, no matter how much he wanted the child with him.

Reaffirming his decision and setting his personal life aside, Kane reined his mount to a halt in front of the Northrop mill. He had no time to further ponder his relationship with his wife. The blackened hull of the warehouse would require all of his attention if he wanted to learn what had started the fire.

Kane dismounted and tethered his mount. He helped Fortune and Price dismount before turning to the burned-out warehouse. With wife and child at his side he strode around the perimeter of the charred structure. A thoughtful frown creased his brow as he tapped his riding crop absently against his thigh, his eyes sweeping over the entire area, seeking any answer to the fire's questionable beginnings.

"If yer alooking for the reason the warehouse went up

in flames, I'd suggest this might give ye a clue," Henry Reed said, stepping around the corner of a charred pile of rubble. "I found it in the bushes over there." He pointed in the direction from which he'd just come and held up a long piece of resinous wood that had been wrapped in rags. The scent of tallow still clung to the few fibers that had not completely burned into ash.

"I suspected as much," Kane said in disgust. He took the torch from Reed and turned to his wife. "Does this prove to you what you're up against here?"

Stubbornly Fortune shook her head. "It proves I'm right in what I've decided to do. If I was wrong, they wouldn't go to so much trouble to stop me."

Bemused at his wife's indomitable spirit, Kane shook his head. "Fortune, it could get much worse than this. We don't know the culprit responsible for the fire. And until he's caught your mill and even your life could be in danger."

"If you're trying to frighten me, then you've succeeded, but I still won't change my mind. As soon as we can get in a new shipment of cotton, my mill will be back in operation again."

Kane glanced at Henry Reed. "My wife seems to respect your opinion, Reed. Can't you explain to her that what she's attempting to do could harm her?"

"My lady, he's right, but if yer still set to go ahead with yer plans then we're behind ye."

"Damn it, Reed, I didn't ask you to encourage her."

Reed nodded. "I know that, sir. But as I see it, either way she'll lose. Her mills won't survive if she backs down."

"You're right, Mr. Reed," Fortune said. "And I don't intend to back down now or in the future. They can burn me out, but at least I'll know I tried to do what I felt was right." Fortune turned to look up at her husband. "Now that my mill is closed until a new shipment of cotton can arrive, I think I'll turn my attention to Northington. People there are living in squalor."

"Fortune, if you've forgotten, you have a family who needs your attention now," Kane said, glancing meaningfully at his son. If he could convince Fortune that Price needed her far more than the villagers, perhaps he'd be able to protect her from harm.

Fortune laid a protective arm about Price's shoulders and gave her husband a tender smile. "I know I have a family who needs my attention, and I can assure you they won't be neglected. However, I also have the people of Northington to consider. Grandfather wouldn't rest in his grave if he knew I continued to handle things the way Manville did."

His exasperation mounting, Kane looked down at his wife. "Madame, should I take this to mean you have more ungodly ideas you plan to set to work?"

"You may take it that way, sir," Fortune said, bestowing an impish smile upon her husband.

Kane rolled his eyes heavenward. Couldn't his wife ever just leave things alone? First the mill owners threaten to close her down and then the warehouse burns. Wasn't that alone enough to prove to her she wasn't invulnerable?

"Fortune, I'm asking you to reconsider. If you keep on, I fear I'll not be able to protect you at all times. At least if you stay at North Meadows, I'll know you're safe while I'm at the construction site."

"I'll take care of Mama for you, Papa," Price quickly volunteered, smiling up at his father for approval. "And I won't let anything happen to her, I promise."

"If she keeps being stubborn, I'm afraid it will take more than what we both can do to accomplish that, Price," Kane said, a frown of worry creasing his brow as he turned once more to Henry Reed.

"Mr. Reed, as my wife seems set to change the world, I'd like to hire you to help her. You know everyone in the village and can hear if there's any trouble brewing she should know about."

"Mr. Reed won't spy on the villagers for you, Kane,"

Fortune said, annoyed with her husband for insulting the man who had helped her reopen the mill.

"I don't mean for him to spy on the villagers. I just want him to keep his eyes and ears open so you won't be harmed. Is that too much for a husband to ask for his wife?"

Fortune blushed and lowered her eyes as a wave of pleasure washed over her. Kane did care for her just a little or he'd not be concerned about her welfare. "I'm sorry, Kane, I didn't understand what you meant."

"As has been the situation in the past and I suspect will be again in the future. I hope someday you'll begin to believe that I'm not your enemy," Kane snapped, his patience pushed beyond the limit. Her attitude vexed him more than he wanted to admit. After all that had transpired between them, Fortune was still able to immediately assume the worst of him. Without waiting for Reed's answer to his proposal, Kane turned and strode back to his mount.

"Papa is angry with us," Price ventured as he watched his father untie their mounts.

"No, Price. He's not angry with *us*—just me." Fortune glanced at the silent Henry Reed and flushed with embarrassment. Arguing with her husband in private was one thing, but in front of someone else was an entirely different situation. Although she knew Kane was right to worry about her welfare, she couldn't let whoever did this frighten her away. However, she would accept Henry Reed's protection as Kane had suggested. After clearing her throat, she said, "My husband is right, Mr. Reed, and I'd appreciate it if you'd accept the job he offered until we find out who burned the mill."

Reed nodded his understanding and gave her a slow smile. "My lady, I'll do me best not to let any harm come to ye or yers."

"That's all my husband wants, Mr. Reed," Fortune said, and turned as Kane returned to her side.

"It's time I get the two of you back to North Meadows. I need to go to the construction site and see if the rain has affected the diggings.'' Kane glanced up at the overcast sky, his brow furrowing with concern. "I hope it doesn't rain any more. After last night the river's already high, but if it rises much more, it could break through the dam between the excavation."

"Mr. Reed can see us back to North Meadows when I'm ready to go," Fortune said.

"You're ready to go now," Kane commanded.

Fortune shook her head. "I'm going to the village and see what I can do for my workers while the mill is closed."

From the stubborn tilt of her chin, Kane knew further argument was useless. The only way he'd be able to get her back to North Meadows before she wanted to go was to tie her up and drag her there. He was tempted to do just that, but he knew the consequences of such humiliation. She'd never forgive him.

"All right, damn it," Kane growled, his voice low with anger. "Since you won't listen to reason, you go to the village, but I'm taking Price back to North Meadows and get him out of this weather. Good day to you, madame."

Kane lifted his son and set him back in the saddle. He mounted and flashed Reed a warning look. "Keep your eyes open."

Reed nodded and raised two fingers to his brow. "Ye've my word on it."

Kane turned his horse and, with the pony's short legs working hard to keep alongside, he and Price rode back in the direction of North Meadows. He didn't like leaving Fortune to her own devices. He wanted her safe at North Meadows. But knowing that she had Reed to watch over her made him feel better. From the expression he'd seen on the man's face when he looked at Fortune, Kane knew his wife's kind heart had gained Reed's loyalty. The man would lay down his own life for her.

Reed's allegiance to Fortune would also serve to make his leaving easier. When he returned to Warhill, he'd know she was protected. Kane drew in a long, resigned breath and pressed his lips into a thin line against the pain that made his heart quiver. He didn't want to leave the only woman he had ever truly loved, yet he had no other choice. He wouldn't risk her life because he was too weak to control his own desires.

After hugging Price and telling him that he loved him, Kane left his son in the same drawing room where he'd found him playing with his toy soldiers earlier. He paused briefly in the foyer and looked up the winding staircase toward the bedchamber in which he'd finally found happiness. He said a silent farewell to the woman he loved better than his own life and quickly strode out of North Meadows before he could change his mind. He had made his decision and he'd abide with it, even if it tore him apart.

Kane drew his mount to a halt at the end of the drive and turned to glance back at North Meadows. Reason told him he was foolish to believe that what happened to Felicia could occur again if Fortune conceived his child. However, during the past years fear had grown within him into a large, ungovernable monster that he couldn't control with logical thoughts. His guilt over his first wife's death was the fodder that fed his fear and made it too strong for him to fight.

"I'm not deserting you, love," Kane mused aloud, his shoulders drooping. "I'm doing the only thing I can to protect you from me." Giving the stallion a sharp kick, he sent the animal racing away down the muddy road. He spurred it to a faster pace and prayed he could outrun the pain in his heart.

"I'll meet you in the village, Mr. Reed," Fortune said, mounting her mare. She drew the animal about but did not urge her forward. Instead she sat watching her husband and his son ride away. A sudden sense of loss assailed Fortune when Kane and Price disappeared around the bend in the road. She felt as if a door had abruptly been closed against her. She knew she was being ridiculous, but no matter how hard she tired to rid herself of the uneasy feeling, it kept nagging at her.

"You're just being foolish," she muttered, and turned her thoughts to the village. Ever since the fateful day when she'd first seen the deplorable conditions in which the villagers lived, she'd resolved to do something about it. Now that she didn't have to worry about the mill, she would begin to see things were improved.

Henry Reed awaited with a group of men and women. They greeted her warmly and introduced themselves in turn. First came Mat Simson and his brother Luke. She'd seen the two large, beefy-faced men on the day Manville had given her a tour of the mill. However, today their sullen, angry expressions were replaced by friendly smiles. Each gave her hand an exuberant shake before stepping back to allow their wives to introduce themselves.

Fortune looked at the two women, wondering at the contrast between husbands and wives. Lucy and May Simson looked more like the Simson brothers' children than their wives. Each woman came only to her husband's elbow, yet from the deference the large men gave them, Fortune correctly surmised who ruled the Simson roosts.

"It's a pleasure to meet you," Fortune said after another round of polite handshakes.

"The pleasure is ours, my lady," Luke Simson said as he draped a heavy arm about May's shoulders. "Henry here said you was a-needing our help."

Fortune glanced up at the tall red-haired Henry and arched a curious brow at him. His already-ruddy complexion deepened in hue from his blush, and he shifted uneasily under her direct stare.

"I thought you might need a few extra hands, my lady," he offered weakly.

"I most certainly do," Fortune said, smiling at Reed's surprised expression. She knew that he expected her to be furious with him for overstepping her authority.

"You do?" he said.

"Yes, I do. I think the first thing we should do is to

organize a work party to begin covering the drainage ditches. Mat and Luke should be capable of seeing to that.''

The two large men nodded their agreement.

''Tell the men they'll receive their regular wage for the work,'' Fortune added.

''We'll do it, my lady, but we still have the same problem as we had before when we wanted to cover the ditches. We don't have any lumber,'' Luke Simson said.

''That's easily solved,'' Fortune said. ''Cut some of the trees on Northrop land.''

Amazed at the young woman's generosity, the two men nodded eagerly. Covering the drainage ditches had been the desire of all the people in the village, but they had neither money nor the materials to do so. And Lord Northrop's nephew had refused to lay out a pence to help them; nor would he allow them cut the timber they needed from Northrop land.

''Then while you men supervise the work, May and Lucy will help me find a vacant building,'' Fortune said, turning her attention to the two women.

''A vacant building, my lady?'' Henry Reed asked, wondering what use she would have of another building when she already owned the mills.

''Yes, Mr. Reed. I intend to set up a school for the children.''

''My lady, the children all work. They ain't got time fer school,'' Luke Simson said.

''Not anymore. I will no longer allow children to work in my mills. From this moment on, the children of Northington will be children and not slaves. I'm raising the wages of my employees so their offspring should not have to work. Is that understood?'' Fortune could imagine what her husband would say about this idea, but a school for the children was one thing she was determined to have. She'd thought it over and knew it was the only way to truly help the people of Northington. They would always work in the mill, but they would not progress without an education.

She'd been fortunate to have William Bartram to teach her, but she could still remember how it felt when she couldn't read or write her own name. She didn't care if the other mill owners as well as her husband would condemn her for what she planned. Educating the children of her workers would be her legacy to the future of Northington, and her way of honoring the family name as the generations before her had done.

The Simsons glanced uneasily at Henry Reed. They understood the flaws in her plans but they didn't have enough nerve to tell Lady Northrop.

"An education is fine, my lady, but many of the children are the sole support of their families. If they can't work, then they'll starve," Reed said. He was pleased with Lady Northrop's plans, but like many of her kind she didn't truly realize how the villagers survived.

Henry Reed's remark made Fortune pause. She'd been so involved in her grand schemes that she'd not taken the whole situation into consideration. However, she would remedy that right now.

"You're right, I should have realized it myself before I made my final decision. Would it be better to let the children work only half a day and then go to school the other half?" Fortune asked. She was pleased to see the Simsons and Henry Reed smile and nod their agreement.

"Then that's the way it will be. Now, if we intend to get any work done today, I'd suggest we get about our business."

"Aye, my lady," the three men murmured in unison, doffing their hats before they turned to do her bidding. A short time later Henry Reed and the Simson brothers had organized a work party and were busy deciding the best method to cover the drainage ditches. At last Henry decided they would fill in the old ditches, then dig new ditches and cover them with heavy timbers and dirt. That way it would be impossible for the children to fall into them, and it would also help to end the stench from the open ditches that now filled the air.

It was a major project but no complaints were heard from the men who volunteered to help. Since Lord Northrop's granddaughter had taken over the mills, their lives seemed to have gotten better, their prospects for the future much brighter. The hopes and dreams they'd once possessed now began to take new roots all because of one young woman. And they'd not deny her anything she asked.

# Chapter 12

*The porcelain clock on the mantel chimed the tenth time* as Fortune let the lace curtain fall back into place and turned away from the window where she'd held her lonely vigil for the past three hours. A pensive frown knit her brow as she curled into the worn leather chair behind the mahogany desk and pulled her light shawl closer about her shoulders. She shivered and hugged her arms about her against the damp chill that the rainy weather had left in the large rooms of North Meadows. Her gaze swept over the rich oak paneling to the bookshelves that held the leather-bound volumes her grandfather had collected over the years. She'd read and enjoyed many of them since coming to North Meadows. And they had helped open up new worlds to her, as she hoped the new school would do for the children of Northington.

Fortune's gaze came to rest on the pile of books she had stacked on the floor that afternoon. She'd returned from Northington full of enthusiasm over how well her plans were already progressing. Although she hadn't been able to find a vacant building to start her school in, her dream had not died. The generosity of the local minister, the Reverend McTavis, had come to her aid. By three o'clock that afternoon, he'd heard, through the village gossip mill,

about her futile search and had offered her the use of the
church. To Fortune's delight, when he learned that she'd
not had a chance to consider who would be the headmaster
of the new school, he also volunteered to teach the children. She'd thought little beyond just getting a place for
the school, much less of teachers and books.

Fortune smiled at the memory of the minister's reaction
when she'd told him of her intentions to make improvements in the mill, as well as the village. For a long moment he'd stared at her in disbelief before he grabbed her
hand and kissed it. His exuberance had embarrassed them
both, and his face had turned beet red as he stuttered an
apology. He'd finally managed to compose himself by the
time he explained the reason behind his reaction.

Ever since coming to the area, the Reverend McTavis
had tried to get Manville to make similar improvements.
It didn't surprise Fortune to hear that her cousin had refused and even threatened to stop paying his tithes if the
good reverend didn't mind his own business. The reverend
had begrudgingly done as Manville ordered. The Northrop
tithes were what sustained Northington's small church and,
without them, he couldn't care for his flock. There would
be no hot bowls of soup to dole out on bitter cold days,
nor would there be warm clothing for those who barely
survived on the pittance they made by working in the mill.

The young reverend with his thinning hair and boyish
grin was a good man. He concerned himself with the most
vital needs of his flock even if he had to accept one evil
over another. He didn't give his approval but worked to
improve things without creating more problems. During
the past years he'd prayed daily for changes, and when he'd
heard Fortune's plans he felt God had finally seen fit to
answer his prayers.

Tense and straining to hear the clatter of hooves against
the courtyard cobbles, Fortune glanced once more toward
the windows. To her regret the night remained silent. Releasing a long slow breath, she sought to turn her mind

away from her own personal worries and back to the business of organizing her school.

After her meeting with the Reverend McTavis, she'd hurried back to North Meadows and had come directly to the study to sort through her grandfather's books. Now that she had a teacher and a place for her school, she was eager to see it begin. She'd chosen the simplest books from her grandfather's collection and prayed that they would be acceptable to the reverend until she could order more suitable material from Bristol.

Absently, Fortune wound a long dark strand of hair about one finger and bit her lower lip as her gaze shifted once more to the window. Her day would end as perfectly as it had begun if only her husband would return.

The clock chimed off the half hour.

Ten-thirty, Fortune mused, and felt a sinking sensation in the pit of her belly. She shifted uneasily in the chair and tucked her gown down over her feet. She'd thought nothing unusual about Kane's absence until the dinner hour had passed and he still hadn't returned. She'd eaten little of the delicious meal of Kane's favorite rare roast beef and had finally given up the attempt when the gravy had begun to congeal on the potatoes. She'd pushed back her plate and had come to the study to begin her vigil.

Now after three hours she was beginning to suspect that he wouldn't be coming back to North Meadows that night at all. Fortune's brow creased in a perplexed frown. She knew Kane had been annoyed with her at the mill, but she didn't think he would be so angry that he'd leave her.

Fortune came to her feet, her own vexation mounting at the thought. She'd be damned if she'd worry herself sick over the man.

"If he can't understand I'm doing what I think is right by the people I employ, then that is his problem," she muttered, striding from the room and up the stairs to her bedchamber. However, by the time she slammed the door behind her, her temper was already cooling and worry about her husband beset her once more. She crossed to the dressing table and stared at her reflection.

"What if something has happened to him?" she asked her image. "What if he's hurt and unable to get help?"

Before the words were completely out of her mouth, Fortune was walking toward the armoire. She threw open the cabinet door made of dark, gleaming cherry wood inlaid in an intricate flowery pattern, and drew out her sky-blue riding habit. In her current state of mind, she would have preferred the convenience of her buckskins; however, the maid had taken them away earlier to be cleaned of the soot and grime from the fire.

Releasing a disgusted breath at the amount of time that feminine apparel took to don, she reached to unfasten the tiny buttons down the front of her gown. Her hand froze on the first pearlized fastener as she heard the soft murmur of voices in the foyer below. She tossed the riding habit aside and hurried from the chamber and down the hallway to the top of the stairs. She had just opened her mouth to welcome Kane home when she saw him hand Vincent something and then turn and walk out into the night.

"Vincent?" she called down to the man closing the door behind her husband.

"Yes, my lady," the valet said, turning to look up at her.

"Was that my husband?" Fortune asked, already knowing the answer without the valet's confirmation.

"Yes, my lady. He thought you were asleep so he left this for me to give to you in the morning." Vincent held up a sealed envelope.

"I'll take it now," Fortune said quietly, sensing from her husband's furtive departure that she wasn't going to like what was written in the message. Her heart began to beat rapidly against her ribs as she descended the stairs. Her hand trembled as she took the missive from the valet and slowly retraced her steps. She didn't attempt to open the letter until she had her bedchamber door closed firmly behind her. She crossed to the writing desk and took the silver letter opener in hand. Then she drew in a deep, steadying breath for courage and slit the waxed seal.

> *My dear wife,*
>
> *As we are always coming to loggerheads over your decision to handle your own affairs, I've decided it is best that I reside at Warhill. As our prenuptial agreement stated, I will continue my lifestyle as before. However, I feel at the present time it is best not to disrupt my son's life again by returning him to his home. It is my dearest hope that in the future he will want to be with me at Warhill. But until that time, you will have my gratitude if you will see to his welfare.*
>
> *What I've chosen to do, I feel, is best for all parties involved. I will visit from time to time and hope you will have no hard feelings toward me for my decision. I, like you, have things that need my attention and I must concentrate on them at this time.*
>
> *Yours,*
> *Kane*

Fortune felt like tearing at her hair and gnashing her teeth but she did neither. She crumpled up the letter and tossed it into the fireplace. As she watched it turn to ash, she wished that she could rid herself of her feelings for Kane just as easily. But she sadly admitted it wasn't to be.

"Damn you, Kane Warrick," she cried, and threw herself facedown on the bed. She pounded the pillows and bed with her fists and feet to relieve her hurt, but venting her frustration did not improve matters. Kane's cold message had finally confirmed that Felicia's ghost had triumphed over her.

"No, damn you. I won't let you win. Kane cares for me—I know he does even if he won't admit it to himself," Fortune ground out as she sat up and brushed her hair out of her face. She raised her chin defiantly in the air and her slate-blue eyes glinted with renewed determination. "He is my husband now, Felicia, and I'm going to make him understand that tonight.''

Fortune pushed herself to her feet and with nimble fingers began to unfasten her gown. She stepped out of the pile of material and quickly dressed herself in the blue riding habit that had fallen to the floor at the foot of the bed. After jerking on the soft, blue leather gloves that matched the habit, she set her hat rakishly on her head and turned to the mirror.

Her chin thrust out and her shoulders squared, Fortune eyed her reflection with satisfaction. One of Tiny's old sayings flashed through her mind and she smiled at her image.

Yes, she was prepared for bear but her bear was not the furry animal her uncle had hunted. Hers was a six-foot-tall, raven-haired, silver-eyed devil who could make her forget everything with only a kiss. Unlike her uncle, she wasn't going armed with a musket but she would have weapons that Felicia's ghost didn't possess. She had life on her side. She was warm flesh and blood. Something Kane could touch and feel. She could give him love, and that was the one thing his memories could not do.

When the bay mare was saddled, Fortune took the shortcut across the field and through the woods instead of riding along the road through Northington to reach Warhill. On a night like this she preferred the shortest route.

The chilly, moisture-laden air had created a soft gray blanket of fog across the landscape. It swirled eerily about the mare's legs and wound misty tentacles around the trees and underbrush to create an unearthly atmosphere.

Fortune shivered and looked nervously about. She'd never been afraid of the ghosts and goblins her uncles used to tell her about. She never actually believed such things existed. They were only tales to enjoy around a warm winter's fire.

Fortune cast another wary glance behind her and admitted that a night like this could easily make her change her mind, especially after her earlier thoughts about Felicia's ghost. Contrary to her beliefs, her imagination was delving into the realm where only specters and the macabre reside, and it was making the hair at the nape of her neck stand on end.

"This is ridiculous," Fortune said aloud to reassure herself. Then she kicked the mare into a faster gait. Her imagination, however, was nearly too powerful for simple logic to overcome. By the time she glimpsed the first light streaming through the trees from Warhill, her heart felt as if it was in her throat, and the insides of her leather gloves were damp from her sweaty palms.

Fortune drew the mare to a halt at the edge of the manicured lawns and breathed deeply to steady her quaking nerves. She couldn't meet Kane trembling like a leaf. She had to be in control or she'd never succeed in what she set out to do: to seduce her husband. She intended for Kane to know by morning that he needed her as much as she needed him.

Stiffening her resolve, Fortune urged the mare down the circular drive to the cobbled courtyard. She dismounted and strode regally up the steps and knocked on the door. The door swung open immediately to reveal the sullen-faced Mrs. Ward.

"I've come to see my husband," Fortune said. She gave the woman no time to refuse her entry and stepped past her into the foyer. A moment later she handed the housekeeper her hat and gloves.

"If you'll be so good as to show me to my husband, I'll trouble you no more," Fortune said, watching with amusement as Mrs. Ward seemed to swell with indignation.

The housekeeper did not voice her objections to Fortune's behavior, but every inch of her thin body reflected her determination to show the younger woman how to behave like a real lady. She stiffened her back, gave Fortune her most haughty, stiff-lipped look, and said crisply, "Mr. Warrick is in his study, madame. If you'll follow me."

Mrs. Ward turned and led the way down the long

marble-tiled hallway to the wide double doors that opened into Kane's study. She rapped lightly against the solid wood and heard Kane bid her to enter.

"Sir, Lady Northrop—I mean, your wife is here to see you," Mrs. Ward said as she opened the door but made no move to allow Fortune to enter.

Kane looked up from the pile of papers on his desk to see his young wife flash his housekeeper an annoyed look as she sailed into the room without waiting for his invitation. With a small wave of his hand, he silently dismissed Mrs. Ward and came to his feet to face the woman who'd been in his thoughts all day. He felt an iron fist grip his heart as he gazed down into her lovely face.

At that moment, Kane wanted nothing more out of life than to take his wife into his arms and hold her. After the hell he'd gone through that afternoon trying to decide how he could protect Fortune from himself, he'd be well satisfied just to hold her and nothing more. However, he knew that if he relinquished even a small amount of his self-control, then he'd be lost. He knew he couldn't touch Fortune without making love to her so it was best to keep her at arm's length.

"Good evening, madame. I assume from your visit at this late hour that you've already read my missive. Am I correct?" Kane asked from behind his desk.

"Yes, I received your letter."

He arched a curious brow at Fortune. "And you just decided to drop by for a chat?"

Fortune smiled up at her husband. She wasn't going to let him bait her. If she let her temper have free rein then her plans were doomed. Gracefully settling herself in the leather wing-back chair in front of the large desk, Fortune asked innocently, "Do you object to my coming to visit you?"

Kane's nostrils flared as he drew in a deep breath and sat back down. He shuffled the papers before him and shook his head. "I have no objections, but isn't it somewhat late to go visiting? Especially on a night like this."

"If the mountain won't come to me, then I'll go to the mountain," Fortune murmured sweetly, relaxing back into the chair with her hands folded in her lap.

"I thought I explained everything to you in my letter. Is there something you didn't understand about our situation?"

"I understood everything you said but I still wanted to talk with you. I had such an exciting day."

Kane frowned. "You did, did you? That's nice. Now if you'll excuse me, I have work to finish tonight."

"You mean you don't want to hear about Northington's new school?" Fortune said, and hid her grin at the look of surprise that flickered over Kane's face.

"School?"

Fortune nodded smugly.

"I'm not surprised."

"You're not?" Fortune asked, slightly puzzled by Kane's calm reaction.

"No, Fortune. Nothing you do surprises me any more. As for the school, I congratulate you for having the courage to do something the rest of us have been too cowardly to even attempt."

Dumbfounded, Fortune shook her head as if to clear it. She couldn't believe what she was hearing from Kane. She'd expected his anger but not this calm acceptance. He'd even congratulated her.

"I don't understand," Fortune said at last. "You mean you approve of what I've done?"

It was Kane's turn to smile. He leaned back in his chair and folded his arms over his chest. "It's very simple, Fortune. I respect your determination to improve things even if I don't care for the way you go about it."

"What's wrong with the way I do things?" Fortune snapped before she realized her tone and mellowed it. "I'm just trying to do what I feel is right." She had promised herself she wouldn't lose her temper and was resolved to keep that promise even if it choked her. There was too much at stake here.

Kane nodded his understanding. "As we all do. Hopefully once I have my mills renovated with steam, I'll also have the means to correct some of the same problems you've started working on."

Fortune sat bemused by her husband's answer. Love welled in her heart until she thought it would burst. Kane planned to follow her lead to improve things for his workers. Deep down she'd always know that her husband didn't condone the terrible conditions that inevitably resulted when men like Nevin Manville had complete control over people's lives. Her cousin used them like animals to make himself rich.

Yes, Fortune pondered silently. Her heart had known the truth all along, and she should have realized it wouldn't have let her fall in love with a selfish man. Buoyed by this knowledge, yet still puzzled about what was coming between them, she asked, "If you feel that way then why didn't you come back to North Meadows tonight?"

Kane shifted uneasily. "I explained my feelings in the letter, Fortune. It's best for all concerned that we keep things as they are at this moment."

Momentarily rebuffed, Fortune felt like surrendering the battle to Felicia's ghost. Kane didn't want her at Warhill or anyplace else in his life. Their marriage, no matter how many intimate interludes they'd shared, was nothing but a business arrangement. No, damn it. It's far more than that to me, Fortune fumed silently. He might think he can easily get rid of me, but I'm not going to let him get away with it. Fortune's expression reflected her resolve. She sat up and squared her shoulders.

Until she knew for certain he didn't care for her, she would not surrender one inch of ground to Felicia's memory. She'd remain at Warhill for as long as it took to wage this one last giant battle to make her marriage into something more than a business arrangement.

"I see no problem with that, Kane," she said, her soft tone reflecting none of her tumultuous feelings. "Now, if you'll be so kind as to show me to my room, I'd like to go to bed. It is getting late.''

"You mean you intend to spend the night here?" Kane asked, and swallowed hard. The reason he'd come back to Warhill was to put temptation out of his way, and now that very same temptation had followed him home. He released a long, agonized breath.

"It was my intention since the weather is so horrid." Fortune paused for effect. "But if you want me to leave, I'll return to North Meadows."

Kane felt his stomach plummet as he glanced out into the dark fog-shrouded night. Fortune was his wife, and he couldn't ask her to return to North Meadows at this late hour and in such weather. It was best she stay at Warhill, he reasoned.

Steeling himself against the thought of her sleeping so near, he shook his head. "No. That is out of the question. I'll have Mrs. Ward to show you to your room."

"Thank you, Kane. I honestly didn't like the thought of going back to North Meadows through all the fog. It's scary."

"Then I'll bid you good night, madame. I still have work to do before I can retire," Kane said. He was so caught up with his own emotions that he failed to realize Fortune might have an ulterior reason for her sudden visit. There were few things in life he'd seen daunt his young wife's courage, especially a foggy night. However, Kane didn't notice anything amiss. He was too busy praying that his plans to brace up the earthen dam between the river and the canal would keep him up all night.

"Good night, Kane," Fortune said softly. She came to her feet and moved around the desk to Kane's chair. She bent and brushed her lips against his beard-stubbled jaw before he could escape. "Sleep well, husband."

When Fortune followed Mrs. Ward from the study, Kane glanced down at his tightly balled fists. Beneath his swarthy skin his knuckles gleamed white from the pressure of his grip. It had taken every ounce of willpower he possessed to keep from reaching out to Fortune when she'd bent and kissed him. Every nerve in his body crackled with the need to race up the stairs and throw his wife on the bed and make wild, passionate love to her until she went limp from rapture.

Kane leaned forward, braced his elbows on the desk, and buried his face in his hands. He slowly shook his head. Tonight would be the longest night he'd ever spent in his life.

Ensconced in the middle of the large canopy bed, Fortune sat with one elbow propped against her raised knees and chin resting in the palm of her hand. A mulish expression marred the soft lines of her face and her full lower lip jutted out in a pout. She glanced at the delicate china clock on the nightstand and frowned. It was now three o'clock in the morning and she'd not heard Kane come upstairs. She'd gotten her wish to stay at Warhill but it had done her little good. If Kane didn't leave his work long enough to go to bed, her plans would be ruined.

Thoughtfully Fortune tapped her fingers against the silken sheet. She'd been confident that the closeness she and Kane had shared in the past week would soon bring him to her room.

"As I told Kane earlier, if the mountain doesn't come to me, then I'll go to the mountain," Fortune grumbled. She threw back the sheet and slid her bare feet to the floor. She slipped on the satin robe that Mrs. Ward had given her to wear over the sheer silk night rail. Fortune had not questioned the housekeeper about whom the garments belonged to. She didn't want to know, especially on the night when she wanted nothing to come between herself and her husband. She had arrived at Warhill to drive away a ghost, not to give it more power.

Tying the sash loosely about her trim waist, Fortune gave her reflection a quick perusal in the dressing-table mirror, pinched her cheeks to bring color into them, and then turned and marched determinedly out the door.

Treading on bare feet, she silently made her way down the stairs to Kane's study. The lamp still burned but her husband no longer worked at his desk. The room was empty. Fortune's shoulders sagged as she released a resigned breath and felt defeat well within her. Tonight she'd given up her pride to battle for the man she loved. She'd been willing to plead with her husband to make him realize they could have a wonderful life together if he'd only let go of his past. However, she now knew that Kane also had to be willing to make their marriage work. She couldn't do it alone. She had given everything and there was nothing left.

Fortune felt tears sting the backs of her eyelids as she reconciled herself to face a life without Kane's love. Turning, she stepped out into the shadowy hallway to retrace her steps to her lonely bed. A flicker of light drew her attention and she moved toward it with the hope of finding her husband. A moment later she regretted her choice.

Kane stood in the soft glow of a candelabra that sat on a table beneath the painting of a young woman gowned in pink satin. Her blond curls lay in ringlets about her lovely face. A red cherubic mouth smiled sweetly but the wide brown eyes held no warmth in their thick-lashed depths.

Fortune felt a shiver race up her spine. She had now seen the likeness of her nemesis, Felicia. Yet it wasn't the woman's beauty that made her heart feel as if it had suddenly turned to ice. It was the haunted expression on her husband's face as he sipped a glass of wine and thoughtfully gazed up at the portrait.

Unable to look at him a moment longer, Fortune started to turn away until she heard Kane speak to the woman in the painting. Her heart stilled and she pressed herself deeper into the shadows to keep her presence hidden from husband. She knew it wasn't right to eavesdrop, even if he was only talking to a portrait, but something in Fortune wouldn't let her turn away and leave him in private.

''Felicia, why did all of this have to happen?'' Kane

mused aloud, his gaze never leaving the dark, cold depths of the eyes of the woman he'd married over ten years ago. Ten years was not a long time but to Kane the past decade seemed like an eternity. Many things had happened since the fateful day when he'd been a happy bridegroom. So much misery had come to pass because he'd thought he was in love with the aloof beauty who'd challenged his masculine pride to possess what no other man had been able to capture. He'd been a fool and he'd regret it for the rest of his life.

"All I wanted was a family yet you wouldn't give me even that satisfaction." Kane shook his head sadly and his fingers tightened about the glass in his hand. "You refused me your love and I've paid dearly for my crime of needing you, of wanting a child. I can't even look at our son without feeling the guilt eat at my soul because I forced him upon you."

Kane raised his glass as if to toast his first wife. "You should be satisfied. You succeeded in making my life as much a hell after your death as before it."

Bemused by what she'd overheard, Fortune stealthily made her way back down the hall and sped up the stairs. She closed the bedroom door softly behind her. At that moment she didn't want Kane to know she'd overheard his conversation with his dead wife. She had learned much about her husband in the last few minutes. Through his agonized speech she realized that she had been battling Kane's own guilt, not Felicia's ghost.

Fortune hugged herself and danced across the floor to the dressing table. She smiled triumphantly. "He doesn't love Felicia." Her moment of rapture suddenly faded with her smile as she sank down on the padded stool and gazed at her reflection in the mirror. Tension again marred her lovely features with a frown as she worried aloud, "But it doesn't mean he loves you, either."

Fortune leaned her elbows on the dressing table and pressed her face into her hands. So many answers now fell into place. Kane hadn't loved his first wife, nor did he love his second. He'd gained a son from Felicia and a canal from her. She'd come to Warhill to find out where she stood in Kane's life and now that she knew, she regretted her impulse. At least with Felicia between them, she had hope. Now there was none.

Disheartened, Fortune pushed herself to her feet and crossed to the large bed. She lay down and pulled the comforter over her body to ward off the chill inside her soul. When dawn lightened the eastern sky, Warhill and its owner, Kane Warrick, would see the last of her.

Kane rubbed at his eyes with the balls of his hands and rolled his head from side to side to ease the stinging ache that burned the muscles along his shoulders and down his back. The clock had just struck six A.M. and he had successfully managed to work all night.

Kane drew in a long breath and blew out the lamp. The dusky gray light of dawn spilled into the study as he settled back in the chair and braced his booted feet on the desk. He'd taken only one break in the long hours since his wife had gone up to bed. Kane frowned at the thought. Seemingly against his will he'd been drawn to the portrait gallery where generations of Warrick images had been preserved in oil and hung in gilt frames. But it had not been his ancestors he'd wanted to see. His first wife's portrait had brought him there in the middle of the night.

Fool that he was, he'd talked to Felicia as if she could understand him. He had first railed at her and then later had found himself begging for her forgiveness, something he'd never done before. Surprisingly, he'd felt much better when he'd returned to his office to work. He had purged himself and, by laying open his heart, had managed to become free of the guilt that had kept him a prisoner for so long.

Kane clasped his hands behind his neck and leaned his head back against the soft leather of the chair. He closed his eyes, anticipating Fortune's reaction to his most recent decision—one he'd made during the long hours since his visit to the portrait galley. He knew things couldn't continue as they had in the last week, but during the night he had also realized he couldn't live without Fortune. Their lives couldn't remain in a perpetual state of turmoil; they had to come to an understanding where they could live together peacefully. They had a responsibility to Price. He deserved a mother and father, not two adversaries who were constantly at each other's throat because they couldn't resolve their own problems.

Kane nodded, firming his decision in his mind. The only way they could live peacefully was for him to be honest with Fortune about his feelings and the reason he could no longer share her bed. He couldn't go on any longer with all his emotions pent up inside him. He felt like a keg of black powder just waiting for someone to light his fuse so he could explode.

Kane admitted it wasn't going to be easy to be near Fortune and not touch her, yet it was better than the alternative of losing her completely should she conceive his child. He prayed for her understanding and hoped his love would be enough to make up for the intimacy his decision was ending between them.

Running a hand through his tousled hair, Kane swung his feet to the floor and stood. He resolutely straightened his wrinkled shirt, tucking it back into the waist of his nankin britches, and then strode from the study and up the stairs.

Without knocking, Kane quietly opened the door to Fortune's bedchamber and crossed to the canopy bed where his wife lay sleeping, curled into a small ball in the middle of the down mattress. With one hand cupping her cheek and her dark hair spread across the ruffled silk-cased pillow, she looked like an angel.

Kane devoured her innocent beauty with his gaze and, against all of his resolutions, felt himself swell with desire.

His expression reflected his agony as he squeezed his eyes closed in an effort to regain control over his own wayward body. It would have been difficult to resist Fortune even if he didn't love her but, because his heart was involved, it was nearly impossible.

Drawing in a deep breath, he looked down at his wife once more and groaned inwardly at the rush of emotions she inspired within him. His fingers ached to feel her soft skin and he craved to taste the luscious lips that were parted slightly as she breathed.

"Damn," he muttered, disgusted with himself. He'd come here to talk with Fortune, not make love to her. Kane turned away, fully knowing he'd not be able to control his emotions if he remained in such close proximity to the woman he loved.

"What is it, Kane? Is something wrong?" Fortune asked drowsily. Roused from her restless slumber by Kane's curse, she blinked up at him and rubbed at her eyes like a small child.

"There's nothing wrong, Fortune," Kane said, steeling himself to face his wife once more. He swallowed hard as he turned back to her and watched her simple gestures. He could feel his own pulse beat in the veins that corded his muscular neck.

Still too sleepy to recall her resolve of only a few hours earlier, Fortune raised her arms to Kane. "Come to bed, husband. It's chilly."

"I don't think that's the best idea right now, Fortune." Kane's vows were growing weaker by the moment.

Fortune curled on her side and pulled the covers up over her shoulders to ward off the cool morning air. She snuggled deep into the down mattress and gazed up at her husband through half-closed lids. "I'm cold, Kane. Come to bed and warm me up," she murmured softly.

Kane rolled his eyes heavenward and clenched his fists at his sides. It was taking all of his self-control not to do exactly as his wife bade him. He shook his head resolutely.

"No, Fortune. I'm not coming to bed. I've come to talk to you."

Fortune squinted at the gray light streaming in through the window. "At this time of morning?"

"Yes, at this time of morning." Kane picked up the robe and tossed it onto the bed. "Now if you'll get dressed, I'll ring for an early breakfast and then we can talk."

"I'm not hungry," Fortune grumbled. She frowned as she sat up and pulled the robe about her shoulders. "In fact, I'm not feeling well at all." She grimace and rubbed her stomach. She had eaten little the previous night and now her lack of food was making her queasy.

"I thought you said you weren't pregnant," Kane said, his tone sharp.

"I don't think I am but I can't be certain for a few weeks yet," Fortune said, Kane's accusatory tone rousing her completely from her lethargic state.

"Are you sure?" Kane asked anxiously as he sat down on the side of the bed and took her hand into his own.

"Kane, I know you don't want to have a child by me, so you don't have to worry. If I should be pregnant, you won't have to claim it. I won't ask anything of you."

"Blast it, Fortune. Whatever gave you the idea I wouldn't want to have a child with you in the first place?" Kane asked.

"You did," Fortune answered simply.

Kane stared at his wife for a long thoughtful moment and then slowly gave a sad shake of his head. "I'm sorry if I gave you that impression, love."

"Then you do want us to have children?" Fortune asked, her spirits soaring from the endearment he'd used.

Kane shook his head again. "Fortune, I would love to have children with you but I'm afraid it's the one thing that can never be."

Bewildered by her husband's answer, Fortune asked, "Why, Kane?"

"Because I won't risk losing you."

"You'll not lose me," Fortune said, misunderstanding his meaning. She leaned toward her husband, draped her arms about his neck, and smiled up at him. "A child could never come between us. It would only bring us closer."

Using a firm hand, Kane pulled Fortune's arms from about his neck and shifted to a safe distance away from her. "Fortune, it's what I had come to tell you. We can't be intimate any more."

"What do you mean?" Fortune asked, gaping at her husband as if he'd suddenly lost his mind.

"I mean exactly what I said. I won't risk you conceiving my child."

"I don't understand," Fortune said, even more bewildered than before. Kane said he wanted children with her but he wouldn't make love to her because she might conceive them.

"Damn it, Fortune. It's not easy for me to tell you. I love you so much that I'm afraid I'll lose you if you have my child."

"You love me?" Fortune whispered, stunned. She blinked up at Kane for a long disbelieving moment before she squealed her delight and threw herself into his arms. She rained kisses wildly over his face, neck, and shoulders before she captured his beard-stubbled cheeks between her hands and took his lips in a kiss that spoke more clearly than any words could.

Against all of his resolves, Kane's arms came about Fortune seemingly of their own volition and drew her against him. Unbalanced, they fell back onto the rumpled bed. His hands slid up over her rib cage to caress her breasts through the thin silk of the night rail as he devoured the sweetness of her mouth. His need to taste more of her drove him away from her lips and down the slender column of her throat to the fluttering pulse at its base. Then he slipped the narrow strap of satin from her shoulder and moved to the exposed ivory mounds peaked with rose. He captured the delicately colored nipple with his mouth, flicking the aroused bud with the tip of his tongue before suckling greedily.

His touch made Fortune's blood instantly catch fire. She arched to his mouth, hugging him close, as she ran her fingers through his dark hair and down over his wide shoulders. She savored the feel of his mouth upon her and his resilient flesh beneath her fingertips.

"I love you, Kane," she murmured against his dark hair, and thrilled at the ripple of excitement she felt pass over him at her words. In that moment she knew the true glory of being a woman, of loving and being loved. Each time Kane had made love to her in the past, he had managed to arouse her to rapture, but the heightened sensations now coursing through her body were beyond compare. They had been created by only one simple word: love.

"God, how I love you," Kane moaned against her as he glided his hands down along the soft swell of her hips and drew the night rail away from the bounties of her luscious body. He tossed the offending garment onto the floor at the foot of the bed as he lowered his head to the valley between her breasts. His hot lips laid a fiery trail along her belly to the dark apex between her thighs. He nuzzled against the silken glen, beckoning her to open to him.

Fortune heeded his call, arching to the heady caress of his lips and tongue and giving all of herself to him. She felt the power of her release building deep in the pit of her being. Like a volcano, it boiled and surged until it erupted with such force that she gripped the sheets, threw back her head, and cried out Kane's name.

Her muscles quivered from her release, and she lay panting for breath when Kane covered her with his lean body and recaptured her mouth. She wound her arms about his neck and tasted herself upon his lips as she wrapped her legs about his waist and took him deep within her. Her passion rekindled and heightened, she met him on equal ground, hip to hip, mouth to mouth. They moved as one, glorying in the golden brilliance of the love they shared. Riding through the heavens on Pegasus to worship together once more at Venus's altar.

"My love," Fortune whispered when her heartbeat returned to normal. She could barely speak over the lump of joyful emotions that had formed in her throat from the exquisite rapture she'd received in her husband's arms. Gently she brushed the damp strands of hair back from his brow. "You have made me the happiest woman on earth."

"Don't say that," Kane replied huskily as he pushed himself away from Fortune and sat up on the side of the bed. "I promised myself this would never happen again and look what I've done."

Hearing the agony in Kane's voice, Fortune instinctively reached out to comfort the man she loved. She placed a gentle hand against the bare back turned to her and said, "I don't understand. We are man and wife. There's nothing wrong with us making love."

The silver depths of Kane's expressive eyes reflected his despair as he turned to look at his wife. He raised a gentle hand to caress her love-flushed cheek. "I know you don't understand. It's what I was trying to explain to you before my own weakness overcame my better judgment."

"Then tell me now," Fortune said softly, turning her face into his warm palm and pressing a kiss upon it.

"I love you, Fortune, don't ever think otherwise, but I won't allow myself to make love to you again." Kane paused and drew in a long breath. "It's too risky. I lost one wife to childbirth and I won't lose you to the same fate. You're far too important to me."

"That's what you've been afraid of?" Fortune asked, suddenly realizing the true depth of Kane's love for her. He was willing to sacrifice his own needs to ensure nothing happened to her. She could ask for no greater proof of his love.

"I don't want to lose you," Kane said again.

"My darling, you don't have anything to worry about. The only way you're going to get rid of me after today is to shoot me," Fortune murmured, and wrapped her arms about his lean waist. She pressed her cheek to his furry chest and listened to the steady beat of his strong heart.

Kane drew Fortune's arms from about his waist and set her at arm's length. "Fortune, I'm serious about this. I've made my decision. I won't sleep with you again. If you feel you can't live with me under those conditions, I'll understand."

"Kane, you can't really mean what you're saying? We love each other."

"I mean every word, Fortune. Felicia died because of the child I gave her."

"And you've allowed your guilt to shadow your life with your child, but I won't allow it to ruin our marriage," Fortune snapped.

"Don't you understand? I'm doing this to protect you."

"Protect me by giving me your love, Kane, not by letting Felicia's ghost ruin what happiness we could have together."

Kane retrieved his britches from the floor and jerked them on. He looked down at Fortune as he stood and buttoned them. "You're not making this easy for me."

"I'm doing my best not to," Fortune answered crisply.

"Damn it, Fortune. I love you and want you more than any woman I've ever met. But I can't allow you to tempt me into jeopardizing your life."

Naked, Fortune scrambled off the bed and stood with hands braced on her narrow hips. She stiffened her back and thrust her chin out at a pugnacious angle. "Then I won't live with you. I won't let Felicia ruin my life, as well as yours. I want children of my own and a husband to hold and love me when I need tenderness. I don't want a man who is so afraid of the past that he can't see it for what it is, the past.''

"For God's sake, Fortune, be reasonable. I'm only thinking of you,'' Kane said, running a hand through his hair in exasperation. He had to make her understand before he lost the only woman he had ever truly loved.

"You're the one who is being irrational, Kane Warrick. Had your father felt the same way, you'd not be standing here now. Felicia's death was tragic but it doesn't mean the same thing will happen if I conceive," Fortune said, stubbornly refusing to allow some misbegotten belief to destroy their lives. She would fight to her last breath to save her marriage and the man she loved.

At the haggard expression in Kane's eyes Fortune's heart melted. She tempered her own stance as she closed the space separating them and placed her hand against Kane's cheek. "I love you, Kane. Please let me be a wife to you in every way, not just your companion."

Kane's arms came about her and he drew her unresisting body against his. A pained expression crossed his face when he squeezed his eyes closed and laid his head against her dark hair. If he looked into her beautiful slate-blue eyes and saw her love shining brightly in their depths, he wouldn't have the strength to deny Fortune's plea. His next words nearly choked him. "I wish to God that I could.''

Fortune felt a chill ripple down her spine as she lay her cheek against her husband's shoulder and released a sad breath. Tears of defeat stung the backs of her lids and she said, "Then you leave me no choice, Kane. I won't live with you and not be able to have all of your love. It would kill me.''

"I understand," Kane murmured hoarsely, and let his hands fall to his sides. He turned and strode from the room without looking back. If he saw the hurt expression he knew to be on Fortune's face, he wouldn't be able to walk away from her as he intended.

The door closed firmly behind Kane and the click of the latch sounded ominously through the room, yet Fortune

stood waiting. She just couldn't believe Kane really meant
to carry out his absurd scheme to protect her.

Her husband wasn't an irrational man, she reasoned. It
wouldn't take him long to realize how unreasonable his
fears were. For that reason she expected to hear his knock
upon the door at any moment. He'd come back to her full
of apologies for making a fool out of himself. Then they
would celebrate their new feelings by making love.

The thought momentarily buoyed Fortune's flagging
spirits. But as the long slow minutes ticked by and there
was no knock upon the door, she found herself unable to
keep up the hopeful pretense.

''I can't allow this to happen,'' Fortune murmured before her tears choked off further speech. She collapsed
onto the bed and gave in to the great racking sobs that
shook her entire body. She wept out frustration and fear.
She'd managed to gain her heart's desire by winning Kane's
love, yet she was afraid she'd never truly be able to claim
it unless he relented.

With tension spent and nothing left except shuddering
sniffles, Fortune sat up and brushed the tousled hair from
her face. She wiped at her red, tear-swollen eyes with the
edge of the sheet as she considered her options. As her
threats to leave Kane hadn't changed his mind, she would
use other methods to alter his decision to keep her at arm's
length.

A sly smile tugged up the corners of Fortune's lips and
a devilish twinkle entered the slate-blue depths of her eyes.
If she couldn't persuade her husband with reason, she'd
use the only weapon left to her: Kane's passion. This
morning had proved that even when he staunchly declared
he wouldn't take her to his bed again, her kisses had the
power to weaken his resolve as easily as his had shattered
hers in the past. The love they shared for each other was
too strong for either of them to deny or resist. It simmered
within them just waiting for a kiss or a caress to explode
it into a fervent passion appeased only by their lovemaking.

"Kane, I will fight you and all the devils in hell to hold on to what I've found," Fortune muttered and stood. The glint of determination in her eyes and the stubborn jut of her chin reflected her intentions as she dressed. Fortune McQueen Northrop Warrick was ready to go into battle once more for the man she loved.

# Chapter 13

*The foggy morning did little to improve Manville's black* mood. He felt like tearing out his hair in frustration when he thought of his cousin. With a swipe of his hand he vented his feelings on the unsuspecting tabby that napped on the windowsill. With a quick twist the cat landed on its fat paws and glared up at Manville, before raising its tail in the air and marching regally out of the room in search of a warm bowl of milk in the kitchen.

"Damn you and her both to hell, you feline devil," Manville growled at the retreating animal. "The bitch is just like a cat. No matter what happens she seems to always land on her feet."

Manville's dark gaze shifted back to the man sitting silent and still in front of his desk. "But she's not going to keep getting away with it. And I'm personally going to be the one to make sure that she doesn't."

"Sir," Wilson said, his voice quivering from nerves as he looked at his ranting employer. "Are you sure you want to go through with this?"

Manville crossed back to the desk and settled his thin frame into the uncomfortable chair he'd had to use since leaving North Meadows. Everything that was rightfully his had been forfeited to his cousin, including his favorite chair. But he was going to rectify the situation soon. He had reached the limit of his patience with Fortune Warrick. His beautiful cousin had failed to heed the warnings he'd sent her by closing the mill and burning the warehouse and, like his uncle, she would now have to pay the price for usurping him.

"I'm positive," Manville said, his face set with resolution, a mad light glowing in his eyes. "And I expect you to do your part to keep any suspicion from falling on me when the deed is done. No one should ever know I had anything to do with Fortune's demise or the death of that bastard she's married to."

Wilson shifted uneasily in his chair. He'd begun to wonder about his employer's sanity of late. In the past he'd always done as the man had told him in order for his family to survive. He hadn't liked the fact that his neighbors loathed him because of his association with Nevin Manville. Nor had he enjoyed being the man's lackey through the years. He still possessed some pride even if he wasn't brave enough to show it outside the walls of his own home. He'd done what he had to do to keep his children fed, and that was the only reason he'd stayed in Manville's service. Until now, Wilson mused silently as he watched Manville pick up the quill pen and dip it into the inkwell in front of him. Things were beginning to get out of hand. He had not bargained on risking life and limb to carry out Manville's orders. The villagers were up in arms about the warehouse fire and if they knew that he'd set it, the least they'd do would be to tar and feather him.

I had also not bargained on murder, Wilson mused and fidgeted again in his seat from the thought. His movements made the chair squeak.

"What's gotten into you of late? Can't you sit still?" Manville asked, looking up from the letter he'd been writing.

Wilson swallowed and nodded.

"Then do it, blast you. I've things on my mind and I don't need to be disturbed."

Damn the bastard, Wilson fumed silently. His face flushed a dull red as he lowered his gaze to the floor and muttered beneath his breath, "One day I'm going to make you regret treating me like a toady."

"What did you say?" Manville asked, turning his attention back to the letter before him. He folded and sealed it without signing his name.

"Nothing, sir."

"As you've nothing to say, I suggest you take this to North Meadows and see my dear cousin receives it immediately. I think she will be highly interested in what it has to say." Manville chuckled, imagining the look on Fortune's face when she came to the mill. She was in for the surprise of her short life. He rubbed his hands together in satisfaction. "Just think, Wilson, after today everything will again belong to me."

Wilson felt his blood run cold at the look in Manville's eyes. He picked up the letter. He had already been told what was written inside. It was meant to lure Lady Warrick into the deadly trap that Manville had set. And he knew she would have no chance to come out of it alive.

Wilson swallowed the lump of dread clogging his throat. He'd done many things for Manville but he'd never killed and he didn't intend to start today, no matter what the man said or did. He had a hard enough time facing his family each night without adding more guilt to his conscience by killing a young woman who'd never harmed him or anyone else he knew.

"Why are you hesitating, Wilson? Is there something on your mind?"

"I don't like this, Mr. Manville. I've done a lot of things I'm not proud of but I won't commit murder."

"You bloody idiot. I don't pay you to decide what you will do. I pay you to do what I say."

"I said I won't do murder for you," Wilson said, somehow finding enough courage amid his morass of quaking flesh to disobey Manville. He laid the letter back on the desk and set his hat firmly on his head. Without another word he turned and walked from the room. Once outside, he drew in a deep breath as if to cleanse himself of the foul lifestyle he'd been leading for so many years. Then he smiled. He was free of Nevin Manville at last. Feeling a need for a dram of ale to wet his throat and steady his nerves, Wilson strode toward the village.

Dumbfounded by Wilson's defection, Manville stood gazing toward the door, unable to believe what had just transpired. His shock was only a momentary thing, however, and soon rage took control of him. He narrowed his eyes and screwed up his face in a scowl as he contemplated the things he would do to his faithless hireling. Wilson would pay for running out on him just when he needed the man most.

"After I take care of the little matter with my cousin and Warrick, then you'll regret ever dredging up the nerve to go against me," Manville mused aloud. He'd see Wilson's entire family suffer. And he would stand back and laugh when the man's children starved to death because their father was hanged for setting fire to the Northrop warehouse.

Picking up the letter, he rang for a servant and ordered him to have it delivered to North Meadows. Without Wilson, he'd have to dirty his own hands by doing away with Fortune himself, but this posed no hardship on Manville. In fact, he looked forward to watching the bitch die. She'd been nothing but trouble to him ever since the first day she set foot in England.

Recalling the fateful night in Bristol, Manville bent and unlocked the bottom drawer of his desk and slid it open. Beneath several papers lay the books he'd had Bad Penny and his cohort steal from the *Mermaid*. He took out the top book and opened it to the dedication page. The paper had yellowed with age but the name at the bottom of the inscription was clearly readable: Sebastian Northrop.

Manville absently perused the words of love that Sebastian had written to his wife and wondered why he'd kept the books. They were the only things connecting him to the robbery. He knew he should have destroyed them the first night because they were proof of Fortune's identity and of his own guilt. For some strange reason they had become a symbol of the victory that would be his when he reclaimed North Meadows and the mills. Manville turned the book over in his hand and shook his head at the oddities in life. With his triumph close at hand, he no longer felt a need to keep the very objects that could ruin all hope of regaining his legacy.

Manville took the remaining books from the drawer, crossed to the fireplace, and with a smirk of satisfaction curling his thin lips, tossed them onto the blazing logs. He dusted his hands together at a job well done. "That solves one problem, and I will put an end to the other this afternoon." He chuckled. "And no one will ever be the wiser."

Happy, Manville turned and walked from the study. He'd enjoy a hearty breakfast and then set about finishing the job he'd paid Bad Penny to do the first night Fortune was in Bristol.

"Good morning, husband," Fortune said as she entered the dining room. Acting as if nothing unusual had transpired between them earlier, she bestowed a warm smile upon Kane and then crossed to the buffet to fill her plate.

"What's so good about it?" Kane ventured, his mood as gray as the day outside. His brow furrowed in bewilderment as he watched Fortune act so carefree. His wife never ceased to amaze him. She didn't seem to fit into any mold. She was as mercurial as the winds and at times just as vexing.

"I say everything is good about it," she said, taking the seat at his right. Without another word she turned her attention to the kidney and eggs on her plate and began to eat.

Kane realized the futility of trying to read his wife's curious mood so he, too, turned his attention back to his food. As he'd found from past experience with Fortune, he'd learn what she was scheming soon enough. The thought had no more than crossed his mind when he felt a silken foot slide up the inside of his leg and come to rest on the seat between his thighs. Her toes wiggled dangerously close to the crotch of his tight britches and he choked on the bite of eggs he'd just taken into his mouth. He gasped for air as he jerked about to look at his wife. She smiled sweetly up at him.

"What in the devil do you think you're doing?" he asked. Firmly grabbing her by the ankle, he moved her foot away from its alarming position.

"Touching my husband," Fortune answered, and ran her foot up his leg again.

"Blast it, Fortune," Kane said, drawing in a sharp breath and recapturing her wayward foot. "Don't do this to us."

"I'm not doing anything to us—just to you," she answered provocatively, giving him a mischievous look.

Kane's fingers tightened about her ankle when he saw the devilment twinkling in her eyes. "I know exactly what you're doing but it's not going to work. I'm not going to change my mind."

"I've not asked you to change your mind, have I?" Fortune said, tugging her foot free of his hand and rising. A cunning little smile curved her lips while she moved around the end of the table and draped her arms about Kane's wide shoulders so that he would have to lean his head back to look up at her. He did so and, much to his chagrin, found his head cushioned by her breasts.

Fortune's laugh was low and sultry as she tightened her arms about him when he tried to avoid contact with her by sitting upright. With gentle fingers she brushed a dark curl out of her path before she dropped a teasing kiss upon the brow that had suddenly grown damp with nervous perspiration. She gazed down into his silver eyes and smiled seductively. "I love you but if you don't want me, then there's nothing I can do about it, is there?"

Kane let out an agonized moan, clasped Fortune's arms,

and firmly unwound them from about his neck. When free of her embrace, he stood so quickly he looked like he'd been shot from a cannon.

"Damn it, Fortune. Are you set on torturing me to death? If you are, then it's working." Kane wiped a hand over his face.

"I wasn't aware I was torturing you," Fortune said innocently.

"Good God, woman! You know exactly what you've been doing. Now if you will excuse me, I have work to do." Kane fled the dining room as if the hounds of hell were nipping at his heels.

Fortune slapped a hand over her mouth to keep from laughing out loud. It wouldn't do for Kane to hear her mirth at his expense. Her husband was a strong man but he'd soon learn that he was no match for her.

Fortune's heart sang and she nearly danced across the dining room to the bell cord to ring for a servant. This morning she'd ride back to North Meadows and give Kane a small reprieve from her attentions. However, when she returned to Warhill tonight, she'd give him no such mercy. So far he'd had only a small taste of what she had in store for him. By the time she was through, he would have long forgotten his scheme to keep her at arm's length. In this battle of love she didn't intend to hold back anything.

Sitting amid the stacks of books and crates that she'd been packing to take to the school, Fortune stared down at the letter the servant had just delivered to her. A puzzled frown creased her brow as she slit open the wax seal and began to read.

*Lady Warrick,*
*If you want to know who set fire to your warehouse meet me at the your mill at two o'clock. Please come alone and don't tell anyone of this letter. It could be dangerous to all concerned.*

The letter was unsigned.

Fortune reread the note, her frown deepening. She could understand the writer's wariness. If this witness had seen the person who set the warehouse on fire and could identify the culprit, his or her life could be in jeopardy.

Again Fortune reread the letter and felt her heart begin to race with excitement at the prospect of learning who had tried to burn her out. She cast an anxious glance at the brass clock hanging on the wall behind the desk. It was now one-thirty. She would have to leave immediately if she wanted to reach the mill before two o'clock.

Forgetting about the books and the school, Fortune scrambled to her feet and ordered her mare saddled. She tucked the letter securely into her pocket and raced up the stairs to hastily retrieve her rain cloak.

Due to the mysterious nature of the missive, she briefly considered sending word to Kane to meet her at the mill but quickly thought better of it. The letter had clearly stated that she come alone and she would do as they asked. She'd not risk frightening the witness away.

A slow drizzle had begun to fall by the time Fortune reined in the mare in front of the quiet mill. For a long, tense moment she didn't dismount but sat looking up at the three-story building. She shivered against the eerie sensation that raced up her spine as her imagination played upon the darkened windowed structure. Like a giant multi-eyed monster, it seemed to lay in wait, watching her every move, readying itself to pounce and devour her.

"Here I go again." Fortune gave a nervous laugh, recalling the ghosts and goblins her imagination had conjured up to frighten her on her ride to Warhill the previous night. She gave herself a sharp mental shake, dismounted, and strode up the flagged path to the mill entrance. She was being ridiculous. She wasn't a child, nor was it the middle of the night. There wasn't anything here to fear.

Fortune mentally reaffirmed her sentiment when she swung open the heavy door and stepped into the still, quiet building. The feeble light that came through the grimy windows did little to illuminate the cavernous room, and she felt the hair on the nape of her neck rise as she scanned the shadows around her. All of her instincts urged her to turn around and go back to North Meadows, but her need to find out who had set fire to her warehouse overshadowed their warning.

"Is anyone here?" she called. When all remained silent, she felt the gooseflesh prickle her skin. She absently rubbed at her arms and cast one last wary glance around the spinning room. Then she turned toward the stairs that led to the second floor and the weaving looms. A moment later she jumped with a start and squealed as a tiny mouse scampered from beneath the looms and ran across her feet.

She pressed a hand over her fluttering heart and let out a long, relieved breath before she warily ascended the stairs to the weave room.

"Is anyone here?" she called again. No answer came. "This is ridiculous," she muttered, returning to the stairs. She'd had enough of this hoax. She was going back to North Meadows. If anyone wanted to talk to her, they could see her there.

"Yes, someone's here, dear cousin," Manville said from the bottom of the stairs. He stood with one foot braced on the last step and a hand resting casually on the railing. He smiled up at Fortune yet there was no warmth in his dark eyes. They glistened like black ice.

"What are you doing here, Nevin? I thought you'd left the area after the courts ruled against your claim on the mill."

"You would have liked that, wouldn't you?"

"What you do is your affair," Fortune said as she descended the stairs and stood at eye level with her cousin.

"For once we are in agreement, cousin," Manville said, making no move to step out of her path.

"Then if you will excuse me, I need to get back to North Meadows," Fortune said, and took another step down hoping he would allow her to pass. The cold and

calculating expression in her cousin's eyes made her uneasy, and she wanted to get far away from him as soon as
possible.

"Why are you in such a hurry? I've come all this way
to speak with you and you're trying to run away like a
frightened little rabbit."

Fortune's chin came up in the air at his taunt. "I don't
think we have anything to say to each other, Nevin. Especially after you tried to keep the mills shut down by
threatening my workers."

Manville chuckled and shrugged. "You have to give me
credit for trying."

"Credit for trying to put me out of business?" Fortune
asked, incredulous. "You must be mad."

"Not mad, my dear. Only determined to reclaim what
is rightfully mine."

"The courts ruled against you, Nevin. You have no
rights here now that I'm married."

Manville nodded smugly. "I had been meaning to drop
by North Meadows to see how well your marriage to Warrick was doing."

"I'm sure you've been concerned for me," Fortune said,
her sarcastic tone emphasizing her doubts about his sin-
cerity. "But to relieve your mind about my well-being,
I'll tell you everything has worked out beautifully. I
couldn't be happier."

Fortune made to pass Manville but he didn't move out
of her path. "Nevin, now that you know how things are
faring at North Meadows without your presence, I would
appreciate it if you would please step out of my way. I
have more important matters to attend than to stay here
and chat with you."

Manville cocked a brow at Fortune and his lips curved
upward in an evil grin. "I know what you have to attend,
my dear. I was the one who sent you the letter."

Automatically, Fortune's hand went to the piece of paper
in her pocket. "What letter?"

Manville noted her gesture. "The one you're hiding in

the pocket of your skirt. The one that said you'd learn the identity of the man who burned your warehouse if you met me here today at two o'clock.''

Her instincts finally sensing imminent danger, Fortune swallowed nervously and backed up a step. ''I don't know what you're talking about.''

Manville snaked out a hand and captured Fortune by the wrist, dragging her roughly down the last three steps to face him. ''You know exactly what I'm talking about. You've suspected all along I was responsible for your troubles but you wouldn't heed my warnings. You were determined to show me that I couldn't force you out of business.''

''Let go of me,'' Fortune ordered, hiding her fear behind a show of bravado.

''You're just like that old bastard, your grandfather. He was always giving orders, but they're not going to do you anymore good than they did him.''

Fortune stilled. ''What do you mean?''

''My dear, stupid Fortune, you still haven't guessed the truth yet, have you?'' Manville chuckled and shook his head, wondering at the girl's naïveté. ''Did you honestly believe I'd let you keep what belongs to me any more than I'd let the old man close my mills after you told him what you'd seen that day? No, my dear. It's not the way I handle my affairs.''

Fortune gaped up at her cousin, resisting his insinuations yet knowing deep inside her soul that he was responsible for her grandfather's death. A foreboding chill rippled up her spine as she said, ''You killed Grandfather.''

Manville smirked at her and nodded smugly. ''I wondered how long it would take that simple mind of yours to figure it out. You see, my dear foolish cousin, I had no other choice. He hated the mills and said he was going to have Mr. Rutherford start proceedings to shut them down. He wouldn't listen to anything I had to say on the matter. All he thought about was the land and you.''

Manville raised a hand and gestured from the floor to

the cobwebbed ceiling. "This all belongs to me. I worked to build it and I've already proved I won't allow anyone to take it from me."

"You're mad," Fortune said, her voice reflecting the horror his admission created within her. Without being told she knew Manville's plans for her. She was to suffer the same fate as her grandfather.

The thought spurred her into action. She wouldn't meekly stand by and let herself be killed if that was what Manville thought. Jerking her wrist free of his imprisoning grip while his attention was directed at the quiet spinning frames, she turned and fled, racing through the darkened room. Her footsteps echoed eerily through the cavernous building as she sped down the dusty isles, searching for a way to escape.

Spying the large double doors that opened toward the charred timbers of the warehouse, Fortune raced to them and tried to unlatch its heavy bolts. Her strength wasn't enough to slide them back. Panicking at the futility of her efforts, she turned, seeking another route of escape. Her dismay and terror at finding Manville standing patiently in her path was reflected in her wide slate-blue eyes. She paled visibly and slowly backed up until the doors were behind her. Bracing herself against the thick wooden panels, she looked at her cousin and shook her head. "You won't get away with this, Manville. I'm not old and ill like my grandfather. Kane will know my death wasn't an accident."

"I don't give a damn what your dear husband knows. Once I've gotten rid of you, I intend to see he doesn't survive long enough to come to your funeral." Manville smiled at the worried expression that flickered across Fortune's face.

"You'll never get away with it," Fortune repeated, and prayed for her husband's sake that she was right.

"You think not? I disagree. You see, your dear husband will be so grief stricken he will take his own life. And people will say the poor bastard just couldn't take his luck with women. His demise will then open the door for me to step back into North Meadows as if nothing had ever changed.''

"You are mad, Manville. Kane has a son to inherit his property.''

"That's true, cousin. And for now the little brat is welcome to Warhill and Warrick's failing business. I can buy them later if I want them. However, I'll regain North Meadows and my mill at your death due to my dear uncle's foresight to have everything revert back to me if you didn't marry within six months or at your death without issue.''

"Nevin, there's no need to harm Kane," Fortune lied, silently sending a prayer heavenward that Manville would believe her. "You'll have no problem from Kane because of the prenuptial agreement we signed on the day of our marriage. He already knows he won't inherit the mill at my death.''

"You're lying just to save the bastard's life, but all of your lies won't do him any good.''

Frantic, Fortune shook her head. "I'm not lying. Kane doesn't want North Meadows or the mill. When he signed the agreement, all he wanted was the strip of land for his canal. It's the only reason he married me.''

"It doesn't matter now what he signed. He has to die because you two have become too close. He'd never believe your death was an accident, and I can't have questions about my integrity brought up when I'm going to need the financial backing from the bankers in London.''

"Your plan will fail, Nevin, because you'll arouse more suspicion if you kill Kane. You're the only person who knows we've been happy. Mr. Rutherford doesn't know how our relationship has changed during the past weeks, and he will tell the authorities that Kane wouldn't kill himself over a woman he'd married just to gain a strip of land. And our prenuptial agreement will prove it.''

Manville regarded Fortune thoughtfully for a long, sinister moment. Assuming the girl wasn't lying, then it might be best for him to wait until everything calmed down about his cousin's death before he rid himself of his other enemy. He'd first have to get his hands on the agreement Warrick and Fortune had signed to make sure that he'd be safe, then he'd make his final decision. If it was as she said, Warrick would have a few more months before he, too, fell victim to a fatal accident.

"We will just have to see," Manville said at last.

A wave of futility filled Fortune. She was faced with her own death, yet her thoughts were of her husband and the small boy who would soon be left alone if her cousin succeeded with his mad scheme.

"Why didn't you just have me killed before instead of trying to break Grandfather's will?" Fortune asked, her voice reflecting her frustration and grief. She regretted her question a moment later. Manville closed the space between them. He grabbed her by the arms and drew her against his thin body. His eyes glowed like black coals as he looked down at her and smiled.

"Because I wanted this," he answered huskily before he captured her mouth in a deep, hurtful kiss.

Fortune moaned her revulsion and tried to escape his bruising lips. She failed. He forced her lips open and attempted to ravage her mouth with his tongue. It was Manville who regretted his actions a moment later. Fortune bit down with all her might, her even white teeth sinking into his lower lip, slicing his flesh.

Manville cried out in pain and jerked away from her. His blood stained her mouth as he drew back his hand and slapped Fortune across the face. Her head snapped back, the blow staggering her senses as the imprint of his fingers rose in scarlet streaks against the whiteness of her cheek. Her knees buckled and she slowly sank to the lint covered floor.

"You bitch! I'm going to enjoy watching you die," Manville growled, towering over her slumped figure. He grabbed a skein of the yarn that had been dumped into the bend at the end of the looms and unwound a length of the coarse cotton thread. Bending, he rolled Fortune onto

her stomach and jerked her arms behind her back. He tied
her wrists securely with the thick yarn and then bound her
feet. Satisfied, he lifted her into his arms and strode toward the rear of the mill where he had tethered his mount.
Heedless to her pain, he tossed her over his saddle like a
sack of flour and urged the horse into the woods behind
the mill and toward the canal construction site.

# Chapter 14

$O$utside the Fox and Hound Tavern the drizzle had changed into a steady downpour. A soft rumble of thunder echoed across the landscape and rattled the lone window that looked out onto the muddy thoroughfare that ran through the heart of Northington. The sound roused Wilson from his inebriated stupor, and he scratched his head as he peered about with bloodshot eyes. A loud belch escaped him and he grinned lopsidedly at the red-haired man sitting at the next table.

Henry Reed didn't return the gesture to Manville's lackey. He hated the man's guts for all he'd done to the people he'd grown up with in Northington. In his view, Wilson was nothing but a cowardly little weasel who would sell his own soul as long as the devil paid him well enough for his services.

Wilson's grin faded under Reed's hostile look. He shifted uneasily in his chair and raised his tankard to the barkeep to order a refill. When the potbellied tavern owner shuffled across the dirt floor and set a pitcher of the foaming dark-amber brew on the table before him, Wilson glanced back at the other man. It had been years since he'd enjoyed the companionship of any of the village men. After he'd gone to work for Manville, he'd been ostracized. Now he was lonely for the company of his own kind instead of the likes of the man who considered him less than human.

"Would you like to join me for a dram, Henry?" Wilson asked, raising the full pitcher.

"I wouldn't drink with ye if ye were the last man on earth, Seth Wilson," Reed said, eyeing the other man with contempt.

Wilson nodded his understanding but with the ale to give him courage, he wasn't dissuaded. He needed to let these people know that he had changed. "I don't blame you, Henry. If I was in your shoes it'd be the same with me."

Henry Reed shook his head in disgust. The man knew how they all felt about him. There wasn't a man in Northington who would sit down and have a drink with Wilson. They didn't trust him as far as they could throw him. He spied on them for his boss, reporting their every word and move so Nevin Manville could use it against them.

"I doubt if ye can really understand our feelings. If ye did ye wouldn't have the nerve to show yer face around here," Reed said. "Ye taint the very air we breathe."

"Henry, I've changed." Wilson nearly whimpered. He desperately needed to be accepted again.

"A snake is a snake no matter if it does shed its skin," Reed said, lifting his tankard and downing the contents in one great gulp.

Wilson's face flushed a dull beet red at the insult. "You can believe what you will about me. I know I've made a lot of mistakes by trying to keep my young'uns fed, but that came to an end this morning. I told Manville I wasn't working for him any more. I may be a coward but I ain't doing murder for the bastard."

Reed looked sharply at the man sitting at the adjoining table. "What did ye say?"

Wilson took a another long swig of his ale in an effort to wash down all the misery spewing up inside of him. The ale loosened his tongue. "I said I ain't going to do murder for that bastard, no matter what he's willing to pay for it.''

"Whose murder?" Reed asked, his heart seeming to freeze within his chest.

Wilson shook his head sadly, the drink and the movement making his head buzz.

"Damn ye,'' Reed growled, coming out of his chair and grabbing Wilson by the front of his shirt. He jerked the man to his feet and held him only inches from his own face as he glared down at him and said, "Whose murder? Out with it before I wring yer neck.''

Wilson shook his head. "I'm through working for Manville, but if I tell you anything, he'll have me killed.''

"I'll kill ye here and now if ye don't tell me who Manville intends to murder," Reed swore, giving Wilson a shake.

Wilson blinked at Reed and muttered, "Lady Northrop—I mean, Lady Warrick." As the words left his lips Henry Reed released him. Wilson fell to the floor at Reed's feet.

"If something has happened to Lady Warrick because ye didn't tell someone sooner, then ye won't live to regret groveling at Manville's feet.'' Henry Reed turned and strode out into the rainy day.

Abruptly sobered by Reed's threats, Wilson scrambled to his feet, tossed a coin at the barkeep for his ale, and hurried out of the tavern. He didn't look back as he made his way to the small cottage at the end of town. Taking his savings from beneath the floorboard in front of the fireplace, he ordered his wife to pack their food and belongings while he hitched the small cart to the oxen. There was no time to waste on sentimentality. They could find another cottage somewhere safer than Northington.

Kane listened to the steady roll of thunder as the clock chimed two. After Fortune had ridden away from Warhill he'd managed to find every excuse in the world not to follow in her wake. However, he hadn't managed to avoid confronting his feelings and realizing that he wasn't strong enough to keep his resolves about his young wife.

Running a hand through his hair, Kane crossed to the window and peered out into the rainy afternoon. In the last hours he had gone over and over their discussion that morning. After the years of guilt over Felicia's death, it hadn't been easy to see the other side of the coin and face the fact that Fortune had been right. God didn't grant guarantees, only life. It was left for each person to live each day to its fullest and let the future take care of itself. Life was too short and precious to waste worrying about things that might or might not happen.

A distant boom of thunder rumbled across the landscape. He could just as easily lose Fortune to an accident as to childbirth. He would be foolish to toss away what time God had granted them to be happy together. Kane had finally found true love, and from this moment on he intended to enjoy it. He would take his wife's advice and not allow the past to ruin their future.

Suddenly feeling as if he were ten years younger and a new bridegroom again with no past to shadow his happiness, Kane smiled and turned away from the window. When he crossed to the bell rope, his steps had a jaunty lightness about them. He couldn't wait to tell Fortune of his decision. It was one he didn't want to keep to himself.

Kane felt like shouting from the rooftop that he loved the stubborn little mountain wildcat who had turned his life upside down before setting it to rights with her love. In her wisdom, she had seen his faults and made him realize what he had been doing to those he loved. She had given him his son as surely as the woman who had given Price birth. She had forced him to understand that he'd punished his son as well as himself with his guilt over Felicia's death. Kane knew he owed his young wife far more than he could ever repay her and he prayed she would be satisfied with the meager offering of his undying love.

A moment later Kane's musings were interrupted by Mrs. Ward.

"Sir, there's a man here to see you." The sour-faced housekeeper's tone reflected her opinion of Kane's visitor.

"Show him in, Mrs. Ward," Kane replied briskly. Eager to be on his way to North Meadows to see his wife, he was in no mood to be delayed by anything—not even the canal. A surprised look flickered over Kane's face when Henry Reed entered the study.

"Mrs. Ward said you wanted to see me?"

"No, sir," Henry Reed said, shaking his head. "I came to see Lady Warrick. Is she here?"

"My wife is presently at North Meadows, Mr. Reed. Is there anything I can do for you in her stead?"

"Sir, yer wife ain't at North Meadows and I'm afraid something has happened to her," Reed said, his tone reflecting his anxiety, his ruddy features marred by a frown of worry.

Kane tensed. "What are you talking about, Reed?"

"I came to warn her ladyship about Mr. Manville. His toady got drunk in the tavern and let it slip that Manville wanted him to murder Lady Warrick."

"My God, we've got to find her before it's too late," Kane said, paling. He ran from the study and was already on his way out the door by the time Henry Reed caught up with him in the foyer.

"Aye, that we do, sir. But yer wife ain't at North Meadows nor is she here."

"Then she has to be at the school or the mill." Kane silently sent a prayer heavenward that he was right about his wife's whereabouts. Then he glanced at the other man and realized he was soaked to the skin. His boots were caked with mud from his long walk, and his limp was even more pronounced because of his hurry, as well as the weather.

"Have my stableman saddle you a mount and give you a rain cloak. Then you go to the church while I ride to the mill."

"Aye, sir," Reed said, clamping his soggy hat back down on his rust colored hair.

"If you don't find my wife, meet me back at North Meadows. She may have returned there while you were on your way here."

Kane didn't wait for Reed's horse to be saddled but rode toward the Northrop mill. Stinging drops of rain pelted him in the face but he paid no heed to the discomfort. His only thoughts were upon the woman he loved and the danger that threatened her. His heart pounded against his ribs with the fear that he might be too late.

"O God," he prayed as he reined his mount to a halt in front of the three-storied building, "please let me find her safe and sound."

A short time later Kane felt as if God had deserted him. His wet clothing covered with dust, he emerged from the shadowy interior of the mill and remounted the stallion. He had searched every nook and cranny of the mill, and there had been no sign of his wife. He turned the horse toward North Meadows. Swallowing back the lump of dread that rose in his throat, he kicked his mount into a faster gait.

Kane's hopes soared when he entered North Meadows and heard his son's voice coming from the study. He smiled with relief as he shrugged out of his rain cloak and strode across the foyer. He knew if Price was here Fortune would be nearby.

Kane felt his stomach knot with apprehension when he reached the wide double doors and saw his son standing with his small fists balled on his hips in front of the large mahogany desk peering up at the man behind it. Kane could see Manville holding the prenuptial agreement he and Fortune had signed on their wedding day.

"You'd better leave my momma's things alone," Price ordered, unaware that his father stood in the doorway behind him.

"Get out of here, you little bastard, or I'll have you whipped for your insolence," Manville said.

"My papa won't let you whip me," Price declared, not giving an inch. "He won't like it when he learns you've torn up Mama's things. You'll be sorry when my papa gets mad at you."

"Damn it, brat. Get out of here and leave me alone," Manville growled as he stood and frowned down at the small boy.

Price stubbornly shook his head, his actions reminding Kane of himself when he was much younger.

Manville's attention centered on the child who had been harassing him ever since he'd started searching for the agreement Fortune had told him about. He moved around the desk, without seeing Kane standing in the doorway. "You little brat, I'll teach you to disobey your elders."

Showing a courage that far exceeded his years, Price didn't move. He stood glaring up at the man who raised his hand to strike.

"I wouldn't do that if I were you, Manville," Kane said, his voice soft yet filled with deadly menace as he stepped into the room.

"Papa," Price squealed, and ran to his father. He threw his arms about Kane's legs and hugged him. "The mean man is stealing Mama's things."

Kane gently patted his son's curly head and loosened Price's arms from about his legs. He didn't take his eyes off of Manville as he set his son away from him. "Go up to your room, Price. I'll see that the man leaves Mama's things here."

"I told you Papa wouldn't like what you were doing. It's not nice to steal," Price smugly taunted Manville before he turned and left the two men staring fiercely at each other.

"You should have listened to my son, Manville," Kane said, slowly closing the space between them.

"Don't come any closer, Warrick, or your son will be an orphan much sooner than I had planned," Manville growled, drawing his pistol from beneath his coat. He was cornered and, like a rat, he intended to fight his way out of the situation. He aimed the weapon at Kane's chest and smiled, secure in the fact that he had his enemy at a disadvantage.

"What do you mean?" Kane questioned guardedly as he eyed Manville, his instincts warning him to distract the madman before moving to disarm him.

Manville gave a diabolical chuckle. "As your sudden appearance here has changed my plans, I don't guess it matters now if you know the fate that was to be yours after you found your wife's body."

"You bastard. If you've harmed a hair on Fortune's head then you're a dead man," Kane growled, his features contorting into a mask of rage. He took a step toward Manville then regained control of himself.

"I'd keep my distance if I were you," Manville said, cocking the pistol. He shook his head and smiled at Kane. "Such devotion. It's sad to think it won't do either you or my dear cousin any good, especially if it keeps raining."

"What have you done to Fortune?" Kane asked, his heart pounding with fear. He was no longer concerned with his own safety. All his thoughts were centered upon the woman he loved.

Again Manville smiled. "I assure you that I've seen she's well taken care of, Warrick." He chuckled again. "Most men who have an insatiable mistress like our dear Madelene would be grateful to me for getting rid of their wives."

"Manville, what have you done to Fortune?" Kane asked again, taking another involuntary step toward his enemy. Filled with the need to strangle the man with his bare hands, Kane didn't wonder how Manville knew about Madelene Deveau. Every sinew in his body cried out to kill the villain; however, he couldn't appease himself until he learned what the man had done to his wife.

"It's a shame to end our acquaintance on such a happy note, but I don't have time to stand here and talk with you," Manville said, and before Kane could protest, he pulled the trigger.

Instinctively sensing the danger, Kane launched himself

at the smaller man, hitting him squarely in the middle at the moment the man squeezed the trigger. The impact knocked off Manville's aim and threw him backward onto the desk. Kane and Manville scuffled there, scattering papers and books to the floor before they tumbled after them. Manville landed on his back and Kane came astride him, pummeling him in the face with his fists until the smaller man was bleeding profusely from his mouth and nose and he was whimpering in defeat.

Disgusted, Kane shoved himself away from Manville and got to his feet. It took all of his self-control not to finish what he'd started as he stood towering over the cowering, bloody-faced man. Yet his fear for Fortune's life stayed him.

"What have you done with my wife, you bastard?" he ground out between tightly clenched teeth.

"Wouldn't you like to know?" Manville said, grinning up at him through broken teeth.

"Damn you, Manville. You'll tell me what you've done to Fortune or you'll be in hell within the next few minutes."

"You can't kill me, Warrick, but even if you did, I'd die happy just knowing that bitch didn't live to enjoy what was rightfully mine," Manville said, wiping at the trickle of blood running from the corner of his mouth.

In one swift move, Kane retrieved the pistol from where it had fallen beside the desk. His eyes glowed with determination as he reloaded the gun and reached down to drag Manville to his feet. He smiled coldly at his enemy. "If that's the way you want it, then so be it."

Kane cocked the pistol and brought it up against Manville's temple.

Manville swallowed with difficulty at the feel of the cold metal barrel pressing against his skull. An icy chill ran down his back at the light he saw glowing in the steely depths of Kane's eyes. It bespoke the fate awaiting him. He knew Warrick's threats were not in vain. His death would soon follow if he didn't tell him Fortune's where-abouts.

Manville swallowed again and nervously wet his lips. He'd spoken bravely about his death a moment earlier, but now that it was so near, he realized he didn't want to die; he didn't have the courage to die. He began to tremble.

"No," Manville pleaded, "don't kill me. Fortune's at the canal site. I left her tied up near the dam to make it look like she drowned by accident so I wouldn't be blamed."

Kane glanced out the window at the downpour and felt his blood run cold at the thought of the danger Fortune faced. The river was swollen to the edge of its banks, and it was only a miracle that the earthen dam had not already given way under the deluge of rain that had fallen over the past days.

"I should blow your head off and save the courts the trouble of hanging you, you bastard," Kane growled as he lowered the pistol and jerked Manville toward a straight-back chair near the window. He forced him down into it and used the golden braided drapery cord to tie Manville's hands to the chair behind his back.

"Sir," Reed said from the doorway, "I can't find Lady Warrick."

"She's at the construction site," Kane said. Taking no time to explain Manville's presence, he thrust the pistol into Reed's hand. "Don't let the bastard escape before the authorities arrive."

Every muscle in Kane's lean body screamed with tension as he rode through the blinding rain. In his haste to reach his wife, the minutes that it took him to ride to the construction site seemed like hours. He spurred the stallion to a faster gait and the animal, sensing Kane's urgency, stretched out his long, powerfully muscled legs and heeded his master's order.

Kane was panting for breath as he drew the stallion to a skiddering halt. He sprang to the ground and was racing toward the deep ditch before the animal came to a complete standstill. Fear and panic made his heart beat frantically against his ribs while he searched the muddy excavation site for any sign of his wife.

"My God!" he breathed when he saw her sitting waist-deep in mud. His gaze swept back to the earthen dam and his heart froze. A steady trickle of water was already eating away at the clay. Even as he slipped and slid down the embankment toward Fortune, large clumps of dirt were being gouged out and more water poured over into the ditch.

Frantic now to reach Fortune before the dam completely collapsed, Kane waded knee-deep in the mud. It took all of his strength to free each foot. It also took precious seconds he knew they couldn't spare if they were to survive.

He could see from the expression on his wife's face that she also knew the danger facing them and he called out his reassurances. "Just stay still and everything will be alright."

"Hurry, Kane," Fortune called, straining against her bonds as she glanced once more toward the swiftly rising water.

"We're going to be fine," Kane murmured as he came to his knees at his wife's side and worked to untie her bonds. He had just freed her hands when the dam burst. The force of the water knocked them against the embankment and threatened to wash them downstream, but Kane managed to grasp Fortune firmly by the arm. They struggled together, fighting against being separated. The strong current tore at their bodies, sucking greedily like a ravenous liquid monster set upon devouring them. Yet they fought on, side by side, working their way up the slippery embankment to safety. Breathing heavily, they collapsed upon the sodden ground.

Soaked and muddy, they lay with hair and clothes plastered to their skin as the rain beat down upon them. Their faces glistened with water as they looked at each other and smiled triumphantly. Together they had battled against death and had won. Together they would share the life that God had seen fit to grant them.

"I love you, Kane," Fortune said, reaching out a wet hand to stroke his cheek.

"And I love you, my Lady Fortune. I believe I've loved you ever since you nearly beat me to death that day in the trading post." Kane caught her hand and brought it to his lips. He placed a tender kiss upon her palm as he looked into her slate-blue eyes. "Can you ever forgive me for being such a fool? Because of my stupid fears I nearly ruined everything for us. I now know the past is exactly that and I won't allow us to waste any more of the precious time we've been given to enjoy. I want all of us to be a family."

"All of us?" Fortune inquired, her wet face glowing with love and hope.

"Yes, all of us. I also have you to thank for giving me a son."

"I don't know what you mean," Fortune said. Puzzled, she blinked against the raindrops beading on her thick lashes.

Kane cupped her chin in the palms of his hands and gazed down into her lovely wet face. "Felicia gave birth to Price but you're his mother. You made me realize how much I love him, and I shall always love you for it."

Tears of happiness mingled with the rain on Fortune's cheeks. She threw her arms about Kane's neck and hugged him tightly before leaning back and looking up at him. "Oh, Kane, now we are a real family, and that's all I've ever wanted."

"It's taken a long time for it to come about but I guess we are now a family. And it's all because of one stubborn little minx who doesn't give up when she sets her mind to something she wants." Kane dipped his head and kissed her lightly on the tip of her nose.

Fortune wrinkled her nose at her husband and her eyes twinkled with devilment. "And you wouldn't change a thing if you could."

Kane glanced up at the gray weeping sky before he looked once more at Fortune. He gave her a roguish grin. "I might change this downpour into a sunny day so I could make love to you here and now."

Thrilled with Kane's realization that the past was dead and with his desire to make love to her again, Fortune sat up and smiled provocatively at her husband while her fingers worked at the buttons at the front of her riding habit. "Who cares about a little rain?"

"That's right. Who cares about a little rain?" Kane laughed. He needed no further encouragement and quickly helped her and himself out of their soggy clothing. Their skin was wet and slick from the rain as he lowered his head to hers and their sleek bodies came together in the ultimate act of love. Husband and wife, friends and lovers, Kane and Fortune were as one in the liquid crystal world surrounding them.

## ABOUT THE AUTHOR

Cordia Byers was born in the small, north Georgia community of Jasper and lives there still, with her husband, James. Cordia likes to think of her husband as being like one of the heroes in her novels. James swept her off her feet after their first meeting, and they were married three weeks later.

From the age of six, Cordia's creative talents had been directed toward painting. It was not until late 1975, when the ending of a book displeased her, that she considered writing. That led to her first novel, HEATHER, which was followed by CALLISTA, NICOLE LA BELLE, SILK AND STEEL, LOVE STORM, PIRATE ROYALE (Winner of a *Romantic Times* Reviewer's Choice Award) STAR OF THE WEST, and RYAN'S GOLD. Finding more satisfaction in the world of her romantic novels, Cordia has given up painting and now devotes herself to writing, researching her material at the local library, and then doing the major part of her work from 11:30 P.M. to 3:00 A.M.